W9-AHY-105

PRIMACY

PRIMACY

A Novel

J.E. FISHMAN

VERBITRAGE
More Than Words

This book is a work of fiction. Names, characters, businesses, organizations, places, events, and incidents are either a product of the author's imagination or are used fictitiously. Any resemblance to actual persons, living or dead, events, or locales is entirely coincidental.

Published in the United States of America by Verbitrage, a writers' consortium.
www.verbitrage.com

Copyright © 2011 by Verbitrage LLC, Series 1

All rights reserved.

No part of this book may be reproduced, stored in a retrieval system, or transmitted by any means, electronic, mechanical, photocopying, recording, or otherwise, without written permission from the copyright holder.

Distributed by Greenleaf Book Group LLC

For ordering information or special discounts for bulk purchases, please contact Greenleaf Book Group LLC at PO Box 91869, Austin, TX 78709, 512.891.6100.

Book design and composition by Jennifer Daddio / Bookmark Design & Media Inc.
Cover design by Whitney Cookman

Publisher's Cataloging-In-Publication Data
(Prepared by The Donohue Group, Inc.)
Fishman, Joel E.
Primacy : a novel / J.E. Fishman.—1st ed.
p. ; cm.
ISBN: 978-0-9833809-0-0
1. Animal mutation—Fiction. 2. Human-animal relationships—Fiction.
3. Animal experimentation—Moral and ethical aspects—Fiction.
4. Laboratory technicians—Fiction. 5. Bonobo—Fiction. 6. Science fiction, American. I. Title.

PS3606.I85 P75 2011
813./6   2011925272

TreeNeutral

Part of the Tree Neutral® program, which offsets the number of trees consumed in the production and printing of this book by taking proactive steps, such as planting trees in direct proportion to the number of trees used: www.treeneutral.com

Printed in the United States of America on acid-free paper

11 12 13 14 15 16   10 9 8 7 6 5 4 3 2 1

FIRST EDITION

FOR MY FATHER

PRIMACY

In the beginning was the Word.

—JOHN

PROLOGUE

He had the poet T.S. Eliot in mind as he felt for his weapon in the winter woods—Eliot, who wrote about shadows falling between emotion and response, between essence and descent.

They crouched among shadows, two men in camouflage. The white and the black. The light and the dark. Above them, a tall chimney spewed smoke toward the low overcast.

A furnace in the kingdom of despair, he thought.

"Smell it," his partner, the black African, whispered.

It was sweet and sharp and carbon-saturated, the scent of something beyond death: of putrid flesh consumed.

The African held a pair of halter-tamed whitetail deer while the white man examined the chain-link fence in the glow of a penlight. He attached the wire in his hand with a clip to a line woven through the fence at eye level, walked six feet, and clipped the same line with the other end of his wire. He repeated the procedure for the second line, which was near ground level. Exactly in the middle, he severed the fence vertically with spring-loaded bolt cutters.

Dit. Dit. Dit. Dit. Dit. Dit. Dit. Dit. Dit.

It gaped open.

"*Pedza*," he said. Done.

They retreated fifty yards with the deer in tow, sat on the ground and waited, leaning against cold tree trunks.

For an hour they didn't move. No one came.

They exchanged a silent nod, then the white man stood with one lead shank in hand. His small doe, stirred from boredom, sensed something new and became skittish. He reassured her with a pat and directed her to the hole in the fence. When they were on top of it he straddled her and deftly unsnapped the halter, pushing her through with a smack on the hindquarters. She hustled into the darkness, kicking up dried leaves.

By the time motion detectors tripped the floodlights he had retreated into the shadows. From lawns to macadam, the grounds inside the fence looked like a moonscape under the glare of the lights, all color washed out to gradations of silver.

Two spotters appeared on the flat roof of the boxy industrial building and scanned the property with binoculars. A third guard moved behind the glass doors of the newly illuminated front lobby. He had a pistol and a two-way radio. He tested the doors with a shove and looked out into the parking lot. There was nothing but the doe cantering across the lawn with its white tail raised. The guards exchanged a few words over the radio and withdrew to their original positions.

The men in the woods waited longer, undiscovered.

The floodlights powered down.

Half an hour later, the black man stood with his doe. He led her to the fence as the first man had, straddled her, unsnapped the halter, smacked her in the rear and received a kick in the knee. Grimacing but silent, he limped back into the shadows as the floodlights surged on again.

Once more the guards appeared on the roof and in the doorway. They registered the second doe, which cantered to its grazing friend. A longer exchange ensued over the radios, then with noncommittal gestures the guards retired.

When the floodlights snapped off again, the men in the woods waited for their eyes to adjust and traded knowing glances.

Fifteen minutes later, they stood poised at the gap in the fence, the deer a hundred yards to their right. They hugged the fence until they had an angle to the side door that would take them within twenty yards of the deer. They waited, a hand on each other's shoulder, and surveyed the dim scene one last time. Then they bolted for the door as the flood-lights buzzed to life again.

The deer skittered toward one another, alert. The guards were slower to appear. By the time they did, the intruders had flattened themselves against the reflective glass wall. The white man, using his partner for a ladder, quickly rose beside the plastic bubble that protected the camera by the door. He fixed a larger bubble over it with a hologram burned into the plastic—a replica of the real camera's view with no one at the door. He climbed down and they flattened themselves against the wall again, marking time.

Looking up, they saw the sleek barrel of a rifle extend over the roofline, then steady.

"I should waste these damned deer," said the voice with the rifle. "How many times are we gonna drag ourselves out here?"

"As many as it takes."

Radios barked.

"Fucking Christmas Eve, too, and all. Venison?" The rifle swung.

"Put it down, man. Discipline."

"These endless fence violations... They'll need another perimeter check in the morning."

The radios crackled once more, briefly. The footfall of the guards faded. A few minutes later, the lights powered down again.

With a small hand torch and his bolt cutters, the white man removed a push bar that held the door fast. Before allowing it to swing open, the African slipped a flat magnet where he knew the alarm contact would be.

The African produced a thick rubber exercise band, missing its handles. They raced up the hall. The lobby had wall panels of brushed stainless steel, gray marble tiles and indirect lighting. In one corner stood an artificial Christmas tree with a dozen wrapped presents piled beneath it. Music played in the background—Nat King Cole crooning "O Holy Night."

A single guard sat at the security desk, facing a panel of monitors. His hair looked greasy from behind. The intruders took him so quickly that he never left his chair and had no chance to unholster his sidearm. The African twisted the guard's gun arm behind his back and wrapped the rubber band around his neck. His partner held the sharp tip of a hawksbill blade to the point of the guard's nose, producing a bead of blood.

"Not one sound."

The guard tried to swallow, but the pressure of the rubber band constricted his Adam's apple. When he attempted to nod his head the knife dug into his nose. He blinked in terror.

They sealed his mouth with duct tape and fastened him to the chair. They took his passkey and rolled him into a nearby closet, closing the door. The African slipped the guard's pistol into his own belt.

The men had memorized the plan of the building. They headed straight for the ground-floor laboratories, which occupied the north side. They touched the guard's passkey to an electronic pad, and the door swung open.

Inside, a whiff of antiseptic mingled with the throat-constricting odor of animal excrement. Living things shifted and rustled in dark corners. As the lights flickered on, the sights and smells and sounds made the two men emotional. The African vomited into a biohazard bin. The white began to fling open cages, freeing rabbits and cats and dogs and monkeys. Some of the animals cowered in their enclosures, even with the doors open. Others lay listless. The two men sped up and down the lines of cages, unfastening every door. Monkeys screeched interminably. Two dogs circled, trailing catheters. A baboon, tied to the side of its cage, hugged itself with one untethered arm. It was covered in bloody bandages and open sores.

The white man paused before the baboon's pleading brown eyes.

"'Sweet mercy is nobility's true badge,'" he quoted. He took out his suppressed 45-caliber Heckler & Koch and winced when the baboon's head exploded, blood and brains splattering the room. The bullet ricocheted off a steel countertop, and remnants of the baboon's skull vibrated the bars of the cage.

Several other animals, too debilitated to move, met the same fate.

The African herded the remaining creatures out the door, down the hall, and into the open air.

"*Dzikinuka,*" he told the walking wounded. Be free.

Back inside, an alarm sounded and the men's eyes met. The guards from the roof were certain to arrive shortly. The intruders replaced the magazines in their weapons.

There was no one in the hall and no sound other than the blaring alarm. They raced past the crematorium door, around a corner and into a room lined with filing cabinets. Sweating now, they threw open drawers and emptied folders onto the floor.

The white man sparked his torch and touched blue flame to several piles of paper. Smoke braided to the walls as the small fire slithered into an open blaze. A second alarm sounded and red exit signs began flashing.

"*Bibinuka,*" he said. Get out.

The guards had the lobby flanked, their guns drawn. The intruders sprinted down a side hall, ignoring calls to halt. They flew through the original door, but the African was a step slow, limping.

"*Rambauchiita!*" he shouted. Go on!

His partner hesitated, extending a hand to assist.

The guards were gaining on them now.

"*Rambauchiita! Rambauchiita!*" the African pleaded.

Firearms snapped. Bullets ripped the air, and the African crumpled.

A dozen animals hobbled in the glare of the parking lot—dazed by unnatural brightness and unexpected freedom.

The white man weaved among them. As he reached the woods, a large explosion lit the night.

ONE

Humans are the symbol-using, symbol-misusing animal, inventor of the negative, separated from our natural condition by instruments of our own making, goaded by the spirit of hierarchy, and rotten with perfection.

— KENNETH BURKE

1
___

One Friday in May, a beautiful cloudless day, Liane Vinson had the shock of her life.

By the age of twenty-five, Liane thought she had become inured to profound surprise. She worked as a veterinary technician in the biggest animal testing laboratory in the world, Pentalon, where she had seen plenty in two years—seen plenty and done plenty. She had starved and poisoned more rats and mice than she could count, some of them her dearest animal friends. She had watched a close associate, Ronald Berg, put toxic ingredients into the eyes of rabbits. She had witnessed dogs living for months with wounds that the scientists wouldn't allow to heal.

She had made her peace with all of it. One day, Liane thought, she might be one of those scientists. Currently, she assisted the head of the primate lab, Adnan Hammurabi, preparing a troop of bonobos for coming experiments.

Liane had her justifications for being at Pentalon. Her stepfather had landed her the job at the end of a rocky and extended adolescence. Her psychologist had urged it upon her for reasons that remained complicated. Also, she needed the money and she needed the routine. She didn't harbor any illusions about whether there were better jobs in the world; she knew there were. But Pentalon, she believed, was a safe choice, and her recent promotion to the primate lab had come with a ten-thousand-dollar raise.

Sitting in traffic at the heavily guarded Pentalon gate in Farmingdale, Long Island, Liane looked out at the protestors and wondered what motivated them. She could see having qualms about what went on within Pentalon's walls, but she couldn't understand the obsession that so drove those people who called themselves FAULT—Folks Against Unnecessary Lab Testing. Day in and day out, they walked the picket line in front of Pentalon, waving their horrible pictures and chanting their protests. One in particular, a redhead in vintage Converse high-tops and a sage-green sweatshirt who seemed to be their leader, never missed a minute. Off hours, she could be seen wandering a camp they had set up in the woods. The camp appeared to lie on public property. Nevertheless, Liane didn't understand why Pentalon's crackerjack security force couldn't get local police to move the protestors along.

Today the guards at the gate were working to turn around an unauthorized truck. Liane stared out at the redheaded woman, their eyes met, and the woman shook her fist in anger. Liane struggled to tune out the vitriol, which came laced with the words *killer* and *abuser*. That stung. She knew she treated the animals in her lab as kindly as possible. In fact, she had in the back of her car a bagful of toys that she'd just salvaged from the trash by her apartment building. She'd boiled the toys in water and antiseptic and would introduce them to the apes as a form of psychological enrichment.

The redheaded woman shook her fist again and rattled a placard that showed pictures of a sad-looking puppy.

Despite the warm fresh breeze, which she'd been enjoying, Liane raised her car window.

Ten minutes later, she passed through security in the back lobby, the entrance reserved exclusively for primate lab employees. She fed her tote through the x-ray machine and walked calmly through the magneto-meter and the blowers that sniffed for explosives. On the far side of the lobby, she used her passkey to enter the primate lab.

Liane stowed her personal belongings in the locker room and washed her hands in one of the lab sinks. She kept inside the yellow step-back lines that created a buffer around the perimeter cages, not out of fear of her gentle bonobos, but only because she knew there were cameras everywhere, and she didn't want a reprimand from Adnan about violating procedures.

Adnan Hammurabi stuck to the rules. For all that, Liane thought, he was a conscientious scientist and a sensitive manager, far from a martinet. When she'd begun the new job, he gave her a tutorial on her new charges, which had just arrived.

"*Pan paniscus*," he'd explained, "is also known as the pygmy chimpanzee, not for its size but for the Bantu people among whom it lives. Like the common chimp, *pan troglodytes*, they're the closest cousins to humans, sharing more than ninety-eight percent of our genetic code. But they're significantly rarer and more, shall we say, humanoid. Although bonobos are arboreal, when on the ground they spend a quarter of their time walking erect. More than any other primate."

As Liane went through the troop this morning, greeting each one and taking their vital signs, she recalled Adnan's unbridled enthusiasm with regard to working with this rare species. She remembered how he walked along when they first arrived, tapping the countertop with the heel of his hand.

"Bonobos are said to closely resemble *Australopithecus*, the bipedal hominid that was one of our closest ancestors—and probably one of theirs. They represent an excellent subject for the study of human disease."

In a little over a month in the primate lab, Liane had learned a great deal about her caged animals. Their average age was under two, years younger than the stage at which they would normally stop suckling their mothers' breasts. At full maturity bonobos grow to about two-and-a-half feet tall and weigh ninety-five pounds, but the ones in the lab had so far achieved less than a third that size on average. In the wild, bonobos generally live forty to forty-five years. Under the right circumstances, Liane reckoned, she could spend the majority of her career studying the group that had just arrived. Long enough, if she returned for her Ph.D., to herself become the lead researcher.

Two of Pentalon's bonobos were twins. She and Hammurabi had

segregated this pair in a small room off their main lab, and she made a point of visiting them often, noting how they shared their experience without being able to touch one another physically. Hammurabi had suggested that *Pan paniscus* twins were an unusual find, and he must have been right, because while Liane found many citations on common chimpanzee twins, she could locate no significant reference to bonobo twin studies in any of the literature.

She was growing attached, she knew, and Adnan had warned her about that. Liane would never forget how he'd put it, in fact, saying, "It's a significant step from the beady eyes of rodents to the soft brown orbs of our cousins. Because they're so close to us on the family tree, it's easy to anthropomorphize. I caution you against this, Liane. Ted Bundy, the famous serial killer, looked to many like a Boy Scout, but that didn't make him one. I once saw a chimp bite off a technician's pinky."

But when she pressed him, Liane learned that the biter had been of the *Pan troglodytes* species, the common chimpanzee—not *Pan paniscus*, the bonobo. Indeed, bonobos were known to be the most peace-loving of all great apes.

Having finished her rounds, she decided to bring her new toys into the twins' room first. They tilted their heads in curiosity, and Liane opened the cage of No. 673A, the male. He climbed into her arms and she set him down on the counter by one of the toys, a simple wooden box with cutouts on each plane in the shapes of different animals. He picked up the box and shook it. Hearing the rattle inside, he lifted an eyebrow.

"Now let's see what you're made of," Liane said, amused.

She took the box from him and opened the hinged lid and dumped out the pieces. The ape gazed for a moment at them: giraffe, antelope, elephant, monkey, chicken, turtle. He fingered the elephant and raised it to his lips. He licked it, tested it with his teeth.

"No," Liane said, "not for the mouth. Here's how it works."

She showed him by turning the box and inserting each piece into its respective slot. Then she dumped them all out on the counter and set the box down in front of him again. He lifted the turtle and pressed it to his lips, running the edge of the wood against the ridge between his teeth.

"No," Liane repeated. "Like this."

She held up the box and found the side with the turtle. She guided his hand and they fit the turtle through the slot together.

"There," she said. "See?"

She wasn't sure that he did. The ape picked up the giraffe and scratched the top of his head with it. He folded his wrist and cradled it under his arm, as if to indicate he was taking possession.

Liane left the room to get her electronic tablet. She'd just finished recording the vital signs of the main troop and needed to do these two. She was gone for half a minute. When she returned, the wooden pieces were all inside the box and the bonobo was shaking it over his head in triumph. That was interesting. She knew bonobos were shrewd and she wondered whether he'd cheated by opening the lid. As if in answer to the question, he snapped the lid open and closed while rocking his head from side to side.

He played his fingers over the box edges while Liane measured his temperature with an ear thermometer and recorded his blood pressure with an armband. She took the box from him and returned him to his cage. He looked disappointed, and Liane opened the cage of No. 673B, who engulfed her in long arms.

"Hello, Bea," Liane said.

The bonobo touched her lips to Liane's cheek and fiddled gently with one of Liane's earlobes.

Seeming eager to try the toy, she bounded from floor to counter and lifted the box in the air, shaking it. Liane picked up the other toy—a hard plastic ball with a narrow slot. She unscrewed the two hemispheres and placed a kibble of monkey chow in the receptacle, then screwed it back together.

"The idea," Liane explained to the ape, looking into her eyes, "is to turn the ball enough times in just such a way that the treat works itself out. Do so and it's yours!"

She demonstrated by rotating the ball over and over, but she couldn't work the kibble free. The toy had been designed to keep a dog entertained, but it seemed just as likely to drive one mad.

"Well," Liane shrugged, "maybe you'll have better luck."

She handed the ball to the bonobo, who cradled it in her palms and sniffed at the slot, then shook it near her ear, listening for the faint rattle. Her hazel eyes searched Liane's face. She placed her hands on either hemisphere and tried to twist the ball open, but her unopposed thumbs proved to be a liability; her grip kept slipping. She sniffed again at the slot and rattled the ball while Liane watched. Then an idea passed across her face. She set the ball down on the counter and gripped it between her feet, which were far more dexterous than those of a human. Holding one hemisphere rigid this way, she used both her hands to squeeze and twist the top of the ball. When it sprung free she waved it for Liane to see, then delicately removed the kibble and slipped it into her mouth, crunching it between her incisors.

"Bravo!" Liane clapped. "You're a clever one!"

The female bonobo clapped in imitation.

The male, in his cage, clapped too.

There was something in the way the twins looked at each other today that made Liane's heart ache. As usual, they so clearly longed to touch one another, and she suspected that her own nearly hairless person made a poor substitute when they groomed her to show their affection. Generally, when they rested in their cages, each clung to a dirty stuffed animal in the approximate shape of the cartoon monkey Curious George. She resolved to rely no longer on foraging expeditions for their entertainment, but to purchase more toys for them herself. Yet even that felt inadequate.

Breaking with protocol, she opened the male's cage without putting Bea away. He leaped into her arms, staggering her backward under both their weights. She fell against the counter, and the apes jumped onto it, hugging one another exuberantly and vocalizing softly. They began to rub their genitals together, and Liane, laughing, tried to separate them.

"Now, now, we'll have none of that in here."

Hammurabi had once described the bonobos as "a little sex-crazed as a species." Liane had read about males fencing with their penises and rubbing their scrotums together, and females demonstrating similar behavior in the wild. Bonobos, she knew, could be the only primate besides humans that has sex in the missionary position. But she'd seen none of this behavior firsthand. Her bonobos were never allowed to touch one another, their cages spaced beyond arm's reach.

Bea looked up, tilted her head and made a noise that caught Liane's attention. The bonobos could be extremely vocal, but this was an articulation that she'd never heard before. It sounded like *en-decko*. Her brother added another novel articulation: something like *bowling-go*. They repeated their respective sounds over and over, and Liane found herself strongly suspecting that they were trying to tell her something.

She studied their faces and reviewed what she knew about animal-human communication. Over the years, several primates had been taught to communicate basic concepts and desires by pointing to pictographs or using American Sign Language; a common chimpanzee named Washoe was among the most famous. But those animals learned from considerable human training, Liane reflected, and skeptics had suggested that they may just be responding to human cues, rather than forming original thoughts and sentences. *Maybe that's what's happening here,* she thought. *Some form of mimicking. But of what? And how?*

"*En-decko. En-decko. En-decko,*" she heard.

Bonobos make lots of noises, Liane thought. Why did these particular sounds unsettle her? But she needn't have answered herself. She already knew these vocalizations differed from anything she'd ever heard from a nonhuman. These sounds greatly resembled *words*.

She furrowed her brow and blinked to clear her head, half wondering whether she'd fallen asleep and begun to dream.

"*Bowling-go. Bowling-go.*"

The apes wouldn't allow Liane to lose focus. They prattled on, seeming to find encouragement in the astonished look on her face.

She captured Bea's attention and pointed to her own chest. "Liane," she said. "Liane."

Bea uttered something that sounded like *liloba*. Was she trying to repeat Liane's name? It didn't seem precisely so. Just gibberish, perhaps, but said with such earnestness that Liane again had trouble dismissing it out of hand.

"*Liloba,*" the brother repeated.

"Liane," Liane said.

"*Moto,*" said Bea.

The apes jumped up and down.

"*Moto. Moto. Moto. Moto.*"

Words in sequence. *Liloba. Moto.* They didn't mean anything to Liane, and yet they appeared to inspire something in the twins. Liane desperately searched their faces for meaning. Had one of them just pointed at her?

2

That evening Liane rode the elevator up to her apartment with an armful of groceries, thinking, of course, of the talking apes, but remaining so stunned that she chose to detach herself from what she thought she'd seen.

She wished she had someone to talk to about them, but she lived alone and had few immediate prospects for companionship. Her work friend, Ronald, said he feared that Liane had fallen into the wrong habits of mind, socially speaking, and thus it was no coincidence that she found herself alone again on a Friday night. She pictured the look he would wear Monday. Tan and buff, slightly effeminate, older than Liane, he had a life partner named Keith and he enjoyed his playtime. She'd tell him she sat around her apartment in Lynbrook all weekend and he'd meet the news with a look between contempt and pathos, then talk about the opera he'd attended or the great dinner he'd eaten.

But there was more to Ronald than fun and games. Just the other day, she'd run into him in the parking lot, where she learned that another tech had messed up the records on four dozen of Ronald's rabbits, all of which had to be euthanized. "That's a lotta *lapins*," Ronald joked, but she sensed that the needless slaughter had affected him. Maybe she would tell him about Bea and her brother, but speaking of the primate lab to others—even other employees of Pentalon—was a major transgression and grounds for immediate dismissal.

She opened the door. Her cat, Nicholas, sprung into the small entry hall and began pacing the wood herringbone floor tiles, his orange tail atwitter. He meowed and brushed across her shins as she walked three steps to the galley kitchen and set her grocery sack on the counter. He purred loudly and rubbed the side of his body along her leg and his cheek against the corner cabinet.

She popped the top off a can of cat food, and the whole apartment instantly smelled like kippered salmon with savory sauce. Nicholas leaped onto the counter. He obsessed as she spooned his meal into a ceramic bowl, and while she unpacked her few groceries, he wolfed dinner.

There was a researcher somewhere out in the Midwest, Liane recalled, who was bingeing cats on meth and then dissecting them to examine the organs. She petted Nicholas, then finished stowing the groceries and flopped onto the couch. The living room barely had space for the club chair and an oval wood table with four dining chairs. Simply framed posters of iconic paintings—Van Gogh, Monet, da Vinci—and one or two mirrors rounded out the decor.

Picking up the remote control, Liane flipped languidly through the channels, but none of it stimulated her. *Maybe curl up with Nicholas and watch pay-per-view*, she thought. Instead she turned off the television and took out a small skillet. It had been a while since she'd bothered to cook from scratch. She chopped up some leeks and tomato, washed a handful of basil leaves, and grated a block of Gruyere cheese. *Voila! Frittata!*

She sat at the table with dinner and her laptop, opening a few bills. There were two magazine renewals, electric, rent, three credit cards on which she paid fifty dollars over the minimum, and the car loan. When she finished she had nothing but a plate of crumbs and an online checking balance under a thousand dollars.

When the clock passed seven, she called her mother, as she did every evening these days. Frank, her stepfather, answered, talking in whispers. He said her mother was resting, and Liane promised to visit soon. Renal failure was sapping her mother's vitality a bit more each day. They'd recently faced disappointment with a replacement kidney that turned out to be bruised in the car accident that had killed the donor, so they were back to waiting, and time might run out.

Xenotransplantation—specifically, the use of pig kidneys in humans—was still years away, Liane knew. It wouldn't save her mother, but it might one day save countless others. Axel Flickinger, the Pentalon CEO, ran a program on that subject in another area of the facility. Or so she'd heard. Like everything at the company, it was all hush-hush.

With a tear in her eye, she wished Frank good night and sent kisses to her mother, then hung up. There was a mixer tonight in the building, and she'd determined to go. In the mirror she might have seen eyes that glistened like drops of toasted oil, and hair that was dark and rich. Her lips were full over a cleft chin. But she didn't look at herself that carefully. She threw on some blush and pale lipstick.

Liane stepped into the elevator with a neighbor down the hall, Mickey Ferrone. It had been a while since she'd run into him. He worked the open/close buttons—the ones that never responded to Liane's touch—as if he were operating the lift in one of those old department stores.

"First floor. Ladies apparel," she said, forcing cheerfulness, but Mickey didn't smile. When the doors slid closed she noticed the pet carrier he had tucked under one arm with a sweating six-pack of beer inside. Corona.

"Hey, you ain't seen my cat, have you? Big blackish boy?"

Mickey sounded like he came from the Bronx. He wore a close-fitting flannel shirt with the collar of his white t-shirt showing, an old pair of jeans and broken-in cowboy boots.

"Not lately. Has he gone missing?"

"If you should see him," Mickey said, "the name's Einstein."

"So it's you."

"What's me?"

"The bellowing."

She heard him calling from the window sometimes—"Einstein! Einsteiiiiiin!"—and it sounded nearly as farcical as one might expect, like the genius' father summoning little Albert in from a game of stickball.

"Yeah," Mickey nodded. "Went out this morning and hasn't come back. I've been hoping to lure him into the carrier, but no luck."

Mickey had grass stains on the knees of his jeans.

"You thought you'd tempt him with Corona?" Liane asked. "What is he, a beer cat?"

"Funny."

The elevator doors opened and the two of them stepped out.

"The beer's for his owner," Mickey said. "Care to join me?"

"I'm on my way to this thing, the mixer."

"You'll want the beer. The wine they serve could make your tongue fall out."

They found the lobby nearly deserted. A few people drank from Dixie cups by a small table covered in crepe paper. There were several pasty cheese squares on a round foil platter, fancy toothpicks strewn about.

"Maybe I'll join you in that beer after all," Liane said.

Mickey set down the pet carrier on a console table. He took out two Coronas, pulled an opener from the back pocket of his jeans, and popped off the caps, handing one beer to Liane. She noticed that a Maori-style tattoo circled his wrist, half hidden by a leather watchband.

"Sorry I got no limes," he said, draining half his bottle and exhaling. "This cat thing's been wearing on me all day. Makes it hard to focus. My only plan was to down the six-pack and go looking for Einstein, maybe sit around feeling sorry for myself. I wasn't expecting a date."

"That's a relief. You don't have one."

"Mr. Oakley over there's maybe more your type," he teased. "He's on the prowl but you'd better hurry. He turned ninety last week."

The words cut deeper then he meant them, and she had no retort.

Mickey gestured with the heel of his beer bottle. "What's the name of *your* cat?"

"Nicholas. How'd you know?"

"I see him coming and going sometimes through your window."

"He enjoys his independence. Like Einstein, I guess. Can I help you find him?"

"Thanks, but I'll be crawling around in the bushes. You don't look like the kind of woman who likes to get dirty."

"That's not true. I *work* with animals." She regretted the moment she said it, unsettled by thoughts of the apes. *Were they really trying to speak or had she taken a step toward insanity?*

Mickey was going on about jobs and animals and what–all, she wasn't sure. She struggled to bring herself back. He was asking what she did for a living. It seemed almost absurd to talk about that under the circumstances.

She bit the inside of her lip. "I'd rather not go into it. You?"

"Horses. Mostly at Belmont racetrack."

Liane looked at his broad chest and thick neck. He had a scar across his left cheek, and his hands were thick as clay. She pictured him tossing bales of hay.

He read her mind, winced, then emptied the rest of his beer. "One for the road?"

Before she could answer he made the opener appear. It was plain nickel and polished by frequent handling. She felt out of practice with men.

3

The next morning Liane awakened at four a.m. and emailed Hammurabi for special permission to come into the lab over the weekend. By the time he got back to her it was seven. He assured her that her passkey would be authorized.

"Something wrong?" he added.

"No," she typed. She'd have liked to qualify that but didn't know what else to add.

The sky glowed orange and gray in the sunrise. She turned her back to it and entered the unmarked door, manned by a single guard at this off-hour.

Minutes later, she was washing her hands in the lab sink when she heard an unexpected noise and looked up to see Axel Flickinger closing the door to the small room where the twins resided. She knew from Hammurabi that the company CEO had taken a special interest in the twins, yet she felt her cheeks flush as she looked up into his bony face. Staring down from what seemed a great height, he was a near-opposite of Liane in most regards. His limbs reminded her of rigid circus stilts covered with flowing fabric, and his gray eyes were so light they resembled platinum rings, vibrating with energy. His mane of hair was as white as the starched shirt beneath his navy-blue blazer. In every respect Flickinger exuded power. The rumor mill claimed that his office had been built as a safe room with three-foot-thick concrete walls and an independent ventilation system. One look at him made that easy to believe.

He acknowledged her with a tilt of his head. "You are Ms. Vinson, yes?"

Liane nodded.

"I trust all goes well?"

Liane nodded again. A few bonobos chittered in the background.

"We have a great many subjects in these two rooms. Quite a troop. Dr. Hammurabi tells me the bonobos have acclimated nicely to your handling."

"They're getting more comfortable," Liane allowed. "They have a way to go."

"It is time we began to earn a return on our investment."

Liane's mind jumped to a troop of monkeys down the hall who had steel caps screwed to their heads. She began to protest, but Flickinger held up a palm.

"I have been around experimental animals all my life. It was not a question directed to you, yes? I have spoken to Dr. Hammurabi. They are ready."

His manner was as unsettling to Liane as the words he spoke. It stirred concern in her for the twins, and she wondered whether Flickinger had initiated experiments on them last night or this very morning. They were so vulnerable still, she thought. *How could they be ready?*

The moment he left she went directly to their room. They were fine, alert, unharmed, and Liane felt ungenerous for having suspected anything.

The male, No. 673A, reached out with his long fingers and pulled at the sleeve of her smock. She opened the cage door and he clambered into her arms, his legs encircling her waist. He leaned over and used both hands to take the hand of his twin sister, who was stretching her arm through the bars of her own cage. Liane ran her fingers through the thick hair atop the head of No. 673A and he buried his face in the crook of her neck, making her chuckle. She tossed a stuffed animal into his cage, and when he leaped in after it she closed the door. She was about to greet his sister, No. 673B, when Hammurabi entered.

"It's you," he said.

"I couldn't sleep. Dr. Flickinger says the acclimation period ends soon."

"Yes. I received a lecture on shareholder value yesterday. I've never felt moved by financial abstractions, but we're not funded by Samaritans. Those who give us money expect tangible results in return, even the government entities. And I think this bunch of bonobos has adapted quite nicely, due in no small part to your sensitive handling."

"So can you tell me what the plans are?"

"Of course. We'll be inserting wire coils into the ocular region and electrodes into the cranium."

"For what client?"

"It's a foreign contract. We'll map retinal reception in relation to neurological function. To limit variability, the bonobos will be strapped into special chairs that I'm having constructed in our machine shop. During critical points in the experiments, they'll have their heads anchored in place for precision. We'll incentivize them to cooperate through a system of minor rewards and punishments. You know how that works. Like training the rats with tidbits and water denial."

Liane bit her lip. "And the twins?"

"They won't be among our subjects. Axel has his own plans for them. You'll continue to condition them for handling, along with the others."

In the context of Pentalon's cloak-and-dagger culture, Liane hesitated to press Hammurabi further. Not having begun work on her Ph.D., she felt like a minor player, one among legions, closer in some ways to the animals than to the scientists whom she served.

Hammurabi glanced at his watch. "Saturday. Don't stay too long. Go home and take a break."

He departed, and Liane tried to put the coming experiments out of mind. She waded into the routine as if it were a weekday, removing the bonobos from their cages seriatim and repeating the sequence of human-ape interactions that she felt gratified to have created.

In the small lab again, she sat with the twins, who eyed her attentively. Liane couldn't imagine those intelligent eyes violated with implanted electrical wires. The fact that such a fate was reserved for the other bonobos, not these two, provided small consolation

Not for the first time, she wondered what they might be thinking as they rested on their haunches in the cages, staring out through the bars. But today neither uttered a word.

4

—

Liane's mother and stepfather resided in a modest house that had sprung up in the '30s with a thousand other Tudors in Laurelton,

Queens. When Liane dropped in, Helen and Frank were sitting on lawn chairs in their single garage bay, facing the driveway and the bumper of a high-riding Navigator. Frank's old Harley-Davidson sat in a corner of the garage gathering dust, leather cracking.

He'd set an old television on the floor. Its improvised cable hookup and its power cord—plugged into an outlet by the garage door mechanism—hung braided from the ceiling like a dystopian vine. They kept the sound off, and the imperfect picture revealed Yankees standing around a baseball diamond, but Frank had his face buried in *Betting Monthly*, the bible of his main hobby. As usual, he wore clay-colored leisure shoes with wide Velcro closures and a short-sleeved madras shirt, untucked to hide his growing potbelly.

Liane's mother, also ignoring the television, wore a housedress and worked a pair of knitting needles. Neither of them rose when Liane strode in. She unfolded a third chair and sat beside them.

Frank lifted his eyes from his magazine. "What's been going on at work this week?"

He knows something, she thought. He was always whispering into the phone. He'd worked with Axel many years ago and had helped her land the promotion to the primate lab. The two men continued to speak, for reasons she couldn't comprehend.

"Why do you ask?" she said.

"No reason."

She wished she had the kind of relationship with him that would allow her to share her observations about the bonobos and their apparent use of words. But she'd signed a confidentiality agreement—and, besides, she didn't trust him not to leak the news to Axel. For several days she'd brooded on it, trying to figure every angle. Since the original incident, the bonobos had spoken twice more in her presence—if speaking it was—she couldn't be certain. It was a primate language or something equally unfathomable to her—not an attempt at English, in any case. But if she were right about that, what did it signify? For one thing, a pair of apes could talk about an animal's experience on the other side of the cage door, she thought—not testimony that

Flickinger would be eager to hear or to have broadcast. And perhaps, too, such declarations would be an unsettling prospect for those in the silent human majority who held a rigid understanding of how our relationship with nature should be ordered. Both the religious world-view and the scientific one placed people at the top of the moral pyramid, partly based upon their ability to speak and reason. An ape that could talk, could really talk, if that was what she'd begun to witness, might be welcome as a curiosity, but it might also alarm those who would see it as a challenge to human supremacy.

"Are you with us, Liane?" Frank asked.

"I was just thinking."

"You were going to say something about work."

"Oh, nothing special, no. Just the usual slice-and-dice. You know how it is, Frank."

"You're saying they cut the monkeys?" her mother asked, setting down her needles and yarn. Her face was swollen, her hair thick and gray; the renal failure had caused her skin to lose pliancy. Liane observed that her shins and ankles were bloated with edema.

"Well, you know, Mom, some of the procedures are invasive. I was just using a figure of speech."

"It's not for a layperson's ears," Frank whispered. "I learned over the years never to take the customers behind the scenes of the sausage factory." He frowned. "Bad for business. Things get misinterpreted."

"You're right," Liane said.

She couldn't help wondering whether Frank was thinking just then of her misguided birth father. His work got misinterpreted, all right—because that's what he'd intended. Frank, she knew, held his memory in contempt.

Helen appeared to want to add something about the cutting but then thought better of it. She picked up her knitting again.

"How's my baby, Nicholas?"

"Fine. Feline."

"You should bring him around."

"He doesn't like the pet carrier. He prefers to leave the apartment on his own terms. And I'm looking at cages all day—I just can't shut him up anymore."

"It's getting to you," Helen said. "I can see it."

"No." She wouldn't admit it. Not now. She'd waded in too deep to turn back, particularly after coming to know the twins. "Just a little stressful at this level."

"You'll get comfortable faster than I'll get used to the nursing home."

"Nursing home? What're you talking about, Mom?"

"I'll be in one soon, I fear. I'm dying, Liane."

"You're not dying," Frank said, "any more than we all are. You have a chronic condition."

Liane looked at the pictures of distorted slot machines in the magazine scrunched between Frank's fingers. She rested a hand on her mother's soft knee.

"Mom, what's come over you?"

"Nothing that hasn't been coming for a long time. The poking and prodding. The needles—look at my arm!—black and blue and yellow. Dragging myself around. I've been in and out of the hospital a dozen times in two years. I used to love to dance—remember how we used to dance when we were dating, Frank? I can't dance anymore. I'm worn down, sweetheart."

"Don't be ridiculous, Helen," Frank said. "Everyone has aches and pains at our age. One second you're sitting here making a Christmas scarf and the next thing you've gone all emotional? The organ donor registry will come through any day now. You'll see."

"No, Frank." Tears brimmed her eyes. She dabbed them with a piece of yarn. "That last kidney was a near miracle. At my age, I'm not high on the list. We were born in the wrong generation for what I face. Some-day they'll be growing organs in monkeys, and then maybe in mason jars—but not in time for me."

"Just because that kidney didn't work out? You'll have another chance. We'll see to it, won't we, Liane?"

"If only," Liane muttered. She couldn't believe how on edge she felt.

She looked from her mother to Frank. For the first time she noticed the uneven gray stubble that covered his chin. He must have missed huge swaths while shaving this morning, and he'd never looked more fragile. Maybe he'd been right about everything, setting her on the straight and narrow. Maybe he'd even been right about her father. But where did any of it lead? *They're both in decline*, she thought. Just as the world before her was growing in size and moment, theirs was shrinking toward a vanishing point. Or maybe it had always been shrunken and she'd just noticed.

They'd once been the fount of all wisdom, but now she ached to think how far in the past those moments existed. Her shrink, years ago…no! She decided not to go there.

Frank touched her on the knee. "You'll make us proud, won't you, Liane?"

5
—

Hammurabi's second implant operation ran into complications when he nicked the anterior ciliary artery of a subject with his diamond-blade scalpel, causing bleeding from the eye cavity that a team of three had difficulty stanching. Liane had begun by assisting from the periphery, but when problems arose Hammurabi requested that she contribute sponge work while the others scrambled with the electro-cauterizer. All became soaked by more body fluid than Liane knew any animal could contain—making a mess of scrubs and surgical gowns.

Afterward, she was alone with Hammurabi in the operating room of the primate lab. She leaned against the green-tiled wall to relieve her fatigue. Perhaps exhaustion loosened her lips. She could no longer contain herself about the twins.

"Dr. Hammurabi, is it possible, in your opinion, that a bonobo would ever evolve the ability to talk?"

"How do you mean?"

"Speak w-words," she stammered. "From their mouths." She was aware that she uttered her own words with childlike hesitancy.

Hammurabi looked down at his tasseled loafers, which always looked impeccable and expensive. He removed his surgical cap and lowered his mask to reveal dark Middle Eastern skin, pockmarked cheeks, and thick black hair behind a receding hairline.

"I think you already know the answer to that and it's emphatically negative," he said. "Certainly, if a bonobo or any other primate had done so, we would know of such a thing. That would be big news."

His usual collegial tone had become didactic, as if he were lecturing a high school student.

Liane peeled off her mask and gloves and tossed them into the biohazard discard bin. She pressed on, struggling for an air of professionalism.

"I'm not asking whether one has spoken in the past," she forced herself to say. "Only whether, in your opinion, such a manifestation lies within the realm of possibility."

Hammurabi shook his head. "Setting aside the issue of language development in the brain," he said, "great apes don't have the physical capacity to speak. Their vocal chords are too high up in the throat to manage sounds the way we do. It's like the difference, if you will, between fine and gross motor control. Just because a person can wave her arms doesn't mean she can move her fingers. Just because she can move her fingers doesn't mean she can write with a pencil. Apes don't have the innate ability to create the sounds that real speech requires. Like any animal, they're more or less at the limit with what they already do."

He stepped on the trash pedal, pulled off one glove, and dropped it in.

"You must know this from your reading," he said. "To the degree primatologists understand them, bonobos do communicate quite a lot of information to one another with their vocalizations. This is especially true in the wild. But nobody would confuse that with the way humans communicate."

"And yet," Liane said.

Hammurabi's eyes widened. "Why are you asking this? Are you

suggesting, Liane, that you have heard a bonobo use something that approximates human speech?"

She touched the front of her surgical gown and felt the fabric going stiff with drying blood. Undoubtedly, from the expression on his face, Hammurabi was reassessing her competence with each new remark. But she hadn't raised the subject lightly. Whenever she was alone with the bonobos and they felt secure, the words now flowed. She hinted this to Hammurabi, and she thought his face betrayed a thread of recognition, as if Liane's questions confirmed a suspicion he already harbored.

He sighed, pulling off the other glove and running a hand over his scalp. "You're not speaking theoretically."

"No, Adnan."

Hammurabi assessed her carefully and peeled off his surgical gown, exposing a remarkably unruffled silk tie and a substantial paunch. He folded the gown inside out by habit before depositing it into the bin.

"Have you told anyone else of your—your observations?"

She frowned and shook her head.

Abruptly, Hammurabi seized her upper arm.

"You mustn't reveal this to anyone! I will investigate. I promise you that. But no more independent study between you and the bonobos!"

She hesitated, considering the meaning of his clutch on her arm.

"Liane," he persisted, "do you understand what I'm asking of you?"

She did. He was asking that she burrow back to her place under the cloak of secrecy. Yet, for the first time ever, she saw uncertainty in his dark eyes.

6

When Mickey Ferrone got home from work he headed straight for the bottle of wine that had been sitting atop his refrigerator for three weeks. Then he did what he always did these days. He carried it down unopened to the lobby and sat in a chair, wondering when he'd ever catch a glimpse of Liane Vinson.

Since he'd spoken with her at the mixer, Mickey had found Liane as elusive as a hundred-to-one payoff. Not that he was a betting man. He was more of a bull than a gambler. He'd already called her three times and left messages, all unreturned. If he figured the odds of a date at this point, he'd be set for a bust—beautiful woman like that. On the other hand, she couldn't shake him forever, not if he covered the mailboxes. Even beauties had bills to pay.

The front door opened and a tall old man shuffled in, curved back, wearing dark glasses. Mr. Oakley. Mickey gave him a smile and a wave.

Oakley pointed to the bottle as he walked over. "Got some good stuff there?"

"Lacryma Christi."

"Hell of a name."

Mickey shrugged. "Campania—near Vesuvius. Legend has it that Lucifer laid bare the landscape and it made Jesus weep in heaven."

"So?"

"So the tears fell to earth, wet the ground. A very special vine grew."

"Gosh, that's morbid. Don't tell her."

"Don't tell who?" Mickey lifted an eyebrow.

"You think I don't know?" Oakley laughed. "I'm half-blind, yet I see more than you kids."

The front door opened again. Mickey rose to his feet.

"What a coincidence," the old man observed. "It's her."

They watched Liane come over, looking distracted.

"What's her?" she asked.

"Not 'her,'" Oakley said. "You. The woman of his dreams."

"Is that right?" Liane said. "You two were talking about me?"

"No." Mickey shook his head. "Not exactly."

Oakley shook his head more vigorously than Mickey had. "We were talking about that bottle of wine he's been carrying around, probably gone off by now in his sweaty palms."

"Thanks for the help, Mr. Oakley. I'll take it from here."

Oakley ignored him. He turned to face Liane and lifted the glasses from his nose. "And you… You could do worse than a veterinarian."

"A vet?"

"She doesn't know," Mickey said. "Hey, can I buy you dinner?"

Her look said that was the last thing she needed. She eyed them both.

"I'm kind of busy right now. How about a rain check?"

7

—

In the calm of midnight, the wired innards of Pentalon emitted a tremulous buzz, ten thousand sensors monitoring every movement.

Vlad Gretch, director of Pentalon security, relished it. If Gretch had a routine—and he made sure never to be predictable—his frequent jogs through the company's halls at night would have been part of it. But mostly he followed his instincts when choosing a time. Yesterday he'd run in the afternoon. The day before at four a.m. Twelve o'clock felt right tonight; a certain magic hung in the air at this hour.

His elevated heartbeat sharpened Gretch's mind. His thoughts, as always, focused on the space between possibility and action. It was Vlad Gretch's conviction that stability was an illusion; that the world—and each of Man's endeavors—teetered ever on the brink of chaos. He'd spent his life, had devoted every waking moment, to forestalling that day. And he'd succeeded so far. A former Green Beret and Secret Service agent, he had medals and commendations to prove it.

As he reached a comfortable rhythm, the squeak of his Nikes fading into subconsciousness, Gretch began to consider the broad context of his current work. It paid to think. A thirty-million-dollar budget and two hundred security employees worldwide meant nothing unless you allowed for the role psychology played in the threats lurking out there—not to mention the threats germinating within Pentalon's very walls.

The adaptability of sentient living things was their greatest strength, Gretch believed—and also their most profound weakness. Everyone above a certain pay grade at Pentalon knew that the cameras intended to protect them from others also had the capability to watch employees. Yet the greatest intellects in the laboratory failed to remember—or their arrogance didn't allow them to accept—that what Gretch saw every day could cut them as deeply as the sharp instruments they wielded on the animals. If they understood that the surveillance systems might extend beyond a few lenses in their view, they didn't behave as such. The smiling, uniformed guards and the visible cameras, blatant in their smoked glass bubbles, were nutrients on which false confidence fed.

Long ago he'd concluded with some amusement that those most wary of prying eyes were not the business executives or the scientists with stacks of graduate degrees. The most circumspect were those with the fewest prospects for advancement. In the unspoken caste system of Pentalon, the janitors, the orderlies, the cafeteria workers, the machinists faded into nothingness as thoroughly as the untouchables of Calcutta. Their overlords ignored them until a bucket needed fetching or a pile of entrails called for removal. But this group knew better than to whisper, even in the darkest corners when no one else appeared to be present. Maybe their street smarts told them something the scientists wouldn't have learned in college: Not all rats in the Pentalon building had tails and walked on all fours.

At a randomly selected door, Gretch laid his thumb over the security reader. When the door opened he high-stepped through the narrow aisles of a large supply room, seeing no sign of trouble. Barely sweating, he reentered the hall and broke into a wind sprint. He doubled back, deked to the left at a T, then went right, opened another door with his thumbprint, jogged around the long oval table of an executive conference room.

The Pentalon quarterly board meeting had gone well, according to Flickinger—and Gretch had confirmed it independently. Pentalon would soon announce that the company had exceeded analysts' projections for a twelfth consecutive quarter. Profits were rising by double digits and the stock price had gone on a tear. The prospect of several major testing contracts hovered just over the horizon, and the rare bonobos would satisfy an enormously lucrative order from the Indonesians, who weren't as fussy as Americans when it came to such things as so-called "endangered species."

Flickinger's growing attachment to the twins worried him, though. While Gretch couldn't tell peach preserves from jellyfish, he knew that, in theory, experiments on twins, with their genetic overlap, commanded exponential premiums. But these twins had something else going on, something that made them a pet project for the boss. And pet projects, like any obsession, opened up vulnerabilities that could be exploited by Pentalon's enemies.

Radicals were out there, wishing the company harm. In fact, if he could believe the FBI reports on his desk, the radicals did more than wish harm—they sought ways to inflict it. In Gretch's five-year tenure, not a single security incident had interfered with the march toward staggering profitability, but that could change in an instant. Bonuses and stock options might cover the inconvenience of metal detectors and the humiliation of being spat upon now and then, but it was a vein of fear that really kept everyone on their toes—from the lowliest technician to department heads and board members. That's why Gretch permitted the protesters at the front gate to stay. *Free speech? Laughably quaint.* He could have them gone in a day, he thought, and he would do so if ever it suited his purposes.

But the boss's obsessions—those were another matter.

The cinderblock hallways instilled a chill at this hour, and it took Gretch a long time to build up a satisfying sweat. He never lost breath, though. He had more wind than an Oklahoma prairie, more strength than three men.

Early adversity had made him strong—long walks home from school through Chicano gang territory on the west side of Dallas. They taunted him at first. Then they took his knapsack and scattered his books on the ground. Then they burned him with their lit cigarettes and beat him and showed him their shivs and their knives and their brass knuckles and their socks full of rocks. They convinced him that they'd kill him one day. And they taught him, without meaning to, that in places where society's rules don't reach, the prevailing powers set their own parameters.

The gang members had outnumbered him. To fight was not an option, so he'd learned to run. He stayed late after school and did wind sprints on the football field when the team wasn't practicing. He started with twenty-yard segments, and by the time he was fifteen, he was dragging a tire behind him. He became a fullback—best in school history. He later ran with his platoon mates and his buddies; he ran with presidents and dignitaries.

Somewhere along the way, his response to the gang morphed into something greater, more gut testing. He grew from despising the footsteps behind to feeling likewise about the footsteps in front, so if anyone got in his way he knocked them down and ran right over them. If they blocked him again, he pummeled them. And if they gave him serious reason to fear, he killed them.

When tonight's exercise laps drew to a close, Gretch had covered several miles and dropped into a dozen locked rooms. In the main laboratory, lit only in small pools away from the animal cages, he sensed a hundred eyes upon him, feral but cowed. He scared them; they scared him. He liked that. He placed his hand on the final security pad and jogged in place at Flickinger's mahogany door. When it slid open, he threw himself onto the cream leather couch.

Unsurprised to see Gretch at this hour—never surprised to see his director of security—the CEO sat behind his spotless glass desk holding a small white rodent in his left hand, toying with it. The mouse was quick, but Flickinger had practiced reflexes. Though his eyes never left his guest, the creature couldn't escape.

Gretch watched indifferently, one leg dangling over an arm of the couch.

"Listen," he said finally, "we've got a problem in the monkey lab."

8
—

For several days Hammurabi's silence about the bonobo twins dampened Liane's spirits like a low-lying cloud. Then, one afternoon, he returned from a meeting with determination in his stride.

"Take a female from the troop," he instructed her, "and the female twin. Prepare them, please, for the MRI lab."

Liane located a sedative and made the injections. When Bea and the other bonobo were out cold, she strapped them to boards. She notified Hammurabi and they wheeled them on a gurney into a small room dominated by a massive white machine.

They slid the non-twin into the center of the MRI ring and focused the equipment on the animal's head and neck. When the machine powered up, Liane felt a vague tremor in her viscera. Standing shoulder to shoulder, she and Hammurabi studied the pictures it produced on a nearby monitor.

"This one's the control, correct?"

Liane nodded.

Hammurabi pointed out several aspects of the neck and larynx. Using the computer they carefully measured the distance from the top of the ape's larynx to the bottom of the C-1 vertebra. They captured a few images and saved them.

"Now," Hammurabi said, "let's have a look at Number 673B."

As they were sliding her into the MRI machine, Hammurabi began to murmur, "Crazy little bonobo. We'll have your secrets. *Wapi, wapi,* indeed."

Liane stiffened. "You heard them?"

He nodded. "Also something that sounded like *wapi Liane.* Certainly a vocalization I haven't ever observed."

"No, it was *liloba* they said," Liane corrected.

"I don't think so. I heard *liloba,* too. Distinct from *Liane.*"

"I never heard them say my name," Liane reflected.

"I've made some sound recordings and transliterated the articulations myself," Hammurabi continued. "I counted twenty-seven distinct vocalizations for which I find no reference in the literature. Whether these signals are communicative or meaningless, I don't know. But they appear to be purposeful. If there is meaning, they're either speaking some chimpanzee tongue or a human language they've picked up somewhere, the way they learned your name. Still,"—he caught himself—"it's far more likely their articulations are merely the repetition of sounds that their unusual vocal equipment can make—sounds that they're testing out, but that have no real significance beyond that, or no grammatical structure, at least, which is what distinguishes human speech."

"But if it's gibberish, how does my name get wrapped up in it?"

"Good question. Have you seen the Gary Larsen cartoon about what we say versus what a dog hears? I have it tacked to the wall above my desk. The master says, 'Okay, Ginger! I've had it! You stay out of the garbage! Understand, Ginger? Stay out of the garbage, or else!' And what the dog hears is 'blah blah Ginger blah blah blah Ginger,' et cetera. Your name, perhaps, if you've repeated it to the bonobos—against all regulations, I might add, but never mind—your name possibly has become iconic for them. And they've picked it up, all right, much as Rover knows his own name. A dog has the equipment to hear, but how much does it process? Maybe these bonobos have the equipment to speak, but that doesn't mean they're speaking in the sense that humans do."

Hammurabi's eyes came to rest on the padded black feet protruding from the MRI donut. "If it *is* real language, though—bonobo language with human-like syntax—we may require a linguist to sort it out. Meanwhile, I've sent off a sample of their blood and saliva for DNA analysis, along with the same from a random member of the troop. The odds of a simultaneous mutation of the larynx and the primate's comparable Broca's area—the part of the frontal lobe that controls language in humans—seems unfathomable, but not impossible. The physical part we'll know definitively in a matter of minutes."

Again they adjusted the equipment as required and stirred the giant machine to action. As the three-dimensional images appeared on the screen, Hammurabi worked the computer mouse and measured the space from Bea's larynx to her C-1.

"Measure three times, faint once," he joked.

Liane had been hanging on every word. The tension made her feel giddy. She knew that much of science existed in a kind of gray area, subject to interpretation and ever-refined theory, with absolute truth eluding the scientist like a receding horizon. But even so, *some* things were black and white.

As she and Hammurabi absorbed themselves in the crystal-clear MRI image, the director of the primate lab worked the electronic calipers, measured and captured the results.

The fact settled on them together, black and white: They were looking at the digital image of a mutated bonobo, with a larynx that sat significantly lower in the neck than normal.

Hammurabi swallowed audibly.

"Liane," he declared, "you may soon become the most famous lab assistant in the history of primate studies."

She felt a degree of uneasy vindication, let out a breath.

"But," Hammurabi continued, "we must proceed with caution. We'll conduct further tests, you and I, perhaps call in some other experts. And prepare a paper for peer review. All, that is, if we can get Axel Flickinger's approval. That may be difficult."

"Why wouldn't he support us?" Liane allowed herself, for the time being, to ignore the nagging implications she'd already considered. "A breakthrough like this could permanently place Pentalon in the annals of science."

"Yes. And fame is the last of all bastions Axel may want to conquer.

Think of how much controversy our routine work generates. To have a pair of talking apes on top of that—an endangered species, no less—in an animal-testing facility, could attract scads of unwanted attention. Not to mention interfering with whatever plans he has for these bonobos."

"But if he plans to incapacitate them in any way, we'll have to stop him now," Liane thought aloud.

"What do you mean, Liane? As the chief executive he is hardly beholden to us. He paid a lot of money for these animals and he follows his own guidance. We're not in a position to tell him how to proceed." He ran a finger around his ear, half talking to himself. "Maybe I can find a sponsor to fund language research."

"I could look into that," Liane suggested.

Hammurabi screwed up his face, exaggerating his protruding jaw. "Axel—" he muttered. "Our time—we are already so overcommitted."

Liane couldn't believe what she was hearing. "A great scientific discovery meets an inexorable—what?—time-management problem? This is bigger than that, isn't it?"

"Surely. But we must always consider the context."

He stared into space for a few moments, then recovered himself.

"These apes will be waking up soon. Please return them to their cages."

She pointed to the animal still in the rack, and Hammurabi walked over to help, facing her over the hairy chest.

"Have you revealed this to anyone?" he asked.

"Of course not. You told me not to."

"We must maintain the secret. You appreciate why?"

"Yes." Together they lifted the boards with the bonobos onto the gurney. "But, if we confirm that these apes have acquired the ability to talk, how do you explain the coincidence of mutating for speech and language simultaneously?"

"One possible misperception about evolution is that it occurs gradually," Hammurabi said, powering down the MRI machine. "Many paleontologists, in fact, now believe that it has historically occurred in leaps—so-called 'punctuated equilibrium'—which may partly explain

why we find many gaps in the fossil record. So if there's a double mutation and those mutations are coincident, it wouldn't be the first time
evolutionary processes have taken such a leap."

Hammurabi drummed his fingers on the edge of the gurney. "Then
again," he said, "there are few people studying these animals in the wild.
If these bonobos can talk, we're likely seeing the culmination of a series of
mutations, not a single genetic change. Perhaps the members of one new
evolutionary branch, for example, have the mental capacity for language
but vocal chords too high in the throat. Or another branch's individuals
might manifest the lower voice box without having the cognitive ability to
use it. Bonobos in that state may've been running around for a thousand
generations at the periphery of the main population. And as long as the
animals' articulations weren't novel, no one noticed."

"We should put the others in this troop through the MRI."

"I've already undertaken a physical examination of their necks.
They're clearly normal."

"So, besides the twins, there's no other bonobo with a mutation?"

"Not inside this lab, no." He pointed a bent finger to the wall.
"But that doesn't mean there aren't any bonobos with a mutation—
out there."

9

He was there again. Mickey. Flashing the sad eyes and toting that
bottle of wine like a puppy with a tug toy. Twice she'd ducked him
before he saw her. Now she marched right up and snatched it from him.

"There! Happy?"

He looked even more dejected and followed her to the mailboxes.

She turned on him. "What is it with you men?"

"Us men? I can't speak for the whole gender. I just thought we could maybe get to know one another better. I got this sense that you and me have a lot in common."

"Life isn't all lost cats. You found him, didn't you?"

"An hour after we spoke about it. How's *your* baby?"

"He's not my baby. Is it true what Mr. Oakley said...that you're a vet?"

Mickey nodded. "At the track. My accent had you fooled—admit it. No one could educate that outta me."

"It's kind of cute. Contrarian."

"This is good. We're having a conversation, not just bantering. Care to share that?" He nodded to the bottle in her hand.

She rolled her eyes at his persistence as they entered the elevator together. "I'll have to keep it short. I'm stressed-out at work."

"The animals?"

"How'd you know?"

"You mentioned it before. What kinds are they?"

She didn't answer. She ushered him into her apartment and pointed him to a corkscrew. They sat on the couch, neutral corners.

He reached over and tapped her elbow. "You were gonna tell me about your work."

"No I wasn't." *The straight and narrow*, she thought, recalling the program after her youthful offense. *Somewhere along the line, it morphed into narrow straits.*

"What are you so embarrassed about?"

"It's not that. I signed a nondisclosure agreement."

"Ah. So it's someone else who's embarrassed."

"You could say. I don't know. They're a kind of chimpanzee. Highly—highly specialized."

"They'd have to be, to run a whole company."

"Ha ha." She grew thoughtful. "These apes...they're practically human. It's disconcerting."

"So why'd you take the job?"

Why indeed? She smiled and shook her head. "It's a long story. I had a turbulent childhood and went off the rails a bit, sort of got arrested."

"How does a person 'sort of' get arrested?"

"No jail time, but it postponed college for me, limited my options—maybe my ambition, too."

"That's too bad. Everyone's gotta have a dream in America, right?"

"If it doesn't trample someone else's dream. Mine, eventually, was just to be normal."

"In my family, 'normal' meant toeing Dad's line. I wasn't so good at that." Mickey ran a hand through his hair and finished his wine. "Limited ambition's a helluva thing. You didn't let a few setbacks keep you from continuing to dream, did you?"

Liane shook her head, but not in answer to Mickey's question. She'd told him a lot without mentioning the denouement of it all: Pentalon.

"I have to take responsibility for my own actions. That's what my shrink said and she was right. I developed this catchphrase: the straight and narrow."

"Ah. And you're there now?"

"Damned if I know."

They laughed together.

"And it involves apes?" he asked.

"I can't really talk about that." She cast her eyes down.

Mickey ran the back of a thumbnail across the scar on his cheek. "You know, Liane, I've destroyed horses on the track while thousands of people watched."

"How horrible!"

He stuck out his lower lip. "Sometimes I go to Brooklyn and ride the ferry back and forth from Manhattan, just to think in the fresh air. I'm guessing your relationship with those primates is something you're not so proud of, either. But I want you to know that I understand what happens when animals meet commerce. I'm not in a position to be your conscience, and I don't wanna be, but if you ever need a shoulder, I'm here."

"Thanks for saying that, Mickey. I'm all right for now, I think."

But as soon as she said it, Liane lost herself in the middle space. When she was studying biology, she'd never pictured her future life this way—pent-up with unarticulated conflicts. All she'd seen was a young woman settling into a stable existence, earning a few bucks, staying out of trouble, maybe making the world a little better along the way. Straightening out the errors of a twisted past.

When Mickey left she pushed the door closed with her butt and watched Nicholas step in through the window. She frowned and wiped away a tear.

Her father—her birth father—had been a scientist. A gentle soul, he'd never hurt anything more than a dish of agar—not intentionally, anyway. But he had aspirations beyond the results he'd seen in the cancer lab. After a couple of decades, the grants dried up and he had to go off in another direction. His next research proved more fruitful, or so it seemed, and the adulation started finally to roll in. There were articles in leading journals, which led to prestigious positions, larger grants, bigger paydays.

The family moved into a house in Sands Point—not a huge house, but surrounded by mansions. Liane was fourteen and shy, but she made a few friends: the children of doctors and Wall Street traders and corporate executives. Their parents were the winners of society. The high school seniors in her district drove brand-new Camaros and Saabs. The parents of her new best friend invited Liane on a trip to Paris that summer.

She never got to go.

It began as whispers behind closed doors. Her mother, back when she was strong, insisted on the answers to questions, questions that often began 'how': "How does this happen, Joe?" "How can a misunderstanding of this kind occur?" "Tell me again: How did the data get corrupted?" Finally, "How could you, Joe? How could you?"

It turned out there was an unattractive explanation for her father's meteoric rise after so much failure: fraud. The papers, the adulation, the money…all the product of a fraud that Liane's father had perpetrated. Before it came out, some doctors had taken actions based upon her father's 'research.' Actions that had resulted in deaths.

In an instant they were ruined as a family—ruined and banished from the high life. A year later, her father lay dead of cancer, an ironic end, it would seem—except that Liane suspected he'd somehow injected it into himself.

Her mother remarried quickly, to Frank, another man who'd built his life on lab work—but honestly, and without nearly so much ambition. Liane couldn't look at him at first. She felt depleted at a most awkward age. She couldn't bear to hold her head up among the in-crowd at her high school. She couldn't bear Frank's too-earnest advice and thinly veiled contempt for her father, charlatan that he'd been. She gravitated to the wrong crowd, hung out with the smokers and rebels and iconoclasts. That's how she'd met Corey Harrow, the guy who would carry her from the hot plate into the cauldron.

10

Early the next morning, Liane found Hammurabi with the twins outside their cages, against his own strict procedures. It was an instant snapshot that would linger with her forever: the director huddled with the bonobo twins—interspecies coconspirators.

The bonobos greeted Liane with enthusiasm, hugging one another and rubbing their genitals together. Liane and Hammurabi dissolved into laughter as the apes chanted, *"awa, awa, awa."* The male jumped into Liane's arms, sending her paper coffee cup tumbling into the sink and nearly knocking her over. He nuzzled her neck.

Hammurabi took the Curious George toys from the cages and tossed them around. When he lobbed one to Liane, the male bonobo snatched it from the air with little effort, leaped down to the floor, then sprung in Hammurabi's direction, trying to get the second toy, too. Hammurabi tossed that one, and it sailed through the air. Liane caught it as Bea jumped up and down, crying, *"en-decko, en-decko."* The keep-away game continued raucously, and Liane absorbed this glimpse of her boss with appreciation. Until this moment, she'd known only his intense work life. She now thought this must be how he was in the yard with his children on rare days off.

They played for a while—the bonobos uttering words, if they were words, beyond human understanding—until Liane and Hammurabi collapsed in exhaustion. The bonobos, still full of energy, returned to their cages reluctantly. Sadness clouded Hammurabi's face. He directed Liane to a chair in the neighboring lab, across the room from the cages. They sat with their knees nearly touching, Hammurabi rounding his shoulders and closing his legs on his hands as if to stay warm.

"I grew up in Baghdad, you know," he said. "Long before all the chaos there. In the bazaar they had a man with a vervet monkey—little fellow with a grayish tan coat and a small black face. The man would play a concertina while the monkey danced for coins. Sometimes we kids gave him raw pea pods that we'd filched off the ground in the market, and I became fascinated by the dexterousness of those near-human hands, with their fingernails so much like ours, peeling open the shells and extracting the peas. The monkey seemed like a child, only wiser. An old soul. I couldn't stare at him long enough. I'd park myself there while my mother shopped"—he lowered his eyelids, seeing it— "and I remained in that spot, like I was standing in cement."

He tugged an ear. "In some respects I owe everything I have to that little vervet monkey. I wanted to learn what made him tick, and he inspired a curiosity that has served me well these many years. But curiosity has its dangers, you know. In Baghdad under Saddam it sent many people to the torture chambers. Here, living in this paradise, the dangers of curiosity always seemed far away. How ironic that it should now lead to my termination."

Liane sat forward. "Your termination?"

He extracted a cigarette from his shirt pocket and lit it, in violation of Pentalon rules. This alarmed Liane almost as much as the faraway look on his face. He was barely present.

"Adnan, please put it out before someone comes."

He took a long drag and flicked the ashes onto the floor. "It doesn't matter any longer." He exhaled slowly through his nostrils, the cloud rising and dissipating near the smoke detector. "Life will go on, but my relationship with Pentalon is finished. Axel found out about the twins."

"That they talk?"

"That we've begun our own studies of them."

"So what?"

He bristled, took another puff, picked a speck of tobacco from his plump lip. "Axel doesn't brook insubordination. We argued and he fired me."

The air went out of Liane. "But how can that be?"

"Like our chattering apes: It can't be, but it is."

"But the primate lab is nothing without you."

"Oh, I doubt that. There isn't a soul on earth who's indispensable. A twenty-eight-year career…" He dropped his cigarette to the floor and tamped it out with a heel. "Something in this environment of oppressive secrecy had to come along and end it. We don't live in a democracy between these walls."

He frowned and opened his mouth to add something, but in that instant four men strode into the lab, jolting Hammurabi and Liane from their chairs. Liane's eyes swept the room. It was Flickinger, Gretch—the head of security—and two guards. All four stood over six feet tall, and the guards had barrel chests. Though they didn't touch anyone, their intrusion upon the stillness of the lab implied a physical threat. The bonobo troop erupted into hooting and hollering. Danger signals. A few shook the bars of their cages.

Gretch cast a wary eye upon them while Flickinger spoke.

"Good morning, Dr. Hammurabi. Ms. Vinson. I am afraid this partnership already has outlived its usefulness to Pentalon. Very sad, yes? You have been a loyal colleague for so long, Adnan. Who would have thought you would throw it all away on a couple of bonobos! Pentalon has already made you a wealthy man. No one will cry for you. Now it turns out the week I gave you to conclude your business was too long, yes?"

Flickinger stooped and picked up the cigarette butt that Hammurabi had ground into the floor. With a scowl he handed it to one of the security guards.

Liane stepped forward to write a different ending, to stand up to Flickinger. "You can't blame Adnan for this!"

She hesitated. She only vaguely had in mind what to say—some kind of grand statement that would reverse everything. As she struggled for words, Hammurabi and his escorts passed through the door, not pausing, not looking back.

Liane went to catch him, but Flickinger hooked her shoulder, spun her around.

"Don't touch me!" she said.

He let go and drew his lips tight. A vein pulsed in his neck.

The bonobos had escalated into a riot of nearly deafening howls. Opening his hand, Flickinger directed Liane into the neighboring hallway, and the primate calls faded as the door drifted closed.

"Those apes can raise a racket," he said. "But you will notice that on this side of the door their voices go unheard. Do you know why? Because they are different from us. Qualitatively. Even the man sweeping the street knows that!"

Liane pressed her teeth together. Inside the lab they'd just exited, the yellow step-back line followed the perimeter. In life there was a line, too. She thought about breaching it, but remembered her promises to the judge, to her psychologist, to her mother and Frank, and to herself. She held her tongue.

Spittle had formed at the corners of Flickinger's mouth.

"Those are *my* apes, young lady! This is not a free-for-all."

"They're special."

"I know that very well. Nothing lands here by accident. In so short a time you have lost all sense of proportion." He narrowed his brow, looking for contrition. She gave it to him and he nodded, gratified. He took a breath. "Dr. Hammurabi is most at fault, yes? Still, a price must be paid. Collect your things. You are back to the rats."

11

An unfamiliar car occupied the driveway when Liane pulled up to her mother's house that evening. Frank sat in his Lincoln by the curb, talking quietly into his ever-present cell phone. He waved as Liane approached, then turned away. Mounting the front steps, she heard the SUV start behind her and tracked the engine's hum as it pulled into the growing darkness.

A woman greeted Liane at the door. She had mocha skin and a round face with a prominent mole on her cheek. Liane introduced herself as the daughter. "You must be the nurse."

"I'm Claudine, the home health aide." Her accent was West Indian. "Helen's resting in her bedroom."

They proceeded to the door of her mother's room, which stood ajar. Her mother lay on the bed with her eyes closed, snoring. Claudine and Liane walked into the kitchen and sat.

"Thank you for being here," Liane said.

"It's my job."

"Of course. She's fading, isn't she?"

"I'm not a registered nurse, but I have seen many sick people. Her condition is weak. She needs a kidney urgently."

"She's been talking about not feeling well, but it seemed more emotional than physical. I can't believe her health has turned this quickly."

"Folks in her state can be surprisingly fragile."

"I should've paid more attention, but half my mind's been on work."

"What is it that you do, if you don't mind me asking?"

"I don't mind, but I'd rather not talk about it." The mere thought of Pentalon made the bile rise. "I'm in the medical field, one could say."

"I see. So we have something in common."

"I suppose."

Claudine poured two mugs of tea and prepared a plate of sugar cookies. The house felt so quiet that the crunch of a cookie seemed irreverent.

"Your father will be back shortly."

"He's my stepfather. My father's been dead many years. It's good to know you're here taking care of Mom. Is it full-time?"

"Yes. I'm staying in the guest bedroom."

"That used to be my room. It wasn't always tan like that. It was all pink once."

"Your mother told me. She's very proud of you."

Liane smiled politely. She noticed a pack of Camels on the table and offered Claudine a cigarette break, but she demurred. They looked off, two strangers, never meant to know one another.

Liane's cell phone broke the silence. The connection was poor, echoing.

"Liane? That you?" It was Hammurabi. "I'm sorry to call so late, but you must come right away."

The tone of his voice said enough. He suggested a meeting place on Sunrise Highway in Rockville Centre. Liane knew the spot.

The phone cut off.

12

At the door of the restaurant, Liane paused to watch steam hiss from clattering woks. She used to come here with high school friends, stumble in after drinking kamikazes to ravenously consume fistfuls of moo shoo pork with extra hoisin sauce. Underage drinkers still crammed around the larger tables, tucking into mounds of shrimp fried rice or curried rice noodles. Several people crowded by the hostess station, waiting to be seated. Liane pushed past them.

Hammurabi occupied a maroon lacquer stool at the bar. He stood and gave her a warm embrace, the sudden intimacy taking her aback. She eased onto a stool beside him and requested a club soda.

"You'll want something stiffer," he said, ordering her a glass of white wine.

She didn't come for small talk or cocktails. She combed her eyes over Hammurabi. His thin hair was tousled and his skin looked pasty.

"What's happened?" she asked.

"I didn't think you'd show. The call dropped."

"I presumed it was you hanging up. You seemed in a hurry."

"It regards the bonobos."

"No doubt." They'd become the center of both their lives.

When her glass of wine came, Hammurabi drank from his rum and Coke, then extracted his cell phone and weighed it in his hand, taking its measure.

"I have to begin with a confession," he said. "For my entire career I've successfully avoided the problem of identification with the animals. I've done so by putting a box around what we do." He tapped his fingers nervously on his glass. "By putting a box around who *we are* and who *they are*—the primates. You don't step outside your box, you don't let them outside theirs, and the question never arises of where the most important distinction lies—the threshold of being, I mean. In *Genesis* God tells man not only to be fruitful, but to fill the world and to subdue it, to rule over the fish and the birds and every living creature that moves on the earth. But our superiority, like any form of authority, is easier to handle if we can impose it from a distance, isn't it?"

Liane drank from her wine. It tasted flimsy and tart. "I don't get what this has to do with the bonobos."

"Yes you do. Rules are what we make, rules!—to keep us in our superior frame of being and the animals in their inferior one. Am

I right? Rule: It's the same word for a set of principles and for dominion over other beings. Long ago Flickinger and I set the rules for the Pentalon laboratories. We put them in place to keep us from anthropomorphizing, to maintain professional detachment. But these are only euphemisms, Liane, so the employees can live with themselves, so we can avoid confronting the prospect that we ourselves have crossed a line laid down not by us, but by a higher power."

Hammurabi tossed aside his straw and finished his drink in a long swig. He signaled the bartender for another while Liane gawked at the golden tassels of the Chinese lanterns that hung from the bar. She felt the back of her neck going warm.

"So that's your confession, Adnan?"

"No. My confession is that I allowed myself to name one of the bonobos. The male twin, Number 673A. For the first time in my professional life and in secret."

"What name did you give him?"

"I called him Isaac. So stupid! Isaac. Remember? The one God asked Abraham to sacrifice?"

"When?"

"From the beginning. I felt some kind of affinity. Hmm." He scratched his jaw. "I almost said, 'kinship.' How strange. I named him furtively, and then I called him that name aloud sometimes when I was alone with the bonobos, against all protocol."

"That doesn't seem so terrible."

Hammurabi placed the cell phone on the bar and tilted it up so he and Liane could share the small screen. He tapped, and a picture snapped into the frame. It showed a bonobo splayed against a shiny silver background.

"A surgical procedure," Hammurabi said. "Axel Flickinger wielding the scalpel. Ronald, the tech who used to work with the rabbits, assisting. He emailed me these pictures as soon as he was alone. They can't be more than a few hours old."

He swept through the photos, garishly lit, grainy, somewhat distorted. Yet unmistakable to the humans who knew these creatures best. It was the male twin, No. 673A—Isaac—on a stainless steel table. Liane watched the images flash before her in sequence. There were only five or six shots, but Hammurabi flicked through them in a loop and back. The unconscious face with its thin lips and perfect stub of a nose. A swath of shaved skin. A gash of receding flesh. A pink wound flared open. A wet gaping hole.

The face, the gash, the wound. Liane stopped seeing in detail. Her vision blurred. The revulsion sent something inside her into spasm.

They turned to one another.

"Laryngectomy," Hammurabi choked out, confirming what Liane wished she hadn't seen, the voice box of the male twin forever removed.

Hammurabi began crying, and Liane watched his dissolution for a time, aware of the tears that ran down her own face. Her breathing was shallow. Her courage stirred only in tiny increments. She felt the murmur of the crowd behind them, heard the random clinking of utensils.

"Why would he do it?"

"The threat my departure implies," Hammurabi said. "It must have accelerated his research plan."

"And Bea?" Liane asked. She caught herself and let slip a nervous laugh, wiped her tears with a bar napkin. "You see, I've also given one of them a name."

"When last seen by Ronald," Hammurabi said, "the sister remained unharmed."

"So far."

He stiffened and sought her gaze. "Liane, we must rescue her!"

She peered into his rheumy eyes. She felt unprepared for any rational possibility that might follow from such pictures. A knot formed in her chest.

"Adnan," she said, "I'm scared. We should call the police."

Hammurabi snorted. "Tell me," he said, "since when is it illegal for a licensed animal testing facility to perform surgery on its inventory?"

"There are regulations."

"Yes, I know. We wrote half of them. They're enforced by the United States Department of Agriculture. None of them, so far as I know, would prevent a researcher from removing the larynx of a primate under anesthesia. And even if it did, what do you expect the Nassau County Police Department to do with that information—raid a multinational corporation at a moment's notice in order to rescue an ape? It's absurd. At this point, only you and I—and Axel—understand the implications of this transgression."

"But the law protects all animals from abuse. You can't treat a dog this way, for God's sake."

"Can't you? We do so all the time."

She knew it was true. She remembered the FAULT placards and rubbed her brow. "Bonobos are officially endangered."

"And you and I are implicated. Besides, it'd take weeks to move the bureaucracy toward intervention, maybe years." He swallowed. "Do you see, Liane? The burden falls on us to get her out of there."

The burden falls... There was a time in her youth when such decisions didn't feel like burdens, when rightness seemed its own reward—and wasn't that why she'd helped Corey when she knew it could cause her trouble? The outsider—like the teenager she'd been when Corey came knocking; like the woman waving signs by the side of the road—views all moral purpose with clarity. Inside Pentalon, on the other hand, seemingly sharp distinctions turned out to be an illusion. It was an entire world constructed of finely wrought nuance. She thought she'd known where she was going, but in reality she'd become lost in the maze. How strange now to have Hammurabi, the rule maker, tempting her to a higher path.

She tossed back the rest of her wine and thought of Bea—Bea watching her brother dragged away by Flickinger. *Flickinger! The great business executive. The expert.* She set the glass down. For the first time in her life, she felt ashamed to be human.

13

On the Cross Island Parkway, Vlad Gretch's Chevy Impala caught up with Hammurabi's big Mercedes and settled into a soft tail half a mile behind. There was no need to keep the car in visual sight; he had him on a tracking screen. In any case, Gretch felt fairly certain where his former colleague was heading.

"You old lecher," he said aloud.

A light rain began to fall. The refraction of taillights and headlights made his job easier still. He followed Hammurabi's car into the Red Ruby Motel on Conduit Boulevard near Kennedy Airport. *Hourly rates—and not the monkey man's first visit.* The scientist pulled into a spot and sat in his Mercedes for a long time. *Getting his nerve up,* Gretch thought—*or something else.*

Hammurabi disgusted him. In Kuwait during the first Gulf War, Gretch had formed his opinion of the Arab character, and it wasn't a flattering one. For a long time Hammurabi seemed to be the exception—disciplined and trustworthy. But over the past few years he'd sunk into personal corruption. He'd put on weight, begun smoking and drinking more, and started getting fuzzier around the edges when it came to company regulations. Two years ago Gretch had tightened surveillance and found new, disturbing things: Permits for handguns. Secret bank accounts. And, most interestingly, an ongoing arrangement with a Japanese masseuse who charged à la carte. Gretch had hoped to get pictures, but the shades were always drawn and the masseuse showed no attachment to any single room. The expense of implanting devices throughout the motel for a little blackmail then seemed unjus-tified. Now, given events of the past week, he regretted that he hadn't pushed forward.

The Mercedes door swung open, and the Arab shuffled across the wet parking lot with his head down.

Gretch unclipped the Spyderco Citadel automatic knife from a belt at the small of his back. The blade was warm, and he knew its edge was sharp enough to slice through a wet sponge. *A fine tool of the trade,* he thought. He snapped it open.

14

The neighborhood projected order with neatly mowed lawns, painted fences and a high canopy of branches stretching from thick sycamores. Hammurabi's house was grander than Liane might have imagined, cinnamon-red brick with leaded mullions in the windows and giant neo-Gothic dormers. She rumbled slowly over the Belgium-block drive-way, which twisted through a wrought iron fence and widened into a circle by the front door.

Braided limestone framed the entrance. An amorphous shape formed in one stained-glass window, and a moment later the big door creaked open.

The woman who answered—blonde, middle-aged, color coordi-nated—kept a hand on the inside doorknob while she gave Liane the once-over. Behind her Liane glimpsed a marbled hall, finely polished. When she introduced herself, the woman's chin rose.

"Addie didn't return home last night," she said. "I thought it'd be better when Axel fired him, but I've scarcely seen him these past two days." Pause. "Monkeying around." She ran her eyes over Liane. "I presumed he was with you. You're the assistant, right?"

"Was."

"I'm Addie's wife. They axed you too?"

"Not exactly. I quit." Her throat went dry as she said the words. It was a proclamation of sorts, a proclamation she hadn't fully faced until this moment. *Ladies and gentlemen, I wish to proclaim that Liane Vinson will depart the straight and narrow, effective immediately.* She cleared her throat. "Yes, I'll be leaving Pentalon forever. As soon as I'm done here." She felt her leg trembling. "Adnan and I had a meeting scheduled for this morning."

"I can't imagine he forgot. You look like the type who'd keep a lot of guys overtime at the lab."

"Our relationship is strictly professional, Mrs. Hammurabi, or should I call you—"

"I believe you. You're just a kid, for Pete's sake. Speaking of which, I have to get my daughter to school. I'll have Addie call you when he gets in touch. He probably fell asleep at the all-night library or something."

"Do you mind if I wait here—outside?"

"Suit yourself. We never lock the gate."

The door closed and a deadbolt snapped shut. Liane turned to the street and squinted into the bright sunshine. In the breeze, a nearby cherry tree shed pale blossoms, the petals tumbling exuberantly along the gutter.

She sat on the step and waved as Hammurabi's wife pulled down the side drive in a sparkling green Range Rover. As the car rolled away, Liane looked down at her lap and brushed some lint off her slacks. For a moment she allowed herself to feel out of place—almost helpless—but then she thought of the twins, subject to forces far beyond their power and comprehension. Human forces for which she shared responsibility.

She dialed Adnan's cell phone and got nowhere. The sun had risen high above the trees, and still no sign of the scientist. The pictures of Isaac on the metal table drifted back to her. *Flickinger didn't even put a sheet under the ape. He won't be doing the same to Bea.* She climbed into her Accord and pulled away.

Half an hour later she drove past the Pentalon gate, gathering her thoughts. She made a U-turn and parked along the shoulder—out of sight of the guard booth—dug around on the floor of the back seat and produced an old Mets baseball cap, which she pulled low over her brow.

She clung to the edge of the woods as she walked.

The FAULT protesters, approached from this angle and on foot, seemed vaguely threatening—like a mob whose intentions might turn ugly in the next moment. In the woods they had Coleman stoves in front of pitched tents with a couple of mutts sauntering around. One woman was banging together a sign between the tents while a man close by stirred something in a saucepan. The majority of protesters—ten or twelve—were lined up with their backs to her by the side of the road where it curved toward the Pentalon entrance. She spotted the redheaded woman with the sage sweatshirt and high-tops.

"Hi," Liane said, approaching. "I work at Pentalon Labs and I could use some help."

15

She donned an old lab smock that she'd found in her cluttered trunk and stood nervously outside the building by the back entrance. Ronald accepted her call.

"Liane, where are you?"

"They won't let me in. I got demoted out of the primate lab."

"I know. They gave me your job. I'm sorry."

"I left one of my personal notebooks behind." That was a lie. "I'm hoping you can get it for me."

A long pause.

"Ronald?"

"Okay. Where is it exactly?"

She explained in fictive detail and dictated her cell phone number.

As she waited, she struggled not to look at the Honda, which she'd parked in an unauthorized spot within sight of the door, a blanket covering the back seat. If the security car swung past this area, she'd have to break away to move it. They could roust her just for standing here. She distracted herself by watching a pair of robins hop along a narrow swath of lawn. One of them pecked at the grass. The other picked up a sprig of straw and cocked its head to check its surroundings. The phone rang.

"It's not where you said. I can't find it."

"Hmm. Any chance you'd let me in to look for myself?"

"Maybe you put it somewhere off the premises."

"Can you just meet me at the door?"

Silence.

One of the robins flew in among the delicate white flowers of a Callery pear, a worm hanging from its beak.

"C'mon, Ronald. It's not that big a deal. I still work for the company, you know."

She could feel him mulling it over. "Okay. Two minutes."

As soon as he disconnected she dialed another number and left the line open as she walked through the door. She flashed her I.D. and turned her attention to the secure door to the lab, weighing the cell phone in her palm and setting her feet in an athletic stance.

Ronald emerged, his brow furrowed.

"Now!" she cried into the phone.

She ran straight through the metal detector and past the two guards manning the equipment. As the buzzer began shrieking, she embraced Ronald and yanked the lanyard over his head and took possession of his passkey.

The guards—recovering from their surprise—began moving toward her, but they had to pause for a bigger distraction as the woman in the sage sweatshirt and two FAULT members burst through the door, wielding their placards like swords. They fell upon the high-tech equipment, turning over the explosive-detection portal and pounding on the other machines. They jousted raucously with the guards.

Liane mouthed an apology as she shoved Ronald away. She touched his card to the security pad and ducked through the open door, pulling it closed behind her. Next to the commotion by the secure entryway, the halls of the primate lab were too quiet. She walked briskly, keeping from breaking into a run to avoid drawing attention. She averted her face as she passed the door to the break room filled with former colleagues. When she neared the entrance to her old lab, she accelerated.

The main room, empty of people, looked as it always had. Polished. Antiseptic. But the wall of bonobo cages projected a different aura when viewed from her new perspective, the animals looking universally forlorn. She took an involuntary step toward the cages. The apes, recognizing her, cooed plaintively, and a renewed sense of purpose propelled her toward the room containing the twins.

She went through that door and there they were. Isaac had a thick bandage around his neck, a hole protected by a gauze flap allowing him to breathe directly through his trachea. He rested in a sitting position, but his eyes were closed in sleep and his chest rose and fell softly. A catheter taped to his back indicated the presence of a sedative pump.

Bea, who had been lying down, jumped to her feet when she saw Liane. She reached both arms through the cage bars and began keening. In one hand she held the filthy stuffed monkey. She touched it to Liane's arm while Isaac cracked open his eyes. The rest of his body remained stiff and inert. Through the slits, his brown irises appeared to have gone dull.

"Poor Isaac," Liane said, tears welling.

"Liane," Bea whined, "*kotala en-decko.*"

"Oh, Bea," Liane said, "if only I could understand you."

She looked around. There was a large FedEx envelope on the counter, unopened, addressed to Hammurabi. As she picked it up, a red light in the corner by the ceiling began flashing.

She opened Bea's cage and the bonobo jumped out and engulfed her.

Liane approached the door and then hugged Bea firmly, knowing how hard the next few steps would be with the powerful ape likely resisting. She stepped over the threshold.

"*En-decko!*" Bea shouted in panic, stretching her arms across Liane's shoulders toward Isaac. "*En-decko! En-decko!*"

As the door to Isaac's room swung closed behind them, Bea clambered up Liane's torso, continuing to scream, "Liane, *en-decko! En-decko!*"

Liane encircled Bea's waist with her arms and began to run as the screeches of the other bonobos ascended in alarmed chorus. The ape worked her limbs with massive prehensile power, but Liane put every fiber of her own being into the embrace as she bolted across the room, shouting over the din: "Bea, we have to! Hold on! We have to!" and Bea continued to scream in terror, "*En-decko! En-decko!*" Reaching for the air behind Liane. Reaching.

When they exited the bonobo lab, Bea relaxed her struggle and rebalanced herself, enabling Liane to get her own feet better under her.

In the hallway, red emergency strobes pulsed and a deafening siren blared. Scientists and technicians were emerging from their laboratories, bewildered, and Liane knew in an instant that there was no percentage in maintaining the pretense of calm that had carried her past the break room moments earlier. She accelerated into a sprint down the hall—heading away from the entrance—weaving among the perplexed white-coated employees who continued to step from their lab rooms. At the end of the hall, a bespectacled executive scientist took in the scene and froze at the sight of Liane charging past with a bonobo in her arms.

"What the ef!" He held up a hand.

Liane lowered her shoulder and plowed past him, catching one of his lower ribs with her elbow and sending him back onto his heels, or worse—she didn't stick around to find out. With Bea bouncing in her arms, she hit the emergency exit at a fast clip. Another alarm joined the growing racket.

They'd passed into an empty cinderblock corridor. Liane overrode her own disorientation and kept running full-tilt until she came to a door with a push bar. She twisted and threw her hip into it and sped through the doorway, but in the next step her feet caught. Woman and ape flailed into the glaring sunshine as Liane landed on something hard and high and dusty. She pushed up onto her elbows and saw that a stack of traction-sand bags had broken her fall. The impact forced the air from her lungs, and she lay there heaving, alone. She rolled over in dread, wondering if she'd lost Bea, but the ape was hanging onto the side of a cyclone fence, looking down in wide-eyed surprise.

The alarms in this outside utility area sounded fainter, but Liane heard voices shouting instructions to one another. A few appeared to be coming from inside, but others originated out in the parking lot somewhere. She shed her lab coat and extended a hand and turned her shoulder to Bea, who instinctively jumped. With Bea on her back, Liane ran for the woods.

Set aside from the employee parking lot with a high privacy fence, this corner of the Pentalon facility seemed an unfamiliar wasteland to Liane. She weaved rapidly between earth-moving equipment and piles of mulch and open utility sheds, her ankles turning in large gray chunks of gravel. When they came to the fence that blocked them from the woods, Bea clambered over effortlessly while Liane struggled to make headway, catching the toes of her shoes in the fence links, which sprung into vibration at every movement, pinching her fingers raw. Then a gate swung, and Bea stood erect in the doorway, holding it open.

Liane jumped down and joined the bonobo and they ran side by side and were fifty feet from the woods when Liane saw people moving between the trees. Her spirits rose with the hope that they were part of the FAULT crew, but as she rushed toward them she spotted the uniforms of Pentalon security.

Fear gripped her. She turned abruptly, crying out for Bea, and with the guards closing in from the trees they propelled themselves along the grass margin between the edge of the woods and the parking lot. Bea's head of thick brown hair danced in the wind as she trundled along in exhilaration. Liane was breathing heavily, sweat coating her forehead.

As they turned the corner of the building, the rear loading dock and its primate lab entrance came into view. There was a great commotion: primate lab employees milling about the parking lot in their lab coats and uniforms, security guards barking into walkie-talkies, three FAULT protesters still fighting to resist apprehension. And there was Liane's Honda, overlooked in the melee, right where she'd left it.

The sight of Liane and the bonobo sprinting for their lives froze the crowd in disbelief. Liane made straight for the car and threw open the driver's side door. Bea stopped dead in her tracks.

"Get in," Liane told her.

The ape stared.

"Oh, man, Bea," Liane screamed, "get in the car!"

Bea stood frozen, blinked twice. "*Boyini*," she mumbled. "*Wapi*."

The crowd was seventy-five yards away. Liane was sure no one else could hear the ape.

"Goddamn it, Bea," she said. "I couldn't decipher you in the lab. I sure can't do it on the fly."

She grabbed for the ape, who easily evaded her.

Three security guards, overcoming their amazement, began to jog toward the Honda.

"Get in the car!" Liane screamed.

The bonobo stood her ground.

Liane let her shoulders sag and jumped in. She started the car and lowered the driver-side window, extending an open hand, pleading with the bonobo while she pulled into DRIVE and began to roll away. The three guards, now running all out, were closing fast. Liane began to accelerate even as she hung farther out the window, pleading with the ape.

"Get in the car, Bea. Come on, honey, get in the car! *Bowling-go! Bowling-go!*"

The guards were nearly on them, but the forward movement of the Accord had altered the angle of approach—to Liane's momentary advantage.

"*Bowling-go!* Goddamn it! *Bowling-go!*" she called to the ape.

She could sense that the guards were within feet of them now, and others had begun to converge from all directions. Liane heard a thump on the roof and floored the accelerator, weaving between security vehicles and shocked onlookers. As soon as she could straighten out and take a hand off the wheel, she depressed the button to lower the passenger-side window.

There was a long moment. Then a brown hand. And in another breath Bea dropped into the passenger seat as if she'd just hitched a ride.

A security car blocked the front gate, its amber lights flashing. A pair of guards signaled for Liane to stop. As she slowed to fifteen miles per hour she saw their bodies tense. One of them had a pistol out and the other waved a billy club. Everything she'd ever learned instructed her to stop the car, but her peripheral vision invited a different calculation.

"Hold on!" she shouted to Bea.

She turned the steering wheel sharply and bumped the two right tires over the curb. As she pressed forward she could feel the under-chassis scraping along the concrete edge. The adrenaline rush had her so charged that she saw stars—then recognized in the rearview mirror that real sparks were shooting out the back.

The guards receded as the car thumped to equilibrium and the open road.

In two minutes she was blending into traffic on the Seaford Oyster Bay Expressway, and her whole body began trembling.

Bea sat in the passenger seat, oblivious, one hand clasping the stuffed monkey to her chest. In her other hand she raised a pair of glasses to her mouth, chewing one end, seemingly deep in thought. An image flashed before Liane of the scientist who'd tried to stop them in the hall. In the chaos, the ape had snatched his spectacles.

"Now we're both thieves." Liane rested a hand on Bea's hairy thigh.

The bonobo sighed and scratched herself. She muttered something under her breath.

It sounded awfully close to *Goddamn it.*

TWO

There must have been laughter amidst the apes when the Neanderthaler first appeared on earth. The highly civilized apes swung gracefully from bough to bough; the Neanderthaler was uncouth and bound to the earth. The apes, saturated and peaceful, lived in sophisticated playfulness, or caught fleas in philosophic contemplation; the Neanderthaler trampled gloomily through the world, banging around with clubs. The apes looked down on him amusedly from their tree tops and threw nuts at him. Sometimes horror seized them; they ate fruits and tender plants with delicate refinement; the Neanderthaler devoured raw meat, he slaughtered animals and his fellows. He cut down trees which had always stood, moved rocks from their time-hallowed place, transgressed against every law and tradition of the jungle. He was uncouth, cruel, without animal dignity—from the point of view of the highly cultivated apes, a barbaric relapse of history. The last surviving chimpanzees still turn up their noses at the sight of a human being.

— ARTHUR KOESTLER

1

—

Dikembe Kasa monitored the sounds of the jungle the way a conductor hears a giant orchestra. When he'd been fighting with the rebels years ago, they bivouacked in a village where one of the elderly women had an old windup Victrola and a pile of scratched Herbert von Karajan records. Though only twenty, the commander had studied music in Lyon for a few years in his youth. He ordered Dikembe to adjust the needle when it caught or skipped. During quiet times Dikembe sat with him in the woman's luxurious hut and listened to Strauss waltzes and Mozart concerti and sonatas by Bach while the commander pointed out the distinct sounds of each instrument. Dikembe never forgot. As he pulled himself along in the dugout canoe, he thought of the Congo peacock's call as the reedy expression of an oboe, of the elephant's cry as the blare of a trombone, of the red-throated bee-eaters as violinists, the gorillas on bass or percussion, the doves standing in for flutes.

It had been a five-day trip home from the edge of the vast Salonga National Park. In the evening he would pull the canoe ashore, hang his meager provisions from a high branch, and find a mature manilkara tree with a comfortable crook in which to sleep, hands folded across the machete on his chest, listening to the boisterous orchestra of the wild.

Dikembe acknowledged three major differences between von Karajan's Vienna orchestra and that of the bush: First, in the jungle the "music" never stopped; second, there were more instruments than anyone could count; finally, no one could see the conductor. Still, the analogy satisfied him. He made his own contribution, drumming the oar on the gunwales to prompt hippos ahead to rise, lessening the danger he would surprise one. He had seen the battered corpses of women who'd gone down to the river with their washing and had been stomped to death by the thousand-pound beasts. He'd witnessed submerged hippos reacting to an unexpected shadow by rapidly crushing the canoe with a single snap of their massive jaws. Like everyone who lived in the bush, Dikembe gave the hippo an even wider berth than he did the crocodiles dozing on the riverbanks. Nearing home, he tapped his canoe again until the hairless pink ears and bulbous eyes breached the surface.

Night had already fallen over the village when Dikembe returned. He removed his boots and enjoyed the touch of the cooling reddish earth on the soles of his calloused feet. The rising quarter-moon lit his way among several dozen structures huddled in a clearing near a dirt road that, after meandering one hundred miles, led to the nearest town with a substantial electrical generator.

His grass hut stood just beyond the outskirts, where his father, long dead, once kept cattle. Dikembe occupied the doorway for a long time, letting his eyes adjust. Daniel was fast asleep on a straw mattress, facing the wall. Odette lay on her stomach across the way from him, one bare leg lifted toward her ribs, her buttocks exposed. Dikembe set his bag on the ground and gently placed a hand on her shoulder. He put a finger to his lips and she smiled sleepily, not moving. Dikembe climbed out of his soiled jeans and descended to his knees on the mattress. He slipped two fingers between Odette's legs and massaged her special place. When he felt her weight shift, he lay down atop her and entered her from behind, running circles with the tips of his fingers over her flattened nipple while he rocked his hips. He climaxed and collapsed beside her, burying his face in the soft flesh of her neck.

In the morning, the three of them shared a large plantain and Daniel, who was eight, ran into the village to play with friends. They had lost three children young. Two who survived, Daniel's older brother and sister, had moved from the village, breaking with tradition. With only Daniel to care for, Odette set to work cleaning a small pile of cassava and pounding it with an ironwood mortar and pestle for the later meal.

Dikembe looked her over. Of medium complexion, she shined with a certain beauty despite her age. Her lips were thick and luscious, her hair closely cropped. Beneath a bright kente her drooping breasts jiggled and swayed as she worked.

"What news?" he asked.

"There's no rice left."

"I got some money from the Englishman."

"Game counting?"

"Yes. The white rhino is way down. The poachers are using the logging roads just outside the park."

She disapproved the moralism of his tone. "People have to eat. What has the government done for folks in the bush? Nothing. Our sons are cannon fodder."

"The poachers are equally short-sighted, interested only in the horns for the Far East trade. They leave the meat to rot because they can't pack it out. You know that. Our ancestors wouldn't recognize this place."

"They would. It's all an expression of hunger." Odette scraped the pestle firmly into the lumpy paste of cassava.

"I have money from the Englishman," he said again.

"I'm exhausted from waiting for you, and my head hurts."

"I'll set out tomorrow myself, then, and come back with provisions."

She flashed her eyes at him. "Take Daniel. I'll go visit with my sister."

She stopped pounding the cassava and blinked. Her head swayed and she looked like she'd pass out. Dikembe took a step forward and dropped to a knee to catch her, but she recovered.

"I'll finish preparing the *baton de manioc* in a while," she said. "I need to lie down."

It wasn't like her. An hour later he tried to rouse her, but she stirred only long enough to identify him. She turned away, listless. He touched her arm and found her to be on fire with fever. Finally, she sat up and worked her jaw. He offered her a cup of water, but after taking a sip she ran out and vomited by a nearby bush.

"Dikembe, I'm not well," she moaned.

He led her back to the hut and bade her to lie down again.

"But the *manioc*," she said.

"Never mind that. I'll borrow from the neighbors."

He set the mortar of half-beaten cassava in the shade and covered it with a cloth to keep the flies away.

In the afternoon, while she slept, he walked into the heart of the village. He asked a cousin to feed Daniel and from his new wad of cash offered a few francs, which were refused with a click of the tongue. Dikembe himself skipped dinner. He had trained himself to go a long time without food.

Before the sun set he and Daniel sat outside the hut peeling the bark from sticks. Odette rose only occasionally to relieve herself in the bushes or to retch.

"Boy," Dikembe said, "before it's dark sweep the leaves out so your mama doesn't have to."

"Will she be better soon?"

"Tomorrow, I think."

He looked in on Odette. Her arms and legs had gone to gooseflesh and she was shivering.

Dikembe put a sheet over her, and when darkness fell he and Daniel shared the other bed. Though he felt exhausted, he lay awake for a long time, listening to the rhythm of his son's breathing. It reminded him of a slow-tempoed maraca, graceful accompaniment to the orchestra of the night.

2

Liane lowered the car windows halfway and let the parkway air blast in and tousle her hair. She shook her head and reviewed her circumstances: the grave condition of her mother; instant unemployment followed, presumably, by diminished job prospects . . . and therefore, an impending shortage of money; plus the insurmountable challenge of maintaining a growing bonobo in an uncontrolled setting—somewhere. On one level it was enough to crush anyone's spirit, yet in a deeper way she'd never felt freer.

She rolled down the windows the rest of the way and relished the wind beating against her face. She looked over to Bea, who stopped playing with the filched glasses and eagerly sniffed the fresh air that flowed through her body hair. Bea closed her eyes as if in ecstasy, no doubt sensing a contrast to the fusty laboratory air. Liane smiled. They were two American females indulging their wild side in an automobile on the open road.

"Look at us," she said. "A regular Thelma and Louise. Just a couple of girls with nothing left to lose. "

Bea gazed out at the passing trees.

The Honda hit a pothole and began shuddering and resisting. It felt like something was dragging along behind her. Liane pulled into the right lane and slowed. At the first opportunity, she steered into the breakdown lane and creaked to a stop. She pressed her face into her hands, contemplating one horrible possibility: *A man. A body. One of the guards, scraping along for miles.* Was Liane now no longer just a trespasser and thief, but a murderer, too? She tried to picture the instant when she'd run around the Pentalon gate. Had she been too distracted by the flying sparks to see a guard disappearing under her car?

"Wait here," she told Bea.

She flung open the car door and slammed it behind her. Bea clambered into the back seat and closely followed Liane's tentative movement toward the back of the Accord.

Liane bent from the waist and peered under the rear bumper. The muffler rested half on the ground. No dead bodies. She touched a hand to the trunk, thinking more clearly. She and the bonobo weren't Thelma and Louise. She needed to make provisions for the animal and she needed to start now. She popped open the trunk and rummaged beneath a layer of blankets and pillows and empty cardboard boxes, finding a large backpack. Then she returned to the driver's seat, took a deep breath, and eased back into traffic.

A few minutes later they pulled into the apartment house parking garage. Liane looked around. All was quiet. She reached for the backpack, a relic of the days when she used to take long summer hikes through the Adirondacks. It was the type one might use for an overnight, with a lightweight aluminum frame and plenty of room inside. She dumped its gnarly contents onto the back seat.

"Okay," she said to Bea. "Get in."

Bea grabbed hold of the backpack as if it were the largest toy she'd ever seen. She shook it from side to side, grunting.

"No," Liane said, grasping the pack with more authority. She peeled Bea's fingers off one by one. "I want you inside this thing so I can carry you upstairs without being seen. Understand?"

Bea rocked her head, grabbed hold of the pack again with both hands, and resumed shaking it. Liane wouldn't let go. They descended into a tug of war, with Bea hooting all the while. After a minute of this, Liane felt like her arms would fall off. She released her grip and turned to the detritus she'd dumped from the pack. She found some old granola bars and a musty bag of gorp. She peeled the wrapper off one of the bars and handed it to Bea, who devoured it and reached toward Liane for the other.

"Oh, no you don't," Liane said.

She maneuvered the pack around, waved the snack at Bea, and tossed it into the wide opening. Bea dove in after the bribe and Liane quickly slid the zipper closed.

"Not as smart as you think you are, huh?"

She wrestled the pack out the door and strapped it to her back and waist. As she walked she could feel Bea's weight shifting around inside, but at least the bonobo remained quiet, probably munching away inside or concentrated on getting the wrapper open. Liane climbed the stairs to the lobby, which was empty, and ducked into the elevator. There was an old lady inside with a miniature schnauzer on a leash. The woman smiled at Liane, who made a monumental effort to appear nonchalant. The schnauzer sniffed the air, looked at the pack and growled.

"Stop it, Linus," the old lady said, yanking his leash. "What floor?" She was standing beside the buttons.

"Five, please."

The schnauzer growled again, his eyes fixed on the pack.

"Linus!" the woman snapped. "I'm sorry. He's usually not like this."

The old lady and Liane focused on the crack between elevator doors. Linus growled a third time.

"I don't know what's come over him." The old lady forced him between her ankles and squeezed.

When the lady's floor came, Liane exhaled. Bea cooed behind her.

"Shh," Liane said.

The back of her neck had gone clammy. She trembled by the door to her apartment, short of breath, pulse racing as if she'd just completed a hundred-yard sprint. Strange images floated back to her. Not images from her escape with Bea, nor even the photos of poor Isaac. Rather, she saw herself at sixteen, her knobby elbows and nail-bitten fingers; her mother and Frank bracketing her on the couch as the detective pressed her to reveal "the young man's whereabouts"; the look of disgust on Frank's face, a look that encompassed not only the trouble she'd found, but every transgression of her father's, as well.

Her mind jumped to the psychologist that the court had assigned to her, a young woman barely out of graduate school, earnest and treacly, telling Liane she still had a life to live if only she'd get in line. She thought of the counselor who'd put her back on the road to college, the advisor who'd steered her into animal testing. All solid citizens, women who thought themselves empowered by the choices they'd made and urged upon others.

If they could see me now, she thought mirthlessly. She hadn't just left the straight and narrow, she'd obliterated it.

Liane felt Bea stir and looked at her apartment door, sensing movement inside. *Nicholas?* She couldn't be sure. They might come for her at any moment. She backed away from her apartment, entered the elevator and rode back down to the garage.

The doors opened. It happened very fast. She sensed the presence of two forms on either side of the garage, one of them moving toward her, his heels clicking on the blacktop rapid fire. She couldn't let them trap her in the elevator. She let out a gasp and ducked behind the concrete box that contained it, running along the garage wall, reaching the rear end of a Chevy Tahoe.

She didn't crouch so much as she collapsed behind that car, the weight of the backpack and of all she'd done buckling her knees.

The clicking heels stopped. Someone with quieter shoes was running at her but she froze in fear. She fell to her knees, bracing herself for whatever would come.

"Liane!"

She looked up into Mickey's face. Was he one of them?

"What's going on? You dropped something?" Then he could see it. "You're hiding?"

She felt Bea shifting her weight in the backpack. Mickey's eyes tracked the motion.

"That man!" Liane choked out. "He's after me. The man in the trench coat. The heels." Her lips were trembling but she couldn't calm them.

"That guy in the raincoat?" Mickey pointed with his thumb. "He got on the elevator. I think he lives on the second floor. An accountant or something."

Her diaphragm relaxed. "You're sure?"

Mickey cocked his head and laid his hands on both her shoulders. "What're you afraid of, Liane? What's in the backpack?"

3

—

Mickey hadn't seen anyone look that scared since he'd witnessed the wife of a jockey he knew watching her husband get thrown and trampled. He couldn't convince Liane to step into the elevator. Her inclination toward secrecy had blossomed into full-blown paranoia.

The fabric of the backpack distorted from inside; it looked like the protrusion of a nose or an elbow.

"That thing ain't happy in there."

"We can't let her out. She may run."

"It's one of the reasons I wanted us to go upstairs."

"You don't know it's safe up there."

"The guy in the raincoat? I told y—"

"Him or maybe someone else." She put her hands on her hips. "I'm not crazy."

He remembered a place off the garage, a storage room with steel cages stacked with bicycles and luggage. He unlocked the gate to his space and Liane shirked the backpack onto a large cardboard box. She unzipped it and a young ape poked its head out and climbed into Liane's arms, cowering.

"Holy crap!" Mickey instinctively looked down at her genitalia. He touched the ape on her knee and made fleeting eye contact. "She's a sweetheart."

"Her name's Bea. She's a bonobo."

"I know. I'm a vet, remember?"

"A horse vet."

"Insult me now. I left the track the other day. I couldn't take it anymore."

"Then we have something in common." She pointed to Bea. "It seems unlikely they'll be renewing my contract."

"So I guess you stole her from your previous employer. Where was that?"

"Pentalon Laboratories."

"Pentalon!" Mickey let out a whistle. "Animal testing company. Pretty major, aren't they?"

"The biggest. Traded on NASDAQ."

"They'll want her back."

"No joke."

"You're afraid they're upstairs looking for you."

"I wouldn't put it past them."

"That they'll harm you in some way?" He took in the depth of her eyes. "If you snatched her, you must have been desperate."

"I was—I am. But I can't talk about that now. I'm sorry, Mickey, sorry for all of it. If you'd seen half of what I've seen...but I don't want to risk getting you involved. You might lose your license or something."

"Let me worry about that." He couldn't help himself. She was the most stunning woman he'd ever touched, even if it was just her shoulders. She had something going, an energy that drew him in. "I'm a sucker for a damsel in distress. What can I do to help? You have a plan?"

She shook her head and threw up her hands. "It's all ad hoc—worse than that. Somehow in all this I've neglected the person most important to me, my mother. She's dying."

"Liane, I'm so sorry."

"She's only fifteen minutes away in Laurelton. I need to see her desperately, but I can't very well drop in with Bea on my arm."

"I'll take the ape to my apartment if you want." He looked at Liane's outfit, tattered and dust-covered. "Better yet, if the coast is clear up there, I can get you some fresh clothes."

"You'd do that for me?"

He pretended to ponder it. "Only if you let me buy you dinner tonight."

"It's a deal." They looked at the ape. "We'll order up."

He took her keys. "Get her into that backpack while I'm gone upstairs. Bea, you said, right? She'll answer to that name?"

Liane blushed. "She might."

4
—

By morning, Odette's condition hadn't improved. She lay motionless on her side and could barely swallow the water that Dikembe offered. He began to fear the worst. Crouching on the ground beside her, he ran a damp rag repeatedly over her cropped hair, hoping to reduce her fever.

Daniel came in and sat on his mattress, gaping at the scene. Odette hadn't the energy to acknowledge him.

"Go out and play, boy," Dikembe said.

Daniel disobeyed. He pulled a piece of straw from his mattress and nervously fretted the end of it with his teeth.

"I said, get out!" Dikembe shouted.

Daniel didn't budge. Dikembe raised the rag in his hand to throw it at his son, but then thought better of it.

"Daniel," he protested, "do you not see what's happening here? Do you want to get the fever?"

Odette, lying on her side, torpidly covered her exposed ear with a trembling hand. The boy continued staring.

"He must go," Odette whispered. "Take him to my sister."

Dikembe looked from his son to his wife and back again. His gut told him she suffered from something more profound than the flu. The idea of Daniel, his last child, contracting a deadly fever was enough in itself to break his heart. He hated to leave Odette, but he knew that he must do so before Daniel risked further exposure.

"My head hurts so bad," Odette said, her eyes closed. The skin of her neck and temples glistened with sweat and her ribs heaved with each labored breath. Dikembe wiped her face with the cool rag. She didn't stir.

"I'll leave some water here in this cup for you and a bowl with the rag," he said, standing. "Put a pot to boil, boy. We'll go to your auntie after washing."

Daniel walked out and put a full kettle on the low fire that burned in a cinderblock pit. He added some sticks, stoked it and blew, as he'd seen his mother do many times. When the kettle began to steam, Dikembe used the hot water to wash his hands and arms in a basin. He usually took the gray water to the small vegetable garden that Odette tended. In this case, he carried the basin along the edge of the village to an area the residents had set aside for their most useless garbage. He poured the water into the ground and kicked sand over the wet spot.

"Now," he told Daniel, returning to the hut, "grab the bar of soap and we'll go down to the river."

They waded in and washed themselves from head to toe, keeping close watch on a crocodile beached on a nearby sandbar. They sat on a flat area covered by exposed river stones, rounded and smooth, and waited for the morning sun to dry them.

"It's not the best hour to be heading out to your auntie's," Dikembe said. "The road will be hot and dusty. We can rest in the shade of the trees. We can stop halfway for a treat. But we must go now."

"I can do it, Papa," Daniel said, "but—" He lowered his eyes.

"What is it?" Dikembe lifted Daniel's face by the chin with two fingers.

"I'm afraid for Mama."

"Me, too, boy. We are men. This is a test of our strength. I will drop you with your auntie and hurry home to care for your mama."

For all that, they trudged along the forest path back to the hut. When they emerged into the open, tsetse flies descended on them.

Daniel waved his hands and began to jog. Dikembe killed two on his forearm and followed.

At the hut, Dikembe filled his canteen with fresh water from a barrel and strapped it over his shoulder. The water was for Daniel; Dikembe wouldn't allow the boy to share it with him. If Dikembe became parched, he'd seek out a vine to sever for its watery sap.

They stood in the doorway, peering at Odette through the dimness of the hut.

When Daniel stepped toward her, Dikembe caught his arm, holding him back.

"Feel better, Mama," Daniel said, nervously kicking the sand. "And send for me as soon as you can."

Odette forced open her eyes. Even in the poor light Dikembe could see they were bloodshot. She blinked and pursed her lips for a silent kiss. Dikembe perceived the glistening of a tear.

"I'll be back by sunset, love, God willing," he said.

The village where Odette's sister lived was a three-hour walk. The sun beat down on their exposed heads, and the trip wore on Daniel. Dikembe walked ahead, urging his son along with threats and small bribes. They stopped at a bamboo roadside stand after two hours walking. Dikembe purchased a coconut and lopped off the top with his machete. Daniel drank the coconut water. Dikembe handed him his knife and Daniel shaved chunks of milky white meat from the husk, passing pieces to his father. They chewed silently in the shade of an acacia, brushing away flies.

"Come," Dikembe said as Daniel began to nod off, "you can sleep at your auntie's."

Daniel groaned but cooperated. They stepped out into the blast furnace of the midday sun, too hot even for the flies to follow. They could smell the red earth bake-boiling, like wet pottery in a kiln, and soon Daniel was dragging his feet again. Dikembe opened the canteen and splashed a tablespoon of the precious water on his son's head. Daniel rubbed it in with his palms, employing every drop.

More than an hour later they arrived at the outskirts of Odette's sister's village.

Dikembe stopped. "It's not a good idea for me to enter the village. Tell your auntie I'll be back for you as soon as I can. Or maybe your mother will come. Now go on. You know the way."

"Can I hug you?"

"Best not. Don't cry. You're almost a man now."

"Okay, Papa."

Daniel's first few steps were tentative. Then, as Dikembe watched, he broke into a run.

5

The car smelled like stale gorp. Liane, already missing Bea, wondered if the ape would be safe at Mickey's place. *But they won't think to search there,* she thought. *It's not like he's my boyfriend or anything.*

The car felt sluggish, the muffler clattering along the street, taking every pothole to heart. As she slowed at a yellow light on Hempstead Avenue, she looked around for police cruisers. *Heck of a time to get pulled over.* A dark blue Chevy Impala switched lanes abruptly behind her, and she recognized the driver. His face struck more fear in her than the police ever would. Could his presence on this street at this moment be a coincidence? Liane shuddered.

She turned left where she would have gone straight and turned right where she would have gone left. She followed the most random path she could trace, leaving the main road, avoiding dead ends, easing through quiet residential neighborhoods with her muffler etching stripes into the blacktop. She came to a red light by a major thoroughfare in Rockville Centre, and a block behind her the Impala slowed to a stop. There was no question that he was following her. She took a deep breath and, when a break came in traffic, ran the red light with a dangerous left turn.

Tires screeched. Horns honked. The muffler shot sparks.

She focused on the rearview mirror, made more random turns, and finally pointed the car back in the direction of her mother's house. But a minute later he was on her tail again. She could see his face clearly, draped in a menacing grin, sending a message.

Fear tightened her throat. She made a right turn onto Sunrise Highway and pulled across three lanes to the far left. She drifted along for a while at normal speed, the Impala never more than one traffic light behind her, the sound of the muffler grating her nerves, reminding her with each bump that she was heading in the wrong direction, away from her mother's house. Reminding her, too, that she couldn't outrun a donkey cart with her Honda in this shape.

She barely perceived the Long Island Railroad commuter train gliding along in the distance. It was a mile away at least, parallel to the road on an elevated track, heading toward her. She made a U-turn at the next intersection, passing the Impala, so close they could spit at one another across the median. The grin hadn't left his face. As he made the same U-turn and continued to shadow her, she focused on the train.

The next station was back near her apartment in Lynbrook, half a mile ahead now, she reckoned. If this had been the movies, she thought, she'd jump the tracks and run along the rails until her tires stripped off and she hooked up to the train and let it drag her along to safety. But in reality she was on the ground in a car that couldn't attain forty miles per hour before going to pieces. In reality the train was not only three quarters of a mile behind her but riding along a bed that was twenty feet over her grade. In reality she was on the wrong end of a slow-motion car chase that didn't lend itself to movie cues. *Still, there* is *a train.* She had a sense that it might harbor her deliverance, and she knew where to find the station.

Ninety seconds, Liane calculated. *Ninety seconds for the train to pull into the station and open and close its doors. Ninety seconds to cross traffic, drive through the underpass, drop the car and race up the stairs to the platform.*

Eyeing the train in her side-view mirror, she eased over to the right lane and drew to a complete stop at the green light with her hazards blinking. Impatient drivers laid on their horns, but she ignored them. She waited for the train to pull within a tenth of a mile, then floored the accelerator.

The Accord groaned, then jumped through the red light and out into crossing traffic, barely avoiding collision with an oil truck. It fishtailed through the overpass and ground to an awkward halt at the base of the station stairs. As Liane threw open her door, she could see the Impala careening through traffic. The casual flowing skirt that Mickey had fetched for her caused wind drag that she didn't need right now, slowing her down and wasting precious seconds as she struggled to take the steps two at a time—a stretch for her short stride under any conditions.

She reached the platform as the train hissed to a stop. There was a delay before the doors opened, and she jogged toward the front, entering the first car out of breath. The seats were sparsely occupied, mostly by day laborers returning from early jobs, their cheeks freshly weathered by spring sunshine. She took a seat near the door facing backward, peering anxiously through the milky scratched glass of the train window, silently begging the conductor to shut the doors.

The electronic indicator tone sounded and the doors finally began to slide closed just as her pursuer reached the platform. She watched him sprint for it and disappear into the train's shadow—she guessed three cars back. There was a long pause. The doors reopened. The tone sounded, then they slapped closed.

Liane's stomach knotted. She felt certain that Vlad Gretch had succeeded in boarding the train.

6

She massaged her temples, thinking through her options. Gretch's grin may have been a front, but she couldn't get it out of her mind. If he meant to scare her, he was doing a bang-up job of it, in just under an hour making her feel like a hunted animal. And how had he stayed on her tail so effortlessly, even after she was sure she'd lost him?

Yet, if he meant to harm her, he could have done so already. Everyone at Pentalon knew of his Secret Service background. He might easily have pulled alongside her car in a quiet neighborhood and put a bullet through her head. He might have forced her into oncoming traffic. *Why hadn't he?* Perhaps he intended only to let her know that Pentalon wouldn't give up the case so easily. He wanted the bonobo, of course, and thought he'd scare her into handing Bea over. That was all.

None of this thinking changed the fact that he was three train cars back, plotting against her in some fashion. What could be easier than following someone on a commuter railroad? They arrived at Laurelton in three stops. While he wouldn't have known her destination in advance, he only needed to poke his head out every time the doors opened to see where she detrained. Once they were on foot she didn't stand a chance of outrunning him. In that context, the Accord felt like a lifeboat that she'd carelessly abandoned.

She had her left heel locked on the back edge of the armrest of the seat in front of her. Across the aisle, one of the day laborers took a swig of the beer that he clutched in a paper bag and belched quietly. His hands were black with dirt, his work boots worn down to the metal toe caps. At first she thought his eyes were downcast. Then she saw that he was staring at her ankle. He ran his gaze up her exposed leg. Liane had never become accustomed to being ogled. The experience made her skin crawl. She lowered her skirt and squeezed her knees together, disgusted, wishing she'd worn stockings. But it gave her a radical idea.

The conductor came around and she purchased a ticket.

"Is there a restroom on this train?"

He pointed his chrome hole punch over his shoulder. "Fourth car back." He punched a paper marker and stuck it in the crease behind her seat, then moved along.

Liane watched him punch the next person's ticket, the chads tumbling end-over-end.

Fourth car back, the man had said. She thought that wouldn't do at all. She rose and walked to the rear door between cars, peering through the window. Gretch wasn't in the next car, but there was a transit cop there, working his way toward the front. How in the world could she convince a cop that a neatly dressed guy had bad intentions toward her? He could refute anything she'd say. And, besides, *she* was the one who'd broken the law.

The train screeched to a halt and the doors slid open. *Valley Stream.* They were now two stops from her mother's station. The tone sounded. One or two people exited and another few climbed on. The doors closed and the train started forward again, rocking.

Liane opened the door between cars, balanced herself, and passed through the next door into the second car. The policeman checked her out, but he was heading in the wrong direction. She passed him closely, brushing her breasts across his arm. If that didn't turn him eventually, nothing would. Her bet laid, she walked briskly, reached the next set of doors, and stepped out between cars. She took a deep breath, not believing what she was about to do.

In the car behind her, she could barely see the policeman's back as he paused and rubbed his neck.

Gretch spotted her from the fourth car. She braced herself between cars in the rocking train, standing on the rubber gasket that protected the gap, which shifted as the train cars on either side tugged and yielded to one another.

Gretch stepped into the third car. In the second, the cop had not yet turned around. Gretch moved toward her position, but he was still nearly a car-length away. Certain that no one could see below the window, she grabbed hold of the long metal handle on the back of the car. With her free hand, she reached up under her skirt and slid down her underpants. She climbed out of them and crumpled them into her hand, straightened her skirt, set her jaw, and pushed open the door to Gretch's car just as the cop spun around and began walking back through the second car.

In the middle doorwell, she met up with Gretch. She gathered her few strands of courage and poked him in the stomach with two fingers. As she might have suspected, his abs were harder than stone.

"So," she said, mouth dry, "the mountain comes to Mohammed."

Gretch laughed coldly, his eyes still and penetrating. *Like a lizard,* she thought.

"My brief isn't to hurt you," he said. "Axel only wants his ape back."

"Who needs an ape when he has a big stud like you."

"Watch your mouth. He wants his damn bonobo, and if he doesn't get her, that jalopy you abandoned back there'll be the least of your worries."

"Do you see her here? Wanna search me?"

"I know you left with the ape, Liane. Half the world saw you. We can do this the easy way or we can do it the hard way, but I'm not going to stop until Pentalon has its property back."

He took a step closer and bored into her with such a determined gaze, it was all Liane could do not to flinch. She could hear contained fury wheezing through his sinuses.

"You think you're hot stuff," he said. "You'd better consider what you're doing real hard. You're risking everything for what? For a chimp?"

There was a loud clack, and he turned to see the door opening from the second car.

Liane took the opportunity to step closer, then she raised a knee sharply into Gretch's groin, a perfect shot. She felt soft matter yielding like a crushed blossom to the force of her patella and heard the air chuff from his chest. He doubled over and she pulled him down on top of her. As she was lying on her back with what felt like a pallet of bricks pressing her into the ribbed mat of the train floor, Liane forced her underwear into one of his fists. He clenched it blindly, gasping, but then in one motion he popped right back up, grinning.

"Help!" Liane screamed, astonished. "Help me!"

The policeman closed in, twisted Gretch's arms behind his back without resistance, and snapped on a pair of handcuffs. Immediately he noticed a fringe of the baby-blue underwear poking from Gretch's hand.

"The hell is this?"

Passengers stared as the train screeched into Rosedale station. The doors opened.

"Both of yuz, out onto the platform," said the cop.

7

A cornered animal, Gretch thought, *is the essence of fear, pure visceral instinct.* He sensed it in the girl.

He was standing on the concrete platform in handcuffs, watching Liane walk away. Not his type, but any man would appreciate the view: muscular calves, narrow waist. At least, he thought, he'd had the presence of mind to drop her underwear through the gap to the tracks below when they'd stepped off the train.

"Just when I thought I'd seen everything," the cop was saying. "Tell me, pal, what type of pervert *does* this kind of stuff? In broad daylight, no less, not even the night shift."

"I'm no pervert," Gretch said through gritted teeth, still a little queasy. "The girl's playing games."

"How do you figure?"

"She has something that belongs to my company."

"What the hell could belong to you *down there?* You a pimp?"

"I called for a cop, I got a comedian. I keep telling you, she nailed me in the nuts and pulled me on top of her."

"And you yanked off her undies for the trouble. That's a neat trick."

"I don't know how they ended up in my hand. I never touched the bitch. She's got more pluck than I thought."

They watched Liane emerge from the station stairwell at street level and climb into a taxi. She leaned forward, instructing the driver. As the taxi pulled away, she gave the two men a long look.

"She played you for a sucker," Gretch told the cop. "*She* attacked *me,* not the other way around."

"Yeah, you look like the vulnerable type. You only got a foot and a half on her."

"The underwear was a brilliant stroke," Gretch reflected. "I have to give her that."

He made some tactical calculations. The taxi was gone and the girl with it. So no matter how this ended with the cop, she was already beyond his immediate grasp. But time remained an essential element. The cop hadn't reached for the radio so far, hadn't called for assistance, hadn't rifled the wallet yet, had therefore foolishly preserved Gretch's anonymity, but that wouldn't last much longer. The old guy in the janitor's outfit on the facing platform presented complications, his face angled so that he surely had to be looking. *Beer can in his hand,* Gretch observed, *an unreliable witness.* Gretch turned his back toward him, positioning to keep his options open, see how it played out.

"Why am I still here? She said she wouldn't press charges."

Complications, he thought. *Liane doesn't want them either. Smart girl.*

"Yeah, don't sound so disappointed. It's not that uncommon with sexual assault. Some of 'em just wanna move on as quick as possible. Avoid having to see the sicko ever again."

"All she's looking to avoid is jail time. She wants to move on because she's a thief."

"I could haul you down to the station for disorderly conduct."

"You have no cause, officer. Besides, I know your boss."

"Yeah? The sarge is a friend of yours?"

"Not the sergeant, the police commissioner. We work very closely with him. He won't be happy if you drag me in for nothing. You can bet your badge on it."

"I'm quaking in my boots. What's he gonna do, put me on desk duty? That'd be a relief from having to deal with goons like you. You think I need this shit, people skipping out on their fares, fighting over who got the seat first, shoving their hands up ladies' dresses? Anyway, I told her I'd hold you for ten minutes."

"So she could get away."

"Or she was gonna press charges. You'd prefer that?"

"She wouldn't dare. She's up for a felony."

"You still haven't told me what she allegedly stole."

Gretch sighed.

The cop gazed at the station clock. "Turn around."

He tapped his fingertips over Gretch's ankles and ran his palms up the legs to the butt. *All because of Flickinger's damn obsession with those apes,* Gretch thought. The cop paused when he felt the sheath with the Spyderco knife, a concealed weapon.

Gretch had to act. He sent a heel sharply into the cop's face, breaking his nose and staggering him backward. Gretch hopped forward and bent and threw his hip behind the cop's knee, his shoulder into the cop's ribs. The motion sent the cop sailing sideways off the platform. With a grunt he fell heavily to the tracks below, where the drunk janitor couldn't have seen him if he tried.

Hands still cuffed behind his back, Gretch jumped down, landing in a balanced, athletic position. The cop was struggling to his feet, half under the platform. He bumped his head. When he reached for his gun, Gretch nailed him in the solar plexus with a swift kick, stunning him immobile. He drove a knee into the cop's neck, straddled him and twisted, locking his knee against the cop's Adam's apple, crushing it with an ironclad scissors hold.

When Gretch had completed the cop's strangulation, he released his legs, then grabbed his keychain and groped for the keyhole behind his back. Beneath him, the railroad ties vibrated. He used his soles to shove the cop onto the tracks as he slid the key home.

The cop's shirt had come untucked and his face was purple. His gun remained in its holster. *Loser,* Gretch thought.

By the time he looked up, the front of the rattling train forced a blinding gust of wind into his eyes. The handcuffs still dangling from one wrist, he flattened both palms on the beveled edge of the concrete platform and braced himself.

8

—

Frank was out front, shaping the boxwood with pruners, when Liane pulled up. He wore a Hawaiian shirt and Bermuda shorts, a betting sheet protruding from the back pocket. She thought he looked like a fat Jimmy Buffett on a bad hair day, but didn't say so.

"What's with the cab?" he asked.

"A little car trouble."

She walked past him and through the garage with its old Harley and rusty lawn chairs and jury-rigged television. She climbed the stairs to the kitchen, where Claudine sat reading a worn Bible.

The home health aide looked at her watch. "Your mother's resting but she'll be needing her medicine soon. Would you like to bring it to her?"

"Sure. How is she?"

"Stable, I'd say."

"Is that a good stable or a bad stable?"

"She's not a well woman, hon, you know that. Her energy's very low. Without a new kidney, and at her age, she'll continue to struggle."

Claudine rose and opened a cabinet, revealing a row of medicine bottles. She shook eight different pills onto a butter plate and handed it to Liane with a tall glass of water.

Helen was asleep when Liane entered the room. Books and tissues and cups and greeting cards sprawled from the placid center. The act of opening the door and stepping inside felt to Liane like intrusion on a sacred place.

She pushed aside a vase of daisies and placed the glass and plate on the nightstand. She relocated a terrycloth robe to a hook on the back of the door, then dropped into a chair. Her mother looked peaceful but remote, like someone passed out on a float, carried by a hidden tide. The motion of her eyes opening sent a rush of adrenaline into Liane's chest.

"Hi, Mom. It's me, Liane."

"I can see that. I still have my eyesight, thank God."

"How'd you sleep?"

Her mother looked at the bedside digital clock. "Don't you usually work later than this?"

"I brought your pills, Mom."

As Helen pushed herself into a sitting position, Liane propped her up with pillows. She handed over the pills and water and watched her swallow two at a time. It was an unpleasant chore, even for the observer.

They sat for a while, keeping company, alternating periods of silence with small talk. Helen tuned the television to CNN and they drifted in and out of conversation about national politics and world events. Given all she'd been through in the past twenty-four hours, the discussion felt to Liane like the worst kind of cocktail party chatter. She fidgeted in her chair.

Finally, her mother yawned. Liane helped her lie down and smoothed the blanket, noticing that she exuded the odor of urine. She rubbed her shoulder, kissed her, and left the room on tiptoe.

She found Frank at the kitchen table with a bowl of cereal.

"How is she?" he whispered.

"Back to sleeping. Mind if I hang out awhile?"

"Make yourself at home."

Needing a moment to think, she went into what originally was the smallest bedroom of the house and closed the door. It had been the nursery, then became a guest room. When Frank married Helen they'd turned it into a cozy office with dark walls, bookcases, and a desk. Liane perched on the edge of the day bed, bouncing a throw pillow on her lap, trembling. Outmaneuvering Vlad Gretch felt too much like beginner's luck, and in retrospect it terrified her. She knew she was overmatched, and she had an unusual creature to protect in the bargain, a creature with her own needs and vulnerabilities.

Maybe Frank could help her, she thought. He had the nurse to take care of Helen, free time on his hands. The prior relationship with Flickinger was a complication, to say the least, but one ought to hold more loyalty for a stepdaughter than for an old colleague, right?

The desk phone rang. She ignored it.

"Liane. Phone! *Liane!*" Frank's voice came from down the hall and through the closed office door, calling with increasing urgency. Nearing. Frank didn't knock. He barged through the door brandishing the phone.

"It's the lab," he whispered, "wanting to talk to you."

Already they've found me. She didn't have time to wonder how. "I'm not here," she said.

Frank blanched.

"You didn't tell them I was here." She threw up her arms.

He looked sheepish, covered the mouthpiece with his palm and tried to hand the unit to Liane.

"You did tell them."

"Yes. Why wouldn't I?"

"Who is it, exactly?"

"Some guy named Ronald. Something about a theft."

"I'm not here. Tell him I'm not here. You thought I was here but I'm not."

"Don't get hysterical," Frank whispered. "If you want me to lie for you, I need to know what's going on."

His face had that look she'd seen before—the look it wore when he used to talk about her father, and, later, when the police had entered their home seeking Corey. It was a look of mistrust. Worse: of moral indignation. If she told him what she'd now done, he'd see her father in the act and condemn them both with a common judgment.

Liane's jaw tightened. She took the phone from him roughly and heard Ronald's voice through the receiver. *"No cops, Liane. Find Shaker—"*

She pressed the OFF button and tossed the phone onto the daybed, then pushed past Frank, heading for her mother's room.

Helen was awake again, occupying a chair with her feet up—always, these days, with her feet up.

"I gotta go, Mom."

"Why so soon?"

"I have to go feed the cat."

"The lab called," Frank said, entering. "She's avoiding them."

"Don't say that, Frank," Liane said.

"I want to know what's going on."

"You put me on the straight and narrow, Frank. Many thanks, okay? But I quit my job this morning."

"Quit?"

"It wasn't working out."

"The new job?" her mother asked in confusion.

"None of it, Mom. They fired the director of the primate lab. They're taking the whole thing in a different direction."

"Then what's this theft business about?" Frank whispered.

"Not in front of Mom, Frank. Just shut up, okay?"

"A theft?" her mother asked.

"It's nothing, Mom. A misunderstanding that—that'll get cleared up soon. It's not something for you to worry about."

"She wouldn't take the phone call," Frank said. There it was again—that tone his voice used to carry whenever the subject turned to her father, the mountebank. That sealed it. She couldn't tell him about Bea; she was on her own.

"I have to leave now, Mom." Liane stared daggers at Frank. "The cat's waiting for his dinner. I'll explain everything another time."

She kissed her mother on the cheek and squeezed her hand. She forced a smile as their eyes met, then left the room with Frank clipping her heels. *They know where I am,* she thought. *They know, they know.*

"Look, I need some wheels and I can't wait for a cab," she told him without pausing. She headed through the empty kitchen. He followed her down the stairs.

"Liane," Frank said from behind her, "this behavior of yours concerns me. I think at the very least you owe me an explanation."

Liane stopped in her tracks and turned around. "I'm not a kid anymore. Just take care of my mother and stay out of this. Right now, I need wheels. How about the motorcycle?"

"The Harley? You ever ride a motorcycle?"

"Once or twice in college."

He paused, deliberating.

"C'mon, Frank. Can't you see that I'm in a hurry?"

"Right. The cat."

He followed her into the garage, the door of which was now closed, making the air stuffy. She grabbed a rag off a shelf and wiped the dust from the seat and the sides of the fuel tank.

"I hope this thing works," she muttered.

"You can't have it." He folded his arms across his chest and scratched himself.

Liane pressed a button and the garage churned open.

"I can't let you have it," he repeated. "It doesn't seem right under the circumstances."

Liane rose onto the balls of her feet and looked him nearly in the eye.

"My circumstances don't concern you. I'm not asking for moral guidance, Frank."

She spotted the helmet on the shelf. That seemed like a good idea.

She pulled it over her head and flipped up the tinted visor as she climbed aboard with her toes barely touching the ground. She turned the key that he'd left in the ignition. Nothing happened. The few times she'd ridden motorcycles they were already running and she'd hopped on for kicks. She tried to picture how they got them going and felt beyond her depth. She took a deep breath. The smell of tobacco smoke wafted into the garage.

From the corner of the house, Claudine appeared, cigarette in hand.

"What are you doing out here?" Frank whispered.

"I was getting a breath of fresh air, Mr. Moore, on my break. But I'm never really off duty. I'm always attuned to signs of distress."

She smiled and stepped toward Liane.

"I can't get it started," Liane said.

"Stay out of it, Claudine," Frank said, wetting his lips. "This is a private matter between me and my stepdaughter. My wife needs you."

"I'll be right with her, Mr. Moore." Turning to Liane: "Did you kick it?"

"Kick it?"

"It uses a kick starter. My brother in Jamaica had one years ago."

Liane pumped the pedal three or four times. It sprang back uselessly. She thought she heard the phone inside ringing again.

"No," Claudine said, clenching the cigarette between her lips to free her hands. "You need to keep the clutch depressed and to apply more force with the leg." She climbed aboard behind Liane, reaching around to put her hands over Liane's on the handlebars. "Like this."

Claudine stomped the pedal sharply and the motorcycle barked to life. She got off and took a long puff of her cigarette, looking the Harley over.

"Remember how to clutch?" she asked. She gave Liane a quick refresher. "Don't forget to ease into it."

Liane nodded grimly and tucked the folds of her skirt under her thighs as best she could, feeling very naked under there. With the motor vibrating she felt like she was straddling a rocket.

Frank leaned into her in order to be heard over the rumble. "Liane," he said, "what the hell's come over you?"

Liane snapped the kickstand up, twisted into first gear and released the clutch. The Harley jolted forward with such violence that it almost deposited her on the garage floor, but she lightened up on the throttle, adjusted her hips forward, and tilted into the handlebars. Then, fighting for balance, she and the Harley trundled up the short driveway and onto the street.

9

Dikembe returned to the hut at the time of long shadows. When he reached inside the doorway to fetch the kerosene lantern, a rotten odor assaulted him.

"Odette," he called. "Odette!"

From within came a faint groan. *So she's alive,* he thought with relief.

He lit the lantern and entered, setting it down on the floor in the center and adjusting the flame.

"Oh, my, Odette. I'm back. It's okay, love."

She was lying on her side with her hands pressed together beneath one cheek. There was a large wet spot on the top sheet in the area of her middle. Dikembe lifted the sheet, and the rising odor caused him to shudder. Her dressing gown was soiled with diarrhea.

"Oh, beautiful Odette," he cried. "Oh, my beautiful Odette. It's going to be all right."

He removed the sheet, gathering it together with the soiled spot in the center. He raised Odette by the shoulders into a sitting position and extended his forearm across her back, cradling her weight while he used the other hand to lift off her nightgown.

"I was asleep," she muttered.

"I know. You made an accident. We'll clean it up."

"My head!"

"We'll clean it up. Be patient, love."

He laid her down again naked on the straw mattress, back into the pile of loose stools, and used his teeth to rend the top sheet, shearing off the clean half. He went to the fire pit and stuffed the soiled part in among the twigs and lit it. Then he put a pot on to boil.

"I'm cold, Dikembe!" Odette called faintly.

He rushed to pour the warm water into a bowl and placed it with the clean fragment of sheet near the lantern in the center of the hut. He wrapped his arms under Odette and lifted her like a bride, conscious of her wetness against his skin, the acid stench of the excrement burning the lining of his nose. Odette twitched and shivered in his arms. He set her on the dirt floor and cleaned her with the sheet remnant and the water, beginning with her hair and face, wiping behind her ears, her neck, the folds of her breasts, working his way down as she shivered, finishing between her toes. When he was done he pulled a linen shift over her head and worked her arms through the sleeve holes. Wrapping her in a clean blanket, he lifted her to Daniel's mattress.

"Neighbor came by," she said. "I sent her away."

"Saying?"

"Stomach virus."

"Oh, Odette!" Dikembe cried. "It'll pass. It will pass."

He found the sheet upon which she'd lain to be a total loss. They had no spare. It pained him to ball it up and burn it along with the other in the fire pit, watching them glow to blue and orange in the darkness. He took a thick stick from the firewood pile and dragged the sheet partially out of the pit. He thought he saw red there among the caramel stains. Unsettled, he used the stick to shove the sheet back into the pit as one of the neighbors walked up.

They exchanged greetings and chitchat. Dikembe told the neighbor about his visit with the Englishman. The neighbor talked about the level of the river, the fish that were biting. Then, all at once, he changed the subject.

"Why is it you tending the kettle?"

"Odette's under the weather," Dikembe said.

"What does she have?"

"Bad bad cold."

The neighbor nodded slowly, ruminating. "Doctor come?"

Dikembe shook his head.

"How long?" the neighbor asked. "No one's seen her for two days. Where's your boy?"

"Gone to his auntie's. Why all these questions? The woman's entitled—"

"What, you'll be doing the laundry next?"

"If I choose. The world is getting modern."

"And so we burn the sheets? Throw everything away like the Americans?"

Dikembe scowled. "Get on with you now. I'm ready for sleep."

But he sat up for a long time after the neighbor left, staring at the perfect cross of stars in the soot-black southern sky, too distraught to consider the neighbor's suspiciousness. After a while, louder moaning began inside. Dikembe extinguished the fire and lay down on Daniel's mattress next to Odette, resting an arm across her, feeling her quiver. He patted her and she quieted. He lay awake listening to her soft crying over the headache and the helplessness. This was worse than any disease they'd spoken of, but there was no point calling the doctor, who would take days to come and provide little comfort. If it was something like Ebola, well, Dikembe already had her quarantined. There was no other mortal response.

As the sun came up Odette appeared worse. During wakefulness she complained of excruciating headaches and muscle pain, particularly in her thighs. Dikembe, despite the neighbors, went outside to cook her a thin soup, grateful that his grandfather had settled on the outskirts of the village, rather than in the center. But the soup was a fantasy; Odette could barely keep water down. When he lifted her to wash away the diarrhea that constantly leaked from her, she felt noticeably lighter than when he'd first returned.

Two days later Odette's legs began to spasm and she twitched in waves. When she was quiet, she melted into the mattress. Dikembe took to sleeping on the bare floor, afraid to crush her. When she was lucid, he propped her up against the wall of the hut. She asked him to promise to take care of Daniel.

"Don't talk like that," Dikembe implored. "We'll get through this."

"Bury me outside the village," Odette mumbled. "I'm being punished."

"For what?" He held up some water for her to drink.

"You are good, Dikembe. You have been a good husband."

Tears made rivulets down her cheeks.

On the sixth day of her illness Dikembe saw dried black crust in the corners of Odette's mouth. When he pulled back her trembling upper lip, he saw blood dripping from her gums and glazing her teeth. He laid a hand on her arm and she opened glassy eyes. Within a few hours she began to writhe in pain on the bed. She coughed and hacked up pink mucous. By that evening blood dripped from her nose and puddled among the straw.

Dikembe wondered about the choices he'd made. Perhaps a doctor could have helped after all. It felt so uncertain now. She moaned and writhed and thrashed and he had exhausted himself with the effort to hold her down, to wash her, to comfort her, to fend off suspicious neighbors who trickled out of the village. Except for the small pile of clothes that he'd set atop his boots in the corner and covered with a piece of plastic, everything in the small hut was tinged with Odette's bloody fluids. Dikembe sat cross-legged, rocking naked in the middle of a dirt floor stained black with islands of spillage. He swallowed and his throat felt raw. The air was as fetid as the underworld and he sensed a headache coming on.

An hour later Odette farted and a river of blood spewed across Daniel's polluted mattress. Her shallow cough ended in a hellish gurgling sound. Dikembe crawled to her and laid a hand on her bruised and weeping leg. He thought that it no longer mattered if he lived or died.

When he sucked in a breath it felt as if someone had plunged an arrow into the center of his skull.

10

Liane wouldn't venture the parkway on the motorcycle. Cruising along at thirty miles per hour, flattening out her turns, the breeze flapping her skirt, and hidden within the giant cocoon of her helmet, she felt much safer than she had with Frank waving the phone at her. She wished she'd asked more questions about his relationship with Flickinger before things got out of hand. The two men had worked together once, but it was hard to imagine them ever having been peers, and she wondered how often they now spoke and how their conversations might flow when they did. Certainly Frank had always been the junior intellect of the two, and whatever acuity he started with seemed lately to be fading. She now feared that he was vulnerable to easy manipulation by Flickinger, a worry that she'd never before considered. And yet Ronald was the one who called—Ronald, who Frank didn't even know.

She pondered the possibility that Ronald's call had been freelance. Maybe he was just pissed that she betrayed him to gain entry to the primate lab. It occurred to her that she hardly knew Ronald at all outside the lab. His life partner, Keith, could be a figment of his imagination for all she knew; everything he'd told her could be a false biography. She'd never seen his house, never met his friends. They'd had an occasional lunch together, talked lab techniques sometimes, more often exchanged innocuous stories of their weekends and vacation plans. At the time, from Liane's perspective, it had been idle but sincere conversation, if more acquaintanceship than friendship. Now, through the prism of growing distrust, she wondered.

Hammurabi, by contrast, hadn't mentioned anything she construed as personal until a mere—was the time of his dismissal not even three days ago? Before then she never could have imagined the circumstances of his home life: the fully American blonde wife, the imposing house with the iron gate. She wondered whether she should detour and pay him a surprise visit. Was he home finally, licking his wounds? He'd never shown any sign of doubt until the morning of the firing—but then again, who shares his darkest side with subordinates? Still, he was the one who reached out to her when he might have called quits to their professional relationship. Instead of cutting it off, he'd led her to the edge of the precipice, imploring her to jump with him, and then had backed away and gone incommunicado. *Why?*

She was turning this over in her mind at a red light when her cell phone rang. She glided to the curb, fished the phone from her tote and flipped open her visor, half expecting a hostile voice.

"Liane," Mickey said, "what took so long to answer?"

She could barely hear him over the clamor of passing traffic.

"Can you speak up?" she said.

"No."

She removed the helmet and used it to shield the noise that came from the street.

"What is it, then? Is everything all right? Is Bea okay?"

"The ape's fine. It's you I'm worried about."

"That's sweet. I'm on my way home." She'd have to skip that dinner, she thought. *How stupid to have left Bea!*

Mickey said something she couldn't pick up.

"Can you speak louder, Mickey? I can barely hear you."

"Negative. Just listen harder. What I said was: there's someone in your apartment."

"Who?"

"I don't know, but they sure ain't the maid service. It sounds like they're tearing the place apart."

"Oh, God. What about Nicholas?"

"The cat? If he's got any instinct for self-preservation, I'm sure he ran for the hills."

She closed one eye and, through a space in the helmet, peeked at the traffic blurring by.

"Liane," Mickey said, "if you want my advice, you'd best not come home."

She climbed off the Harley. Her eyes darted around the street, and she pirouetted in place for a 360-degree view.

"Are you able to get out of your apartment?" she asked.

"Maybe. I looked out a second ago and didn't see anyone in the hall."

"Okay."

She pressed her fingers into her forehead. *Think!* Ronald's call—"something about a theft," Frank had said. What she heard through the receiver: "No cops. Find Shaker." Shaker Moyo, he'd meant. So Ronald wasn't a tool of Pentalon. He was helping her puzzle this through from inside. *Shaker Moyo: FAULT operative.* What a danger for Ronald even to have spoken the name, given the position he was in. Shaker Moyo had been Corey's accomplice when they burned down the lab. He'd been shot in the leg by a guard during the arson, pinned down in the parking lot and later brought to trial for manslaughter.

"Mickey, a few nights ago you mentioned a place where you go to think sometimes."

"You mean the—"

"Don't say it. Meet me at the entrance there in an hour. Can you do it?"

"Yeah, I guess. You know, there's just so deep I can get before I have to know exactly what's going on. We're near that point."

Liane pondered. A few phone calls to the State would undoubtedly reveal Shaker Moyo's whereabouts, rotting in some maximum-security prison somewhere. And he might lead her to Corey Harrow, who remained free, she believed—she'd have known if they'd caught him; it would have made the news. If Corey were still into animal rights, he'd have an idea what to do with Bea. And, even if he weren't, he'd have to help her—they'd been so close. He'd nearly been the father of her child. It was shortly after her abortion that he'd burned down the lab and gone into hiding.

"If you can get Bea to me, you'll be off the hook if you want, Mickey."

"It won't be a picnic, Liane."

"I'll be at that place in an hour, okay?"

"Right. This is crazy. I'm in, though—I'll be there too." A pause. "One more thing. What's the deal with this animal, anyway?"

"How do you mean?"

"If it wasn't, like, impossible, I'd swear she's been calling your name."

11

It had poured buckets all evening. Mickey used the big bath towel in which he'd wrapped the bonobo to dry one of the outdoor benches on the water taxi from Red Hook, Brooklyn to Manhattan. Most of the commuters were inside, half asleep, hiding from the weather as the canary-yellow ferry chugged along. The breeze off the East River tasted fresh and Liane felt wired from too little sleep.

Bea kept nuzzling her and quietly saying, "Liane *moto*. Liane *moto*."

One of the ferry staff came out, looking serious. He was dark, squat and broad-shouldered, a native Spanish speaker in white boaters. "Yo," he said, "no animals allowed on board."

"No?" said Mickey. "Not even seeing eye dogs and such?"

"That's the exception," said the ferryman. "This don't look like a dog and neither of you peoples looks blind."

"My friend here is dexterity challenged."

"Dexterity?"

Liane nodded. Bea imitated.

The ferryman took it in. "You got any paperwork?"

"No. The chimp's her helper. It's a working chimp."

"That right? He works at dexterity? Doesn't look like he's doing much."

"She's on break."

"You messing with me?"

"I'd never," Mickey said, reaching into his pants pocket. He extracted a wad of bills and peeled off a twenty. "We already left the dock. We're not looking to make trouble."

"I can't accept any dough," the ferryman said. "Put it away before someone sees. Just stay outside with the monkey, okay? No going inside, even if it rains again, okay? I don't want any problems with my boss when we reach New York. Keep low getting off, too."

The ferryman left, shaking his head all the way back to the cabin.

Liane turned to Mickey. "You handled that well."

"That guy only wants a plausible story to tell if anyone calls him on it."

"Plausible? If he repeats the tale you told, he's going to end up looking pretty foolish."

"Yeah, but we'll be gone by then. Anyhow, that's nothing compared to what we may be facing."

"We? You said last night that you'd see me to the other side and that'd be it."

"Well, let's now say I'm warming to the proposition. The ape's a kick. And I don't want to see any harm come to you."

After Mickey had asked about her mother's health she'd told him most of the rest of the story in his BMW last night. They'd ordered dinner from a McDonald's drive-through. Liane bought a salad for Bea, but she showed more interest in the chicken nuggets. They'd slept fitfully in the car under a broken streetlamp, and this morning the bonobo had the runs all over the rear shelf. She'd sat on the front headrest looking guilty, whining, *Bosoto. Bosoto.*

"So you never have any idea what she's saying?" Mickey had asked.

"Only when I hear my name."

Mickey had played the sport about Bea's accident, and Liane tried to clean up the mess with some paper napkins, but she suspected that none of them would want to be around when the sun hit it.

"I'm really sorry about your Beemer," she said now.

"Aw, it's nothing. I've had my hand so far up the asses of large beasts that I looked like a one-armed magician. After that, what's a little chimp shit between friends?"

"I seem to be hard on vehicles lately. My Honda must be a total loss and I may've destroyed my stepfather's Harley on the way over here. It started making a pretty big racket when I crossed into Brooklyn. Then it petered out just as I got within striking distance of the ferry landing."

"If it'd been sitting a long time in the garage, the gas was probably just stale. Where'd you park it?"

"Fifty-seventh under the Gowanus."

"Ouch. Never mind the engine, then. You'll be lucky if any part of it lasted the night."

"Damn. Frank's gonna kill me."

"From the tale you told, I'd say that's the least of your troubles. These Pentalon people don't sound like they'll be pulling any punches. Don't you think we should consider going to the authorities?"

"What authorities?"

"There's a committee in the Ag Department that sets the rules for the treatment of lab animals, as I understand it. Maybe we can get them to do something."

"Even if they go after Pentalon over the bonobos, what're they going to do with Bea? She's a threat to the whole infrastructure of lab testing just by existing. A talking ape means the end of primate vivisection, which the Ag Department won't countenance. They look out for *people*."

Mickey bit the inside of his lip. "I get what you're saying. The next step in primate evolution is probably not something that's high among bureaucratic priorities. While they wring their hands I can see Bea rotting behind bars."

"It's so unfair! Isn't it supposed to be government's role to protect the weakest among us?"

"You kidding? Half the research animals in America are owned by the United States military."

She frowned. "You're right. I've read some of their studies."

"Our only choice is to render unto Caesar what's Caesar's and unto God what's God's." He crossed his legs and shook his foot, gazing out at the harbor. "You know, they legally race horses drugged up. I couldn't watch another stallion break down because of the injections I gave him and then pretend to be surprised that it turned out bad."

"They'll get someone else to do it."

"Already have. When you put them down, they call it euthanasia, but that's bullshit. Horses in the wild are often what we'd consider lame, but they manage to survive. These catastrophic injuries at the track ain't natural. I couldn't be part of that exploitation anymore. That's why I left—and that's why I didn't like to talk about it when I was still there."

Liane stared out past the iron rail. From the middle of the river, the eastside buildings hunkered like giant trolls and the Brooklyn Bridge looked like a magical fairy path. Bea, flat on her back, seemed to be contemplating the sky's piebald overcast.

"I'm glad you and I reached the same conclusions," Liane said. "I quit Pentalon but I'm not ready to quit the whole deal and abandon Bea. If the government won't naturally be on our side, we have to find a way to get the attention of someone in power who knows the difference."

"Fine, Liane, but we can't exactly write a letter. The bureaucracy won't take kindly to this news."

"So, if the bonobo's trying to communicate and we can figure out what she's saying—*big if*—they might not even see how this could entirely change our view of ourselves as a species?"

"What I'm more afraid of is that they might understand all too well. Like the way they buried that Area Fifty-One UFO deal."

"In which case, we'd be totally on our own."

"Yeah," Mickey nodded, "or worse. On the other hand, you can't stay on the run forever with an ape, Liane. And she'd be only marginally better off locked away in hiding with you, still unable to live any kind of life."

Liane had puzzled through most of this during her motorcycle ride.

"There's someone who can change the game for us. The problem is that it's going to be a bit of work tracking him down, and it'll be next to impossible if I have to attempt it with a close cousin in tow who isn't even potty trained. Especially if the lab or the police are looking for us."

"What exactly'd you have in mind?"

"I need a place to stash Bea. I think it would be for a day or so."

"I was afraid you'd say that. I can't take her back to my place. Pentalon will be all over that building like fur on a grizzly."

The ferry's momentum shifted, jerking them toward the bow. The humans had to set their feet to keep their balance, but Bea remained sprawled on Liane's canvas tote with a grip on one of the bench rails. As the boat pulled into dock, the commuters shuffled toward the exit in their raincoats and business suits. Liane and Mickey waited until most of them had cleared. Then Mickey threw the towel over Bea and hustled her off the ferry.

"Hey, what d'ya think of this?" he asked, transferring Bea into Liane's arms on the street. "Friend of mine from vet school specializes in exotics and has a clinic on First Avenue uptown. He always seems to have a primate or two around."

"In New York City?"

"Might be illegal, but you'd be amazed what people keep in their apartments. Tortoises. Ferrets. Two-hundred-pound potbellied pigs. Maybe we can get my buddy to admit Bea. She could spend a couple of nights there while we sort things out."

He took out his cell phone and began to course through his contact list.

"Hold on," Liane said. "Don't think I'm completely paranoid, but maybe we should avoid using our phones for a while."

Mickey scratched his head and looked off into the distance, seeming to take the measure of Liane's logic.

"That's cool," he said finally. "We'll figure out another way."

12

Axel Flickinger sat at his desk behind a small cage and a specimen jar. He removed a dead white rat from the cage, dangling it by the tail, watching it slowly rotate.

"What killed him?" Gretch asked.

"He died on schedule. He has more mercury in him than a barometer." He replaced the rat and set the cage aside. "Tell me once more, yes? What exactly happened on the train?"

Gretch narrated for the third time. He left out the part about killing the cop.

"I can write you a prescription for Jimmy and the boys," Flickinger offered.

"Never mind. I'll live." Truth be told, Gretch was enjoying the residual pain.

"So you have no idea where either the girl or the bonobo is?"

"No, but I'll nail them."

"We cannot allow this person to jeopardize all that we have built. What did you find in her apartment?"

"No sign of the ape and it's impossible to tell exactly when Vinson last set foot in there. If she does return, by the way, I'll know instantly. Also, I tipped off the police and they impounded her car. She'll have to resurface somehow for transportation if she wants to get anywhere. When she pops her head up, we'll cut it off."

"You sound too confident, Mr. Gretch. Do you fully appreciate how much harm this pair can inflict on our operations? If the bonobo shows up on *The Today Show,* blathering on like a toddler, the movement we have so long sought to marginalize will explode into the mainstream and we will be considered radioactive by all the hypocrites who pay to keep our lights on."

"Why not get the bonobos out of here? It's an Indonesian contract, isn't it? Send them to Jakarta."

"Perhaps one day, but most of them can't be moved right now." He picked up the specimen jar and stared through the glass. There was something inside, pale pink tissue.

"What's that?" Gretch asked.

"The male twin's larynx."

"What were you hoping to accomplish by removing it?"

"I want to compare it to a human larynx I had ordered. If they are similar enough, we can breed those two—when you get the female back. Then we will have a proprietary genetic line that we can take in a dozen directions."

"You can't skip that now that you've stirred up the girl?"

"We do not retreat in the face of a peon, yes? It is not like you to suggest so."

"I have a bad feeling. Can we use the leverage point—your acquaintance, Frank Moore?"

"We can try. I have the sense that he hid something from me, and I have grave concerns with regard to our clients. They expect us to keep a low profile, even in crisis."

"And we will."

"We did not build this empire with sticks and spit, yes? Pentalon needs to turn over half a billion of notes every quarter. If bad publicity causes our bondholders to run for the exits, it will not matter that we own half the Department of Agriculture. And if that bonobo goes Hollywood, every congressman I currently supplement will act like he never heard my name."

"So I'll make Liane Vinson and her ape my priority."

"Not her ape, Mr. Gretch. Mine."

13

It was nine o'clock in the morning and already unusually warm. The streets of Chinatown teemed with people: a stew of every ethnic group imaginable, wearing all manner of clothing—from business suits to Japanese kimonos, from cut-off shorts to guayaberas—steaming as the sun boiled the dirty wet sidewalks of Canal Street. In this crowded morass, few people bothered to take note of the young female bonobo riding atop Mickey's shoulders, hanging onto his hair with one perfect brown hand. She seemed strangely in place among shops cluttered with live chickens and fish, gutted pigs and exotic vegetables.

Mickey and Liane dodged down a side street to escape the press of flesh. They paused at a curbside fruit vendor. While Mickey applied a bear hug to keep Bea from leaping atop the display, Liane purchased a bunch of bananas and some apples. The fruit was still cool from the truck. They stepped under an awning to relish it.

"Mmm," Mickey said between bites, "looks like the third world, but it's hard to find a pay phone down here these days."

"What we need are some untraceable cell phones," Liane said, tossing a banana peel into the trash.

"Even if they're devious enough to have you tapped, I still think that my phone would be clean. There's no reason they would even know I exist."

"If Vlad has the kind of access I think he does, he could be combing my phone records as we speak. And he'd see an incoming call from you. At a crucial time, too."

"Okay. What say we go into one of these all-purpose electronics stores down here—we must've passed six of them already. Buy us a couple of them prepaid jobs?"

They walked around the corner and paused by a storefront whose windows were papered over with colorful advertisements for international calling plans and hand-lettered signs in four Asian alphabets.

"Bea and I'll wait out here," Liane said.

"Oh no you don't. I'm not letting you two outta my sight."

He lowered the bonobo from his shoulders and she walked through the door erect, holding Liane's hand, with Mickey following. *Just your average American family out shopping for untraceable cell phones,* Liane thought.

Ceiling-high shelves groaned under Buddhas and incense burners and lucky porcelain cats. There were dusty boxes of toasters and curling irons and answering machines and electric shoe buffers and snow-globe paperweights. Bea's eyes opened as wide as any curious child's. They stepped to a glass case near the back, where a slender Asian man perched on a stool.

"Tell me how can I help," he said, sweeping his dark eyes over his visitors. His diction may have been a little off, but he barely had an accent.

Mickey gazed at the array of cameras and phones in the glass case. They didn't look like they came with long warranties. "We need two prepaid phones," he said.

The man pointed through the glass with a pair of delicate fingers. He had one pinky nail that was two inches long.

"These are ones, twenty-nine dollars," the man said. "Twenty minutes call time, free incoming. Or for twenty bucks more, one hour call time. Two for eighty-five, no tax if you pay cash. Or," he added, looking Mickey in the eye, "you can trade for the monkey."

"We'll take the longer call time," Mickey said. He removed his wad of bills and peeled off five crisp twenties. Liane considered contributing but concluded she'd better preserve her cash.

"All right, I can do very good phone, thirty-day guarantee, two hours call time. You trade for the monkey," the shopkeeper said.

"One hour call time is fine," Mickey said, pushing the money forward.

The man splayed his fingertips on the glass and rested his long pinky nail on Andrew Jackson's right eyebrow.

"That monkey, the more I look, is valuable, very. I'm thinking the phones plus two hundred dollars for you."

Liane bade Bea climb into her arms and backed away. They held one another around the waist.

"The ape's not for sale," Mickey reiterated. "I'll just take the phones now. Please!"

Keeping his hand pressed to the money on the counter, the man bent down and removed two phones that were packaged in clear plastic clamshells. He set them on the counter and examined them with care.

A heavier man appeared from behind the back screen. He paused with his arms folded.

"How about for the monkey four hundred dollars plus phones," the first man said. "A lot of money, that."

"I told you, pal, the animal ain't for sale."

"Let's go," Liane said, as the larger man stepped forward.

Mickey scooped up the phones. "Keep the change," he said over his shoulder.

Liane looked back just long enough to see the two men making eye contact. Outside, she transferred Bea to Mickey's shoulders.

"Phew," she said. "I think this bonobo's growing heavier."

"And she's strong as an ox already. I thought she was gonna have her way with that fruit vendor."

They left Canal for a quieter block, unwrapping the cell phones as they went.

Liane handed Bea another apple.

"Come on," Mickey protested. "She's dribbling on my head!"

He put Bea on the ground and Liane held the ape's free hand while Mickey looked up the number of his friend.

14

The train station at Thessaly resembled an old public works project from the Soviet Union: flaking steel and thickly grained concrete, colors so muted that even the brick of the outside walls appeared more gray than red. A line of thunderstorms had passed through, and the disturbed sky lingered to the south, mottled in shades of yellow and brown. Puddles remained in the depressions of tarred railroad ties, and branches torn from trees lay scattered against embankments and fences. Only a few people had departed the train with Liane, and they disappeared while she got her bearings.

The whole place felt eerie. She looked around for transportation and spotted a taxi stand with siding peeled down to the knotted plywood and sign letters faded to ghosts. The sun pierced the clouds and a gust came up, throwing grit into her eyes and shaking her skirt. Everything she could see was paved over; there were no trees visible in the direction she faced. It amazed her that rural New York State could feel so urban in microcosm, and she thought of the street in front of Mickey's friend's Manhattan clinic, pleasantly shaded by narrow gingkoes. With a breeze rushing from the river, the air there tasted fresher than it did in this worn-out speck of a town.

She'd left Bea and Mickey at his friend's veterinary clinic as planned. Mickey had marched in cradling Bea in his arms and informed the receptionist that the ape was a special case without revealing a word of truth.

When Mickey's white-coated friend came in, Mickey concocted a story on the spot involving smugglers and corrupt officials and animals dying in shipping containers. The story featured Liane's selfless rescue of this unfortunate young primate, with the take-home message that they needed a place to crash with the bonobo for a few days, no questions asked and no privacies violated. Mickey's friend looked skeptical but acceded to fraternity. He'd left them with the bag of groceries that Liane bought on the way and a couple of sleeping bags. There was also a cage, which they'd made a big show of placing the bonobo into while Mickey's friend stood in their presence. As soon as he left, though, they set Bea free.

Mickey's friend lent them a laptop, and they used the wi-fi to surf the Internet. Liane soon discovered that Shaker Moyo was serving fifteen to twenty years at a state penitentiary in upstate New York. When the vet clinic went quiet for lunch just before noon, she'd snuck out a side door.

In Thessaly, the gritty wind let up and an unmarked, run-down Buick, big as a houseboat, pulled to a stop at the taxi stand. Liane flagged him down and leaned through the passenger window.

"Where to?" said the driver.

"The prison."

"Where else." He grinned at her with teeth so well-spaced you could store nickels in his mouth. He patted the empty seat beside him.

Liane looked over the rear bench. There was nothing there but an old coat. "Mind if I ride in back?"

"Suit yourself. I won't bite either way."

The door creaked when she opened it. There was a puddle of water on the vinyl mat, she guessed from the recent downpour.

"My name's Handy."

"Nice to meet you, Mr. Handy."

He broke into a long laugh and Liane angled herself to examine him in the rearview mirror. His face was round and smooth, with reddened cheeks that could have been painted with rouge. It was hard to guess his age. His eyes were beady under crooked bangs. If he'd been an animal, she thought, he'd be a giant prairie dog.

"No, Handy's the first name. Sorry to make fun. It's been a long time since anyone called me mister."

Liane didn't respond. She laid a hand on the armrest.

He began to whistle but stopped abruptly. "You don't look much like the kind of visitor they tend to get at Thessaly."

"What makes you think I'm visiting? Maybe I'm here for a job interview."

He gave her a prolonged look in the rearview mirror, making no effort to hide his curiosity. "Well, you sure don't look like guard material. Could be a social worker, I guess."

Liane didn't bother to argue about her intentions. She wished Handy would keep his eyes on the road.

"You need the office entrance or the visitors'?"

"The visitors'," she conceded.

"It's around the side. I can wait if you want."

"Thanks, Handy."

A few minutes later they turned and began to parallel a high chain-link fence covered in razor wire. A vast brick structure came into view, octagon-shaped with crenellated towers on every corner. Her driver knew the uniformed man in the guard booth. They exchanged a salute, and Handy turned right and accelerated along a service road that ran between fences. He was waved past another checkpoint, then pulled up in front of a low-lying modern building that connected to the older part by a narrow, windowless extension.

Liane walked across a gravel lot and entered on the ground floor. The security regimen inside the lobby made the system at Pentalon appear space age. The x-ray conveyor belt squeaked and the metal detector portal looked first-generation.

"Number sixteen," a guard said, handing her a slip of paper.

Liane was so focused on reading the labels above the cubicles that she only belatedly noticed the man sitting on the other side of her station. His skin appeared very dark against the orange jumpsuit. His nose was broad and his face was shaped like a dish, round and shiny.

He wasn't smiling.

15

"I don't know any Liane Vinson."

"But you agreed to see me."

"It gets lonely in here."

"I was Corey Harrow's girlfriend before everything went down."

"Is that right? What do you want?"

"I'm looking for him."

Shaker Moyo sucked his teeth. "You said he was your boyfriend."

"That was a long time ago."

"Tell me about it. I'm rotting in here. I had a girl, too, who ran off with some tool in the Green Party when I was still downstate. Now nobody comes to visit. I haven't seen a soul from the outside in fourteen months."

"I understand."

He glared at her. "You don't understand anything!"

Liane watched him stew for a minute. She was glad to have the Plexiglas. "How'd you meet Corey?" she asked.

"At a gathering in Denver. We were both hardcore. The easy explanations for doing nothing didn't satisfy either one of us. He didn't mention me?"

"Honestly, I only heard your name at the end. We didn't talk so much about his friends in the animal liberation group after he left high school and got deep into it. He came back from the training camp and it was like he was all grown-up. I was still a kid."

Moyo fussed with a sleeve of the jumpsuit. "Even a kid knows right from wrong."

"Yeah, but a kid doesn't have the power to act. Not in a way that makes a real difference."

"Be the change you want to see in the world." Moyo pulled at an eyebrow. "That's Gandhi."

"Gandhi wouldn't have approved of your actions, though, would he?"

"Everyone makes mistakes. What about all the bad things that happen day in and day out? Why does the mistake of one moment weigh more than all the daily injustices?"

"It's a good question," Liane said. "I don't know. Maybe because a man died."

"And now I'm ruined, too."

"The FAULT people couldn't help you?"

"The FAULT people put their cause first. I'm deadwood now."

"Are they in touch at all?"

He paused and raised his eyes to the ceiling, then looked back at her. "How do I even know you were Corey's woman?"

"I helped him escape and paid a price. We met on a little island in a park where we used to hang out when we were still dating. I brought him food and a flashlight. When I hugged him I felt the gun in his waistband. I was naive. We sat on the ground and my jeans got covered in goose poop. When I got home, the cops were already waiting."

"The poop was a telltale," he nodded. "Accessory after the fact. You went to jail?"

She shook her head. "I got off as a juvenile. Nobody from my adult life knows about it."

"You know what you aided?"

"Just what I read in the papers."

"The guy we locked in the closet, he got fried. For years I saw his face every time I closed my eyes. I watched the paramedics wheel him out. His skin—it was a pus bubble. They went over a bump and I saw it move like Jell-O. Horrible." He buried his face in his hands, looked up at Liane from the spaces between his fingers. "Sometimes I wonder which one of us made out better. That'd be a fair question for someone to write a paper about. We get students through here sometimes, you know. I thought you might be one. They drain our brains clean and then they go. I doubt that happens to Corey, wherever he is."

"He said you were a true believer. If I remember right, he said he paused to help and you told him to run."

"Bullets were flying. I went down. *Rambauchiita*, I said." He dropped his eyelids. "*Rambauchiita.*"

"What language is that?"

"Shona. I taught some to Corey. We were like family then, brothers. Not anymore."

"What does it mean?"

"Just run, man. I got hit. There was no escape for me."

"Where is Shona from, Mr. Moyo?"

"You can call me Shaker. I'm from Zimbabwe, from a village near Lake Kariba and the Matusadona." She recalled now that newspaper articles at the time had made a big deal of his foreignness. "I had an uncle who lived in Chicago way back. He used to send us postcards of the Sears Tower. He had a job delivering flowers for some rich people in Cleveland, Shaker Heights. My mother thought the name sounded exotic."

"Does your uncle ever visit?"

"He was shot by the police on his way to work ten years ago. They said he flashed a gun—never found." He sucked his teeth.

"I'm sorry."

"You don't know what it's like in here." He wrapped the table with his knuckles. "I had a woman lawyer. You remind me of her in some ways—another nobody who can't help me. So why should I help *you*?"

One of the visitors got up to leave, and a guard on the other side of the Plexiglas led the prisoner away. Moyo's eyes darted about the room.

"What about the cause?" Liane asked.

"What cause would that be? Only cause I have now is survival, man." He sucked his teeth again.

"Listen, Shaker," Liane rasped, "I'm sure nobody's happy with the way things turned out. And as for that change we're supposed to be, it's a hell of a lot harder if the good people won't stick up for one another. Remember that song from *Hair*? It's easy to be hard."

"*Hair?* Sticking up? The good people?" He sniggered. "Maybe you haven't noticed that I'm on the wrong side of the barrier here. You presume to talk to me about powerlessness?"

"I just thought you might be in a position to help me—in spite of it all. I thought you were Corey's friend. I know the movement is still alive out there."

"Yeah, well there aren't a lot of animals that need protecting in here, Liane, unless you count the *cucarachas*. I had ideals once. Now I have Crips and Bloods and MS-Thirteen and skinheads and psychopaths. That's my existence."

He slapped the table and rocked his chair onto its back legs.

"You know, I miss some things," he said. "I miss women, sure, but also other things that a visitor can do something about, like pencils and paper. Haven't had pencils with real sharp points in a long time—just dull nubs. Pointy pencils I need, that you can write with real fine. And how about a fresh book to read? And Kit-Kat bars, like they sell out by the waiting area. Visitors buy stuff like that for the inmates. You didn't bring so much as a piece of hard candy! Even the women who cheat on their husbands do better."

The bell rang and the guards stepped forward. One of them took Moyo by the elbow. The prisoner turned to go and then paused.

"Pistachio nuts," he said. "That's another thing. I haven't eaten a pistachio in five years and you come in here asking for favors. Salted pistachio nuts fresh in the shell. Mmm-mmm. Makes my mouth water just to think of it. A friend would bring me a pistachio, that's what a friend would do."

Liane pushed her chair back. She watched in awe as Moyo and the guard faded into the expanse of fortified corridor, pausing just once to unlock a wire-mesh door.

16

It was hard for Dikembe to grasp that the tangle of dissolved flesh on the mattress beside him ever could have been his wife, Odette. She'd frozen with her mouth and eyes open, and that was how she silently lay. There was only the sound of the mourning doves outside the hut, beseeching the world on her behalf. And the buzz of flies. They landed on her and he waved them away. He curled into a ball on the dirt floor, weeping.

For two days he waited there for the headache to develop into other symptoms. Neighbors called to him from outside the hut. Dikembe called back, telling them to go away. He ignored the rising stench, which changed in character with each hour. He monitored his internal workings the way he once paid careful attention to the orchestra of the jungle. There was a cramp in his left calf; he straightened his leg and after a while it went away. There was a pang in his stomach; he drank some water and it stayed down. There was the headache; it snuck away during the night. Only gradually did it dawn on him that he may not have contracted the virus. He was hungry and thirsty and bone-tired and distraught, but he wasn't ill.

Dikembe lit his lantern and searched the hut for something to eat. He located a few crackers and chewed them slowly. He found a square of chocolate that he'd set aside for Daniel and let it melt in his mouth. He found a small container of corn meal, but it was inedible dry. He spit it out and drank the last of his water.

He dug out a piece of cloth in which Odette often wrapped scraps of leftover food. There was a bone in it, striped with dried remnants of meat—probably being saved for soup. He held the bone to the light of the lantern and examined it. He recognized it as the femur of a small monkey. Once, he'd spent two weeks counting Allen's Swamp Monkeys for the Englishman. After that, he made Odette promise there would be no more bush meat prepared for the family. Yet what had he done in the bargain? He'd committed his own offense against nature, and perhaps far worse, involving bonobos, much rarer than the monkey whose femur he now held. He tossed the bone to the floor in disgust and looked across at Odette's dimly lit corpse. He couldn't hide the tragedy from the other villagers much longer.

Dikembe used the small sheet of plastic that covered his clothes to gather them up without touching. He held them under one arm and cautiously proceeded through the spreading dawn to the river. He immersed his head and ran the bar of soap over his hair, agitating it into a lather. When the soap dribbled into his eyes, stinging them, he didn't at first blink it away. He washed and scrubbed for a long time.

As the sun rose, he saw hippo eyes in the middle of the river and crocodile nostrils not twenty feet away. Upriver, a herd of elephants silently crossed, thick silhouettes like a string of paper cutouts. The crocodile disappeared below the surface and glided away. Dikembe climbed ashore and sat on the flat stones that he'd last shared with Daniel.

Voices drifted down the path. Though he was only half dry, Dikembe pulled on his clothes. He was lacing his boots when two women from the village descended to the riverbank.

"*Mbote*," one said. Hello. Her name was Charlen. The other was Jannie.

The women had baskets of laundry resting on their heads. They placed them on a boulder.

"Where Odette?" Charlen asked.

Dikembe felt his face go slack. After all these days of struggle, the sight of the neighbors magnified his loneliness.

"Gone," he sobbed, fighting for composure.

"You mean—"

"Deceased," Dikembe said.

"Odette? Not Odette!" Jannie said. She put her face in her hands and began keening.

"We suspected," Charlen said. "How did it happen without you asking for help? We called and you wouldn't come."

"I was trying to protect everyone."

Jannie gasped as if she'd seen an apparition. She seized her laundry basket and raced up the path toward the village.

"Trying to protect *yourself*, more like," Charlen said. "Dikembe, how could you?"

"First I thought that it would pass," he said. "Then it was too late. She's still in the hut."

Charlen took a step back. "And you are ill, too?"

"No. I wish it had taken me instead."

"You've endangered all of us."

"Walk ahead," Dikembe said, extending his open hand, "so you won't breathe my air."

They saw smoke rising over the treetops before they emerged from the path. The quiet village morning had yielded to frantic activity. Flames crackled among the thatched grass of Dikembe's roof. Men— his neighbors—leaped around, poking the fire with sticks, encouraging it. A few women with brooms swept the ash and stray embers that had already begun to fall, swept them back toward the hut, as if the last traces of carbon could themselves contaminate everything. Dikembe sat forlorn on the ground, his arms on his folded knees, watching the immolation. He knew he would do the same thing in their place.

It took a long time for the roof to collapse. When it finally did so, the villagers threw dried palm fronds and sticks atop the wreckage, piling it into a vast bonfire, the heat of which Dikembe could feel even from a distance. Odette's body was in there amidst the flames. He imagined the heat as her love, come to radiate upon him.

By the time the moon appeared, the hut and its contents and his wife had been reduced to a fine gray powder. Nothing remained but the scarred cinderblock walls of Odette's cooking pit, standing like an ancient relic. He lay down on his side and that night the mosquitoes feasted on his unmoving body.

A poke in the ribs awakened him. When he rolled over and opened his eyes, he saw that it was morning and five men towered over him with sticks and clubs. He knew all of them as well as he knew his own lost brothers, but he made no effort to say any of their names.

"There's nothing of yours here now, Dikembe." One of them stomped on Dikembe's outstretched hand with his boot. "Nothing to keep you."

Dikembe pulled his hand out, scraping his knuckles, and rolled over onto all fours. Someone kicked him in the stomach, taking the wind out of him. They watched him labor to catch his breath. He struggled to his feet.

"I made a mistake," he said shakily. They would think he meant Odette, though he intended something else entirely.

The circle parted and Dikembe pushed through and pointed himself toward the road, his stomach still in spasm. He'd have to get Daniel first, then he had some ideas on where to go. There was small treasure in his shoe, and most of the cash from the Englishman remained in his pocket. He resisted an urge to feel for the wad with his hand.

A hard shove came from behind and Dikembe flailed forward, accelerating into a jog.

The first rock glanced off his shoulder. The second hit him square in the small of his back. There was a pause. Then the thud of a third and a fourth and a fifth stone. The sixth and seventh missed, skittering past into the trees. The eighth one was larger and nearly brought him down. He broke into a run as he reached the road, but the men had stopped following him.

17

From the platform, Liane saw the train emerging through a crease between hills. A part of her wondered why she'd ventured up to the boondocks at all. The FAULT organization had a public, law-abiding face. Theoretically, she could have called the 800-number or gone to San Francisco and walked into their headquarters. But she doubted they'd acknowledge Corey's existence, let alone put her in touch with him. And, as for Bea, she couldn't imagine placing her in the trust of total strangers, however well-meaning they might appear on the surface.

Her mind drifted to the prison. She'd gotten nothing from Moyo by showing more compassion for a bonobo than for a fellow human being. Liane left the platform and walked back toward town, determined to give Shaker Moyo another try in the morning.

Earlier, she'd passed a modest department store. From the front, it had all the charm of a shopworn five-and-dime, but it was getting near closing time and she wasn't about to start searching around. A bell attached to the door clanged when she walked in. A middle-aged man with a thin mustache stood behind the counter, wearing a plaid vest. She began to browse. The man offered to help.

"We close in ten minutes."

Liane went into the changing room with a pair of boys' tan chinos and a plaid button-down shirt.

"I'll take these," she said, emerging. "Can I wear them out?"

"Sure. I'll cut off the tags."

Glancing at herself in the floor-length mirror, she decided she looked too much like a boy. She found a cotton crew-neck sweater, yellow, went into the dressing room, and swapped it for the shirt. *Better.* She chose some underwear, a toothbrush and toothpaste, and a box of pencils, then set all of it on the counter.

"Do you have ladies' shaving razors?"

"No, ma'am, sold out."

"Men's?"

He shook his head.

"How about deodorant?"

He reached for a shelf behind the counter and took down a stick of the only women's brand.

"Our clientele's a little different around here," he apologized.

Liane combed the store for a few more items. She found a pencil-sharpening block with Sponge Bob on the side. There was a sparse shelf of paperback books. She grabbed a Stephen King. She stepped back to the counter and eyed several handguns in the glass case.

"Do you have writing pads or loose paper?"

The man said no. Liane put her hands on her hips and looked around for anything she might have forgotten. On the whole, it was slim pickings.

"Do you have anything at all with a sharp edge on it?"

From under the counter the man produced a mason jar filled with pearl-handled switchblades.

Liane fingered one. "Can you show me how they work?"

He took it from her and pressed the release button. *Swick!* A narrow pointed blade snapped out so quickly it seemed like a special effects trick.

"Wow," Liane said. "Is it sharp?"

"You betcha. Watch where you flash it, though. They're of marginal legality."

"My specialty."

"What's that?"

Liane wrinkled her nose.

He bagged the blade with her old clothes and the toiletries.

The store didn't accept credit cards, and the combined purchases consumed the majority of her cash.

"Is that motel across the street any good?"

"Sure, fine. They keep it nice and clean."

She crossed the street and walked up to a drive-through ATM by a bank next to the motel. Her checking account balance read $903.48. Her last paycheck had never cleared—quick work on Flickinger's part. *Damn.* She withdrew four hundred and checked into the motel. The woman behind the counter had dyed orange hair, pale wrinkles, and a pleasant demeanor. She recommended the bar-and-grill two doors down for dinner and took forty dollars from Liane for the room.

It was meagerly furnished and synthetic. The bathtub showed cracks and gouges and mineral accretions where the spigot dripped. She brushed her teeth and climbed into the shower. There was no shampoo, so she washed her hair with the acrid-smelling soap that the motel had provided. She snapped open the switchblade and used the edge like a barber to shave her legs and armpits. The bath towel, thin and brittle, irritated her where she'd shaved, but she soon welcomed the feel of the new clothes. They were a luxury under the circumstances, and she wished she'd bought a t-shirt or something soft to give Shaker. But then she supposed that may violate the rules. All the prisoners she'd seen had worn jumpsuits.

She imagined Corey wearing one. If he were alive and in the United States, it was only a matter of time before he ended up behind bars, like those Sixties radicals who'd changed their identities and were discovered decades later, living in the suburbs with three kids and significantly less hair. When she'd last seen Corey he'd said he might flee to South America. She wished she'd thought to mention his name to the woman who helped her break into the primate lab. She might have revealed something—if she knew—about Corey's whereabouts. Now, barring a trip to San Francisco with Bea, she had it all riding on Moyo.

She picked up the cell phone and dialed Mickey. It rang twelve times without an answer. The phones had no voicemail, and she remembered that the examination room was situated in the clinic building's interior. Her stomach growled, and she decided to head for dinner.

It was dark out, and Liane had to pick her way through three pot-holed and poorly lit parking lots to reach the bar-and-grill. The place had all the character of a company cafeteria, she thought, albeit with dimmer lighting and a liquor license. The bar was wrapped in Formica with attached diner-style stools. She slipped into a booth: dark wood worn practically to splinters, a soiled vinyl tablecloth under paper napkins.

There was a man, half-crocked at the bar, wearing glasses thick as bottle heels with fishing flies stuck to his sweater. He turned and stole a peek at Liane. "You got to order from the bar," he said. He was drinking something amber in a rocks glass.

Liane thanked him and approached the bar on the opposite end. A few other patrons sat scattered about the place, but the bartender was nowhere in sight.

The man sidled up closer and belted down the remainder of his drink. "I don't know where he went to. Hard to get good help in these parts."

Liane snorted in sympathy. The man leaned into her personal space, his breath a noxious mixture of cigarettes and bourbon.

"They could use a waitress," he continued, leering at her. "I bet you'd be good for business."

"Thanks," Liane said, backing off, "but I'm just passing through."

"Prison wife?"

"You nailed it. He gets out tomorrow and I hope he won't kill again."

The bartender stepped in and the man retreated to his original stool. Liane ordered steak and eggs. She attacked it between sips from a glass of lager. The eggs tasted fresh, but the steak was shot through with gristle. She was giving up on it when Handy, the driver, walked in. He'd waited by the prison and had given her a lift to the train station earlier for ten bucks. Now he made straight for Liane's table and greeted her like an old friend.

"That guy at the bar ain't bothering you, is he?"

Liane shook her head, still chewing. "I can fend for myself, but you're sweet to ask."

Handy seemed to Liane like an innocent. Though he was high functioning, he projected the vulnerability of a Down syndrome adult, too sweet for a bitter world.

She pointed in the direction of the prison. "How do they treat them in there?"

Handy shrugged as he took a seat nearby. "Three squares a day. Better than I get sometimes."

"You have your freedom. Or is that just another word for nothing left to lose?"

"Not in my book." It didn't seem that he got the Janis Joplin reference. "I'd die in there, to tell you the truth, like a trout dies in a fishbowl. I don't know how they go on. But in some small ways they got it better than most of us."

"You know anyone inside?"

"No, ma'am, not the prisoners, if that's what you mean."

Liane pushed her plate away and he looked at her as if she'd violated some unspoken code. "You're not gonna finish that?"

"I'm full. Ketchup?" She slid the plate and bottle in his direction and sat and watched him eat for a while. His table manners reminded her of Bea, but she had more important things to worry about than civilizing the natives.

She paid the check and said her goodbye and walked back to the motel. It had rained while she'd been inside, but the sky now hung clear and puddles glistened in the moonlight.

She bought a gumball in the motel lobby, but by the time she reached her room all flavor had leeched out.

The TV didn't work. She sat Indian-style on the bedspread, sharpening pencils for Shaker Moyo and watching the shavings curl into the wastebasket.

18

Special Agent Henley Pulsipher crossed Independence Avenue in Washington, D.C., with the confidence of a man who knew all of importance within his sights. Pulsipher cherished information the way bees love honey. He gathered it, processed it, used it, reveled in it. He purchased it wholesale when he could, retail when he had to. He'd pick it up for free when offered, squeeze it from anything inanimate or living when it wasn't. To know about things was to take their measure.

For example, he knew that the United States Department of Agriculture, where he worked, occupied two square blocks near the Washington Monument. He knew that it was the only cabinet-level agency located directly on the Mall. He knew that the neoclassical office building had once been the largest in the world, until the construction of the Pentagon in 1942. And he knew the department's budget down to the penny—if anyone could.

Up the broad limestone steps of the formidable stone structure climbed Pulsipher. He drew little attention as he swung his leather briefcase at his side and proceeded across the barren lobby and down a hallway, where he disappeared through an office like any other and stepped into a hidden elevator for his short ride to the basement.

Pulsipher's own miniscule piece of this colossus was a ten-by-ten windowless office with a gunmetal gray standard-issue desk, matching steel shelves, and a pair of battered guest chairs from the Eisenhower administration. The modesty of this setup belied the true nature of Pulsipher's power. His was a secret realm, tasked with shielding this portion of the executive branch from foreign governments and criminals and outright crackpots. In this endeavor, he had latitude to do whatever the achievement of his mission required—emphasis on *whatever*.

Yet a search of government records would turn up no trace of Special Agent Henley Pulsipher's real name. To friends and relatives he was a minor bureaucrat who spent his days counting specks of grain. Congressional staffers found him always away from his desk, for his official office was on another floor entirely. General Services Administration auditors had no access to the corridor where he performed his real work. And the FBI couldn't touch him.

His life, as they say in the District, was a black box. He had a one-line code of conduct and a single brief: to prevail. And, as a corollary: to do so in a way that wouldn't ever scar the Department. He reported directly to the Undersecretary of Agriculture, and they communicated only in manners that left no record.

As he set a decaf latte on his desk, Pulsipher had Corey Harrow on his mind. Corey Harrow, who had eluded the master for nine long years. Corey Harrow, whom he knew beyond doubt to be the secret head of Folks Against Unnecessary Lab Testing and, more important, mastermind of their terrorist operation. Corey Harrow, of whom he possessed all but one crucial bit of data—the man's whereabouts. This bothered Pulsipher, but it didn't discourage him, because Pulsipher believed he had an advantage over Harrow and his ilk: He understood fully what this rivalry was about, and the FAULT operators didn't. They thought the battle pertained to the fate of animals or morality or some such nonsense. Pulsipher knew it was really about power. Power to regulate. Power to destroy. Power to decide. The power of one species over all others.

The phone on his desk vibrated. As always, Pulsipher waited for the fourth ring before picking it up. He listened. Here was an interesting nexus of data, the ex-girlfriend popping back up on the grid, having visited Harrow's old accomplice and used her bankcard at an ATM in upstate New York.

He pondered that for a few minutes with his hand resting on the receiver. Then he made a call.

19

Liane opened her eyes and surveyed the dark bathroom doorway, the rumpled bedspread at her feet, the green polyester chair, and the morning light filtering through sheer curtains. She rushed to get dressed and pack her tote.

Out the back door, growing sunshine coaxed mist from the damp macadam and dispersed it without mercy. Off to one side of the parking lot were Handy and the creep in the sweater who'd come on to her at the bar. The sight of them together disturbed Liane, but it occurred to her that she had no strategy for getting to the prison.

Handy nodded in her direction while the guy with the thick glasses, visibly drunk, locked his eyes so blatantly on Liane's chest you'd think she had the day's winning lottery number displayed there. But with few options available, she folded her arms across her v-neck sweater and closed in.

"Hey, Hands. Can you give me a ride to the penitentiary this morning?"

"I got a fare that called me a few minutes ago."

"I'll take her if you won't," the man in the sweater growled.

"No, I couldn't, sir," Liane said. She turned back to Handy. "I'll pay double if we can leave right now."

"No need to do that. I'll squeeze you in."

The three of them walked to Handy's Buick.

"I'm riding along," the man in the sweater said.

"No you ain't," Handy said. He raised two palms and too forcefully pushed the man, who stumbled backward, surprised, and fell onto his butt. Through the thick glasses his eyes bulged like cartoon orbs on a pair of springs. He rose unsteadily to his feet and rocked forward as if he planned to rush them, but he couldn't seem to figure out how to get his momentum started.

Liane went to the front passenger door and climbed in. Handy got behind the wheel, locked the doors and turned the ignition key, grinding the car to life.

The man in the sweater, finally in motion, sprung forward and pawed the window, yanking on the uncooperative rear door handle. Meanwhile, Handy shifted into DRIVE and eased forward slowly. His friend, left no choice, ran a few clumsy steps and then released his grasp. Liane kept her attention on him until they were well past.

"Morning of the living dead." She shuddered.

"Don't mind him," Handy said. "He's just mad cause he ain't caught any fish this week. I didn't mean to push him so hard."

"I've never been so stared at in my life."

"Oh, come on. I'd think you'd be used to it by now."

She wasn't. She'd never be.

The prison came into view.

"I don't suppose you could wait," she said.

"Sure I can."

"But your other fare…"

"I'll pick them up later. They ain't in no hurry."

She thanked him and, to mitigate the hassle at security, tucked her tote under the seat as the Buick glided up alongside the fence, where sprigs of wild blue aster had just begun to bloom. Defying the flowers, Liane thought, the penitentiary looked as menacing as ever.

20

Liane pushed the bag of pistachios through the slide-drawer that was built into the Plexiglas screen. It was a tight fit and she had to pump the drawer a few times to get it over to Moyo's side. A guard with a wiry goatee, leaning against the wall with his hands behind, looked on, amused.

Moyo seized the bag, pulled it open, and snapped apart four pistachio shells, popping the meat from them into his mouth in quick succession. He ate with his thick lips closed, forming a perfect seal, his tongue working through his cheeks, lapping up every crumb. He broke open three more and chewed them with greater deliberation. Then he tossed in four more, letting them linger on his palate before chewing. He shook the bag and examined it, calculating what remained.

"Never had one of these before I moved to the States," he said, gathering the empty shells into a pile on the table with his long fingers. "Used to take a little spitball and put it under one of the shells, then do like this."

He segregated three shells and shuffled them rapidly, open side down.

"I was living in the Henry Horner projects with my uncle. Not a lot for a kid to do. We'd buy a bag of nuts and make it last the whole day, my friends and I, playing the shell game. Whoever guessed right got the next nut to eat. I learned it's not always easy to tell which shell has the ball under it. You have to watch from your peripheral vision, not concentrate so much on the misdirection. See here. I'll put this little flake under one and you watch for it." He shuffled them quickly. "Which?"

Liane pointed.

"You sure?" She nodded and he picked up the shell. "Not so good, you see. Don't watch my fingers. Don't watch the shells. Look at the table and see what's happening in the plane beyond your focus."

She tried again, failed again. Moyo pressed past her anxiousness. He shuffled the shells along the table a dozen times, and she got no more than a couple guesses right. Moyo fell into a fit of laughter and clapped his hands.

"The misdirection, you see, became your master. You must learn to look through it."

She regretted that she'd given him the nuts. The next train for New York, she knew, departed in less than an hour, and she hadn't been able to reach Mickey on the phone before hitting the prison vending machines for Moyo's cravings.

Liane tried to stay calm. "I brought you some other things, Shaker."

"That right?"

She pushed the Stephen King paperback through the drawer. He thanked her and bent the spine back and propped it open on the table, reading. Without taking his eyes from the book, he grabbed a handful of pistachios and began cracking them open and eating. Reading and eating.

Reading and eating.

Liane wanted to scream. She directed the box of pencils through the drawer.

Moyo enclosed them in his long fingers. He opened the box with one hand and slid a pencil out without removing his eyes from the book. He bounced it on its eraser.

"You see," he said, "yellow Number Two, green stripe, sharp point, Ticonderoga. All with the peripheral vision. Did you bring anything else, paper maybe?"

"No." She was so annoyed by now she wouldn't tell him she'd tried. "I forgot the Kit-Kats, too."

"Hard to write without paper."

"Shaker, I feel like I'm sitting here by myself. Do you want me to go?"

"As you wish. I thought you came for something." He looked up at her.

"You know what? I don't think you have what I came for."

"If it's a way to get in touch with Corey, then I guess you're right. I told you I have no contact with FAULT any longer. So why'd you return?"

He directed his attention to the book again, working the pistachios, bouncing the pencil behind it, perhaps. She wasn't sure exactly. The book, propped up, hid most of his hands. Once in a while he popped a pistachio into his mouth.

"I said," he repeated, sucking his teeth, "why did you come?"

"I don't know," she said, wishing he were half as interested in her as the drunk guy in the sweater had been. Then maybe she'd get somewhere. "I thought maybe you were only playing coy yesterday. Guess I was wrong." On an impulse she pushed her seat back and stood. "I got a train to catch."

Moyo rose, too, pressing his knuckles into the table, raising his voice. "Back to the *monkeys?*"

She hadn't said a word about that. She fell back into her chair.

"There's my girl. A nerve worth touching." He took her measure. "Did I tell you how I got into animal liberation?"

"No."

"It's a sad story." He worked his hands behind the book, popping a few more pistachios rapid-fire into his mouth. "About a dog."

"I don't know that I want to hear it."

"You should hear it."

"I don't know that I have the stomach to hear it."

"You'll want to stay for this, damn it!" He slammed an open hand on the table and the pile of pistachio shells jumped.

Liane looked nervously at her watch.

"I'll give you the short version," Moyo conceded, continuing to work his hands. "These pistachios," he said, "aren't as good as I remember. You can't ever go home again."

"You were saying?"

"There was a cop who worked the K-9 at the Horner houses, a real mean son of a bitch, like one of those Nazis from the concentration camps with his German shepherd. He'd just walk up to people and have the dog sniff their privates while he stood there smirking. We'd be hanging on the street—not drug dealers, just kids—and he'd walk up and ask a question, and if you didn't answer quick enough he gave the dog a signal and the thing would go crazy on you, barking, baring its teeth."

"Charming."

"Yeah. But there was one little kid who refused to be intimidated. This one kid would sneak the dog pieces of kibble when the cop was busy talking to someone. He'd make eye contact with the dog and let him sniff the back of his hand. But the K-9 cop, after a while, caught on to it. He resented the fact that this kid—only eleven—had found a way to make nice with the thing that was supposed to be there to put everyone in their place. You see?"

"Sort of."

"So one day he comes upon the kid walking alone down the street. There was a fair around the corner that had everyone's attention, but the kid was bored and wandered off. Big mistake, you see. He walks by the cop with his dog and tosses the shepherd a piece of kibble that the dog—forgetting his training—takes right out of the air like a pet."

Moyo cracked a pistachio, tossed it up and caught it in his open mouth, chewing as he studied Liane's face.

"They're just in front of an alleyway, no one around, the noise of the street fair floating over. The cop backs the kid into the alley and signals the dog and the dog growls, but it's half-hearted-like. So the cop yanks the dog's short leash and gives him a knee in the ribs to fire him up, but the dog's not cooperating much. The dog's sort of suggesting, hey, don't make me snarl at my buddy. And the cop, losing it, says something that's, like, meant to get the dog to tear you apart. And guess what?"

"The dog turns on the cop?"

"Nah. The dog just stands there and looks at the cop—whining. Not wanting to defy the cop but not willing to attack the kid. And the cop, calm as you please, like he's lighting a cigarette or something, takes his baton from his belt and without warning cracks the poor dog across the mouth, teeth ticking onto the sidewalk, blood splattering."

Moyo raised a fist in the air, as if he were preparing to punch through the Plexiglas. Over his shoulder, the guard eased himself off the wall. Moyo lowered his hands behind the book and fidgeted them. The guard relaxed.

"And then," said Moyo, "he gives the dog the command again and the dog just shies away from the cop, but he's on that short leash—he can't go anywhere. And the cop hauls back with anger and starts shouting the command and whaling on the dog's head with the baton—like he's pounding a tree stump."

"Oh, God."

"Cracks the shepherd's skull open." He shook his head. "When the kid gets up the courage to run past him, the last thing he sees is the dog unconscious on the ground, being pulverized to shit, never moving to defend himself."

"Jesus! What was the upshot?"

"Never saw the cop again. The K-9 unit came right away and took the carcass away in a police van, I heard."

"And the kid?"

"The kid? You haven't figured it out?"

"God, I'm so sorry, Shaker."

He stopped working his hands. He picked through the bag of pistachios, finding ones that had slipped from their shells of their own accord and tossing them into his mouth.

"Bitter," he said.

"What?"

"Where'd you get these nuts from, Liane?" Louder.

"Excuse me?"

"These are stale, they're bitter!"

"Keep it down!" the guard called.

"Trying to poison me, are you?"

"No. I just bought them out front. You're crazy."

"Trying to hurt me!" He took the bag with long trembling fingers and held it open at the edge of the table, sweeping the shells back inside with a few swipes of his hand. He zipped it and shook it and stuffed it into the drawer, sucking his teeth. "Take your damn nuts back!"

"Shaker, I thought we were getting somewhere."

"They're yours. Take them!"

"But, Shaker—"

The guard stepped forward as Moyo shoved the drawer through, rattling the screen.

Liane peered down at the bag.

Moyo stood. "You come in here talking about Corey!" he screamed, several guards now converging on him. "With your poison!"

They hustled him out so quickly that Liane hadn't yet moved when the guard with the goatee returned.

"These guys go stir-crazy in here sometimes." He picked up the book and pencil box. "There's no accounting for it. You want these back?"

"See that he gets them, if you don't mind."

"Okay. He's got plenty, though, back in the cell."

"Really? That's okay."

She began to walk away.

"You can't leave those here—the pistachios. It's against the rules."

"Right." She nodded and scooped up the bag and walked rapidly from the place.

The Buick was waiting, Handy behind the wheel, tapping his fingers to a silent beat.

Liane looked back at the prison. She pulled open the car door and crawled in.

21

The witch doctor's village was an hour's walk from where Dikembe retrieved Daniel. Now the boy stood beside him, quietly crying, as Dikembe shuffled his feet outside the hut, waiting his turn.

"Pull yourself together," Dikembe said.

An old woman, face worn to leather, came through the doorway and shambled away.

Dikembe and his son stepped inside.

The hut was spare with a few masks hanging on the walls, some finely patterned cloths and pillows, and rows of jars filled with dried plants. The air exuded pungent herbs and incense. The witch doctor, balding with a scraggly beard, sat on a plain wooden chair with his hands folded in his lap.

"Go to him," Dikembe instructed Daniel.

The boy eased forward and the witch doctor placed a hand on the back of his neck.

"You may recall," Dikembe began, "that my wife, Odette, came to you a few years ago with a difficult pregnancy."

"I remember," the witch doctor said. "How is she?"

"Dead of the virus."

"I'm sorry to hear it. Today you have come for?"

Dikembe explained that he wanted the witch doctor to examine Daniel. The witch doctor nodded solemnly and looked into Daniel's eyes and ears and mouth. He laid a hand on the boy's head.

"He's a healthy young man," he said. "For an extra ten francs, though, I can give you an amulet."

"That would be good."

"Is there anything else?"

"Yes. About Odette. I loved her very much. She said something near the end that disturbed me. She said I was a good man and she was being punished. What do you think she meant?"

"I'm a healer, Dikembe, not a spirit talker."

"All right."

"Tell me, what do *you* think she meant?"

"After she died I found a monkey bone. We argued sometimes about the bush meat. I've been working for an Englishman in the park, counting game and such. He says the bush meat can spread disease."

"Disease can be evidence of a misapprehension about what nature wants from us, that's true. If you're asking whether the monkey meat made Odette ill, the answer is I don't know. The problems these days are bigger than whether to eat bush meat."

"I think the bush meat is wrong for us."

"It wasn't always so. It's been said that a man never steps in the same river twice."

"I never heard that. An old Bantu saying?"

"No. Heraclitus, an ancient Greek philosopher. I learned of him at the Sorbonne. My point is that the world changes. Drought, poaching, these new diseases—the balance of nature gropes to restore itself."

"I had less right to criticize Odette than I allowed," Dikembe said. "I committed my own sin against nature. What's a man to do?"

"Only what lies in his reach. The problems of the world, they are bigger than any of us. Fix what you can fix."

From a plastic bucket behind him the witch doctor selected a carved wooden disc, hollow, with a neck like a miniature vase. He opened one of the jars on the floor and put a small pinch of herb into the mouth, stuffing it deeper with the point of a sharpened twig. Under his chair he found a narrow leather band and threaded it through a hole in the amulet. He tied it around Daniel's neck.

"There," he said, touching the carved fetish with the tip of his finger. "That looks good. Twenty francs, please."

22

Liane rode along in glum silence, a stranger among her own thoughts, not listening while Handy chattered aimlessly. They were a block from the station when she noticed a commotion of police cars with their lights flashing, parked at angles along the shoulder of the road and in the parking lot. They were stopping every car that turned that way. There were state troopers and local uniforms and some guys in navy windbreakers with big white letters stenciled across the back. Liane didn't dawdle long enough to read what they said. She ducked down and grabbed the switchblade from her tote and placed her cheek on the middle of the car bench and pointed the knife at Handy's crotch, screaming, "Left turn, Handy! Keep driving! Left turn now!"

Liane could see Handy's reflection at an oblique angle in the rear-view mirror. He looked as surprised as she felt, but he followed her instructions, accelerating at a measured pace as the car straightened out of the turn.

A mile or two beyond town, she eased herself up and peered around the headrest and out the back window. The road was wide open. If the cops back at the station were looking for her, Liane hoped they were asking after a woman with an ape. That might slow them down, at least.

"I'm sorry I had to do that, Hands."

"I nearly pissed my pants."

"I'm glad you didn't."

Handy sighed. "Where to, boss?"

"How much gas do you have?"

"Nearly a full tank."

"Enough to take us to New York?"

"I don't get great mileage in this thing, but I guess I might."

"Hop on the parkway as soon as you can."

Liane took out her phone and began to dial Mickey, but then reconsidered. What if his friend got suspicious about the bonobo and turned them in? Maybe they'd traced her through Mickey to Thessaly.

"Fuck!" she said aloud. "What a waste!"

"What's that?"

They merged onto the Taconic, a verdant road with sharp hilly curves that gave way to flat straightaways, begging drivers to floor it.

"Stick to the speed limit."

"I always do."

She felt on edge. She fiddled impatiently with the radio, feeling hemmed in. From the guy in the sweater to her parents to the psychos at Pentalon, it was like the whole world was crushing her. And the way Shaker Moyo went off when they were having such a delightful heart-to-heart about shell games and, oh, cops beating their dogs to death. *What a joyous world!*

She took out the pistachio bag and began cracking the nuts and munching them, dropping the empty shells into Handy's ashtray. She didn't find them bitter at all. On the contrary, they were addictively sweet and pleasantly salty. What the hell had Shaker been talking about? *A complete lunatic, not just a little bit,* she thought.

"I'm hungry," Handy said.

She gave him a few pistachios and he fumbled with them on the steering wheel. She cracked open another and popped it into her mouth. She ate five or six more, slowly, looking out the window and dropping the shells into the ashtray.

"So it's true what Jerry said about you," Handy said.

"Jerry?"

"Our friend from the bar. Said you might be a bad-ass."

She had to chuckle over that one. "A bad-ass, huh? *He's* such a prince."

"That's what the man said, not me. Though I might have my own opinion now."

"And what's that?"

"Well, no chick's ever pulled a knife on me before. You could've just asked nicely."

"I apologized already. I'm not in a position to take any chances."

"You always this explosive?"

She laughed again and dug out an empty shell and playfully beaned him in the side of the head.

"Hey!" he said.

It felt childishly gratifying. She dug out another empty and did it again.

He surprised her by catching the second one in midair. He rolled the window down and tossed it out.

"No littering," Liane said.

"It's biodegradable."

"We're all green when it's easy."

She rummaged through the bag of nuts again, found another empty, weighed it in the palm of her hand. There was something written on the inside: 37. She closed her fingers around it quickly, as if someone might snatch it from her, formed a pincers with her thumb and forefinger, held it up to the light. Sure enough: 37. Recognition dawned on her. She burrowed into the bag again, looking for empties, found another one right away: 71. She thought of Shaker, working his hands with the sharp pencil behind the book, talking of peripheral vision, then going bonkers. *No! Not going bonkers,* she thought, *he was* playing *bonkers.* Not able to tell her outright in front of the guard that he knew something. Pretending to have nothing more to do with FAULT. *Acting crazy. Acting.*

Misdirection. That had been the clue. The insight made her frantic. She dug madly through the bag then slowed down, trying to appear nonchalant for Handy, searching with focus.

"Whatcha doing there?"

"Just having fun."

"Don't throw any more. It ain't safe. We could crash."

"Okay, Hands."

She found a few more with writing, all double digits, then became meticulous. She dumped the pistachios out on the seat between her legs and returned the whole nuts to the bag one at a time. The empty shells she examined more closely, surprised now when she didn't find writing, as if pencil scrawls on the inside of a pistachio shell were the most normal thing in the world.

When she'd finished there were nine in all—eight double digits and one other: the number 107. She pressed the back of her skull into the headrest. It had to be a code of some kind.

23

By the time they reached the Bronx it was midday and traffic was thick on the Major Deegan, strings of cars with Jersey plates inching toward the George Washington Bridge exit and trucks squealing and creaking into every choke point.

"This normal?" Handy asked, throwing the car into PARK for a dead standstill.

"Huh? I suppose."

The heat shimmering off the sun-drenched dashboard and the fumes and the moment had put Liane's head elsewhere. Having passed several hours in reflection, she was again not entirely convinced of Shaker Moyo's sanity. Maybe the numbers on the nut-shells were his idea of a joke or revenge for having disturbed his isolation. But where had the monkey reference come from? Could that have been coincidence? If Corey were still part of the movement then the redheaded protester in the sage sweatshirt might have spread the word of Liane's role in Bea's kidnapping. And if that knowledge got to Moyo so quickly, these FAULT people were more sophisticated than she'd ever imagined.

"It's hot as hell in here, Handy," she said. "Turn up the air conditioning."

"No can do. I'm low on gas. See here?" He pointed to the gauge.

"We're only a few miles from where you can drop me."

He shook his head. "I'm a country fella and I'm showing dead empty already. The light's on and everything."

"You should've stopped in Westchester."

"Yeah. I got you out of some kind of scrape back there in Thessaly, didn't I? You must be in a heap of trouble to have the feds after you."

"How do you know that was for me, Handy? There might be half a dozen people up there on the Most Wanted list."

"Maybe. That a list that features you?"

"Not that I know of, but tomorrow's another day."

"Well, what'd you do?"

She drummed her fingers on the armrest.

"You remind me of my daughter," he said.

"You're not proud of her?"

"She's all right."

"Tell me about her. Does she have a mother?"

"Everybody has a mother. She lives with hers."

"A job?"

"She's studying to be a hairdresser."

"No kidding." Liane dropped the visor and fluffed her hair in the mirror. "How about pets? Does your daughter have any?"

"She has a Dobie. She spends most of her life chained to a tree, far as I can tell."

That made her feel melancholy.

They began to creep forward and Handy saw an opening and pulled into the left lane. Traffic was moving more steadily there, but still slowly.

"Do you tell her the truth, Handy?"

"Who?"

"Your daughter."

"About what?"

"About how ugly life can be?"

"No, ma'am. She'll figure that out soon enough."

He reached over and turned the air conditioning completely off, then rolled down his window. The air outside wasn't as hot as the sunshine suggested, so Liane opened her window too.

"The Willis Avenue Bridge exit's up here."

"Yes, ma'am."

They were off the expressway and within sight of the bridge ramp when they spotted a gas station.

"My stop," Handy said, rolling over the shallow curb. "I'm past fumes. Dead empty."

Liane tossed him the bag of nuts, knowing there was nothing left there of value to her. She had the numbered shells in a pocket of her chinos.

Handy lifted the plastic bag from his lap and examined it like it contained manna from heaven. Liane paused to absorb the gap-toothed grimace on his face. *How strange to have pulled a knife on him just two hours ago,* she thought. He looked miserable and out of place in the big city.

A taxi driver in front of them prepared to pull from the pump and Liane flagged him down. She shoved open the car door and passed Handy forty bucks. "I'd give you more, but I'm short."

"It's all right. Least I had an adventure."

The taxi driver looked Pakistani, or maybe Egyptian, with a pock-marked face that reminded her of Hammurabi. She opened the rear door and climbed in, and the taxi swung back toward Handy's car to exit.

"Stop beside this guy for a second, please." Liane rolled down her window as they crawled even.

"Listen, I feel real bad about pulling that switchblade on you in Thessaly."

"You were in a pickle. I understand."

"You're a good guy, Hands."

"Likewise." He smiled. "If you ever get into another situation…"

Liane shook her head. "You're a prince, but I don't plan to be back."

24

On the FDR Drive, when the taxi hit more bumper-to-bumper, Liane called Mickey on the prepaid cell phone and finally reached him.

"Liane, Jesus! I'm in a panic here. You're a day late and I'm out of supplies, living off rabbit chow."

"Rabbit chow?"

"What's keeping you?"

"I'm close-by. I tried you on the cell yesterday and this morning, but no answer."

"It's balky in here. I got myself pressed into a corner right now to make it work."

"You haven't been using it?"

"Hardly. I had in mind to call for a pizza last night then thought better of it and hung up. They're getting suspicious around the clinic. We can't stay. I was gonna bolt soon with or without you."

"Don't do that. Let me think."

"Meanwhile, I wake up last night to Bea screaming, *kotala en-decko,* whatever the hell that means. If she starts that while someone's by the door we're done for."

"Where does that leave us?"

"I don't think you should come to the clinic. Other than that, I'm open to suggestions."

"We need a place to work out a plan." She hesitated. "I'll call you back in an hour."

"That's just great. I'll be in my corner."

The taxi dropped her on an eastside block. She hit the street with determined steps, pretending to know where she was going. On Lexington she shaded her eyes and peered through the plate glass of a restaurant, like a homeless person. The inside looked welcoming in a modern urban way. A few people sat at one end of the bar. She went in and took a stool several seats away from them and ordered the sliders with a bottle of San Pellegrino.

The bar patrons were a couple of heavily made-up women and a salesman type in a herringbone sports coat. The salesman progressed through a litany of jokes involving most of America's ethnic groups and, in one instance, a gorilla. His final routine featured an obnoxious dwarf and a genie on the beach. As the bartender set the food in front of Liane the salesman delivered his punch line: "And then I requested a two-foot prick!" The four of them erupted in laughter.

The bartender asked Liane if he could get her anything else.

"Yes," she said, eyeing three miniature burgers, glistening mesclun salad and a pile of sweet potato fries. "Another order of this to go and some vegetables." As the bartender walked away, she wondered whether Mickey had been joking about the rabbit chow.

The sliders tasted succulent, and the irony of having made her last two meals of red meat was not lost on Liane, who imagined Corey must still be of the vegan persuasion. She ate quickly, paid with a credit card, then used the ladies' room.

Back on the street, pedestrians straggled along upper Lexington: well-dressed Europeans swinging refined shopping bags, nannies pushing strollers, teenagers in small groups, sweaty men pedaling grocery cart cycles. One of the carts was chained to a post in front of an apartment house. She wished she had the nerve to steal it or the cash to pry it from the delivery person with a bribe. She could stuff Bea inside with a few bags of groceries and be off like the old crone who pedaled herself into a witch in Oz, no less absurd than the situation in which she found herself.

A man with a large parrot perched on his shoulder passed her on the sidewalk, the bird's long tail feathers rustling in the draft from a passing bus. She stopped and turned to follow him down the street with her eyes, but no one else gave him more than a glance. She called Mickey and he picked up on the first ring.

25

"So which part is the brilliant plan?"

They were standing on the broad sidewalk west of the Lincoln Center garage, Bea clinging to Liane like she was the last tree in a flood. The moment Liane had rounded the corner Bea had leaped from Mickey's arms and trundled down the sidewalk, pouncing and nearly knocking Liane over, then running her fingers along her face, playing with her ear, issuing a series of *motos* and *bowling-gos* and *malobas*—the last one a word they hadn't heard before. Liane wondered whether Bea made up her own language as she went along.

Mickey had voiced more practical concerns, saying, "Whatever. We gotta find a way to shut this ape up." He'd seemed a bit irascible, not exactly what Liane expected. But soon Bea had subsided into gratified cooing.

Now a pair of women in heels broke stride and gave Liane a wide berth.

"My God," one whispered, "that chimpanzee is rubbing her genitals against the woman."

Mickey gave them a look. "Oh, like they never saw that before," he said, loudly enough to be heard.

The women quickened their steps.

"You were about to explain why this was a good idea," Mickey said to Liane.

"Right. I was thinking Big Apple Circus. They usually pitch a giant tent back here and put on regular shows featuring acrobats and small animals."

"I know what the Big Apple Circus is. They're seasonal, for Christ sake."

"I guess that would explain why the plaza's empty. When they're in town, the patrons can mingle on the sidewalk with the clowns and such right before the show. I was thinking we would blend right in."

"So here we are, fugitives from justice with an ape, running for our lives, and your stroke of genius was to join the freaking circus?"

"They can't all be gems." She looked down at the sidewalk. "You don't seem as nice as the last time I saw you."

"No? Forty-eight hours in a windowless room with a talking bonobo might put an edge on a person, don't ya think? Plus, I had no idea what happened to you."

"I explained that already. I brought you dinner, if it's any consolation. My mother tells me it's the way to a man's heart."

"It might be."

She transferred Bea to Mickey's arms. They walked to the park and found a bench. Liane reached into her tote and pulled out a piece of poster board that she'd bought on her way to their rendezvous.

"What's that?" Mickey asked.

"Plan B. Justification for the bonobo."

She unfolded the poster board. It said: My Monkey Can Guess Your Age. One Dollar. She propped it on the bench next to them and extracted the take-out, along with some paper napkins. They spread a picnic on the bench.

Mickey and Bea had no sooner begun to dig in than a tall man glided up on Rollerblades.

"Okay," he said, scratching the back of his shaved head. "How old does the monkey think I am?" The man reached into a back pocket and produced a damp and crumpled dollar bill.

Liane wasn't sure what to say.

Mickey swallowed a mouthful of burger and took a swig of water.

"Monkey says thirty-two." He cleared a molar with one fingernail and extended the other hand for the dollar.

"But the monkey hasn't done anything," the man protested, rocking one foot back and forth on its wheels. "It's just sitting there."

"Is thirty-two correct?" Mickey asked.

"It happens to be."

"So you owe a buck. Give it over."

"But the monkey didn't do anything."

"No? How'd we get it right, then?"

"Lucky guess, I'd say."

"Nah. The monkey's never wrong." Mickey tapped his temple. "She communicates with telepathy."

"She's not even a monkey," the man said. "She's a chimpanzee."

"What's the difference?"

"Monkeys have tails, for one thing."

"Everybody's a critic. You gonna give over the buck?"

"Not to you. To the talent."

"Okay."

He held the dollar in Bea's direction. She looked up, mashed vegetable clinging to the hairs on her chin, and accepted it. "*Kotala*," she said. "*Elongi.*"

"Now you're messing with me," the Rollerblader said before Liane could react. "I saw the woman's lips move. It's just bad ventriloquism. And not even English."

"Still," Mickey said, the picture of calm, "this monkey guessed your age, didn't she?"

"It's a chimp, damn it! And the woman's speaking Bulgarian or something."

Mickey gave an exaggerated shrug, as if to say, *what'd you expect for a dollar—the world?* The man skated away.

"He seemed intelligent for a while there," Liane said.

"That guy gave me an idea. Maybe Bea's not speaking a chimp language."

"Go on..."

"Maybe she and her brother were speaking a language that they picked up before they came to the lab. Bulgarian it ain't, but if we can figure out where they originated we can communicate with her in their language—or someone can."

"I know where she came from, sort of. Unless she's from a zoo or a secret breeding program, bonobos in the wild live in a narrow range. They're found only in the Democratic Republic of Congo."

"Wow. No kidding. Isn't that heart-of-darkness territory?"

"I don't think they like to call it that anymore."

"It's a former Belgian colony. But I know a little French, and unless they taught me wrong in high school, that isn't what Bea's speaking."

"No. It could be a tribal language. Maybe we can find one of those African guys who sell counterfeit watches on the street."

"That won't help. They're all from Nigeria and it's more than a thousand miles from Congo."

"We need to get FAULT involved."

"Well, how'd you make out with the guy in the prison?"

"Something of a puzzle." She told him everything.

"The feds!" Mickey whistled. "Shit. What makes you think they were after *you*?"

Liane threw up her hands. "I just happen to roll into someone else's FBI sweep?"

She began gathering their trash as some tourists came over. Bea squatted in the grass to relieve herself, then headed for the trunk of a tree. Mickey jumped up and ran over to intercept her, and their interaction devolved into an awkward wrestling match, elbows flying, dirt and leaves attaching themselves to their backs. The tourists—a couple with cameras over their necks and a kid in a Knicks t-shirt—looked on like it was all part of the show. The kid waved a dollar.

"Sorry," Liane said, folding up the sign. "We're closed."

"Aw, heck," the kid said, "can't the monkey just do one last guess?"

Mickey jogged up with Bea in a bear hug, breathing heavily. "The monkey says nine," he huffed.

"That's correct." The kid reluctantly parted with his money and the tourist family strolled away.

Liane wished everything in the universe were so simple. "How the hell do you do that?" she said to Mickey.

"The force is with me." He paused. "But I'm no Luke Skywalker. We're asking for trouble if we continue to put this bonobo in a setting with people around. Or trees, for that matter. Don't you think we need some place to crash tonight, figure things out?"

"I'm a step ahead of you for a change, Mick."

She had the phone out and was dialing a friend's number.

26

"This girl from college," she said, disconnecting. "Wall Streeter posted to London and doesn't like to rent her apartment out, but she shares it with friends. We're in luck that it's vacant at the moment."

"Must be late in London."

"I think I woke her, but we're in. She said she'll fax permission to enter—stat—and the doorman has the key."

On the way, they detoured to Third Avenue, where Mickey thought he remembered a pet store. The staff fawned over the cute young ape, oohing and aahing. When Bea started to say something, Liane hustled her over to the noisy cockatoo in back. They left the store with Bea jammed inside a pet carrier.

"She'll outgrow that thing in a week," Liane complained.

"In a week, one way or another, this situation will be resolved or I'll be a —" He stopped and grinned.

"A what?"

"I was going to say 'a monkey's uncle.' Then I realized that I sort of am one already."

"That's funny."

"Not really."

The building was a tall modern sliver thrown up between pre-wars on Madison in the Sixties—not too long a walk with Bea and requiring no tortured explanations to cab drivers. They took the key from the liveried doorman and rode the elevator up in anxious silence, Liane beginning to get that trapped feeling again already. But when she bolted the door behind them, the tension drained from their bodies.

"Thank God," Mickey exhaled, setting the carrier down and looking around. "Something that resembles normal."

The apartment was a one-bedroom with a book-lined living room and an eat-in kitchen. Liane checked out the bathroom, picking up the soap and deeply inhaling its floral scent. In the medicine cabinet there was a cartridge of disposable razors. The sight made her giddy.

"Before we do anything I need a real shower," she said.

"I'm right behind you," said Mickey. Then, when she shot him a look: "Hey, it's a figure of speech."

"You'll let Bea out of the carrier?"

He walked over and took both her hands. "Listen, no offense—I didn't lock her up at all when we were at the clinic together—but I need a break from the little one."

"I understand," Liane said curtly. She dropped Mickey's hands and went over to the carrier and freed Bea. She took the bonobo into the bathroom with her, closed the door and set her on the closed toilet. A few minutes later, as Liane was drying herself, Bea reached for the towel and Liane tousled the ape's hair with it. Bea climbed into Liane's arms, and she cradled her like a baby. The ape nuzzled Liane's still bare breast with her soft lips, causing Liane to shift and push Bea away, but as she did so a searing pain exploded through her nipple. She couldn't contain her scream as she dropped Bea, whining, to the floor.

"Liane? You okay?" Mickey called.

"Yeah. I'll be out in a second."

But her left nipple burned in unrelenting waves, doubling her over, bringing tears to her eyes.

"Bad," she said to Bea. "Bad girl."

She finished drying and wrapped the towel around herself. When she opened the door, Bea trotted out and jumped onto the couch, covering her head with a throw pillow. Liane felt sick.

"You're pale," Mickey said. "What the hell happened in there? You hurt yourself? *She* hurt you?"

Liane turned from him, opened the towel and examined the nipple through tearing eyes. Best she could tell through the fog, a welt was forming there. She touched it and it felt damp. When she closed the towel over it she thought she'd faint.

"Liane?"

"It was stupid. I picked her up. She was weaned too young. She tried to suckle."

"From your—from you?"

An open invitation to a snide remark, but she didn't have it in her.

"You don't look well," Mickey said. "Did she break the skin?"

"I don't know. I'm not sure."

"I could take a look."

"Is that all men ever think about?"

"Liane, I'm serious. I *am* a medical professional."

"You're a vet. They're tits, not teats." But she felt so vulnerable. It required every ounce of strength to contain her emotions. And the throbbing remained a torment. "Okay," she half nodded, leaning against the wall, "no funny business."

"I would never." He approached. "Which one?"

She pointed to the left.

"Ready?" Mickey said. "Let's see."

She watched as he delicately clasped the edge of the towel between thumb and forefinger and inched it down, like he was removing the dressing from a surgical procedure. The pink nipple popped free. There was a welt at the edge of the areola.

"I can't do this!" Mickey exclaimed, hiding his eyes.

She covered herself quickly, the pain finally easing to remnants of heat. "Did you see anything?"

"Yeah," Mickey gasped, "of course."

"I meant the—"

"I know what you meant."

"Do you think it's all right?"

"Yeah, it'll be okay."

He walked into the kitchen and poured himself a glass of water. Liane followed.

"That was a bad idea, wasn't it?"

"Yes."

"How did it look?"

"Beautiful." He gulped the water, half hid his face with the glass. "Too beautiful."

"I meant the bite. Do you think she broke the skin? It's hard to tell with the swelling."

"It's—I don't think so. The bonobo, though, Liane, you have to remember she's a wild animal. Not a pet."

She found Neosporin ointment in the medicine cabinet and applied it, taking a closer look at the wound in the process. With her eyes no longer tearing, she could now see that the bite hadn't penetrated flesh. She wiggled into her bra. The ointment had already relieved some rawness.

When she came out, dressed, Mickey had also recovered from the trauma. He was wearing nothing but a towel he'd found in the hall closet, and the tattoos on his upper arms accentuated the roundness of his pectorals. He had a slight bulge at the belly with a runnel of fine hair flowing up from his navel.

"My turn," he declared, stepping past her and taking the bathroom door handle. "Keep the ape outta here while I'm naked, okay? I don't wanna lose nothin' that doesn't come in pairs."

"Ha ha."

Liane looked at Bea, fast asleep on the couch in primitive innocence, the throw pillow still half covering her head. There came an initial thump through the wall as the shower started up, then the sporadic slaps of water hitting the tub bottom. Her mind drifted back to the pistachio shells. Could it be that Corey, whom she'd learned to consider her lifelong curse, might now become her savior? She removed the shells from her tote, sat on the couch by the sleeping bonobo, and spread them across the coffee table. The numbers seemed random. Rather than seeing a pattern, she homed in on the dark lines of graphite that formed Moyo's careful writing, European style, the 1's adorned with flourishes near the top. She wondered for the first time what kind of education he'd had before coming to the States. Enough that the south side of Chicago couldn't take it all away.

She thought: *Henry Horner Houses. Shell games. The beaten K-9 dog. Peripheral vision.* Clues? Her head ached with the immensity of it all.

Bea stirred, crawled into her lap and reached for one of the shells.

"No!" Liane snapped.

The ape withdrew her hand. A moment later she searched Liane's face with her hazel eyes, said, *"Bowling-go,"* and began grooming Liane's head, picking through with delicate fingers but finding nothing.

Liane returned the favor, pretending to look for fleas. "Don't you worry, Bea. We'll get you to safety. Somehow."

27

Mickey opened the refrigerator door and stood silhouetted by the light from within.

"Slim pickin's," he said, holding up a box of Cheerios and a carton of soymilk. "Think your friend will mind?"

"No," Liane said. "We could order up."

"Rather not. The fewer people who see us here, the better."

She took out three bowls, but Mickey wagged a finger.

"No sugar for the bonobo," he said. "She'll be up all night. There's a box of Triscuits in there she can have."

Liane gave Bea the crackers with a bottle of water, and she sat on the floor munching contentedly. Mickey explored the freezer and discovered three fruit pops. Once they'd finished eating they engaged in a sword fight with the sticks until Bea bit two in half. She showed her teeth in a taunting smile.

"Kids today," Mickey sighed. "Hey, I saw something in the freezer that only grown-ups can have."

It was a chilled bottle of vodka. They sipped it on the rocks from wine glasses while trying to make sense of the pistachio shells, shuffling them into every combination.

"You'd think it's a phone number," Liane moaned, "but how are we supposed to form a ten-digit phone number out of nineteen digits? I can't get over the thought that Shaker Moyo is a lunatic, plain and simple. He's messing with us."

"Seems like a lot of trouble for a crazy person to go through. Crazy like a fox seems more like it. Maybe he wanted to stall you a little bit, give himself time to send the heads-up to your ex."

"My ex?"

"Isn't that what he is?"

"We were so young then. Exes are for adults to have."

They stared at the numbers a long time: 16, 83, 59, and so on. Mickey refilled their vodka glasses. "If it's a code it has to have some kind of pattern. Like one of those deals where you add two numbers to yield the next, and so on—whatever you call that."

"Fibonacci numbers. But how do you get anything useful out of the sequence?"

Mickey shuffled the shells around again, threw up his hands. "He couldn't just write it down on a page from the book you gave him!"

"Too obvious. The guard was watching."

"Well, it's a helluva way to communicate, if you ask me. Did the guy think you had six months to figure this out? We're on the lam here."

The vodka spread warm fingers in her chest and the pain had subsided in her breast. She couldn't imagine how alone she'd have felt if it weren't for Mickey, and she would have liked to feel good for a while, not just relieved to be away from danger. She went to the freezer. The frozen vodka bottle was almost empty.

"Knock it off?" she offered.

Mickey frowned his approval and she poured him twice her share.

"Maybe with a fresh look in the morning," he said, casting his eyes about. "I'll put the ape in the carrier and take the couch."

"That's not fair," Liane said. "There's plenty of room on the bed."

Mickey did his best to look cool.

They went into the bedroom and she pulled off the comforter and they lay atop the blanket, not touching.

"In some ways I can handle the idea that these Pentalon characters have it out for us, but it really scares me to think the feds are after you," Mickey drawled.

Liane got up and stumbled to her tote in the living room. She'd almost forgotten about the FedEx package from the lab—the DNA report that she'd read on the train trip to Thessaly. She took the manila envelope from the bag and carried it back to bed, then sat cross-legged, flipping the pages.

"I've forgotten more than I remember about alleles and such," Mickey said, arms folded across his chest, eyes studying the ceiling. "You understand all that stuff?"

"A little. The twins' FOXP2 gene seems to be more similar to ours than to a normal bonobo's. That's one of the genes that's essential to language. Big stuff. The guy who analyzed the results has a note here for Hammurabi to phone him stat."

"Did he call?"

"Not on this note. It's dated the day he got fired."

"So this dude in the lab runs the report, can't believe what he sees. He tells Hammurabi to call him, but when he doesn't hear back, he can't keep it to himself. If he's a smart guy he knows Bea has the potential to change society's whole relationship with animals, shake our moral universe to rubble. He calls the feds and tells them there's a bonobo out there who's a world beater, so now it's a race between them and Axel Flickinger."

"Bea versus the human race."

She set the report on the nightstand and extinguished the lamp. One could have read by the light cast from the street.

"What I'm also wondering…" Mickey said, "if we keep sleeping with our clothes on they'll be able to find us just by the smell pretty soon."

"You're right."

When Liane stood up to undress she became aware of how drunk she was. Still, she crawled under the covers in her bra and panties and found Mickey's mouth with her lips. He tasted aromatic. It was the last thing she remembered.

28

Special Agent Henley Pulsipher felt as out of place as a penguin at a polar bear convention. He was sitting in the back booth of a rundown bar in an African-American section of Northeast Washington when another white man walked in. The man had a baseball cap pulled low over his brow and wore wire-rim eyeglasses that Pulsipher knew he didn't need. All he was missing, Pulsipher thought, was a neon target on the back of his head. But at least he had two Secret Service types with him. And one of them was a black guy. Their .357 SIG Sauer P229s were "printing" through their suit jackets.

They retreated to a booth across the room when the Undersecretary waved a hand. He was wearing a windbreaker and torn jeans, but his shoes looked too rich and important, giving him away. Then again, Pulsipher thought, the man hadn't bothered to hide his escort, either.

"I got some shocking information," the man said, "about the chief executive of a certain animal testing company. A guy who's fertilized a lot of careers around here over the years. I think you know who."

Pulsipher nodded.

"That thing of his that's gone missing—turns out there's something unusual about it."

"It's endangered," Pulsipher said. "You're worried, if this gets out, about internecine warfare between Ag and Interior. It could harm the animal testing infrastructure."

"Yeah, well, that's the half of the problem we knew about yesterday. It's much worse than that." He dropped his voice. "The thing talks."

"How do you mean?"

"I mean it may be more human than half the people you'd find on the streets of D.C. after midnight. It's the greatest threat to mankind since Neanderthals."

"You can't be serious. It's two years old, sir. You're expecting it to take up arms against us?"

"I'm speaking philosophically. Morally. A talking animal's no joke. It calls into question many of our values." The Undersecretary's cell phone rang. He pulled it from his pocket and glanced at the screen. "I have to take this. Give me a minute."

Pulsipher walked to the bar and ordered a club soda. He nodded to the Secret Service guys when he took the first sip then turned away.

He was disappointed in himself, dismayed that the Undersecretary had been able to surprise him with this bit of information. He knew the intelligence reports on his desk were stale, and yet he'd wasted the morning running through them.

Other than a quick trip to that backwoods town in upstate New York, Pulsipher hadn't left Washington for a month. So much time in the office could get a person too deep in the labyrinth of his own head, where every fart sounded like thunder and flights of misdirected logic sent you to a souk in Riyadh when you should be surprising someone in a cabin on the Argentine Pantanal. Bad enough the NSA—with all its eyes in the sky and pattern-seeking communications sweeps—was so backed up parsing Urdu phone calls that it took three days to get the information he needed on a line trace. Now Pulsipher felt like he'd allowed himself to be lulled into complacency, and the Undersecretary had trumped him.

In response to another wave, Pulsipher crossed the room without his drink, suddenly feeling like a lapdog. The Undersecretary started talking again before Pulsipher's ass hit the booth. He explained that, in a nation where perception was often reality, the powers that be saw very high stakes in the potential publicity around exposure of the animal-testing infrastructure. Americans cherished their paths of least resistance. Most didn't mind necessary slaughter when it was kept off their television screens or hidden behind high walls. But when pictures started getting beamed into their living rooms, all bets were off.

"I've had to brief the Secretary," the Undersecretary said. "He wants us to keep a close eye on that company. And he wants it captured or gotten rid of."

"It?"

"The animal and any friends it has with the same talent. What do you know about the girl's whereabouts, the kidnapper?"

"She's somewhere in Manhattan. I'm trying to narrow it down."

"What else?"

"Guy who's after her on behalf of that company, Vlad Gretch, is a volatile dude. He gets to the girl first, he'll tear her face off."

"Where's he stand on the bonobo?"

"That's up to the businessman who called you, I suppose."

"You better get to her first, then."

The Undersecretary rose. He nodded to the Secret Service men and they were gone from the bar in an instant.

Despite the neighborhood, Pulsipher walked a few blocks before hailing a cab back to his basement office. Once inside, he stepped to a photograph that his youngest son, Jimmy, had taken with his older brother's Leica camera. Jimmy was ten and his older brother, Brip, was fourteen. Brip had greater technical command of the digital camera; he could tell you everything about apertures and shutter speeds. But Brip was blind to the right-brain side of life, and Jimmy, somehow, had intuited that you couldn't figure everything in the world with equations. Jimmy's photograph of Rome, taken from atop the Duomo of St. Peter's, was not a great technical accomplishment, but it had a kind of poetry in it that Brip never would've achieved. And poetry, Pulsipher had come to understand, drove a greater portion of humanity than most people acknowledged. The sad part was that poetry could get you killed just as easily as a technical calculation might. Maybe even more easily.

Pulsipher peered into the imperfectly perfect study of Rome that his younger son had rendered with the Leica. He could make out the walls of the Vatican in the foreground and small pieces of more ancient walls that the earlier empire had built. He could discern, barely, the ruins atop the Palatine Hill, and not far from that the massive marble ornamentation of the monument to Victor Emmanuel. He wondered who had plundered what from the Palatine to build what cathedral, what monument. And those decisions, now made anonymous by time, were taken in which palazzo? The picture wouldn't tell him. To arrive at that answer required human intelligence—assets on the ground—what the spooks, with their absurd love of acronym, called *humint*.

Pulsipher thought hard about that. He decided to go home and pack a bag.

29

When Liane opened her eyes she was facing the ceiling with the bed covers tucked under her chin. It wasn't like her to lose herself to alcohol. The cotton mouth was an unfamiliar feeling, as was the sense that she may have done something regrettable last night. She pulled her right hand across her body to scratch an itch and found her bra was still on. So the nice kiss truly was the last thing that happened—perhaps.

The covers on the other side of the bed had been cast aside, the mocha percale barely wrinkled. Rather than think of Mickey, Liane's mind drifted back to Corey as she originally knew him. The idea that a kid could change the world, her old shrink had suggested, was a lie whose grandiosity made her father's fraud seem puny. Both of their chosen paths could get people killed—and, indeed, both of them had.

Liane couldn't defend her father's cynical behavior, so she'd opted to defend her boyfriend's idealism instead. But the right answer to her father's dishonesty, the shrink had argued, was to become a solid citizen, a person who plays within the rules. As an adult, until the moment she'd felt compelled to rescue Bea, Liane had followed exactly that course.

It was this court-appointed shrink who urged Liane to channel her love of animals into a field that would satisfy that interest while yielding human benefits. Frank, with his scientific connections, had further pressed her down this path, down what they both called *the straight and narrow*. And Liane had taken the bait and swum forward like a fish on a line. Only Corey, long out of touch, would've had an inkling through his own obsessions that predators infested the waters in which Liane chose to swim. She was a minnow among barracudas.

In the final analysis, Liane didn't know whether Corey had truth on his side or was lost in his own big lie. But Bea needed a protector, and neither she nor Mickey had the resources to meet the challenge. Corey, she thought, if he were still out there somewhere, would suit Bea. His purity of views might counterbalance the cynicism that drove Pentalon and its network of support.

Liane rose and went to the bathroom. She emerged to find Mickey at the kitchen table and Bea on the counter over his shoulder. He passed the ape Cheerios, two at a time.

"What's the story, morning glory?" He wore a silk bathrobe over his white t-shirt and boxers. The robe was too skimpy.

"My head hurts," Liane said.

"I found some Excedrin by the toaster. It helps."

"We didn't do anything last night, did we?"

"Vodka. Talk. Last I remember was a terrific wet kiss." He indicated her breasts. "I wish you'd stow those weapons, though. They could put someone's eye out."

"Only because that someone's eyes are so wide open. I *am* wearing a bra."

"Not for nothing, but—what, I'm supposed to walk around like a blind person, feeling along the walls? That could be more dangerous. Please, Liane. It's too sheer. I'm in pain here."

She returned to the bedroom and pulled on the sweater and chinos she'd bought in Thessaly.

"Better?" she asked, returning.

"How's the bite, by the way?"

"Improved, I think. Where'd you find the robe?"

"Hanging inside the closet door."

"You look like Tony Soprano."

"Want I should shuffle down the driveway to get the paper?" He poured some Cheerios into a dry bowl and handed the whole thing to Bea. "I've been working on the code this morning while you slept. Is it possible there was another shell?"

She thought back. "I may have tossed a few before I realized they had writing on them."

"That's what I suspected. If I'm right, it's a simple puzzle. See here."

Mickey had the shells re-aligned on the coffee table, five-space-four. "The numbers in the tens column progress in order, except that the sixty-something is missing."

"So?"

"So the tens column is just telling us the order, see? That's why the last number's one hundred seven. It's the tenth place."

"Gee. How didn't we see this yesterday?"

"Patterns can seem ridiculously obvious once you know how to look."

"So if you're right and I threw away one of the marked shells we only have ten possible numbers to try—zero through nine in the sixth place."

"Bingo, baby." He handed her the phone. "I'll get dressed while you dial."

30

It was a long way from the witch doctor's village to Kinshasa, but Dikembe felt compelled to make the journey. He knew he could never return to his village, and the important thing he'd last done in the crowded city—though months ago—hung heavily over him.

They began on foot, walking at first in near silence, Daniel fingering the dangling amulet.

"What will this do to protect me, Papa, what?" he begged.

Dikembe didn't know how to answer. He didn't know whether he believed in magic anymore, or even in Jesus. For his own sanity, his memories of Odette's illness, not yet a week old, had receded just out of reach. They were present but hard to discern, like a wound covered with gauze. Only Daniel's future now drove him. That—and rectifying an injustice that he owed the world.

"What of the virus?" Daniel persisted. "How will this pinch of dust stop something so big?"

"The virus is tinier than dust," Dikembe said. "It's so tiny we cannot see it. To the virus that charm is very big indeed."

"But, then, we are bigger. And the virus can still hurt us."

"Smart boy. That was before you saw the witch doctor. Now you are possessed of some mean juju. If the virus comes, the charm will bare its teeth and tell it to move along and take someone else."

They walked for hours, occasionally passing others on foot. The shadows grew long, marginally cooling the steamy air. Dikembe feared they would have to spend the night in the bush with no weapon for protection from wild things.

The sky glowed russet as they approached a small village, where Dikembe bought koki from a woman by the side of the road. They sat on a discarded wooden box and unfolded the banana leaves and ate the steamed paste with their hands.

Dikembe decided they'd have more luck hitching a ride if Daniel tried to thumb down a vehicle alone. When they heard the roar of an engine, Dikembe ducked behind some trees before the truck's dust cloud got too close. The beams of its headlights looked stiff enough to hold a person's weight in the thick air.

The truck rumbled to a halt and the driver hung out his window.

"Where to, boy?"

The truck's storage bay was wrapped in canvas and the back had three rusty chains strung across it.

"The big city," Daniel said.

"I don't go to Kinshasa center. If you have money I can take you to the outskirts."

Dikembe emerged then. "Fine. We can pay."

They negotiated a fare and Dikembe handed the driver half before they trotted around to the back, holding their breaths in the dirty exhaust. Dikembe gave Daniel a boost and used one of the chains to pull himself up. The cargo consisted of sacks of flour piled halfway to the ceiling and half a dozen people sprawled atop them with no room to stand. They coolly acknowledged Dikembe and Daniel, who lay down in the stifling air, made cloying by the flour dust.

For four days they rolled along, jostled by potholes and miles of unrelenting washboard. When the road was smooth, which was rare, they closed their eyes to rest more soundly. When it was rough—most of the time—they stared out the back, fighting to keep their teeth from chattering into fragments.

Late one morning, after the sun had crested the roadside trees and begun its relentless baking of the canvas roof, Dikembe awakened to notice the road behind them had grown more congested with cars and trucks, motor scooters and bicycles. He crawled to the opening of the truck bay and squinted against the sunshine. There were more buildings than they'd yet seen along the side of the road, standing close by one another in motley disarray, like the mustering of reluctant recruits.

He tapped Daniel and pointed. "Almost Kinshasa."

31

Liane strode down Madison Avenue, past office buildings and apartment buildings and the glass and stone facade of the Morgan Library. She didn't look like someone who might be running for her life, only a young woman with purpose in her step, drawing the sidewalk under her.

She turned west onto Twenty-Ninth Street and stopped before a small neo-Gothic church. There was a waist-high old-fashioned wrought iron fence around it, painted black, and the sign in front identified the building as Episcopal, The Church of the Transfiguration, but also as "The Little Church Around the Corner." She tried the first gate and found it locked, but the second gate swung open. The garden, just off the sidewalk, seemed oddly quieter and more peaceful than the street only steps away. She located a stone bench under a small bower and sat, looking at her watch. Five minutes early, she waited with her hands folded in her lap, like a good schoolgirl.

Mickey had been right about the simplicity of the code. Sitting on the edge of the bed Liane had begun with a zero in the sixth place and dialed in order, reaching two wrong numbers and one not in service. On the fourth try a man said only, "Speak."

Liane, all these years later, knew before the complete articulation of that single syllable that the voice belonged to Corey Harrow. The sound of it made her heart skip in spite of herself, but no small talk followed, no reacquainting. Corey told her where to meet him and hung up.

The stone bench felt cool on Liane's hamstrings. The sensation took her mind back to the bone-chilling cold of that day when she'd sat on the damp ground with Corey, on the island covered with goose poop. When they'd stood and embraced and she felt his gun against her hip Corey didn't seem much like the revolutionary he'd claimed to be. He was more lost boy than Che Guevara. She saw fear on his face and it made her want to protect him, almost at all costs, despite the fact that their relationship had already begun to deteriorate. For a long time after that, though, she regretted the help she'd given him. Her mother and Frank couldn't speak Corey's name. Her actions in helping him were an injury added to the insult of her birth father. Yet, given the course of recent events, Liane couldn't help thinking now that the price she paid to abet Corey's freedom may not have been too much after all. There was, as the gurus say, kismet behind it.

Liane glanced at her watch. Corey was five minutes late. She put his tardiness out of mind and watched the brown sparrows and yellow-gray tufted titmice flit about the foliage. Flowers bloomed in the church garden—white bearded iris, purple delphiniums, pink double peonies, red roses, white oxeye daisies. The oxeyes reminded her of the flowers by her mother's bedside. Last time their petals had been browning at the edges, curling in on themselves. *What might they look like now?* she wondered. Had her mother discarded them? Had Frank or Claudine? How much time had passed since she last stood in that room, felt its oppressive force? It was a challenge to remember the turning of the days.

She dug through her tote and located the cell phone that they'd bought in Chinatown, fished around some more to find the disconnected battery. Precautions. She and Mickey had decided never to text one another, which seemed too risky, too easily captured by the powers that be. Also, Mickey said he'd read that authorities could use GPS to pinpoint a phone with the battery in it, even if that phone had been turned off. So they'd taken to using this procedure, but it had drawbacks. She could reach Mickey only on the apartment landline.

Something bothered her now. If the feds were after her they must have the ability to trace a call to or from her mother's house. She should keep the prepaid phone clean, she decided. She put it away and took out her normal cell, snapped in the battery and dialed. Frank answered on the second ring.

"Liane. Where are you? We've been worried sick."

"I'll buy you a new motorcycle one day, Frank."

"What, you crashed the Harley?"

"No. Just lost it."

"Where?"

"I'm not telling you."

"Your mother's not well, Liane. You need to come home."

"I can't right now. Would you put her on the phone, please?"

"She's sleeping. She's not conscious most of the time now. You have to come see her." Frank's voice cracked.

Liane rubbed her brow with a knuckle. "I don't believe you. You're trying to trap me."

"Why would I do such a thing?"

"You betrayed my trust."

"To whom?"

"You know. You're with them, on their side."

"Liane, I don't even know what you're talking about."

"You don't know about the bonobo?"

A long pause, finally: "Somewhat. But your mother's health is nothing to do with that now. She's in a bad way, Liane. Truly. Are you alone? Is someone with you?"

"How could you be so manipulative, Frank!" She used the back of her hand to wipe away the tear that ran down her cheek. "I trusted you like a father."

"I've only tried to help. Stop with this nonsense and come home to your mother. She needs to see your face."

"Put Claudine on the line. Is she there?"

"Yes."

She heard the phone set down and waited. On the street in front of her, two taxis sped around a slow-moving van. A rustle came over the receiver.

"This is Claudine speaking."

Liane hardly knew the woman, but at the sound of her voice she let out a long sob.

"You okay there, precious?"

"Oh, God." Liane was crying uncontrollably. She knew she couldn't do this here. She attempted to suppress her sobs, hurting her ribs.

The traffic light on the corner turned red and the cars piled to a stop. The sparrows flitted. A bee visited one of the daisies.

"Is it true, Claudine? Frank says—"

"I'm afraid so. The doctor was here this morning. It's become a hospice situation."

"What about the dialysis?"

"No longer prescribed."

"No dialysis? Isn't that a concession of defeat?"

Nothing but the faint crackle of static. Then: "I'm sorry, Liane."

"Oh, God. Why now? Has she asked for me?"

"Many times. Are you okay?"

Liane didn't answer. "Tell her," she began. "Tell her— Shit!"

A man moved into her line of sight, walking rapidly, wearing jeans and a polo shirt with the collar pulled up under a mane of long, loose-hanging hair. He went straight past her to the church door with no acknowledgment. But she knew him.

Liane folded her body forward until her chin rested on her knees. In a moment she stood and followed Corey into the church.

32

He was sitting in a pew three quarters back when Liane entered, pausing to let her eyes adjust to the dimness. The church had a refined Nineteenth-Century interior, a vaulted wood ceiling above pointed arches. With the hanging fixtures turned off, stained glass rainbow light bathed the space. Three or four scattered parishioners knelt in pews closer to the chancel. Corey also had his head bowed, his forearms resting on the back of the pew in front of him, but he didn't kneel. Liane slid in next to him. She didn't think to cross herself.

Silence.

Corey's long hair spilled over his face, hiding it, and formed curlicues on his arms. He was thin. The glimpse Liane had of his neck and shoulders indicated more sinew than muscle.

"I feared you weren't coming," she said to the side of his head.

"You underestimate me."

"Last time I saw you, you had a crew cut."

"Last time you saw me, I lived in a different time. And so did you."

She reached over and lifted a lock of hair from his polo shirt. It felt soft. Weightless.

"Don't touch me," he said. Her hand recoiled. "We're here to pray."

"For whom?"

"Just act like a believer, Liane."

"What makes you think I'm not one?"

"I don't care about your religious views. We don't want to stand out is all."

Liane faced forward. The altar glowed golden. She half admired Corey's discipline. "Why this place?" she asked.

"Because we know where the cameras and exits are."

She looked around and spotted a tiny red diode blinking high on a pillar.

"That one's nonfunctioning," Corey said flatly, not lifting his head. "It's for show."

"Who's *we*?"

"Let's not play games. You know who. The ape's of tremendous value to the movement."

"What do you know about her?"

"Everything of significance except her whereabouts. Is she in your possession?"

"Yes. What do you see as your interest in this?"

"We're going to make her a TV star, Liane."

"She doesn't speak English."

"We'll teach her."

"Can I see your face, Corey?"

"This isn't about me or you. Or us."

"No. But I still want to see it."

He didn't move, continued staring into his own knuckles.

"Tell me about your life these past ten years. Has it been hard for you?" she asked.

"Nobody would prosecute you, Liane. They don't want this public. You'll never have to live as I live."

"I wasn't thinking about myself. Not everyone in the world who doesn't take up arms against injustice is a selfish asshole. You and I had something once, or have you forgotten? We may have moved on, but we can still care about each other."

He gathered a breath. "Tell me where you have her stashed."

"Not yet. Where do you stand with FAULT? Are you a formal part of it?"

"You won't find me on any organizational charts, if that's what you're asking. The role played by people like me doesn't get committed to paper and put in a file somewhere to be discovered later by the other side."

"You're part of an underground army, then."

"One could say that."

"And Shaker Moyo too?"

"Shaker Moyo is indisposed. I think you know that. How is he?"

"Don't you know? I thought he was your best buddy."

"I can't exactly waltz in there myself unless I want to stay forever. That should be pretty obvious. Unfortunately, he's a sacrifice to the greater good."

"The ultimate sacrifice," Liane said.

"No. The animals make the ultimate sacrifice."

"To the scientists, not to the cause."

"That's not exactly true. We could free half the animals in testing labs tomorrow through coordinated attacks. But there are many more in line to replace them the next day. We need a more permanent solution. So, in that sense, today's imprisoned animals are suffering for *all* their own greater good, while we await the bigger opportunity."

"And what of my bonobo?" Liane frowned. "Would she also be just a means toward the permanent solution you're speaking of?"

"I wouldn't put it that way. Not *just*."

"But I thought you people stood for the sanctity of the individual."

He finally turned to face her. Except for the thick goatee, he didn't look that different from the person she'd once known. But his eyes burned with a colder fire.

"This isn't high school anymore, Liane. We're not in the debate club. Tell me where you have the bonobo."

"You sound a lot like Flickinger's lackey, Vlad Gretch. Whose lackey are you, Corey?"

"I don't think you fully understand my importance to FAULT, to the cause. Anyone involved with us would scoff at your characterization. They revere me. It's almost embarrassing."

"So you're more analogous to Flickinger. The top of the heap."

"Every man or woman—every thing—has the role that the gods

have cast for it. I have mine. You have yours. That brilliant bonobo, too."

"Silly me. I thought you could help me save her, free her."

He shook his head, cleared the hair from his face with an index finger. "Save her? Yes. But freeing her isn't in the cards."

"Then we have nothing further to talk about."

She straightened her legs and felt herself rise.

"You don't want to defy me," Corey sighed.

She looked at the ornate gilt cross standing erect on the altar table, then back at Corey, who remained seated.

"Look at you," she said sharply, "the long hair and beard. You want to think you're the Christ figure or something, but he didn't sacrifice anybody but himself. It's not my bonobo's place to suffer for your ideals."

"She's not your bonobo. You stole her."

"She isn't yours either. Sacrifice yourself if someone has to suffer."

"But I already have." He paused to search her face, perhaps measuring her resolve. "Call me if you change your mind."

The church was ten blocks behind her when regret set in. Why had she allowed the conversation to end in anger? There were better things she could have said. She might have found a way to open his heart.

As she walked she reached into the tote, snatched up the cell phone, and dialed. An automaton came on; the number was disconnected. She tried twice more, disbelieving. She had half a mind to turn on her heels and head back to the church. But she knew Corey would be gone.

THREE

It should be obvious that the fundamental objections to racism and sexism made by Thomas Jefferson and Sojourner Truth apply equally to speciesism. If possessing a higher degree of intelligence does not entitle one human to use another for his or her own ends, how can it entitle humans to exploit nonhumans for the same purpose?

— PETER SINGER

1

"Tell me you're kidding," Mickey pleaded.

They sat shoulder-to-shoulder on the apartment couch with Liane's hand pressed between both of Mickey's. Bea had climbed the bookcase and perched at an improbable angle on a high shelf, flipping through a financial dictionary, saying *"buku, buku."* Liane's eyes brimmed with tears. She knew she'd made a difficult situation nearly futile.

"Tell me you're yanking my chain," Mickey said. "You blew the guy off? What were you thinking?"

"I looked into his eyes. There was no humanity left there. I couldn't place Bea in his care. I just couldn't."

"And what's she gonna do in *your* care? Certainly not thrive. She took a crap in the kitchen sink this morning. She's a wild beast, Liane. We've been through this. You're not her mother."

"Don't patronize me, Mickey. I'm not looking to keep her."

"What I'm saying . . . there are limits. It can't go on forever. She's a hindrance."

"She's our mission."

"At the moment, yes. But tomorrow? Next week? Next year?"

"They're easily house trained. People keep primates at home sometimes."

He rolled his eyes. "You're off the deep end, now. She's not a chimp you picked up at the exotic pet store. She's contraband!"

Mickey's face had gone red. The scar on his cheek stood out white and pale, like a strip of cartilage boiled to the surface. She reached up with her free hand and touched the tip of her pinky to it.

"Tell me what happened," she said, "to give you this mark. There's a story behind it, isn't there?"

"You're changing the subject."

She pouted.

"Fine." He let go her hand and leaned forward, looking into the middle space.

"Most people don't understand how ugly a racetrack can be," he said. "They see the horses from afar, their coats glistening. They presume they're happy out there—reminds folks maybe of their own sprints to the finish line in high school track or something, wind blowing through their hair, rushing endorphins. But there ain't a single horse out there who chose to be on the track, because no domesticated animal ever chooses. You serve man or you perish."

"They can choose not to cooperate, not to run as fast. It would limit their utility."

"Yeah, but they don't think six steps ahead. They only know what's in store for them tomorrow because it follows the routine of a thousand yesterdays. If they don't run well, maybe they're lucky enough to get sold to a show rider who'll still force them to work. If they're not good enough for that then they'll end up as steak on the plate of some French guy or—more likely—so-called beef with gravy in the can. Wink wink."

"Dog food."

"You got it. Out in nature they might frolic some, canter around, but mostly a horse's motivation to run is some component of fear. In the wild they're fleeing predators. At the track they're escaping the bat or trying to keep up with the herd. So, at best, a kind of absence makes them race. You know? There isn't a whole lot that's life affirming about it, despite what the sportscasters say. And when they're not running the track, even the greats spend a lot of time standing in a stall with barely enough room to turn around—a big cage. You start out in the profession because you love these animals. Well, you're as likely to love 'em to death."

"Reminds me of Adnan. He got into primate research because monkeys fascinated him as a boy. He ended up with a lot of blood on his hands."

"I'll say."

"But that's the big picture. What's it got to do with you, Mick?"

"Couple years ago there was a trainer and jockey who I thought were pushing this horse too hard. She was a filly with beautiful strong hindquarters, but she'd developed a problem with her stifle—their equivalent of our knee. We had her on bute, which is like aspirin, and I was giving her regular injections of hyaluronic acid, which is supposed to help lubricate the joints. None of the technical stuff matters. Bottom line: the horse was finished. They wanted to get one more race out of her and I tried to stop 'em. The jockey was up and the trainer was trying to push me away. I had a hold of the guy's reins just under the horse's chin and I wouldn't let go. I wasn't a track official; it wasn't my call. The jockey cracked me across the face with his crop. It caught me just right, opened up the skin."

He ran his knuckles across his cheek, reliving it.

"Did you hit him back?"

"Not then. The horse ran and I was proved right. She pulled up and had to be destroyed a few hours later. Another vet made the decision. They wouldn't let me near her, said I'd jinxed it. At the end of the afternoon I went to the hospital to get stitched up. They told me if I'd come right away the scar wouldn't have been so prominent—but what the hell."

"It's kinda handsome. It adds to that rugged look of yours."

"Listen to you, blowing smoke up my ass. Well, a few days later I got drunk and beat the crap out of the jockey, threw him all over the tack room."

"Score one for the good guys."

He shook his head. "I wish. The man only weighed a hundred pounds. It was like kicking an aluminum can down the street—more exhausting than fruitful. Plus, I lost a lot of business over the whole thing."

"You did right."

"One insight I had? Right ain't so easy to define. That horse's time was up, expired. Old age was never in the cards for her. She was either gonna die by injection or by bolt pistol after a long, scary van ride. At least this way she went down in familiar surroundings."

"Still, I think if you met Corey today and had only a minute to make a decision you would've come to the same conclusion that I did."

Mickey looked into her eyes. "You could be correct," he said. "We're a couple of softies. Where's it gonna get us?"

"Don't go all maudlin on me now."

Their faces grew closer, so close she could study the specks in Mickey's irises.

"I'd like to kiss you when we're sober one of these days," he said.

"What're you waiting fo—"

He swallowed her last word with his lips.

A buzzer went off. They jumped up, disoriented.

The buzzer screeched again. Bea let out a cry and dropped the book to the floor. She climbed down from the bookcase in seconds and launched herself into Mickey's arms.

Liane looked at the intercom. "Wrong apartment?"

"Could be," Mickey said, biting the inside of his lip. "But do we wanna take that chance?"

Liane walked over and pressed the button below the speaker. "You rang my apartment, I think."

"Yup. Four well-dressed gentlemen to visit. I sent them up."

"But we didn't answer."

"I knew you was home. I figured you were in the bathroom or something."

They could almost hear the doorman's lame shrug. Their eyes met, processing it in the same moment.

"Go!" Mickey shouted. "Go!" He still had Bea in his arms. He seized the carrier with his free hand and stuffed her inside as Liane grabbed her tote and opened the door into the hallway.

They took three steps toward the elevator. Its bell dinged. The fire stairs were too far beyond it.

"This way!" Mickey said, turning Liane in place with a tug of her shoulder.

Behind them a gear yanked open the elevator just as Mickey ducked through the nearest door and pulled Liane in after him.

2

"I thought I might hear bells when I kissed you," Mickey rasped, "but that wasn't exactly what I had in mind."

They were standing toe-to-toe in a cramped trash closet, Bea in the carrier sandwiched between them, a bare compact fluorescent bulb casting blue-white light from the ceiling. On a Formica shelf rested newspapers and magazines for recycling, broken-down cereal boxes, stacks of wire hangers. On another shelf lay a carton half filled with black coaxial cable and a basket containing discarded electronics. Cardboard bins with blue liners stood underneath, plastic and glass bottles gathered inside them. There was barely enough room to turn around.

They heard a sudden whoosh and clatter. They flinched, held their breaths. Fetid air forced its way through the seams of the trash chute door and tickled the hair on their foreheads.

"Just someone's garbage bag coming down." Liane exhaled softly.

The odor of rotten food filled the room.

"*Bosoto,*" Bea said from within the carrier. "*En-guy.*"

"I'm gonna open that door a crack to look out," Mickey whispered. They rotated gingerly in the small closet, keeping the carrier between them.

Liane sensed danger. She poked three fingers through the mesh of the pet carrier door, wiggling them to distract Bea. There wasn't room to look around the side of the carrier, but she felt the flesh of Bea's palm and fingers making contact, squeezing gently, exploring. She thought that she should have stopped to pray at The Little Church Around the Corner. The air there smelled sweetly of candles and the light was ethereal. *How soon we return to the sour muck,* she thought. But it wasn't the smell that made her want to throw up. It was the knowledge that they'd been found out.

They maneuvered to lower the carrier to the floor and Liane crouched over it. She watched Mickey turn the handle and crack the hallway door, leaning an eyebrow against the edge. He closed it quickly and quietly.

"Four suits," he said, holding up his fingers. "Just as I looked out one picked the lock to your friend's door and three pushed their way in with guns drawn."

"Guns. Wow." She rubbed her temples. "We need to get out of the building."

Mickey looked out again. He closed the door and shook his head. "Big big guy standing guard outside. We wait."

"They'll find us."

"They'll find us faster if we don't shut up."

Bea continued to fiddle with Liane's fingers. Liane's knees began to ache, and she leaned her back against the wall for relief. She wondered whether it was the government's men or Pentalon's goons inside the apartment, maybe tearing the place apart like Mickey said they'd done to hers, but either way they were trapped.

Mickey listened intently for further trouble. It made her anxious just to look at him. She closed her eyes.

How'd they find us? she wondered, touching the back of her head to the wall. Did Mickey's vet friend turn them in? Had they been followed all this time, their pursuers waiting for this moment to spring? Was it her phone calls to Corey? But if someone had Corey's number all along, why wouldn't they have picked him up ages ago? Or was it the call home to Frank that someone traced back? She withdrew her hand from the carrier and dug through her tote. There it was: the cell phone she'd used to call Corey the second time, from the street. She'd put it back with the battery still engaged. *Damn.* She opened the trash chute door and dropped the phone down. Three long seconds later they heard it clatter at the bottom.

Mickey lifted an eyebrow. He cocked his head toward the hallway door again, looking worried.

She'd never been any good at hiding, Liane thought. On rainy Sundays as a little girl she played hide-and-seek with her father sometimes, and she'd always leave a toe sticking out from behind the curtains or the top of her head poking above the back of an upholstered chair.

"I may hear something," Mickey mumbled.

Running had always been more her thing; in the schoolyard no one could catch her.

"We need to get away from here," she whispered.

"They're still out there."

"The other door." She pointed to the trash chute.

"Carrier won't fit," Mickey said, shaking his head.

"We'll leave it. Put her on one of our backs."

"Look at the size of that hole. My shoulders are too broad. I'll never get through there."

Liane paused. "I'll go on my own. We'll split up. Communicate via cell when this moment blows over."

"You just threw the phone away."

"I still have the other one."

"No." Mickey shook his head again. "Mine's still in the apartment. Plus: eighth floor—nine stories straight down to the basement."

Liane looked from him to the box of coaxial and gestured.

"Uh-uh," Mickey said.

"There appears to be lots of it. It's thick and I'm light."

"Not that light. Not with Bea along for the ride."

She pulled the box from the shelf and stuffed it into his arms. In the desperate silence, the sound of the cable shifting inside resembled a ghostly scream.

"They pull this stuff with big trucks," she said. "It'll hold me for a hundred feet if *you* can. Will you be okay if I leave you?"

"Like you said: The bonobo's our mission."

"If I could think of another way, I wouldn't suggest this."

"I'm a big boy. I can fend for myself better alone than with you and Bea in tow."

He said it without conviction, Liane thought.

A noise came from down the hall.

"Hurry up!" Mickey said. The decision made, he braced his rear end against the door and started stripping cable from the box. The spool inside whirred until the floor of the trash closet looked like a pit of black snakes.

Liane pulled open the chute door and peered into the void. It snapped shut.

"The door's on a spring," she said.

Mickey produced his metal bottle opener from a back pocket. He used it to wedge open the chute door and wrapped several yards of cable under Liane's arms. Then he lifted her by the waist. It took some doing, but they got her propped atop the open chute door, facing into the room, her sneakers gripping the edges of the frame.

"Bea," Liane said.

"I'll open the carrier door. She'll come."

Another noise from the hall.

"Okay. I'm ready."

"The ape's no feather, Liane. She'll produce torque when she jumps on you. Brace yourself."

"I will."

He pulled the cable halfway taut and looped it over the door handle to make a primitive pulley. Liane closed the fingers of one hand around the cable and with the other hand clawed a corner of the chute doorway. Its edges were sharp. She knew she couldn't maintain her grip for long.

Emotion fluttered across Mickey's face.

Bea hooted as if a game were commencing.

"Hurry!" Mickey fiddled with the carrier door while fighting to maintain a grip of the cable with his other hand.

Liane eased down and positioned herself with her knees against the chute wall. She had her hands stacked atop one another on the cable, which she'd wrapped around one forearm. She thought she should say something Mickey would remember forever—something about kisses and hearing bells. Maybe long-overdue apologies. She looked into his eyes as she inched down to the point where her weight on the end of the cable was pulling him slightly forward.

Their gaze connected achingly across the small space between them. *Ten inches.* It might have been a chasm.

3

The moment her door sprung open Bea shot forth, knocking the carrier into Mickey's shins with the thrust of her legs. *Liane didn't even have to call her name,* Mickey thought. *The ape knows who butters her bread.*

He watched her come sharply to rest with one leg on the chute frame and another on Liane's shoulder. The surge produced a vicious tug, lifting the cable from the door handle and tipping him off balance. If the room weren't so small, he might have dropped Liane twenty feet or more, like a dead weight over a cliff. As it was, he barely managed to get the sole of one shoe flat against the wall under the chute opening. His face stopped an inch shy of the chute door's sharp corner, making him feel as if he were fighting also for his own life. And maybe he was.

By pushing off with this foot and throwing back his weight, Mickey pulled his arms closer to his core, a more solid posture. But even from that position he barely possessed the strength to wrap the cable around one forearm and impede the course of his plunging cargo.

One of Bea's hands had a firm grip on Liane's hair, and the other flailed like a rodeo rider's. Liane's face disappeared so quickly that the final image didn't register with Mickey. *Like a snapshot at the fag end of a film roll,* he thought. *Beyond recovery.* And her last word, maybe forever, had been only, "Ow!"

Before he tried anything more he croaked a whisper down to her: "Liane, you all right?" But she didn't answer with words, only groaning.

Part of him wanted to pull her back up, but he could hardly keep the cable from slipping through his fingers, let alone reverse the force of gravity. The bottle opener wedging the door deformed, warping under pressure. Mickey's free knee had landed atop the unstable plastic carrier. He attempted to kick it away, but it only interfered more, tripping him and making a clatter.

The dead weight on the end of the cable was fatiguing his arms. He heard voices in the hallway, and they didn't sound friendly.

The bottle opener buckled into a kinky C. Italic. The cable—poised on the edge of the chute door—also began flattening in an ominous way. He set his feet, untangled his arm, and paid it out, one inch at a time, then faster, laboring to keep it from slipping too quickly while backing himself toward the hallway door. He got there and twisted his shoulder around to wrap the cable over the door handle stem again. It held, but he nearly dislocated his elbow in the effort.

The voices drew closer. He used the door-handle pulley to accelerate the feed hand-over-hand, straining with all his might to control Liane's fall. Who would've known a small woman and a young bonobo could weigh so much? He peered into the dark square of the chute opening, its concrete walls stained with the foul drippings of an entire high-rise community, watched the black cable vector into the hole. When he turned his head to look back at the door handle he spotted the shadow of a foot on the threshold. He threw his back against the door just as the handle turned, paying out the cable faster, faster, hoping for the slack of a soft landing with every feed.

The handle turned. The door moved. Mickey threw himself against it.

The handle turned again. Mickey, reaching for anything to improve his leverage, found the shelf with the piles of papers and cardboard. It collapsed in a heap and he pushed himself to his knees and threw his hip against the door again, paying out the cable, paying it out. Thinking only: *Liane, Liane, Liane.*

The bottle opener trembled. The door handle turned. Mickey got himself fully upright just in time, desperately pressed his hip and shoulder in resistance, strained to control the cable. Then the door burst open, throwing him off his feet, slicing open his forearm on the corner of the fallen shelf. The door to the chute snapped shut on the cable, severing it, and Mickey and the big big guy stared at the closed chute in frightful anticipation.

Two seconds later, a dull thud echoed up the shaft.

Mickey cried out, "Liane. Oh, Liane!"

The big big guy in the gray suit reached down with two gigantic hands, seized Mickey by the shirt, and hoisted him to his feet.

4
—

Mickey, cleaved by the bottomless sense of loss, worse than he ever would have imagined, refused to calm down. They wrestled him into one of the kitchen chairs and strapped him tight with zip ties.

He closed his eyes and a sense of doom overtook him, and he thought: *Once again Michael Charles Ferrone gets more than he bargained for.* His mother, auburn-haired dark Irish with the purest white skin, used to tell him to be careful what he wished for. "You might get it." With all the Wall Street dough flying around Westchester County, his father had built a big business, employing over a hundred people. But the Ferrone boys always worked. For the longest time Mickey only hoped to get away from the tedium of building stone walls, which he'd done every summer since he was old enough to lift a ten-pound rock to his waist. In the northern part of the county, where most of their customers lived, his father would catch Mickey daydreaming over the cows and horses and sheep in surrounding fields. He'd walk up and slap him on the cheek, letting his calloused palm linger for the duration of the sting, then instruct him what to do next. His father was like a force of nature, a stubborn Italian who asserted his prerogatives. So once he'd yielded to his youngest son's desire to attend veterinary school, Mickey never looked back, only forward to another wish—to work with the horses whose power and elegance had possessed him. That choice hadn't turn out as hoped, and he sometimes envied the gobs of money his brothers raked in, but more than that, the sense of purpose with which they drove their Hummers and wielded their Blackberries. Their big families filled six-bedroom houses, worked the joysticks of Nintendos, frolicked around stone-encrusted pools—acted like they owned the world. And maybe they did. To visit them made Mickey wonder whether his mother had been right, whether he'd chased the wrong dream. It wasn't their bank accounts and big houses he so much envied as their certainty about everything. He thought he'd finally found that feeling when he first set eyes on Liane.

There had been women before her, but none of them satisfied. Like bland meals, they just made Mickey crave spice. Liane, on the other hand—Liane! The sight of her turned him into a speechless buffoon, he knew, like the guy in *West Side Story* who couldn't say "Maria" without breaking into song. She awed him. So much so that, at first, he feared touching her. And then, though he'd never possessed her, he feared even more losing her. He couldn't tell her so, but it'd been Liane who inspired him to leave the track, to search for ways to express his authenticity. Even as she struggled with her own uncertainty Liane exuded a sense of possibility. To be in her presence had felt like a drug to him, still did. And where had it gotten him?

He roused himself, thought: *yeah, a drug—like the kind that makes people jump off buildings presuming they can fly.*

"Liane," he blubbered. "Gotta save Liane."

"She your girlfriend?" said the big big guy who'd lifted Mickey off the floor of the trash closet. "We're working on that."

"Gotta save her now!" Mickey cried, straining to stand. His efforts tipped the chair over. Nobody moved to pick him up.

"Our colleagues are down there," said the big big guy. "They'll deal with what's left of her."

"No no no no no!" Mickey wailed, beating the chair against the floor.

"Calm yourself down." The big big guy poked Mickey in the ribs with the toe of his shoe. "If they find her alive they ain't gonna kill her."

Mickey absorbed that. He certainly wanted to believe in the prospect of Liane's safety. But there were too many *ifs* to account for. He ran his tongue across his front teeth and bit his lower lip. After a while the big big guy pulled the chair back up onto four legs.

"There," he said. "Behave."

"Not as tough as he looks," the other suit said, flashing a badge. He took off his jacket, revealing a shoulder holster with the butt of a pistol protruding.

Mickey looked around. The bowl he'd fed Bea from this morning still rested on the kitchen counter. The book she'd dropped lay splayed on the rug, open with its spine up. He struggled to pull himself together, sensed the tears leaving salt tracks on his cheeks as they dried. It took him awhile to regain composure.

"Am I under arrest?" he asked finally.

The cops—if that was what they were—didn't respond.

Mickey asked again, more firmly.

Still nothing.

"What're you, the strong silent types?" They were getting his Irish up. "I'm an American citizen."

"That right?" said the guy with his jacket off. "Well, we didn't think you came from Burma."

The restraints rubbed. "I asked you if I'm under arrest."

"What for?" replied the suit with his jacket off. He was nearly as large as the big big guy. His fleshy neck overhung his shirt collar.

"I dunno," Mickey said, "accessory to some kinda theft, maybe. After the fact."

"The chimp? I wouldn't worry yourself about jail for that."

"You know about her, huh?"

"C'mon, Dr. Ferrone. We didn't come to New York to climb the

Statue of Liberty. Give us a little credit. Is the chimp with Ms. Vinson or was that carrier for your pet squirrel?"

"If I'm not under arrest I don't have to tell you anything. You're holding me for what?"

"This is bigger than criminal charges. You two heroes have gotten yourselves into more trouble than you know. Think of it this way. You've wandered into a factory with some really huge machinery. When the gears turn, people who ain't standing on the right side of the line get their fingers pinched. Or worse: They lose an arm or a leg. Speaking of which, how's the cut?" He turned to the big big guy. "See if you can find anything in the bathroom to clean up Dr. Ferrone's arm, will ya?"

The big big guy returned in a moment with alcohol and cotton balls. The alcohol stung at first.

"All better. See? We're on your side."

"Lotta fuss over a damn chimp," the big big guy said. "What's she got that I don't got?"

"I dunno," said Mickey, feeling somewhat recovered, "brains?"

The big big guy cracked him across the jaw.

5

All was blackness and stench.

Liane, already close to the bottom when the cable gave out, nevertheless had lost her balance in the sudden fall and ended up lying on her back. Bea landed an instant later on Liane's stomach, forcing the air from her.

Liane's lungs burned, and something damp and slimy clung to the bare backs of her arms. She struggled against it before she could breathe, envisioning all imaginable horrors. Then she realized that the substance was thin plastic, wet inside like a living thing, but nothing to fear. She'd come to rest on a pile of garbage bags full of household trash—the detritus, she imagined, of people like Mr. Oakley and the old lady she'd met in the elevator when she had Bea in the knapsack. She closed her eyes and forced herself to swallow.

"Bea!" she called into the darkness. "Where are you?"

The bonobo didn't answer, but Liane heard her stressed breathing.

Liane pushed against the trash under her, struggling to right herself. She felt weak and achy. Her scalp throbbed where Bea had gripped it, tugging painfully at her hair all the way down. Her ear and her collarbone and her knees and her hips hurt from slamming against the concrete wall of the chute. Her arm and her hands felt raw from the abrasion of the cable.

But the fall itself didn't appear to have done her much harm, the trash bags having softened her landing. She thought of the noise that the cell phone made when she'd thrown it away. It must've hit something and bounced to the harder floor. *Where is that floor?* She groped around and found a metal wall to her right and one behind her head. She sensed that she must be in a big box. *Of course: the building's compactor.*

"*Bosoto*," Bea whined somewhere in the dark. "*Kobima*."

The air of the compactor room was thick as rotten soup. Liane shuddered to think what must be skulking in the dark. She attempted to push herself up. Her hand found a space in the layers of bags and plunged in up to her underarm, a swath of plastic clinging repulsively to her cheek. Something tickled her wrist and she hastened to extract herself. She'd just managed to work her body into a sitting position when the weight of an animal, warm and hairy, landed in her lap. She repelled it, twitching her legs and throwing out her hands, and it batted at her chest, grabbing for her clothes. The two of them emitted otherworldly screams, and then the thing was gone from her. Or was it?

Presently aware that her eyesight had adjusted to the darkness, she noticed the glow of white trash bags below and all around her, like a sea of phosphorescence. She looked up to see the silhouette of Bea, the faintest glint of light reflecting off her corneas. The bonobo sensed Liane's gaze and whimpered.

"I'm sorry, Bea. I didn't know it was you. *Bowling-go.*"

It was the second time Liane had used one of Bea's words back at her in earnest—the first being when she was trying to get her into the car in the Pentalon parking lot.

"*Bowling-go,*" Bea repeated, sounding still a little hurt. "Liane. *Kobima?*"

"I thought you were a rat—the biggest rat there ever was. I should know better."

She reached up to the top edge of the wall. It was made of steel, sticky but cool in relation to the stifling air. It had a rounded edge that she could easily wrap her fingers over, but there was nothing solid with which to push off her legs, and she didn't have the arm strength to pull her whole weight to the top. She tried three times and the effort exhausted her. She sat back down and buried her face in her hands, thinking how much she already missed Mickey. "You all right, Liane?" he'd called down into the shaft, and she could hear the strain and panic in his voice. Winded by the blow, managing her own pain, she couldn't get an answer out before the cable started moving again and she could then focus on nothing but the stomach-churning motion as she receded from him.

Only minutes had passed, but Mickey must be caught by now, or dead. If either, it would have happened only to save her. And whoever it was was coming. Coming for her and Bea. *Right now.*

"The door," she told Bea. "Open the door."

The bonobo just sat.

"Light," Liane said. "We have to get out of here. *Bowling-go.*"

"*Bowling-go* Liane," Bea said. "*Kobima.*"

"*Kobima,*" said Liane. "Whatever that means. *Kobima.*"

Bea shifted her weight, turned and disappeared over the steel wall. Three seconds later Liane heard a door creak open. Harsh light flooded the compactor room.

6
—

Dikembe could sense that Daniel was scared. His eyes darted among moving bicycles, motor scooters, buses, and cars. People—city people—walked toward him as if they'd run him over. He halted frequently in his tracks, didn't yet understand the sidewalk sidestep. But he would adjust, Dikembe knew, just as he'd already begun accommodating the absence of his mother.

Nzete etengama bomuana, as the saying went. "A tree bends when it is still young." The fear would soon subside and curiosity would again rise in the boy's mind.

Dikembe himself already missed the jungle. The music of the city was nothing like the sound of the orchestra that he heard in the natural environment. It was invasive, discordant: the clopping of donkeys, the rumble of motors, the shouting, the sirens, the banging. They jarred Dikembe, set him on edge. If this were an orchestra, he thought, it was one directed by Satan and inhabited by devils. He found it hard to believe that the Creator meant for man to live this way, roads covered in tar so that the rain would not penetrate, high rises taller than trees.

In any event, Dikembe hadn't come to Kinshasa to wax philosophical. He'd come to right a wrong, to save a pair of bonobos that he'd endangered. He would do it for himself, but also for Daniel, to give him a vision of a different world—a world where people didn't burn forests or consume bush meat, a world where men respected their own responsibilities as husbands of everything on earth. That was the world the Englishman had showed him. It wasn't a perfect vision,

Dikembe knew, but it suited him. He'd right the wrong and then he'd return to where the Englishman had his permanent camp in the jungle wilderness. But first, to be able to proceed, he must right his own offense against nature.

After considerable walking they arrived at the vast animal market, where fish teemed in cloudy tanks, the gutted carcasses of sheep and monkeys and pigs hung from grappling hooks, and twitchy chickens clucked in tiny cages, their molted feathers collecting on the ground.

Daniel furrowed his brow and commented on the fancy dress of the city people. "And why's everyone rushing about so?"

"They're busy," Dikembe answered. "They don't follow the rhythm of the bush. They make their own rhythm, and it's almost always fast— like the soukous music."

"We should've brought my drum."

"One thing they don't lack is percussion, boy."

Dikembe was searching for a particular shop, where not long ago he'd disposed of the captured bonobos. They wended their way through slow-moving traffic to cross in mid block. The front of the shop, open almost completely to the street, looked like a hundred others, save for the faded green paint on a pair of faux colonial pilasters. There was a young man standing just inside, haggling with a dashiki-clad woman already weighed down with shopping bags. The subject of their negotiation appeared to be a set of steaks marked as smoked elephant meat. Dikembe and Daniel pushed past them to a doorway protected by a beaded curtain. A girl of about twelve, gangly as a sapling, stood just inside. She cast her eyes imperiously over Daniel.

"We're looking for Pierre," Dikembe said.

Her attention lingered on Daniel, who looked up at her in turn.

"Mind what I'm saying, girl," Dikembe persisted. "Show me to Pierre. We don't have time to waste."

She crossed her chest with one arm and curled long fingers around her scrawny triceps. "In the very back," she conceded, walking away.

"Strange girl," Daniel said.

"Keep your mouth closed now," warned Dikembe.

They proceeded through a room hung with pelts, mostly those of big cats and various types of antelope. Daniel's attention went to an ashtray made from a gorilla's hand. He ran his finger over the palm, pinched the stiff fingertips.

"No touching," Dikembe snapped.

In the next room, live animals in cages lined the walls. Amidst them an enormously round man sat behind a desk covered by a leopard-pelt blotter. His skin was blue-brown and his head was the size of a basketball. He wore a broad, welcoming smile.

"How can I help?"

"We did some business not long ago," said Dikembe.

Pierre searched his visitor's face. He placed a chubby hand atop his desk and opened it to gesture toward a pair of chairs that faced him. They were upholstered with okapi pelts.

"Now I remember," he said. "You're a seller. Please sit down."

Dikembe hesitated. He expected a difficult discussion and felt that accepting any hospitality from Pierre amounted to an early concession.

"It is better to sit," Pierre pressed.

Dikembe slipped into a seat while Daniel propped himself on the edge of the other chair.

"Some tea?" Pierre offered.

Dikembe demurred.

"A lollipop for the boy, at least." Pierre pushed forward an elephant-foot bowl.

Daniel snatched up a cherry one before Dikembe could object. He tore off the cellophane, licked it once on each side then slid it with great contentment into his mouth.

"You look unhappy," Pierre observed, directing his attention back to Dikembe. "Some dissatisfaction with our last transaction?"

"It's only a change of heart. I'd like the apes back."

"What apes?"

"The ones I sold to you. The bonobo twins."

"The bonobos?" Pierre leaned back and released a hearty laugh, so genuine and contagious that it brought a grin to Dikembe's face, too.

"I'll pay back every cent you gave me," Dikembe persisted. "If you need a bit more, for the trouble, I'd understand."

Pierre settled down and spread both hands flat on his desk, his round belly cresting the edge of it. "The bonobos are gone, my friend. I resold them the week you brought them in."

The news hit Dikembe hard. In all his thinking of this unfortunate business, it had never occurred to him that he couldn't reverse his deed.

"There are more where those came from," Pierre said. "We have no bonobos presently, but there are plenty others to choose from. I can sell you a macaque or a mandrill right now. You can have both for less than I paid you for the bonobos."

"They were special, and so young," Dikembe said, looking off into space.

"I'm told I may have a baby gorilla coming in tomorrow or next day. I can set that one aside if you like."

"No. You don't understand. It's the bonobos I want back. The twins. Nothing will substitute."

"But it's impossible," Pierre smiled. "Surely you understand. They're long gone from here."

"Did they go to the bush-meat trade, then?"

"No, sir. As I promised you—and paid—they were much more valuable than that. They're off to a dealer in the west. To America, probably."

"You don't know exactly?"

"Why would I?" He threw up his arms. "They've entered the circle of commerce."

"But what would an American want with them?"

"There are collectors everywhere, scientists, pharmaceutical companies doing important experiments. Possibly they went to a zoo."

"I can't bear it. Is there no way to recover them? I can pay a premium. I'll get the money."

Pierre sighed. The smile had now faded. "I don't know why you should be so attached. One can't be sentimental about these things."

"I have cursed myself!"

"If it's any consolation, be grateful they went west. In the East they'd be done for, ground into potions or featured at a banquet. This way, who knows, your bonobo friends may tap the fountain of youth, live forever."

Dikembe looked to Daniel, who had nothing left of the lollipop but a wet white stick.

Pierre reached behind his desk and held out a small garbage pail. The outside was covered with scales, shades of tan with broad brownish spots. Dikembe recognized the pattern. It was the tanned skin of an African rock python.

7

In the light cast from the basement corridor Liane got a better look at the compactor box in which she'd come to rest. The walls of the box—rectangular and smaller than she'd thought—were the color of putty; the piles of bags beneath her were so shallow she could see glimpses of the blackened floor below; one side of the mechanism, attached to controls and levers, rose nearly to the ceiling. Most important, there was a single foothold molded into one interior side. It enabled her to boost herself over the wall.

Bea stood in the doorway, watching. They took each other's hand as Liane peeked down the brightly lit corridor, where a series of painted pipes paralleled the ceiling. Three quarters of the way down, the pipes made a sharp turn and disappeared through a wall. Beyond the elbow, at the end of the hall, stood a door with a push bar. The sign said: EXIT TO STREET. NO RE-ENTRY.

"Perfect," Liane whispered.

Bea cocked her head and lifted an eyebrow. They heard urgent voices somewhere behind them, the jingle of equipment and the rustle of clothing. *Men. Running.* Chasing them. Liane tightened her grip on Bea's hand and sprinted for the door. They emerged onto an interior ramp, ten yards long. She ran up the ramp to the next door and burst through to the sidewalk.

The first sensation was the sheer energy of the street—the sunlight, the air, the moving traffic. Then, before Liane got her bearings, there came physical contact—a shove to the upper arm, nearly knocking her off her feet, followed by a firm hand on the back of her neck. Finally a flash of movement—a dirty white van streaking to the curb, a hand crossing her sightline—and a stinging in her eyes that forced the lids shut, blinding her. She was shoved from behind, held up on either side as she stumbled forward unseeing, felt herself lifted and tossed. She landed on her side on a flat surface and heard the unmistakable tinny clank of van doors slamming. There was a squeal and a sharp motion as they accelerated into traffic.

The van cruised along for some time, stopping and starting, in no seeming hurry. Liane rubbed her eyes and noticed an acrid smell in her runny nose, spicy in a noxious way, like ant killer. She pushed herself up, still blind, and crab-walked until her back found the side of the van, then sat cross-legged, squeezing her lids closed and struggling to blink open her eyes. They felt like they had needles stuck in them. She lifted her shirt and wiped tears from the corners.

"Bea!" she called into space.

The bonobo climbed into her lap and wrapped an arm around the small of her back.

"She's a cute one," said a boyish voice.

"Yeah," said another, higher pitched. "But don't anthropomorphize the animals!"

They had a good laugh over that.

Liane forced her eyes open as the stinging subsided. Her vision remained blurry, but she could discern a compact woman coming toward her, broad-shouldered, wearing heavy black boots with shiny metal embellishments.

"I'm Tara," she said, squatting. Hers was the voice that had sounded more masculine. She held out something and Liane accepted it. A damp washcloth, cool to the touch. Liane pressed it into both eyes at once, ran circles around her sockets.

"Don't rub too much. You'll only irritate them." Tara returned to the passenger seat, continuing to look back. "Sorry about the pepper spray. We didn't feel like we had time to hang on the sidewalk, winning hearts and minds, if you know what I mean. The effects'll wear off in a minute. No harm done."

Liane didn't respond.

"This here's Pattie, with an eye-eee," said Tara.

"As in eye-eeh eye-eeh oh," Pattie chortled—the more feminine voice and, Liane could now see, attractive, too, with platinum blonde hair down to her shoulders and a substantial chest. She wore a red sleeveless shirt and tan shorts. The assorted silver rings on her fingers clicked against the steering wheel when she went hand over hand to turn it.

"Don't get out of line," Tara continued. "We'd rather not have to kick your ass and tie you up. It might upset the ape. Understand?"

"No worries. I'm not likely to bolt from a moving van."

"Especially since we've removed the inside handle on the back door. You'd have to go through us to get out, and I don't like your odds, to look at ya."

Liane took in the thickness of Tara's neck, the heft of her upper arms. She nodded agreement. "Where're we going?"

"Hah!" laughed Pattie. "Probably we should blindfold her, shouldn't we, Tara?"

"The boss says it doesn't matter. She can't see much from the floor, anyhow. Can you, Liane?"

"You know my name?"

"A course. We don't just go randomly snatching people off the street. What d'ya take us for, dogcatchers?"

"Ape catchers, more like," Pattie snorted.

While the two women again shared a laugh, Liane looked around the van with clearer eyes. It was true that she couldn't see much out the front windshield from her angle—mostly the tops of buildings cast against an azure sky—and the women in front had royal-purple curtains drawn over their side windows. The van was sparsely outfitted, bare metal sides in back, dinky plastic cup holders in front, a hard thick rubber mat lining the bay. Busted air vents rattled with the jarring from each pothole. There were a few pieces of frayed rope scattered about the floor, some clear plastic sheeting, a roll of duct tape, the remains of someone's lunch.

"You done with that?" Liane asked.

Tara glanced down at the brown paper bag.

"Italian sub, what's left of it. Knock yourself out."

Liane picked up the bag. She handed the quarter of a sandwich with teeth marks to Bea, who dug right in, wiping the mustard off and eating the meat first, then the limp lettuce, finally the bread.

"Where's Mickey?" asked Liane.

"Don't know anything about that," Tara answered.

"You're not with those guys back in the apartment?"

"Don't know about them, either. We're told you've been on the run with this bonobo for quite a while."

Liane patted the back of Bea's arm. "All of a sudden we're a whole lot easier to find. I wonder why."

"Can't speak for anyone else," Tara said, as trees loomed through the windshield. "But *we* did it the old-fashioned way. We followed you from your meeting with Corey."

"Corey?"

"Oh, please." Pattie said. "Don't act like you don't know him."

8

After twenty minutes in bumper-to-bumper traffic, Liane felt the van hit a turn, and Pattie throttled it up. The van slowed to a coast, then Pattie feathered the brake and they turned sharply and jumped a curb, jostling from side to side. In another moment they pulled to a halt.

"Pattie'll take the chimp," Tara said, ducking into the back. She produced a canvas hood from her pocket and slipped it over Bea's head, cinching it loosely around the neck before Liane could object.

"Just a precaution," Tara explained, "so no one gets hurt."

Bea whimpered, shook her head, pulled at the hood.

When Pattie stepped to the back and wrapped Bea in a bear hug from behind, Liane yielded to the force of it and let the ape go. Tara opened the van door and they piled out.

The van had parked between an arborvitae hedge and a low-slung building constructed of large granite blocks, roughly hewn. The building matched much of the architecture within Central Park, where Liane guessed they'd stopped. As they climbed down from the van, she sensed pieces of a familiar landmark through a space in the hedge, but she couldn't work it out. The van, she saw, had a green maple-leaf logo on the side with an identification number stenciled below.

"You guys are with the Parks Department?" she asked, puzzled.

"We'd like some people to believe we are," said Tara. "We park wherever we like and we never get ticketed. When the City does the occasional audit, we get wind and take a trip out of town, make the van disappear for a while. Pretty cool, huh?"

"Ta-*rah*," Pattie chanted, like she'd said it a thousand times, "too much in-for-*may*-tion…"

"Oh, hell," Tara replied, "she's a friend of Corey's. If he'll let her see the cave then she can know about the truck."

She walked just past the maintenance building to a small doorway hewn into a mass of nearby bedrock—like the entrance to a root cellar. She pulled aside a weather-beaten wooden door, half off its hinges, to reveal a solid steel one with a key lock. Half ducked down, Tara filled the breadth of the entryway like a bear entering its lair. She inserted a key in the cylinder and they piled into a small hallway hollowed out of the rock.

"This way," Tara said.

As they walked, the hallway widened and the ceiling height increased, but none of it ever got very big. The whole area seemed proportioned like the inside of a big boat. The damp bedrock walls gradually gave way to plaster and tile, the lines becoming straighter and the geometry more consistent as they progressed. Tara led Liane into a small room with a metal-framed cot, a compact desk and a low-slung futon couch. The walls were bare and there weren't any windows.

"You'll wait here," Tara said.

Liane became aware that Pattie had carried Bea in a different direction. She stepped forward, but Tara pushed her roughly in the chest, depositing her on the couch.

Liane stood right back up defiantly.

"I don't know exactly what's going on here, but we will *not* be kidnapped," she said, looking up into Tara's red-cheeked face. The woman had a faint mustache, like a teenage boy before his first shave.

"Looks like you don't have much choice."

"Where have you taken Bea?"

"I wouldn't worry about *her*," said Tara. "We're animal lovers. Nobody's gonna do any harm to a bonobo around here. It's *people* we're not so fond of."

She stepped out into the hall and closed the door firmly behind her. It was arched at the top, solid oak with iron hardware rusted where the black paint had flaked off. A moment later Liane heard the clap of a dead bolt. She tested the handle anyway. It wouldn't budge.

9

Mickey had never been knocked out cold before. He awakened with eyelids so heavy it felt as if lead weights were holding them down. When he managed to crack them the light pounded his retinas in pulses. His jaw ached with the pressure of swelling, and his stomach churned in waves of nausea.

Looking around desperately, he found the kitchen trash bucket open at his knees. He leaned forward and retched into the plastic bag.

"Good ol' Hefty," someone said behind him. It sounded like the big big guy.

"You've done enough damage for one afternoon," said a new voice. "Wait out in the hall, both of you. We'll call if we need you."

Mickey recovered himself in time to see the suits disappearing through the front door. He twisted around in the chair and tugged at the sharp-edged, unyielding restraints, aware all at once that it wasn't only his eyes, his jaw, and his neck that hurt. He felt like he'd gone twelve rounds with a mixed martial arts champ.

A man came into view. He looked innocuous enough, medium height with dark hair and a rounded chin. Wire-rim spectacles framed blue eyes. He wore a sports coat and slacks, no tie. His shoes were Timberlands, if Mickey had to guess, like the ones the man in the TV commercial wore to run the Boston Marathon. *Rubber soles. Very sensible,* Mickey thought, *in case a guy needs to chase someone.*

"If you're through with this," the man said, indicating the bucket, "I'll get it out of our way."

"Liane," Mickey moaned.

"She's gone," the man said.

"Gone?" Near panic.

"Went AWOL. I'm sure that'll amuse you. Are you done hurling? Can I remove the bucket—get you anything?"

"Yeah," Mickey said, running his tongue around his cheeks and spitting, "yeah. I could use some water."

The man pulled aside the trash and held up a bottle of Dasani with a sports top. "Atlanta's finest," he said.

Mickey opened his mouth and gratefully received the stream of water until some of it dribbled down his chin and ran onto his crotch.

"Oops," said the man. "You're looking a bit of a mess, Dr. Ferrone. This Good Samaritan thing isn't all it's cracked up to be."

"Sounds like cop talk for *go fuck yourself.*"

"Don't be silly." He crouched, met Mickey's eye. "If there's any fucking to be done here, you won't get to do it to yourself, not anymore. I'm not a big fan of Amateur Hour—and it's worse in reruns."

"Then...what?" Mickey said as the man straightened.

There was another person off to his left, watching with concern. He was chubby and olive-skinned with pockmarked cheeks. He wore a well-tailored suit, fine silk tie, expensive shoes. His hands were clasped in front of him, at rest on a considerable belly.

"Hello," he said. He didn't look like a pro at this. On first impression he seemed less than pleased to be here.

The two men converged in front of Mickey.

"My name is Henley Pulsipher," said the first man, "Special Agent for the Department of Agriculture."

Mickey leaned back in his chair, closed his still-heavy eyes, and whistled. "You gotta be shittin' me. The Ag Department needs special agents—for what?"

Pulsipher let a smile cross his face, but it was quickly gone. "I presume you're a lot smarter than you look," he said, "so I'll say this once, knowing you'll remember it: I'm here to gather the information I need to recover a bonobo. If I succeed, your girlfriend may get saved in the bargain, but I wouldn't make wedding plans yet."

"I'm not. Believe me."

"This story could still have a happy ending, and you haven't done anything unforgivable so far. But we're running out of time, by my calculations. Plus, there are a couple of bad players in the mix. A misguided idealist and a psycho you don't want Liane facing alone—trust me on that. So what's it gonna be?"

"I'm hardly in a position to negotiate." Mickey shrugged. "The ape's important, but if I have to choose, I choose Liane."

"That's what I want to hear."

The olive-skinned man unbraided his hands and pulled at his chin. "Tell me about the condition of the bonobo."

Mickey detected a slight foreign accent. "Who're you?" he said. "You don't seem like the government type."

The man grinned. "I should've introduced myself earlier. My name is Adnan Hammurabi."

Mickey looked to Pulsipher, trying to gauge the guy's seriousness. "Formerly of Pentalon?"

"One and the same."

"You didn't show to your meeting with Liane. We thought you flew the coop. Not for nothing, but seeing you now, in the pink, has me thinking that you set her up."

"Not true in the least. But nor can I say I'm happy about how things have unfolded."

"No, huh?" Mickey let his skepticism rise to anger. "My friend risked her life because you didn't show. She threw herself down a garbage chute ten minutes ago to save that animal, and here you are in your tasseled loafers telling me *you're* not happy! If I wasn't tied down, I'd throttle you."

"Emotional outburst aren't going to save Liane or the ape," Pulsipher said. "Information might."

"Perhaps in that vein," Hammurabi said, "it would help for me to provide this man with an explanation."

Pulsipher threw up his hands, beseeching the gods of justice. "Suit yourself."

"I'll be quick. You see, Mickey, Liane and I both knew that the unharmed twin—the one she calls Bea—was a major biological find. We knew the bonobo's place wasn't in an animal-testing lab, that she should be studied for the benefit of mankind—of animal kind, you might even say. I had every intention of getting Bea out of there. I just ran out of time."

"But you had time to lay it all in her lap."

"I was already working with the federal government to expose the abuses at Pentalon. Flickinger, in recent years, began to cross many lines, and the acquisition of endangered species was just one of them. But the CEO is no man to be trifled with. He's one of the fifty wealthiest people in America. He has his protectors."

Pulsipher interrupted. "We couldn't just send agents in. The federal bureaucracy has more leaks than a used condom. Quite frankly, this bonobo's not ever going to surface again once we get hold of her. She'll live out her life in secrecy. We needed an airtight plan. We had to proceed with prudence."

Mickey tried to adjust his weight. "So why the sudden call to action by Adnan here? You can't have it both ways."

"Flickinger accelerated his experiments as soon as I left," Hammurabi said. "After what he did to the brother, we had to get the sister out at once, which is what I intended to do, with or without the federal agents. When I went to my regular meeting with them, though—the night before I planned to join up with Liane—they said they wouldn't let me do it."

"Too dangerous," Pulsipher said.

"They detained me," said Hammurabi. "They told me Flickinger's security guy was preparing to cut my throat."

"This is bullshit," Mickey protested. "Why not just pick the guy up?"

Pulsipher interrupted again. "On what charge would that be—having bad thoughts? Vlad Gretch is clean as a goddamn whistle. He maintains the highest federal security clearance, top of the food chain."

"You couldn't just grab him for a little while and let him go when the dust settled?"

"This is still America, Dr. Ferrone. We don't charge into corporations and seize their property. We can't pluck people off the street with no warrant."

"But you're willing to pull out all the stops to haul in Liane and me."

"We can back that up. You were in possession of stolen property. She still is. Plus, I'm the first to admit—not proudly—she doesn't have friends in high places."

"So you gave her enough rope to hang herself." Mickey shook his head. "What a couple of heroes you two are."

"I know how it must look to you," Hammurabi said, sighing,

"especially if you have feelings for the woman. But it never occurred to us that she'd take matters into her own hands. I thought when I didn't show up that she might return home and have a good cry. That's all. At worst, maybe she'd go to the press, but what reporter would believe her? And if some newspaper or website did try to check it out, well, Pentalon is pretty difficult to penetrate—they've spent fortunes on that."

"Tighter than a nun's ass," Pulsipher emphasized. "So we thought. And so thought Gretch."

"Pentalon did a psychological profile," concluded Hammurabi, "and deemed Liane more passive than she's proved to be. She never did anything on my watch to contradict that impression. This thing with the bonobo must have struck a real chord."

"That may be an understatement," Mickey admitted.

"Right," said Pulsipher, "so here we are."

"To continue," Hammurabi said, "please tell me what you can about six-seven—ah, Bea's condition."

"What's to tell?"

"Does her coat look healthy, her eyes, her gums? In your professional opinion, of course."

"Yeah. Why wouldn't she?"

Hammurabi exchanged a glance with Pulsipher.

"Okay, so she's no longer on a controlled diet," Mickey conceded. "We do take good care of her, though. We've busted our nuts to make sure no harm came to her. That should be obvious."

Pulsipher nodded thoughtfully and turned to Hammurabi. "We get the girl, we got the primate."

10

For an hour Liane sat intermittently on the futon, staring at the solid oak door, and paced, examining every inch of the room. It was Corey's room, she suspected, his hideout. The walls were bare—no adornments and no visible ventilation, other than the crack under the door. The desk drawers held a few handfuls of men's clothing, which she sensed were Corey's.

On an empty hope she removed the cell phone from her tote and dialed Mickey, but there was no coverage in the cave. *Trapped again,* she thought. Trapped once by her father's dishonesty; trapped by Corey into becoming an accessory to his crime; trapped as a technician at Pentalon; trapped in helplessness by her mother's illness; trapped every step since her desperate surge toward freedom with Bea. Trapped at first on *the straight and narrow* and trapped now—after everything—while leaving it behind.

The bolt slapped and the door swung open sharply. The small room filled with people: Corey in the lead with three women around him—planets orbiting a star.

"Sorry to have to do this," Corey said.

Though she was still getting used to the goatee, he looked a little more familiar than he had in the church.

"You cut off your hair," Liane observed.

"Don't be ridiculous. They were hair extensions that I wear when I go out in public. They're my disguise. They draw attention from my face."

"I see. Why didn't I think of that? I keep making the mistake of assuming you're the man I once knew. Now I find myself held against my will."

"You can go whenever you want. But the bonobo stays with us."

Liane assessed his forces. The two women from the van had positioned themselves near the door. A redhead stood beside Corey. Crow's feet bracketed her violet eyes, and she had a deep tan.

"I know you," Liane said. "I'm glad to see you didn't end up in jail."

"It's a vandalism rap," said the redhead, weaving her freckled arm around Corey's in a familiar way. "I made bail the next morning."

"That's good. I'm sorry you had to spend the night in prison."

"It was well worth it. We had a blast busting into Pentalon. Flickinger came out as they led us away in handcuffs. The expression on his face—it looked like he was having a stroke."

"Thank you for helping me—" Liane gestured for a name.

"Sarita. I didn't do it for you."

Corey unlocked his arm from Sarita's and drifted toward the corner.

"Bea thanks you, then," Liane clarified.

Sarita rotated to browse the faces of her friends. "Listen to her," she said. "The arrogance!" She returned to Liane. "You don't speak for Bea. She's not your possession."

"I never said she was."

"She's as much mine as yours. Without FAULT's help you never would've sprung her."

"You're right, but now my concern is Bea's welfare. What's yours?"

A whoop from Corey interrupted them. While they'd spoken he'd sat on the edge of the cot and pulled the DNA report from Liane's tote. He had it open between his knees.

"'How many goodly creatures are there here,'" he quoted.

"Still into the Shakespeare, I see," said Liane.

"Ever," said Sarita. "It's one of his charms."

"So it's true," Corey said, raising his eyes from the report. "The bonobo has mutated for speech."

"You doubted that?" asked Liane.

"We haven't been able to get her to say a word."

"She's shy around strangers."

"This report will play well in the media."

"Maybe it's all you need," Liane hoped aloud. "Maybe you don't need to trot her out."

"Don't kid yourself." Corey stood. "This is the age of images. The bonobo's a great deal more photogenic than this report could ever be."

Liane approached him. "Where do you have Bea? Can I see her?"

"Why not? Maybe you can do a demonstration for us."

"She's not an entertainment act, Corey. I just want to be with her. She's probably nervous without me. You know what nerves can do to an animal's health. I could calm her."

"It's not a good idea," said Sarita.

"It's preferable to a cage," Corey said.

"The ape should begin growing accustomed to being without her," Sarita protested. "She doesn't belong to her. She belongs to the world."

Corey approached Sarita and took her hand. He put his face close, raised an index finger to his lips, and touched finger and lips briefly to hers. Then he pulled back and reproached her silently.

"Go get the bonobo," he told Tara and Pattie.

When they exited, Sarita's hostility filled the room. Standing next to Corey she seemed like a bundle of bridled passions, ready to slip the constraints of civility at the slightest provocation. Liane decided to change the subject.

"What is this place?" she asked.

"Just a hole in the rock," said Sarita.

"When they were building Central Park in the Nineteenth Century," Corey explained, "the workmen used it for shelter in inclement weather. During the Cold War, someone had the idea to put a door at the entrance and make rooms, turn it into a fallout shelter, stock it with supplies. Then institutional memory faded. The cave doesn't appear on any maps and every city worker thinks it falls under someone else's jurisdiction. Isn't it neat?"

"I find it a little claustrophobic."

"It's necessary for now," Sarita said. "Besides, we get out regularly, even Corey. He's been to the woods, you know."

Liane thought first of the woodland by the Central Park lake, out the door somewhere, but then she pictured the encampment by the daily Pentalon protesters. "Are you talking about the pine woods by the lab?"

"Yup. He's broken bread with the FAULT helpers out there, even slept in the tent a few times. It keeps their morale up."

The idea that Corey could have been so close that Liane may have passed within a hundred yards of him on the way to and from work stirred a thought in her mind.

"We're near the zoo," she said half to herself. "We're near the Central Park Zoo, aren't we?"

"Close as one can get without being inside it," said Corey, "and we know a couple people there who can help us with the ape. They even have bonobos next door at the moment, visiting from Milwaukee. So—see?—we've got the ability to look out for her well-being. It won't be so bad."

"You're affiliated with them?"

"Of course not. We're not big fans of the zoo system in general, but we have to choose our battles. Most modern zoo folks mean well, so we rarely target them. Here, we're neighbors is all, even if few of them know it. We do have supporters among them. Our supporters are every-where—even the most unlikely places."

Pattie carried Bea into the room, set her down on the desk, and removed the hood.

Liane's heart clutched as Bea looked around. She leaped into Liane's arms, knocking her to the couch. She nuzzled her neck, fingered an earlobe.

"Interspecies love," Sarita spat.

"Can you get her to talk for us?" Corey asked.

"Give her some time to adjust," said Liane. "Then, maybe one on one."

"Not exactly ready for her screen test," Sarita said.

"If we leave you alone with her," Corey apologized, "we have to lock the door."

Sarita walked out.

"Just don't forget me," Liane said.

"I could never," said Corey, and for the first time she saw a flash of the man she once knew.

As soon as the door closed, Bea jumped down and circled the room, peering into all four corners. She returned and sat next to Liane on the couch, frowning.

"*Awa boyini*," she said.

"Yep, another tight spot," Liane said. She may have been, as Corey claimed, free to go, but she wouldn't depart the cave without Bea.

11

When the hidden camera revealed Ronald Berg alone in the break room, Vlad Gretch pulled the keyboard from under his desk and entered a few strokes, locking those doors. He took his time walking down the corridor, pressed a palm to the entry pad, and strode in with his shoulders squared, startling the senior technician.

"Oh, it's just you." Berg put a hand to his heart. "You scared me."

Fear, Gretch thought. *Careful.*

Berg discarded his surgical mask and sat on the bench. He opened his locker door and changed clothes, stepping into a pair of loafers and pulling on a light windbreaker.

Gretch stood with his hands in his pants pockets, watching silently.

"What's the matter, Vlad? Cat got your tongue today?"

Berg's smugness had always offended Gretch, but never so much as it did at this moment. There was a hidden matrix holding the world of Pentalon together. Now, suddenly, tremors were stressing that matrix and threatened to become a full-blown earthquake, uncontrollable, overwhelming the defenses Gretch had elaborately constructed. And this man, he'd come to suspect, occupied a place near the epicenter.

"Please sit down," he told the tech.

"I can't. I have an appointment to go to." But Berg didn't move. He knew better.

Gretch folded his arms. Suddenly, he thought, signs of dissolution were everywhere. It had begun with Hammurabi's insubordination but it grew much bigger than that, and rapidly. He'd waited three hours for the primate lab director to emerge from the motel room, but it hadn't happened. Gretch flashed an old badge and questioned the front-desk clerk, got her cooperation to search the motel, even interrupted a couple of hookers with their johns. No sign of the monkey man. And when he'd come out the Mercedes was gone—the tracking device he'd carefully hidden, smaller than a pack of cards, deposited on the wet blacktop of the parking lot.

Right after that came the business with the girl stealing the ape. *Very bad.* Then, when the FAULT vandals made bail, Sarita, their leader, failed to show up again on the picket line. He'd had her followed from jail to somewhere on Manhattan's east side before she lost them. But, after seeing her freckled mug for more than a thousand days straight—yes, three years—Gretch saw her disappearance as a sign that FAULT had something more brewing than the pot of beans on that Coleman stove in the woods.

Now his sources told him that certain operatives of the federal government had placed Pentalon in their sights. He'd returned to the office to oversee resetting corporate encryption and to take other precautions. But before he went out again, he had a couple more items of business to attend to. Berg was one of them.

"There are forty rabbits missing from your old lab," he told him. "Any idea what might have happened to them?"

"Yes. Another tech screwed up the paperwork. They had to be destroyed."

"Nice try, but they never made it to the incinerator."

"How do you know?"

"There's no record. No one remembers it."

"And that's got what to do with me?"

"It's not the first time charges of yours have gone missing, Ronald. Is there anything you need to get off your chest?"

"Just a hundred-pound barbell. I'm late for the gym." He pushed against the door, but found it locked. "Hey!"

"I'm not done with you," Gretch said. "Are you really going to the gym, or are you off to see your friend?"

"The gym. What friend would that be?"

"Maybe I could work you out right here, just one colleague to another. Should we start with crunches?" He stepped closer.

"You don't scare me, Vlad," Berg said, holding up his chin. "You talk tough, but this isn't the schoolyard. I don't have to take guff from you."

"Right after Liane Vinson stole that bonobo, you made a phone call to her parents' house. Why? How'd you get the number?"

"It's in the phone book."

"No, it's not." Gretch seized him under the collar. "It's unlisted."

"Okay. She gave it to me a long time ago."

"You never called her before, as far as I can tell. Funny that you should choose to reach out right after she breaks into Pentalon, isn't it?" Gretch lifted Berg off the floor by his shirt, so only his toes were touching. "And who should've let her into the monkey lab but Ronald Berg. The coincidences amaze me."

"You're easily amazed then. She tricked me, that's all."

Gretch lowered him to the floor and probed Berg's eyes. He knew firsthand how clever Liane could be. If he'd only thought to tap Berg's phone, rather than track the records later, he'd know for sure. Still, Berg didn't smell right.

"Tricking you doesn't explain the phone call, fairy boy."

"She was a friend. I worried about her."

Gretch grunted and snapped his fist into Berg's stomach and watched him fold like an umbrella, heaving for air. He left him on his knees on the floor of the locker room—drool hanging in long strings from his open mouth.

Gretch stomped the step switch and walked into the lab complex, passing through its corridors in a contained rage, taking deep breaths to dial back the adrenaline. He went through several doors and emerged into the bonobo lab.

Most of them sat up when he entered. Some had bandages covering one eye. A few were hooked up to intravenous pumps. The experiments hadn't missed a beat after Hammurabi left. It was Flickinger's organizational genius.

Gretch grabbed a clipboard and ran it along the bars of the cages as he walked, raising a racket. The bonobos erupted as he went by. He dropped the clipboard flat on the counter, and it popped like a gun, silencing them. Their reaction made Gretch smile. He pushed open the door to the small lab, where No. 673A, Isaac, still resided, alone.

The door closed behind Gretch. He threw open the cabinets, rifling their contents, searching for any clue he could have missed that might enable him to anticipate Liane's next move. Isaac sat up and tracked Gretch with his eyes. His morphine pump removed, he was free in his cage.

Gretch ignored the bonobo, turning his back to the cage. He opened a pair of cabinets with both hands, stepping back to search the top shelf. Just then, he felt a sharp pain in his scalp. It staggered him backward, and his head crashed against the bars of Isaac's cage. The ape had him by the hair. Gretch tried to pry the fingers off but struggled for leverage. The ape's digits were long and amazingly powerful. Gretch couldn't unbend more than two at a time, and they re-engaged as soon as he moved on to the others.

The bonobo had Gretch twisted into contortions with his arms groping behind him. It not only clutched his hair but began pulling out fistfuls, making Gretch scream. He reached back to gouge the ape's eyes, but the bars interfered and the animal eluded him. As Gretch writhed, the pain in his scalp exploded. He groped behind him and located the cage lock, protected from the ape's reach in a Plexiglas box. It took a minute to open the box and blindly work the lock, and in so doing he ceded more advantage to his adversary. A tug slammed Gretch's head against the bars of the cage and he let out another cry and shuddered. The bonobo maintained its grip.

Finally, Gretch got the cage door open. It swung forward with the ape attached, improving Gretch's angle. He lunged backward and grabbed a hold of the bonobo's leg, but Isaac reached a hand forward and began scratching at Gretch's left eye. Gretch twisted around and tugged the ape's leg, which was now near his cheek. Resisting the pain of his hair, he jerked his head rapidly and sank his teeth into the bonobo's thigh, tearing the skin and tasting the briny blood as it ran into his gums and flowed to the back of his throat.

Isaac, with no larynx, couldn't cry out, but an eerie shriek emanated from his chest. He maneuvered around the cage door with one hand still in Gretch's hair and Gretch's mouth still locked on his thigh. He latched his teeth onto Gretch's right ear, and Gretch pirouetted across the small lab, crashing into walls and cabinets, flailing at the beast perched on his head and shoulders, working his hands in an effort to keep the ape from scratching out his eyes. He spun around by an open cabinet door, and its corner caught Isaac's head with a crack, loosening the animal's grip.

The momentary advantage gave Gretch a chance to reach for his Spyderco knife. He flipped it open and lunged up with his other hand, finding the ape's neck and jamming a thumb into its breathing hole. In another second he had sliced deep into Isaac's arm.

Isaac let go of Gretch and jumped to the counter, blood spewing from a slashed artery. He spit out a chunk of human flesh. Gretch, scratched and aching, felt for his own right ear and found the top of it missing. He'd brawled on more than a few occasions in his life and always prevailed, but this bonobo showed more fight than he'd ever seen. He cleared his throat and spit a stream of mucous and ape blood onto the floor. The bonobo, dazed from the fight and the rapid loss of fluid, began to rock on the counter, dozing off.

The fight had gone out of the beast and Gretch could have left it there to die, but he stepped forward and rapidly sank his sharp knife into the bonobo's torso, gutting it. He dumped the body—wet and twitching—into the sink.

In the bloodstained room, he cleaned his knife with soap and hot water. He studied his reflection in the stainless steel countertop and undertook a preliminary dressing of his wounds. Done, he washed the gore off his shoes, retied them and stepped into the main lab, where the bonobos looked upon him in silent awe. No life remained in what had been the twins' room, but tufts of human hair drifted like ghostly catamarans in puddles of blood.

12

After a couple of hours alone with Bea, Liane heard voices down the hall, echoing, angry. They were distorted by the strange acoustics of the rock, but she knew one of them must belong to Corey. A moment later he came in alone.

"What're you guys arguing over?"

"The movement's full of passionate people." Corey held out a hand toward Bea and watched her recoil from him. "When you concern yourself every day with life-and-death matters, tempers run high. We argue a lot."

"No offense, but Sarita sure seems hotheaded. Was she the other person doing the screaming?"

"What do you care?"

"I fear she values Bea more for what she stands for than for what she is. Have you reached any conclusions on Bea's status?"

Corey locked the door with a key, then sat on the couch, resting an ankle on his opposite thigh. The cloak of certainty he'd once worn appeared less solid to Liane now. He pulled at his lower lip with two fingers as he studied her.

"We've tried a lot of approaches over my years with FAULT," he said. "Letter-writing campaigns, protest marches, ads, lobbying, threats. And more serious things. Some of them work for a while. We raise a little money, irritate the system, occasionally get a regulation changed. But nothing creates a tipping point. The torture and killing go on as before."

"There's a place for humane research," Liane said.

"Humane? Don't tell me you're buying their arguments! All those product tests? They're all about determining toxicity levels. Manufacturers do them to limit their liability, not because they really need them to tell whether the oven cleanser causes harm to humans. They—quote unquote—sacrifice two hundred beagles and what happens? Their asses are covered and the product still gets on the shelf. A two-year-old kid decides to drink it and dies anyway, but the CEO can fend off the lawsuit and build a bigger second home for himself. It's nothing to do with protecting humanity or giving ordinary people a better life."

Liane sat on the edge of the bed, allowing Bea to groom her hair and fondle her earlobe. It tickled. Liane pushed her away.

"But who decides what makes a test legitimate?" she said. "That judgment can't fall to Corey Harrow. And to close down all animal research based on a few egregious examples seems equally wrong. What about all the good reasons people use animals for study—the new pharmaceuticals, medical implants, vital body parts like the heart valves from pigs. Not every client that uses Pentalon's services is trying to cover his tracks."

"Wrong again!" Corey exclaimed, uncrossing his legs and sitting forward. "You don't get it, Liane. People are so different from one another that I could pull a couple off the street and feed each a peanut and one would fall into anaphylactic shock while the other asked for more. So what good does it do to dissect a captive rat after feeding him a thousand pounds of peanuts? The rat shares way less DNA with us than two randomly selected humans. Have *you* worked on any project that provided direct human benefits?"

"No. But it takes years. I wasn't around long enough to draw any conclusions."

"Fair enough, but you might have asked that question before you got into this on the wrong side. It turns out that testing animals does no good statistically at all. One study found that they may as well flip a coin to determine drug side effects, that's how random the results are. It's a waste of time. Worse—a waste of life."

Liane stood and walked to the wall, thinking it over. Part of her wanted to agree; another part sought to defend her earlier choices.

"I can't dispute what you're saying chapter and verse, Corey, but there have to be reasons. If nobody pays Axel Flickinger, he doesn't do the things he does—at least not on the same scale. And all those scientists who dedicate their lives to animal tests...they can't all be wrong."

"Sure they can. The experts said the sun revolved around the earth until Galileo came along." He shook his head, leaned back on the futon. "They don't test on animals because they've had some deep insight. They test on animals because that's what they've always done—because *it's who they are!*"

"You don't even know them, Corey. Adnan Hammurabi is one of the smartest people I've ever met." She thought of Adnan and his disappearance.

"Yet, you wisely resisted him. Look what you've accomplished, Liane. You saved the life of a very special primate."

"A lot of good that's done her so far."

"C'mon. She's alive. She's loved."

"By me. Not by her own."

"She's better off than she'd be otherwise. We've taken a huge step in the right direction, thanks to you. I've learned over the years that we can't do it all at once." He massaged his eyebrows, ran his fingertips down his cheeks. "So many creatures have died for my failures."

Liane saw torment on his face. Was it true empathy for the animals, she wondered, or only pity for himself? She let that thought go.

"I can see how it would frustrate you," she said. "It's a gut check to think from the perspective of the animals. And there are thousands of them in labs."

"Many millions, actually."

"It was breaking my heart at Pentalon and I was so wrapped up I didn't even know it."

She walked back to Bea, who sat atop the bed with a quizzical expression on her face. She petted the bonobo's shoulder and attempted a reassuring look.

"*Moto bomo*," Bea said softly.

Corey whipped his head around. "What was that?"

"We think it must be a tribal language from her native land."

"Probably Lingala. That's the most common tongue in Congo." He choked up. "Holy Mother—I never thought I'd see this day."

They stared at one another, weighing the gravity of it all.

"Can you get her to do it again?"

Liane shook her head. "She only seems to talk when the moment strikes her. Maybe that's because I don't speak her language—I don't know."

"Like Nim Chimpsky! He'd only continue signing if the person responded with ASL." Corey's expression changed. He moved over a few inches and patted the couch. "Liane, will you sit with me?"

She decided to join him, and as the cushion yielded to her weight it tilted her close, so their knees touched. It was a funny feeling to Liane, one of vestigial intimacy.

"Is Sarita your girlfriend?"

"There's nothing formal, but yes. She's been my significant other for a while now, but we don't go for monogamy."

"She's attractive."

"No less than you."

"I'm sure if I came to know her better I'd warm to her."

Corey laughed. "She's an acquired taste. We all are around here."

"You didn't used to be." She touched his knee. "You were so calculating in the church."

"It wasn't personal. I have a job to do. Nothing can interfere with that."

"I once thought—it was silly," Liane said, "that you and I would stand in a church together, side by side, for a different purpose."

"The life I chose doesn't lend itself to a house in the suburbs with two and a half kids."

"I know that. This was before—before you changed so."

Their eyes met. He took her hand. "I don't feel that I changed, Liane, so much as I grew into myself. What about you? How'd you end up at an awful place like Pentalon?"

She had the old explanation, how her parents and her shrink had pushed it. But that didn't suffice now. In Corey's presence she saw it more clearly.

"It was penance, I guess, for having helped you."

"But why did you think you had to atone for that?"

"You murdered someone, Corey!"

He grimaced. "I can't argue that fact, technically speaking."

"That sounds so cold."

"Don't say that. You don't want to go there."

"Why not?" Liane said. "Fate has cast us together, put us in this place. Why can't you talk to me?"

"Because it involves a truth you don't wish to hear."

"How dare you presume that."

He looked at Bea. "You had an abortion without consulting me. Our baby, Liane."

"Oh, for God's sake." She rolled her eyes. "We were practically children."

"I was nearly a man. I thought myself one, anyhow. You took that away from me. I've thought about it a great deal since, why I'm so obsessed with protecting these animals. It has something to do with that, with what happened."

She nodded. "I understand. Shielding the vulnerable. I suppose it's the choice I've made now, too."

"You might still join the cause, you know. We could use you. You're closer to believing, aren't you?"

"I'm not such an easy case." She stared into the middle distance. "I see contradictions."

"Like what?"

"The exploitation of others in your own way, the manipulation, the harassment of scientists, physical threats, violence. You don't promote one life by devaluing another."

"The experimenters started it. We're just balancing the scales. It's not perfect." He shrugged. "Emerson called foolish consistency the hobgoblin of little minds."

"So I'm small-minded."

"I didn't say that." He paused and peered into their clasped hands. "I spend my days arguing, Liane. Let's make us the exception from now on."

He reached across and touched her arm, leaned over and kissed her on the lips. But for his scratchy beard, it felt natural, like an old routine coming back to her. She opened her mouth to receive his tongue, then thought of Mickey and pulled away.

"So what of Bea?" she asked.

"That ape's a chance to shift the paradigm. The movement needs her desperately. She's a gift to us from nature."

"What happened to her belonging to the world?"

"There you go with that foolish consistency again. The bottom line is that Bea will usher in a huge triumph for animal rights. You must see that. If you don't, well—we hold the cards now."

"I could expose you."

"I don't think you'd do that. And we'd remain a step ahead of you. I've avoided expert trackers all these years. A lab tech with a vendetta isn't going to bring me down."

She let go his hand, but he seized hers right back.

"There's another way," he said. "If you'd work with us, it'd make our task easier and Bea happier, no doubt. She's imprinted on you in some way. You could help teach her English, care for her."

"And then what?"

"I think you know. We'll go public with her. She'll change mankind's perception of the natural order more than any primate ever has."

Liane dropped Corey's hand for the second time, stood up and walked over to Bea, allowing the bonobo to climb into her arms. She tapped the plaster of the nearby wall, hearing no resonance from it, just dullness. The other side was solid rock.

13

The signal was faint but real as Gretch circled for a parking spot by the curb. Garage parking was out of the question. It generated records that investigators could later discover, as well as witnesses. He'd patiently and methodically used his transponder reader to comb the neighborhood where Sarita had disappeared. If prudence now called for a few more times around the block, he thought, so be it.

Gretch found a space by the Pierre Hotel and parallel parked. He checked the contents of his black fanny pack. It contained a handful of monkey chow, a leash and collar, zip ties, a nylon bag, miniature binoculars, a bottle of aspirin. There were also handcuffs, a 9 mm Glock automatic, a Swiss Army knife, a syringe of diazepam, and a Columbia River tactical knife. He zipped the fanny pack closed and strapped it on. He wore the automatic knife, as usual, at the small of his back, and a Kimber Ultra Carry .45 caliber in a shoulder holster under his jacket. The pistol, he knew, would stop a man and most animals with a single shot. Gretch enjoyed its hardness against his ribs.

Over one shoulder he carried a leather-wrapped case with a flexible antenna sewn into the strap. The case held his portable transponder reader. Thin knobs and toggles protruded from the sides, and through a window on one face he observed its activity.

The reader told him that 673B was close by. He desired more than anything to bring the ape back to Flickinger alive, but he also wanted to kill the girl and the FAULT operatives he figured were still helping her. If Vinson wasn't alone, he'd have to make quick work of things, using his firearm. But if circumstances warranted and her accomplices were few, he might employ a knife, kill silently. *There's nothing like the sound of a surprised body receiving the blade,* Gretch thought. *It's the sound of a person's worst dread rising to attainment.*

He touched the bandage on his left ear and traced his fingers to the scratches near his eye as he walked down East Sixty-First Street. There was no hiding his physical wounds, but those were the least of his thoughts. Chaos threatened. Killing the girl wouldn't fully restore order, but it might arrest the disintegration.

He paused on the corner to look at the monitor and surveyed the street. When the WALK sign glowed green, he strolled across Fifth Avenue and entered Central Park.

14

The sound of footsteps in the hall awakened Liane from a fitful sleep.

The door unlocked and Corey walked in with Sarita. Their entrance awakened Bea, who sat up groggily on the couch. Sarita went straight to Bea and threw the hood over her head. Bea protested meekly, and Sarita marched from the room with the bonobo in her arms. *Like a trophy,* Liane thought, shuddering.

She stood up and approached Corey. He wore the long hair, which now looked ridiculous to her.

"What's happening? You're going out?"

"I never stay anywhere too long. It's harder to hit a moving target."

"Where's she taking Bea?"

"Just feeding time."

"I could've done that."

"She's already attached to you. We need to broaden her horizons so she doesn't get too depressed when you're gone."

"So you'll win her over with food?"

"That's the easiest way."

"It's how the scientists do it."

He pulled at his beard while he studied her. "Have you decided whose side you're on?"

Coldness had returned to his eyes, as if donning the disguise also transformed something within. She wished she could find a way to reach his soul. For Bea's sake, of course, but other concerns surfaced. She had to find out about Mickey somehow, learn whether he was all right. And there was the matter of her mother and the last call home, which weighed on her more with each passing moment. If her mother were dying, she thought, she must go to her at all costs. And if she weren't dying, how would she know for sure without going?

"I don't have any loyalty to Pentalon," she told Corey. "It went away the second I saw what Axel did to Bea's brother."

"That's a start."

He still looked cross. She knew she needed his help, but she had so little leverage. She glanced down at her feet, still bare from bed, pulled at the flannel shirt she'd borrowed from the desk drawer. She unfastened two top buttons when he looked away, then reached for the watch she'd placed atop the desk while she slept, dropped it between them as if by accident and hastily bent over, fumbling with it for a long few seconds, feeling her breasts jiggle, giving him an irresistible chance to look.

As she stood Corey raked his eyes over her with the hunger of a wolf—more salaciously than Mickey ever had. She got on her toes and kissed him with an open mouth, putting out of mind the roughness of his beard. She thought she knew how a whore must feel, inhibition overcome by the need for something more tangible than sex. They were all prostitutes, weren't they—Bea the only innocent victim in a world where ends always justified means.

Corey's hand found her breast. She pressed herself closer to him, feeling the rising hardness of his groin. They fell to the bed. It was so easy when you willed it, she thought. But then a sharp rap came at the door. He flinched and stopped pawing her.

"What is it?"

"Corey!" It was Tara. "Sarita wants you!"

"In a minute!"

He pushed himself up and Liane hid her relief. She couldn't get Mickey out of her head. But she'd accomplished her immediate task, aiming an arrow and finding a chink in the armor. Corey's expression had softened.

"Wow," he said, straightening his hair, "just like old times."

"Corey," she said, desperate to drive that arrow home, "I've been meaning to ask how your parents are doing."

"Dead," he said flatly, "both dead. Pop went quick from a heart attack not long after the lab fire. My mother died in a car crash a few years ago. I missed both funerals."

"Remember my parents, Corey? My mom, Frank?"

"Sure."

"They're old now, you know. And my mother's real sick. I spoke to Frank yesterday. It seems she's on her deathbed."

"What is it?"

"Kidney disease. She's struggled with it for a long time."

"You should be with her."

"I can't."

"I told you you were free to go."

"I know. It's not that." She buttoned her shirt. "I feel like a bad daughter, wrapped up in my own dramas. But it's complicated now with all that's happened. I can't just drop in. Flickinger's looking over Frank's shoulder, I think, and the feds are definitely after me. I have to believe they're staking out my parents' house."

"I wouldn't doubt it. They followed my brother for years, hoping to stumble on me. They cling like fungus. But it's not you. It's the bonobo they want."

"You're not suggesting that I can just walk into their dragnet so long as I'm alone."

"No." He began to pace. "Once you're in that net they won't let you go until you've led them back to Bea. It gives me an idea, but I need to know for certain about you."

"Get me to my mother. If I escape the feds in one piece, and Bea remains safe, I'm on your side."

"You mean it?" He scratched his beard. "Maybe you always have been, Liane."

15

"What now, Papa?" Daniel said, looking up into Dikembe's face. "Where do we go?"

"That lollipop," said Dikembe. "You don't accept anything from a stranger like that without permission, boy. You know that."

"But he wasn't a stranger. Pierre was your friend."

"No. We did business once, that's all. He's not a good man."

"He seemed happy."

"Because he's prosperous, not because he's good."

"If he's so bad, then why did you deal with him, Papa?"

Dikembe stopped on the street and faced Daniel with his hands on his hips. "Why, indeed. I made a big mistake. I took something from nature, two bonobos, and not for our survival, only for money. Once I had them I sensed they were special too, not your average apes, but I kept on with it anyway. The decision weighs on me now and I'm unable to correct it."

"You still have the money?"

"Most of it. Yes. And some diamonds, too."

"Diamonds!"

"Shh. I took them as partial payment. What's here on my person is all the possessions we have, and it's a long way to our new life. We can't return to the village. Your brother and sister maybe can help us, but they're poor themselves and far away. They have their own families to feed."

He didn't mention his plan to find the Englishman. In the dust of Kinshasa it seemed like a distant hope.

"Let's go steal a chimp from that bad man," Daniel suggested. "We could set it free in the jungle. Wouldn't that help make it right?"

"Stealing is wrong. Nothing right comes from wrong. We'll go around here and find a place to stay for a few days. We'll eat and rest and build our energy. Then we'll leave the city for the bush. Okay?"

As they walked Dikembe saw the exhaustion in his son's face, perceived the dragging of his feet. He lifted his eyes to the towering modern buildings nearby, as far removed from his experience as the open ocean would be to a Bedouin. There was nothing for him there, he knew. But the expanse of nearby slums—battered tin lean-tos crowded against one another in endless swaths of mud and sewage—were also not an option. He decided to head north for the river.

When they could smell the water, they stopped at a food stand and made a snack of deep-fried palm grubs, white and creamy. Dikembe washed his down with Primus beer.

The coffee-colored river was broad and choppy under a growing overcast. They walked along the shore, passing rotted piers and the rusting hulks of beached barges. Daniel's eyes became wide. Then lightning flashed over the river. They felt the first drops as they neared a building with a battered hotel sign hanging by one corner. The sign twisted as the wind picked up and the squall descended upon them. Fat raindrops soaked them, and Dikembe danced through the puddles to put a smile on his son's face.

Soon they floated into the hotel lobby, riding the wave of their own laughter.

16

The old neighborhood didn't look any different, rows of Tudor cottages desperate to evoke a simpler time.

Frank's Lincoln was nowhere to be seen. Claudine's parked car rested by the curb.

Liane pulled to a stop across the street and surveyed her surroundings. The trees had leafed out, casting deep shadows under a glaring sun. She rolled down the window. It was the most scorching day of the year, humid, tropical, and so early—still May. *The bonobos at the zoo,* she thought, *should feel right at home.* But those in the climate-controlled lab wouldn't know the difference. They faced only another day of rationalized torture.

Liane glanced into the cage in the back seat of her borrowed car. When she looked up, the street was quiet, nothing moving but the rustle of leaves, no sound but the sharp call of a blue jay.

The unwieldy cage rocked as Liane crossed the street, her arms fatigued. She set it on the ground and rang the doorbell twice. When no one came, she tested the knob. It was open and she pushed in, walking first to the kitchen and setting the cage directly on the table. She thought to call out, but it felt wrong under the circumstances. The house was dead quiet except for the irregular ticking of air ducts and the wheezing of the sedated ape's soft respiration.

The door to her mother's room stood ajar. Inside, the curtains were drawn and a single bedside lamp glowed orange. Claudine sat in a chair, reading the Bible with a lighted magnifying glass.

"We thought you'd never make it," she whispered.

Liane studied her mother, eyes closed, face swollen, paler than pale. "Honestly? I'm surprised to be alive."

"You look it, too."

"Don't make me laugh. You'll only make me cry."

Claudine pointed with the magnifier. "She's very weak now."

"Is there a better time of day?"

"No. I'm sorry. She won't improve." She closed the Bible, kissed it.

Liane said, "Just to warn you: there's something large on the kitchen table."

Now, with no sign of the feds, Corey's whole scheme seemed unnecessary. Maybe, as Frank said, her paranoia had gotten the better of her. But she was here now; she'd needed the crutch.

"Don't be surprised by what's in there," she told Claudine, "but don't get too close either."

The nurse looked puzzled.

"And don't ask me to explain," Liane added.

"I'll leave you two alone. If anything happens that you can't handle, call me."

"Likewise."

The door closed, only the faint light cast by the lamp remaining. From a certain angle, it made her mother's face appear golden, ethereal, masking the paleness Liane had noticed just a minute ago.

She pulled the chair closer and sat with her knees touching the side of the bed. Her mother's chest appeared motionless. Liane stared, waiting for a breath. Waiting anxiously. Waiting. She was about to jump up and call Claudine when the movement came, slight, almost imperceptible. Liane had observed primates under deep anesthesia, their respiration suppressed. Her mother breathed even more shallowly.

Liane reached out and, without making contact, traced the side of her mother's face from temple to cheekbone to jaw to chin. She looked barely like herself now, the sodden flesh of her cheeks sagging to her earlobes. Yet her essence was there somewhere.

Her mother's closed eyelids, creased and flabby, had skin tags that

Liane had never observed closely before. *Another affliction of old age.* She was peering at them when the eyes opened, soft and rheumy and too tired to register surprise.

"You're here," her mother said.

Liane turned to her tote and removed a single fresh daisy. "It'll have to do, Mom. It was all I could carry." She laid it on the sheet over her mother's chest.

"More precious this way," her mother said. "May I have some water?"

Liane took a glass from the bedside table and extended its straw to her mother's lips. Her mother barely turned her head, sipped briefly, pushed the straw away with her tongue.

"I always thought a single flower held more beauty than the whole bouquet," she said. "You were my flower."

"I hope I still am, Mom."

Liane set down the glass and placed both palms on the pliant flesh of her mother's upper arms, leaned across and rested her head on her mother's chest, aware that she was crushing the flower between them in the process.

"Don't cry," her mother said. "The time for crying is past."

"No, it's not. It may never be."

She so wanted to tell her mother of her life these past days, of Bea and Mickey and Corey, of the insights she'd had and the ones that still eluded her. Perhaps her mother should know about her departure from the straight and narrow, about how right it felt in spite of everything. But this moment didn't belong to Liane.

Her mother swallowed heavily—Liane could feel it through her chest. The woman didn't need to hear about talking bonobos, she thought. She didn't need to know of the dangers that still sought her only child.

"I made mistakes," her mother said.

"What mistakes?"

"Too many to mention."

"Then don't."

"I want you to know that every minute of it, even before you were born—" she swallowed "—it was you who were in my heart."

"Thank you, Mom." Liane felt the wetness of her own tears, soaking the sheet.

"I hope I didn't ever push you to do anything you didn't really want."

Liane couldn't help thinking of Pentalon. "It all works out in the end," she said. "I'm dating a new guy."

"It's nice to have men around. They make us feel less imperfect." She closed her eyes for a moment, opened them. "Frank loves you."

Liane sat up and took her mother's forearms in both hands. "Why do you say that now?"

"Because he does. Because he's a man of a certain generation. Because he can't say it himself, not in words."

"I'm sure he does. In his own fashion."

"Understand something: He didn't take your father away. Your father did that all by himself."

"I know, Mom. I do."

"When I'm gone," her mother said, "I want you to love Frank like a father."

"Haven't I?"

"Never. Will you now?"

Liane hesitated, knowing it was true. She forced herself to agree.

Her mother smiled faintly and closed her eyes for a long moment.

When she reopened them, she seemed focused on something in the room but not of it, as if she could see a faraway place through an invisible hole in the air. "It's dark," she said. "Why's it so dark?"

"The curtains are drawn. It's really daytime out there."

"They close them because—" she swallowed "—the light hurts. Everything does."

Liane caressed her mother's arm. The loose skin bunched at her fingertips.

"More water?"

Her mother shook her head. "Open the curtains, Liane."

"But you said it hurts."

Her mother emitted a long, deep sigh. It came from a place Liane didn't know. It scared her.

She rose. "I'll get Claudine."

"No!" Not loud, but emphatic. "Please, no. She's an expert. But she's not who I want now. Open the drapes."

"If you're sure, Mom."

Liane pulled them aside a few inches, allowing a shaft of white light into the room. It stung her own puffy eyes.

"More," her mother said. "All the way."

She grabbed each side of the curtains and threw them wide. The harsh sun poured in.

"Ooh," her mother said. "So bright."

"Should I close them again?"

"No," softly, "the pain means"—she licked her parched lips—"I'm still alive."

"Is there anything else I can do for you while I'm up, Mom?"

"Yes, my sweetheart, my love. Come to me."

It sounded like an urgent plea. Liane stepped quickly to her mother's bedside. She slid her palms up her mother's forearms, their hands nesting in the crook of one another's elbows. Her mother squeezed her there and Liane returned the pressure. Their faces were a foot apart. She would have heard the quietest whisper, but there were no more words, just the relaxation of her mother's face into a smile as subtle as the Mona Lisa's.

When the last long sigh came, she felt it as much as heard it.

"Mom?" Liane called softly. "Mom?"

She brushed the gray hairs from her mother's forehead, touched her cooling cheek with the flat backs of her fingers, searched the flaccid face. When her back began to ache she let go, stood, and kissed her mother on the temples, the lips, the eyelids. She knew it was her last chance. Her tears dripped on her mother's waxy cheek, and she wiped them away with a thumb before they ran into the pillow.

The light had changed. The sun floated lower in the sky. Liane looked at the clock. She'd been in the room for more than three hours.

She went to the window. Down in the yard, something moved in the bushes.

17

Gretch roamed Central Park and settled with satisfaction on a bench on the Mall. As he adjusted his reader, the phone rang. It was Flickinger.

"Any luck, Mr. Gretch?"

"When it happens, luck will have nothing to do with it."

"That was quite a mess you made of my bonobo, yes?"

"Damned thing attacked me."

"I had plans for that beast and you ruined them. When plans go awry, Mr. Gretch, people get hurt, money is lost."

Gretch started to tell him about the ear then thought better of it. Flickinger, he knew, didn't care about collateral damage to the paid help, except to the extent it inconvenienced him. Gretch wanted no one's sympathy, anyway.

"I trust you didn't have to mop it up yourself," he said.

"No, no," Flickinger assured him. "One of our associates handled it. The concerns I have lie elsewhere."

"No doubt." A pigeon landed on the bench next to Gretch. He swatted it away. "I'm closing in on them. We'll contain the situation."

"But I am not speaking of the bonobo or the girl. There is the other consideration. A matter I thought was settled."

"Is it something else you need me to do?"

"Something you failed to do. I had two fund-raisers to attend last night: a Republican governor in the Midwest and a Democrat senator in Washington."

"You hit them both in one night?"

"I used the jet. The point is that I ran into a few old allies and began to put some pieces together. The puzzle is incomplete, but one thing seems certain: Our Arab friend is still out there, plotting against us."

"Oh, that." Gretch sensed a headache coming on. "Do you know where he is?"

"I know where he is not."

"Yeah. I missed my shot."

"Then lied to me."

"I didn't want to worry you unnecessarily. I thought I'd get to it before the bill came due."

"You thought wrong. You are zero for two, Mr. Gretch. Even the bonobo nearly got the better of you."

"But I'm still alive, Axel. And your precious little chimp's marked for the incinerator."

"He claimed his pound of flesh, but it is the others who will cause us bigger problems."

"And we'll settle that preemptively if you'd let me go."

"Sadly, the chance for preemption has passed. Chaos is closing in. Do you fear it?"

"Damned right I do."

"It's closer than you think."

"I have two jobs in front of me, that's all. When I finish here, I'll jump straight away on the next one."

"It is all a write-off at this point." Flickinger sighed. "We have to cut our losses now, yes?"

Gretch pocketed the phone and ran his fingers through his scalp. He'd rubbed in a salve before he left the car, but it still hurt where the ape had yanked out his hair—hurt so much outside his skull that he felt the pain inside, too. He pulled three aspirins from his fanny pack and swallowed them without water. They tasted sour. He rose from the bench, checked his monitor, and followed the signal south.

18

Her eyes were dry by the time Liane emerged from her mother's room. Dry and achy. Salt puckered the back of her throat. She went to find Claudine.

Frank was with her. They appeared startled, as if they'd only now discovered the bonobo dozing in its cage on the table. With a glance at Liane's face, Frank sensed that the long-dreaded moment had arrived. His mouth went slack.

"No," he said, "not yet."

He looked ancient, desiccated. Liane nodded her head.

"No," Frank repeated, his face sinking into a frown. "I'm not ready."

He rushed toward the bedroom as if time yet mattered.

"Ah, precious!" Claudine exclaimed, extending her arms to embrace Liane. "I'm sorry."

A knock came from somewhere, followed by a sense of motion, at first unseen. Then they descended on her, a sea of black windbreakers, strangers in surgical masks and goggles armed with pistols and official identifications. Two of them went right for the cage. Claudine released Liane as a man wearing glasses and a sports jacket stepped forward.

"Liane Vinson?" he said through his mask. "You're under arrest."

19

Depleted of all emotion, she slid calmly into the back seat of the unmarked sedan. She remained calm for the ride into the city with the misery lights reflecting off the cars around them, calm, too, for the elevator ride to a high floor in a downtown office building.

It was seeing Mickey in restraints that unhinged her.

"Liane!" he blurted. "Thank God!"

An agent in a suit led her to a hard chair next to Mickey, and they sat and cried together in shared relief and sadness and joy.

"Cue the tearful reunion," said Pulsipher, rolling his eyes. He'd introduced himself to Liane at her mother's house, during the arrest. She'd watched him carefully then—his studied cynicism, his elevated attentiveness—but now someone else had her focus.

"Mickey," she said, "your face."

"Aw, what? The jaw? It feels better already."

It was mottled black-and-yellow on one side.

"They beat you up?"

"Just one punch. At least, that's all I remember."

"It's my fault."

"Hell, we're in this thing together now, ain't we?"

The office, sparsely furnished, featured fluorescent lighting and floor-to-ceiling windows with a view of New York Harbor. Ellis Island and the Statue of Liberty floated majestically amid scattered whitecaps. As Liane examined her new surroundings, an agent wearing a surgical mask carried in the cage and set it down on the carpeted floor.

"Bea! Holy shit!" Mickey said. "So the jig's really up."

"Yes," Liane said, searching for words, "—my mother…"

"No!" Mickey groaned, reading her face.

"I was there at home. That's how they got me—or, us."

"I'm damned sorry."

"Thanks."

"Fucking tragic couple of days, to go through all this and have it come to nothin'."

Pulsipher strode across the empty room, taking charge. He ordered everyone to leave. "Send in the doc," he said to the last guy.

"You're in for one more surprise," Mickey whispered to Liane. "Your old friend."

Liane didn't get it until Hammurabi entered. A surgical mask covered half his face, but she'd have recognized him anywhere.

"Is it necessary," he said to Pulsipher, "for this woman to be hand-cuffed?"

"That's the procedure." Pulsipher shrugged.

"*I* will vouch for her," said Hammurabi.

"What? Like you did before? Let's stick with our objective here, shall we? What's your assessment of the bonobo?"

Hammurabi ignored Pulsipher and turned to Liane. "Hello," he said, "so nice to see you again. Though, the circumstances…" He threw up his hands and the surgical mask puckered, suggesting that a sheepish smile had spread beneath it.

Liane gasped, at a loss for words

"Yes," said Hammurabi, reading her mind. "A long story, filled with many apologies to you, when I have a chance to tell it. You made the right decision." He nodded toward the cage.

Pulsipher stepped between them. "Dr. Hammurabi, the ape needs to be moved from here posthaste. You know that as well as anyone. Can we please get on with it?"

Liane set her jaw and looked out the window. A barge glided below, pushed by a tugboat toward open water. From afar, the harbor appeared peaceful, the whitecaps like brushstrokes, almost poetic.

Hammurabi pulled a pair of rubber gloves from his pocket and handled the padlocked cage-door latch. "Open it, please."

"Uh-uh," replied Pulsipher. "Back at the secure lab only."

"But I can hardly undertake a proper examination without touching the animal."

"Understood," said Pulsipher. "You're covered. Now no one's going to impugn your judgment. But the ape doesn't leave the cage and that's the way it has to be. Just give us a preliminary opinion and we'll get her out of here."

Hammurabi leaned toward the cage. The bonobo, awake, followed him with her eyes.

"Has she said anything?"

"Not in our custody," said Pulsipher. "She was asleep at first. Then, well...you're sure this thing's legit?"

"Of course I am. They don't chatter on like Alvin's bloody chipmunks. The speech comes in fits and starts, as it might for a toddler." He peered into the cage. "Her hair's the right color, and the hazel eyes... the complexion. Her face looks a little different than I remember it. The snout's a bit longer. But it must be her, yes. She's grown since I left her." He straightened up. "She looks healthy."

"Okay, good," said Pulsipher. He opened a door and summoned two of the agents. One of them lifted the cage off the floor and marched from the room.

Liane hesitated, then cried out, "Don't be afraid, Bea!"

Pulsipher pulled off his mask, as did Hammurabi. The agent stepped toward Liane.

"I understand why you took the bonobo from that lab," he said, "and why you thought you had to run—from Pentalon, even from us. Tell me what made you come in from the cold today."

"You can't be that dense," Mickey exclaimed. "Her mother was *dying*, for cryin' out loud."

"But she brought the ape with her. She didn't have to." He turned back to Liane. "You knew we'd be watching, yet you brought the bonobo."

"What was I going to do? Mickey was gone. Who would I leave her with?"

"Before you came, where were you?"

"What difference does it make?"

"I decide what makes a difference. Where were you?"

"Around and about. I rented a room."

"There'll be a paper trail."

"I paid cash, used a false name."

"You got an address?"

Liane shook her head. "I forget. The stress..."

"Fine. Not that important at this juncture." Pulsipher paced across the room and back. "So, why not leave the ape there while you visited your mother?"

"I couldn't. They panic when left alone, pull their hair out, won't eat. And if anything happened to me on the way, Bea would starve to death."

"You're holding back. There's more to it than that."

Liane shook her head again. "You're right," she conceded, "there's something else. The more I thought of my mother, the more I doubted the course I'd chosen. She had kidney disease and they couldn't find a replacement. I watched her suffer for a long time—not even so much the physical consequences, but the psychological, not knowing when or how it would end. I know that there're scientists doing animal research for transplants. When I realized they could save someone like my mother one day, it gave me a change of heart."

The civilians stared at Pulsipher, who stood with one arm crossed and his chin in his palm. He nodded.

Liane looked into her hands. The metal cuffs weighed on her wrists, and her fingernails needed polishing. Her mind went to Flickinger, impeccable in every way. How could she have thought she was a match for him?

Pulsipher sank his fists into his jacket pockets. "You're lying," he concluded, "but I'm going to let you two go."

"That's good," Hammurabi said without disguising his relief. "It's the right thing."

"Pentalon won't press charges," Pulsipher said. "And my department doesn't want the publicity of an arrest and trial, either, considering what we're dealing with. So I can't hold you."

He opened Liane's handcuffs with a key, then pulled small wire cutters from his jacket pocket and snipped Mickey's plastic zip ties.

"There's a doctor in the next room who'll examine each of you. Then you can be on your way."

"You're shittin' me," Mickey said, standing stiffly.

"Understand something," said Pulsipher. "You'd best forget any of this happened. We'll clean it up. By tomorrow, no one will find a trace."

"You'll clean it up?" said Liane.

"It's what we do. Any attempt to resurrect this, and you'll be marginalized as crazies, like all the other conspiracy theorists running around this country, inhabiting fringe websites."

"Can you assure me that no harm will come to Bea?" Liane flexed her wrists.

"I'm not obligated to assure you of anything. But to the extent I know what the bonobo's in for, I can say that she'll be studied, not harmed."

At the door, Pulsipher paused uncomfortably. "Listen," he said to Liane, "with regard to the thing at home: I'm sorry for your loss."

After the examinations, they emerged into a lobby with an empty reception desk. Hammurabi awaited them, holding Liane's tote.

"The feds forgot to give you this."

"Thank you."

"It's for the best, you know." Hammurabi glowed as if they'd won a prize.

Liane glared.

She was still processing the toll—who was alive and who dead; who was missing and who was accounted for. She took Mickey's hand and they left her former boss standing in the lobby. For once, she thought, she knew something that Hammurabi didn't.

20

It was late at night when they emerged onto West Street in lower Manhattan.

"Phew!" Mickey sighed, stopping by a street vendor. "Buy you a pretzel?"

Liane nodded. "Light salt."

They stood there a minute, chewing.

Mickey rotated his arms from the shoulder in wide circles, then twist-stretched his torso. "I feel like a sadist's ragdoll. Hard to believe what we've gone through. And then it's over, just like that."

They began walking down the street.

"Those cats been out on their own for a week, eight days," Mickey said. "How long?"

"Poor things. It's bound to be a while yet."

"I feel terrible about your mother, too. How're you holding up? You want a shoulder?"

"I'm sure I will later, but there's more work to be done."

"Yeah. That apartment of yours, for one thing. I can help clean it up. Anything big, I know a guy. We'll get on top of it in no time."

"Not right away, Mick."

They turned onto Warren Street. Traffic was unusually light. A few cars rushed by.

"You believe that guy Hammurabi?" Mickey continued. "I mean, all due respect to your prior relationship, but what an asshole. First time I saw him, I threatened to throttle him. But my hands were tied at the time."

"Well, I'm glad you didn't go through with that idea. I don't want you in jail, and we may still need him."

"You're not thinking of going back to work for him!"

"No. Nothing like that."

She took his hand as the Parks Department van pulled to a screeching halt beside them. Tara and Pattie leaped out. Tara went for Mickey.

"What the—" he said.

She lifted him off the ground with a bear hug just as Pattie threw open the rear doors. They dumped him inside and Liane followed on her own.

The doors closed and they peeled away.

Pattie tossed back a towel and Liane held it to a cut that had formed on Mickey's temple. She removed it, looked at the smear of blood there, applied pressure again.

"What the hell just happened, Liane?"

"Looks like you rapped your head on the van door. You could say you were kidnapped. It gives you deniability."

"For what?"

"These women are from FAULT—and not the division that sells bumper stickers. I've been with them the past two days. They abducted me for real when I escaped the compactor."

"Sorry about the head," said Tara, looking back.

"It's not so bad," Liane said, "is it, Mickey?"

"Oh, it's just peachy."

"We had to act fast. We never know who could be following us," Pattie said, looking into the side-view mirror. "Hey, what happened to your hands?"

Mickey pushed the towel away and opened his palms. "You talking about the wrists? That was from the zip ties they had me in. The other's burns from the cable. Presumably Liane told you about that."

"No." They shook their heads.

"Figures," Mickey said, "all that trouble and no credit. I cut my arm, too. See here?"

"Shh," Tara said. She turned up the radio.

"I'm not gonna shush," Mickey said, raising his voice. "My friend here has some explaining to do. All of you owe me an explanation, in fact."

"I said, shut up!" Tara said, twisting the knob again.

She had on an all-news station. They were doing traffic and weather.

"I'm not gonna shut up!" Mickey shouted.

"This guy's beginning to bug me," Pattie said.

"You people have some fucking nerve!" Mickey shouted. "I'm not gonna shut up until I get some answers. What the hell is going on? Where are we headed? Why are we in this van?"

Liane began to answer, but too late. Pattie slammed the brakes and the two women converged on Mickey, hastily wrapping his wrists and feet in duct tape and slapping a strip across his mouth.

"No way!" Liane bellowed, reaching toward the tape on Mickey's face.

"Touch it and you get the same!" Pattie yelled, pulling the van into DRIVE.

Tara twisted the knob yet again, the radio now blaring. It was just past the top of the hour, the announcer halfway through the headlines.

"*In local news, three dead in a shooting in the Bronx. Mixed reaction to the mayor's windmill plan. First heat wave of the season continues. And a visiting primate goes missing from Central Park Zoo. More after these messages.*"

Tara turned it down. "Word's out."

A look of confusion glazed Mickey's eyes.

Liane peeled the tape from his mouth. "So you see?"

"Not exactly."

The van pulled to a stop. Tara stepped into the back with a razor blade and cut Mickey free.

21

The cave buzzed with energy, like a castle under siege. Tara led them into a room Liane hadn't seen before, spare as the others, with a stainless steel examination table in the center. Bea sat atop it, Corey standing nearby. Sarita held up a hypodermic needle.

"What the hell are you doing?" Liane said.

"You pulled it off!" Corey exclaimed. "And I take it this here's the guy who's been helping you out."

Liane made perfunctory introductions. Sarita tapped the syringe to get the bubbles out.

"I asked what you're doing to Bea," Liane said.

"What we should've done Day One," said Corey, "if we hadn't been so caught up."

Tara and Pattie crowded Mickey and Liane as Corey wrapped his arms around the bonobo, holding her down.

"No!" said Liane.

"No, no," said Bea, shaking her head. "No."

"Did I hear what I think I heard?" asked Mickey.

"Come now," Sarita said to Bea. "This won't hurt a bit."

She lowered the needle to a shaved spot by Bea's left shoulder blade as Corey tightened his embrace.

"Ouch," said Bea as the point penetrated several times. She opened her mouth and clicked her teeth, just missing Corey's nose.

"Lidocaine," Mickey observed. "It'll just burn for a second."

Sarita set down the syringe and soaked a square of gauze in alcohol. She wiped the area and picked up a scalpel.

Liane stepped forward, but Tara barred her with an arm.

"You have no right—"

"Oh, hush!" Sarita said. "It's for her own good."

Corey held Bea still as Sarita made a shallow inch-long incision. She dabbed up the blood with gauze and pressed it there while she picked up tweezers. A moment later she extracted a square integrated circuit the size of a quarter. She dropped it into a surgical bowl with a clink.

"Pattie," Corey said, "pass her the suture kit."

"She a vet?" Mickey interrupted.

"No. She was a vet tech once, though."

"Not for nothing, but the way she holds the scalpel, I can tell. Why don't I do that? I've had a lot more practice."

Corey and Sarita looked at each other.

"You don't want her to scar," Mickey added.

"Okay," Corey shrugged.

Sarita stepped back.

Mickey laid a hand on Bea's thigh. "How ya doin', kid?"

He splashed some alcohol on his hands, pulled the plastic sealer off the suture kit, threaded the needle and went to work. He was finished in ten minutes.

"See," Sarita said to Bea, "that wasn't so bad."

"Bad," Bea echoed. "So bad."

Mickey took surgical scissors and cut two pieces of adhesive tape into butterflies. He positioned them over the stitched incision. "All better," he said, as Corey released Bea. The ape looked around, felt for the wound behind her back, jumped down and clambered into Liane's arms, whining.

Corey lifted the wafer from the bowl, wiped it clean and displayed it. "An advanced, extended-capability, active RFID tag."

"RFID?" Mickey said.

"All the primates at Pentalon have them. Radio Frequency Identification, like the things they use at Wal-Mart to track inventory, only this one's souped up."

"I had no idea," Liane said.

"The middlemen put them in before Pentalon takes possession," Corey explained. "The wound heals fast in the young animals. Once the hair's grown back, you'd really have to be looking for these chips to find them. But with a proper reading device, that's another thing altogether. They're like transponders."

"So Flickinger can know where the animals are at all times," Mickey pondered.

"Not completely," said Corey. "They can't be read through deep rock, which is why I let this slip until now. Plus, there are limits to the range. Used to be, the passive ones could only be picked up from very close, no more than a few hundred meters under optimal conditions. The active ones, though, have a tiny battery built in, giving them a range up to ten times that. The advanced models, with *extended* capability—who can guess? They improve all the time, and knowing the way Pentalon does business, I'd suspect this item's best in class. I wouldn't be surprised if the cutting-edge RFIDs, tracked with a powerful reader, can be located from many miles away out in the open. If you know the frequency."

"Liane," Bea said, "hungry."

"Get the ape some chow," Corey told Tara.

Liane watched Tara leave the room. "When did Bea start speaking like this?"

"Only this morning," Sarita said, "when I went in to check on her. She seems to be picking up English fast, though. No full sentences, but still pretty remarkable."

"So, if I can jump in here for a second," Mickey said, turning to Liane. "The bonobo that you brought to your mother's house, that the feds now have...that was, like, Bea's double, stolen from the zoo?"

"Not quite," Liane said. "There are three youngsters next door in the troop that's visiting from Milwaukee. One of them looked kind of like Bea. We were lucky that she had the right complexion, but we had to dye the hair and put colored contacts in her eyes."

"And all that business in the office building—you calling out to the bonobo, using the name Bea, acting like you cared about her?"

"That was—pretend," Liane said. "Fortunately for us, Hammurabi couldn't get too close for his examination."

"Hmm," said Mickey. "You also had me fooled with that act. Hammurabi said he noticed the face was different, then shrugged it off. I guess he was inclined to believe what he wanted. After a thorough examination, though, the feds'll be pissed and we're back on the treadmill."

"All we need's adequate time to get this ape the publicity she deserves," Corey said. "We've just enough window to refine the plan, then it'll be too late for the government guys to act first."

"Hold it there, pal." Mickey raised a palm. "I never said I was part of this."

Corey wheeled on Liane. "What the fuck? You didn't check with him?"

22

The aspirin hadn't helped much. Gretch's head pounded harder with each step toward his goal. He blamed the stress, blamed Flickinger. Trouble was bound to follow the talking apes, and now they had trouble in spades. Not just the string of profitable quarters at risk, Gretch suspected, but the survival of Pentalon itself and the balance of power that it had been Gretch's job to maintain.

He crossed the East Drive, dodging taxis and bicycles in the dark, peered down into the screen of his reader. The signal was much stronger than it had been on the Mall. He looked around to get his bearings, noticed the wire mesh of an aviary stretching above the stockade fence and the trees. *The zoo. Of course!*

Gretch walked more deliberately now, one eye ahead, the other on his monitor. The signal had grown stronger than ever.

23

"So you volunteered me for this?"

They were locked in the room, awaiting Corey's judgment.

"Not specifically," Liane said. "I didn't think you'd appreciate being abandoned twice, though."

"I'm overcome. That's just so courteous of you!"

"Nobody's twisting your arm to do anything, Mick. You can split if you want."

"And you?"

"I have to stay close to Bea."

"If I were to leave—not saying I'm gonna—why would Corey let me go? I could easily turn him in to the police."

"I don't think he *will* let you go right now, but I overheard them suggesting they'll abandon this cave pretty soon. When they do, you can flee back to your place."

Mickey probed his bruised jaw with his fingers. "The swelling's gone down," he said. "My place is with you."

"Since when?"

"I've known since the beginning."

She took his hands, kissed the burn marks on his palms, then rose to his jaw, his lips. "How does the battered body feel?"

"Better for your kisses, though you missed a few spots. What happens to Bea?"

"I promised Corey, if he helped me get back to my mother, that I'd give him a hand in return. He thinks I'm with them now."

"Are you?"

"It all depends. Bea's the one caught in the middle of all this."

"She's not caught in the middle, Liane. She is the middle."

"The redhead, Sarita—Corey's girlfriend?—has taken a proprietary interest in her. It gives me a bad feeling. Maybe we can try to influence these guys."

"They're ideologues, Liane. Good luck with that." He looked around the room, tested the locked door. "But, hell, we've come this far. I haven't broken any bones yet."

They kissed again and Liane thought of her session alone with Corey just yesterday morning. It made her blush. When they pulled away, she saw that Mickey noticed. He was about to say something when they heard the latch thrown.

The oak door swung open. "You two," said Tara, "into the meeting room."

They followed her down to the end of the hall, to a damp chamber roughly hewn from the rock. Bare light bulbs in rusted cages were the only illumination. Warped doors laid horizontal over cinderblocks formed a kind of conference table, and log benches made the seats. A whiteboard hung at one end, words scrawled in red block letters:

UNYIELDING COMMITMENT

RIGHTS NOT WELFARE

OVERCOMING DISTINCTIONS

The room filled quickly, some familiar faces and others unknown to Liane. Seats were claimed and bodies pressed forward along the cool walls. Mickey and Liane stood in a corner, uncomfortable sitting. Corey fronted the whiteboard, ardor showing in his face. He looked like a union organizer from the days of Samuel Gompers, Liane thought. Passion incarnate.

Sarita marched in with Bea on a short leash. She settled next to Corey. Bea crouched on the table with eyes darting among the strange faces. She recognized Mickey and Liane, straightened to go toward them, and met the resistance of the collar. Liane took a step forward and Mickey tugged her back.

"Folks," Corey began, holding up a fist, "since the founding of this organization thirty years ago, we've claimed to speak for the animals, who can't speak for themselves. We never wavered. We know where the truth lies, that animals have as much right to live free as humans do. But there were limits to our voice."

"No more!" Sarita shouted, and the room erupted in a cheer.

"The scientists keep moving the goalposts," Corey said, holding up his hands. "They argue that animals don't use tools, and then we learn that they do. So they say animals can't reason the way humans do, and we learn that's untrue also, that some animals will even lie like humans to get what they want. The scientists move the goal again. They say animals act only for themselves, never for the group. And then we learn that some species demonstrate altruism. They argue that it's speech that makes us unique, and when we give them the parrot Alex speaking a hundred words, the chimps Washo and Nim Chimpsky using sign language, and others, they tell us that doesn't count; those animals aren't *really* speaking."

"Boo!" someone shouted from the back. "Open their eyes!"

Bea looked at Liane, then clambered into Sarita's arms.

"Open their eyes we *will!*" Corey pounded the table. "They now tell us animals don't have souls, they don't contemplate their own condition. One day soon, we will ask this bonobo, the first who can speak for herself. We'll have our answer. And they, people, *they* will have theirs!"

The group cheered. Mickey, hands resting on the wall behind his back, shuffled his feet. Liane looked at Corey and Sarita. The FAULT leaders glowed triumphantly.

"It could very well be," Corey said, "that pigs will never speak for themselves. That puppies and rats and rabbits will never give voice to their thoughts, their desires, their pain. But this bonobo will! No more primates behind fences and the high walls of torture chambers. The walls, folks, will soon be breached!"

A cheer went up again.

"They tried to keep us down," Corey continued. "When we exposed them, they pushed us away. When we pushed back, they drove us underground. No more! Very soon we break to the surface again. Not to speak for the animals, but to let this animal speak for herself!"

The group erupted again then settled down as Sarita set Bea on a log and stepped forward.

"But we do it," she said, "as we always have. With careful planning. With unrelenting discipline. Let's not kid ourselves, folks. There are forces on the move, allied against us. The scientists, industry, the governments of the world—all are our enemies. They want Corey dead or behind bars. They want me, they want all of you."

"They won't get us!"

"They haven't and they won't! Why? Because we match their cruelty with our compassion. Their wish to be left alone with our right to protest. And their so-called scientific methods with our methods of disruption!" She paused to survey the crowd. "When we abandon this hideout, we'll leave not out of weakness but out of strength. An hour from now this cave will be empty, but only because the next phase begins, when we take the fight to our enemies!"

Sarita extended her index finger and raked it in the air across every face before her.

"We have prepared for a long time," she said. "What we do soon will make our prior acts seem minor skirmishes in comparison. Beginning next week, the experimenters won't feel safe at work or on their way to work. They won't feel safe at home. For sixty days, their labs will burn, their cars, their homes. Their infrastructure of death will crumble. And this time, it won't be so easily rebuilt."

"What about the ape?!" someone called out.

"The ape," Corey said, as Sarita took Bea in her arms again. "The bonobo! Sarita goes off in secret for the next two months and teaches her to say what we need said. When the last fire's still smoldering—while it's fresh in their minds and we have everyone's attention—she begins a tour that would make any publicist envious. On television, the

Internet, newspapers, magazines. The voice, folks, rises to clarity at last. The voice of the animals!"

"More violence?" Mickey whispered, leaning in to Liane as the group ended with a final chant.

"It's the first I'm hearing of it," she said.

As the meeting broke up, she and Mickey approached Corey and Sarita.

"We can't talk," Sarita said. "We gotta go."

"But what about me?" Liane asked Corey. "Where do I fit into things? What about us?"

By *us* she meant Mickey and her, but Corey lifted an eyebrow. "There is no us," he said, "only the cause."

"You people are gonna blow up a bunch of labs?" Mickey exclaimed. "You've got this beautiful creature in your possession and the prelude is a spasm of destruction?"

"Not a spasm," Corey said. "This will be carefully orchestrated."

"And what about Bea?" Liane said. "She's just another instrument of yours?"

Sarita pulled Corey's shoulder so he faced her. "I thought you said they were with us."

"I did. They are."

"This business of Sarita going into seclusion with Bea," Liane persisted. "What's that about?"

"We have to split up for safety's sake. Sarita will reach out if she needs help."

"Corey!" Sarita protested. "That was never the plan."

"You could use the assistance. We can't handle her alone."

"I don't trust her." Sarita threw her chin at Liane. "She's too close to the bonobo. She doesn't see the big picture."

Corey looked from Sarita to Liane. "We only have a few minutes," he said. "Sarita and I need to step away and hash this out."

"Can you leave Bea with us?" Liane asked.

Corey put his hands on his hips, exasperated. "Sure," he said. "But, just in case, I'm locking the door. Wait here."

"Wait here? Where are we gonna go with the door locked?" Mickey pushed his chest forward.

Corey narrowed his eyes and stalked from the room with Sarita in tow. The door slammed.

They listened for the throw of the latch.

24

Fog rolled off the Congo River their first morning in Kinshasa—fog so thick that it obscured the near shore and lay its foul breath in the hotel lobby. Dikembe and Daniel put the river behind them and walked back toward the city center, stopping along the way for a breakfast of rice and fried bananas and oily smoked fish. By the time they arrived at the market, a hot sun had chased away all droplets of water. Its white heat pounded the teeming city, distending the air and the mosquitoes.

Dikembe and Daniel returned to Pierre's shop. The rail-thin girl was out front, shooing flies from cuts of antelope meat. In one corner, a small crocodile thrashed against the short chain that fixed a hind leg to a bolt in the wall. Dikembe nodded to the girl and proceeded straight toward the back. He was pushing aside the beaded curtain when the girl said, "He's not there."

"When does he come?"

"Don't know. Soon."

"We'll wait."

They sat quietly, gazing around. The cages were empty save for a pair of gray parrots and a baby gorilla. The parrots squawked without warning, startling the visitors. The gorilla restlessly paced its small cage, glaring at them from the shadow of a prominent brow ridge. The air was unmoving, musty. The gorilla paced for an hour, paused, squatted and urinated, resumed its aimless activity.

"You'd think he'd tire himself out," Daniel said.

"He's newly captured," Dikembe said. "His mother probably was killed. He doesn't know what to do about his lost freedom. Eventually, he has to sleep. When he awakes he will show even more distress, maybe panic, throw himself against the cage."

"What will happen to him?"

"He can't survive outside without his mother."

They waited another hour or two. The girl entered, eyed them, scratched a hip through her thin dress. "He's not coming," she said.

"How do you know?"

"When he doesn't come by now he's not coming."

"I'll leave a note," Dikembe told the girl reluctantly. He stood and reached across the desk for pencil and paper. His school learning was rudimentary. He wrote:

> *If you find old bonobo twins,*
> *you reach me, please, at Landmarq Hotel,*
> *Kinshasa, Room 405.*
> *If not, I buy new bonobos.*

He set the pencil down atop the paper and guided Daniel from the shop by the back of his neck.

They returned to the hotel room in the late afternoon and lolled on soiled mattresses. Flies buzzed in circles around the slow-moving ceiling fan. Daniel fell asleep. Dikembe stared at the bubbling plaster of the ceiling, thinking that their trip to Kinshasa had been a foolish errand, born of romanticism. They'd purchase supplies tomorrow morning, he thought, and look into catching a boat upriver as soon as possible.

He fell asleep dreaming of the river, of trips he'd taken with his dugout. Once, in the middle of a swamp, a storm arose suddenly and he'd gotten caught in the mangrove roots, nearly capsizing. He could feel it in his dream, the eerie flirtation with that tipping point, and he stretched an arm to hold onto the high side of the boat. But in his dream the angle of the boat became impossible to rectify. He lost the battle and found himself falling. Only the crack of his elbows on the hard floor awakened him to his actual plight. With his cot overturned, he found himself being pummeled by three sets of fists and boots. Daniel cowered in the corner as the blows rained down on Dikembe, who curled into a fetal position to protect his head and his core.

The men kicked at his back and stomped on his legs from thigh to ankle. They beat his arms and torso with a plastic pipe until it split against his back. Then one of them reached into Dikembe's pocket and removed his wad of francs. They picked him up off the floor, and when he half straightened, they reached into his other pocket and took the rest of his cash. The pain in his ribs was acute. He struggled for air.

The three men dropped him to the floor again and stood over him, breathing heavily. Dikembe peered out at them from between his forearms, tasting blood on the inside of his cheeks.

"Pierre sends his love," said the tallest of the three. "He regrets this morning will be the last he hears from you."

Dikembe looked to Daniel, who was crying quietly in the corner, his eyes wide with terror. The shortest of the men followed his gaze, nodded, stepped to Daniel and patted his wet cheek. He fingered the fetish that hung from Daniel's neck, curled his fist around it, and tugged sharply. The thong snapped and Daniel cried out as the man pocketed the amulet.

"Fine boy." He laughed. "But knuckles work better than charms."

25

To Mickey, unaccustomed to the stridency of the FAULT leaders, the clap of the door slamming sounded definitive. He looked over to Liane, who had unclasped the collar that held the leash and sat on a log bench with Bea in her lap, letting the bonobo groom her, patting Bea's head and running her fingers over the hair of her scalp. It looked like the preface to an emotional goodbye. In his heart, for Liane's sake and Bea's, Mickey didn't want it to be that. Intellectually, however, he saw it a different way. He approached them and rested a hand on each of their shoulders.

Bea said, "Hey, Mickey,"

"Hey, kid. Three of us alone together at last."

"Ouch," Bea said, reaching around to touch her back.

"No more ouch," said Liane, tears welling.

Bea shook her head and showed her teeth.

Liane set her down on the table and leaned against the wall. "We can't allow Bea to be a pawn in their schemes, whether we end up going with her or not. We owe her more than that."

"Listen," said Mickey. "We can't even consider accompanying Corey and Sarita. We think we've had trouble before, that was nothing compared to abetting terrorism and murder."

"But if we let them take Bea, we may never see her again."

"She'll be all over the news in a couple of months if they have their way. Maybe we can work something out, meet her in the green room."

"That's not funny."

"I don't mean it to be."

"And how much will she suffer between now and then? We have to get her to freedom."

"It's impossible."

"Look at her, Mickey. How could we live with ourselves?"

"Okay." He sat on the table. "What does freedom look like for the world's first talking primate?"

Liane shook her head. "I wish I knew."

He hesitated. "Presume we could walk right out of here. If we can get Bea away from them, where do we take her?"

"Back to her own kind. To the Congo. Maybe she has other brothers and sisters out there in the jungle. Her parents could still be alive, her cousins. It's her natural home."

"No way." Mickey shook his head. "The feds by now gotta know they have the wrong ape in their possession. Even if we can sneak back to the apartment building and grab our passports, we're bound to get swept up at the airport. And if there was any chance at all they could miss us, it sure ain't gonna happen with a bonobo in tow."

"Then we have to convince Corey that he's betraying his own principles."

"Didn't you sort of try that? I don't see that argument working out too well. Stealth's more our thing."

"Thessaly," Bea said.

"Thessa what?" asked Mickey.

"Thessaly," Bea repeated.

"That's where Shaker's in prison," Liane noted. "She must've overheard them talking about him."

"Shake her," Bea said. "Out."

"Shake who out?" Mickey wondered.

"Belkin," Bea said.

"Belkin?"

"Maybe more Lingala," Liane mused. She rested her hands on Bea's shoulders.

"English," she said. "What does *belkin* mean in English?"

"One," Bea said. "One. Two. Three."

"She's counting now," Mickey said. "Damned impressive. If we weren't locked up and days from violent revolution, I might be inclined to appreciate this moment."

"How about Canada or Mexico?" Liane pressed. "We grab Bea and go. We evaded Pentalon and the dragnet before, we can do it again. The borders are more porous than the airport."

"Well, if I have to choose my poison I'd opt for Mexico, where Bea would prefer the weather, at least. I got about sixty grand in a brokerage account. That should get us south of the border and then some. We lay low down there for a while, ship out later to Africa. Sounds like some kinda plan."

"A half-assed one." Liane absently tugged Bea's hair.

"Better than you started with." Mickey shrugged. "Involves no garbage chutes."

26

Corey barged in, swept the long hair from his face with a finger, and scanned the room.

"Okay. We've no time for any more bullshit."

Sarita entered and threw the hood over Bea's head.

"No," Bea said, pulling at it futilely. "No more."

Sarita buckled the collar and leash around Bea's neck.

"Stop!" Liane cried. "She doesn't like that."

"It doesn't matter what she likes," Sarita said. "This is bigger than her, bigger than all of us. That's the part you don't seem to get."

Liane searched the faces around her: Mickey, whose cheeks were reddening; Tara and Pattie, hovering by the door; Corey, whose eyes now looked more adamant than the surrounding rock; Sarita, a woman on fire.

She went to Corey. "Take us with you."

"We decided not. We don't trust you or your friend here."

"I could've turned you in to the feds just yesterday, but I didn't."

"Cut the crap." His eyes were dead, blank as a china doll's. "If you'd turned me in, you would've lost the bonobo to them. That's the reason you didn't do it. You don't give a rat's ass for —"

"That's enough!" Mickey lunged and caught Corey across the mouth with his fist. Corey fell hard as Tara and Pattie jumped Mickey, holding him down with his arm wrenched behind his back in a half nelson.

Corey struggled to his feet. He shook his head, spit on the ground, felt for his lip.

"That was stupid," he said, turning to Liane. "Any prayer you had to change my mind? Your man here just blew it."

"Where's your heart, Corey?" Liane pleaded. "Think of this animal!"

"I am. I'm considering all the animals."

"But they're not a totality. They're individuals. Isn't that what rights are about?"

"You think I don't know that, Liane? The problem with you two is that you let sentimentality overwhelm your judgment."

Liane flicked at Corey's false hair. "You're just like them, just like the scientists you claim to disdain. A big phony. You rationalize violence to others in support of your so-called principles. Just like them, you see Bea as the means to a greater good that only you can define."

Corey looked through her. "This said from what moral high ground? You're no better."

"I'm not using anyone."

"Aren't you?"

"We gotta hit the street," Sarita said. "We've wasted too much time here."

"Hold them till we're clear," Corey instructed Tara. "Then go to ground."

He turned to Liane one more time. "In five minutes you can stop worrying about this ape's well-being and start thinking about your own. They can nail you for assisting a fugitive. Again."

He lifted Bea into his arms with Sarita still holding the leash.

Mickey strained to free himself from Tara, who tightened her grip, contorting his shoulder joint.

Liane took a step to follow Corey, but Pattie pushed her back roughly, sprawling her across the table.

"End of discuss-*shun*," she sneered.

The last thing they heard from Bea was a plaintive cry, echoing down the hallway. It was muffled by the hood and distorted by the rock, but Liane thought it might have contained her name.

27

If it hadn't been for the bandage on his ear and the scratches on his face, Vlad Gretch would have blended right in with the morning crowd at the zoo. He wore casual slacks and a sports shirt open at the collar. He bought a box of popcorn from a cart and munched it as he strolled, frequently checking his monitor. He paused by the sea lions, who glided laps around their watery track, sporadically poking their whiskered noses into the hot air. He stopped to look at the snow monkeys, swinging among the branches of their island in the middle of the pond.

The popcorn had a rubbery consistency. It tasted stale, almost metallic. Gretch walked to a trash bin and deposited the box. He entered the tunnel where the polar bears swam, the slabs of their giant paws poking a big plastic ball. The signal was strong here, though garbled. He crossed to the tropic zone building and watched the colobus monkeys and the visiting bonobos. In the wild, he remembered from an overheard lecture, chimps often kill and eat the colobus. It gave him perverse satisfaction to know that fact, to know that the zoo environment, despite what they'd have one believe, was no more natural than Pentalon's.

Gretch touched the back of his head, which was oozing thin pus but hurt less. The signal showed weaker on this side of the zoo. He crossed this quadrant off his mental grid.

An odor hung in the air, the mixture of cooking grease and sweets. The stale popcorn had unsettled his stomach. He walked to the nearby Leaping Frog Cafe and purchased a hot dog with mustard and sauerkraut. He wolfed that down as he headed northwest, past the black-necked swans and the snow monkeys again.

The hot dog didn't help matters. If anything, it made things worse. Gretch resisted a sharp stomach cramp as he pressed on. In the neighborhood of the river otters, he found the signal very strong. The trees and bushes were thicker here, allowed to grow wilder. On a hunch he peered past the exhibits through a crack in the stockade fence. He turned some knobs and held the shoulder strap antenna over his head. The lines on the monitor danced.

He jumped the short fence of the hedgehog enclosure, sending the animals lumbering for the corners, and put his face against the fence. It was some kind of maintenance building just outside the zoo, attached in back to one of the zoo buildings, the fence tightly abutting either side. Just next to that building, he caught movement.

A battered door, fixed to a gash in nearby rock, swung open as two women stepped out.

Gretch reached for his holster and unsnapped the guard, leaving the pistol in place.

One woman, the redhead, he recognized immediately as Sarita. The other was taller with straight hair. She carried something—a black sack—that partially hid her face. No, not a sack—it was a hooded ape. Gretch took the compact binoculars from his fanny pack and adjusted them quickly. Now he saw the beard, and he couldn't believe his eyes. It was a face he'd studied for years, a face he'd committed to memory. *What luck to find the bonobo and Harrow together in one spot!*

Gretch stowed the binoculars and evaluated the scene. To reach his target would require exiting the zoo and walking all the way around. *No time for that*—Harrow was headed for an old Pontiac Grand Am behind the hedge. Atop the fence hung razor wire angled outward—*an uncomfortable path*. Gretch walked to the end by the building and wrapped a large hand around the post. It was anodized aluminum, he presumed, powder-coated black. Impossible to bend. He applied pressure anyway and the post shifted. The concrete that anchored it was weak, crumbling in the ground. He gave a strong yank and pushed, prying the base from the earth and crumpling the chain-link nearby with the extension of a single arm. He stepped through and unholstered his Kimber.

Harrow and the redhead were climbing into their car. Gretch prepared to point the pistol, but just as his arm began to straighten another cramp seized his bowels, the worst pain he'd ever felt. It doubled him over, blinded him. He hugged his midriff with both arms as the hot dog asserted itself, churning in his stomach, propelling acid into the back of his throat. It required superhuman effort to choke down the bile.

The pain lashed him once more, then subsided. He looked up.

Corey Harrow's car was gone.

But the RFID signal showed stronger than ever.

28

They found Mickey's BMW late that morning where they'd left it in Brooklyn, half a dozen parking tickets stacked under the windshield wipers. He slid them free and flung them into the back seat.

"This lawbreaking gets to be a bad habit after a while."

Liane didn't crack a smile. She pulled her tote off her shoulder and stuffed it between her legs on the floor. Failure pressed tightly on her chest, and it sickened her to recall the way she'd thrown herself at Corey, inviting him to touch her that way again, all for nothing.

They'd left the cave by a rear exit that Tara had guided them toward. It had dumped them out on the Sixty-Fifth Street Transverse, where cars rush by nearly at highway speeds. They'd walked to Fifth Avenue and hailed a cab at Sixty-Third, taking it all the way to Brooklyn.

With the sun shining, Mickey's car smelled like baked chimp excrement. They rolled down the windows and Mickey turned the fan on high, but nothing helped much. They stared out the windshield for a long time, frozen.

"You know, it hits me that we can't even go home," Mickey said.

Liane put her elbow on the armrest and buried her chin in her palm.

"I mean," he continued, "first off, the feds ain't gonna give up on that bonobo. Unless they're closing in on Corey and Sarita, they gotta be presuming that we still have her. Ditto for Pentalon—and those characters don't sound like quitters. If we haven't heard from them for a while, maybe it's because Vlad and Flickinger are monitoring our apartments, presuming we're likely to go back there eventually, waiting for us to play into their hands."

Mickey shook his head and rested a forearm atop the steering wheel.

"I sure hope those bastards haven't done anything to our cats," he muttered, turning to absorb Liane's glumness. He watched a couple of construction workers walk down the street, hard hats tucked under their arms, and disappear around the corner. A young woman in tight running shorts and a tank top ushered a Norwich terrier along the curb.

"Life goes on out there," he said, reaching over to pat Liane's leg. He couldn't stand that she wasn't talking. "Where you wanna go? Would you like to see Frank?"

"If they were staking out my mother's house before, they're staking it out again. We'll have to turn ourselves in. Maybe they'll take pity on me and let me attend the funeral."

"Should we find a hotel, get ourselves cleaned up first?"

"Sounds as good as anything."

Mickey pulled from the curb and eased the BMW down the street. "We did our best. You'll see Bea again. When FAULT starts booking appearances, we'll track her down and find a way to visit."

"If we're not in jail." Liane watched him merge into traffic on the BQE. "Where to, exactly?"

"There's a place in Great Neck. We can check in with cash and spend a quiet night."

"And in the morning?"

He shrugged. "Our heads'll be clearer, at least."

Liane pulled her seat forward and propped her knees against the dashboard. She still looked depressed as hell, Mickey thought. He couldn't blame her. He shared her sense of loss.

"Look at the bright side," he said. "At least none of the guys in masks have a hold of her."

They were passing over the Kosciuszko Bridge. Liane peered absently through the steel girders to the gray water below. She sat up.

"Those surgical masks and goggles the feds were wearing... I'm so accustomed to seeing them that I didn't think to ask why they used them when they picked up the bonobo they thought was Bea."

"I dunno. Procedure...precaution?"

"Precaution against what?"

"Passing germs to the ape, I figured. Like you did in the lab."

"But the bonobo had already been exposed to so many humans in uncontrolled circumstances. How were a few more going to harm her?"

"Not an excess of caution?" Mickey blinked. "They did give us physicals on the way out, which was strange. I thought that was in case we later accused them of abusing us in their custody, but maybe they had another reason. Come to think of it, when I met Hammurabi before that, he asked after Bea's health."

Liane began rooting through her tote.

"What're you doing?"

"Looking for a phone number."

"They weren't wearing those masks to protect the ape," Mickey thought aloud. "They were wearing them to protect themselves."

"That's what I suspect." Corey had kept the DNA report, but Liane found the crumpled stickie she needed at the bottom of her tote. "This lab guy who tested Bea's blood? Maybe this note marked *Urgent* has nothing to do with the mutation. Maybe he had a different message to deliver."

"Disease." Mickey gasped. "Bad disease."

"Could be." Liane nodded. She snapped the battery into her cell phone, turned it on and began dialing.

29

Liane told the technician who had analyzed the blood samples that she worked for Hammurabi. The tech confirmed their hunch that Bea carried a powerful virus—a new variety of the deadly *Filoviridae* family. He seemed surprised to learn 673B was still alive. Could be, he said, that the mutations he saw in the speech area were part of a series that also protects the bonobo from the virus, the way the mutation for sickle-cell anemia shields carriers of that gene from malaria. But given the functional discrepancy, he said, the correlation seemed unlikely. The immunity may have an entirely different source.

Liane hung up. "Just so. Mandatory reporter."

Mickey looked in his side mirror, then the rear, and changed lanes abruptly, squeezing between tightly spaced cars and waving off the horn that followed.

"We've been so damn naive," he said.

"Hemorrhagic fevers like Ebola and Marburg don't spread through the air," said Liane. "It requires the ingestion of body fluids."

"She bit you!"

"She didn't break the skin. You saw so yourself. Care to look again?"

"If you want me to crash the car."

"Anyway, they're fast burners. We'd know if we had it. Maybe this version doesn't cross species."

"I hope you're right. Even so, we have to warn Corey and Sarita. We have a moral obligation."

"Well, if we can find them we will warn them. You look nervous," she said.

"I'm starting to wonder what else I don't know. You just used the cell phone, which means they could now have a bead on the direction we're headed."

"I unclipped the battery as usual when I was done."

"Pulsipher let us off the hook awful easy, and now he knows he's got the wrong bonobo. And where the hell's this Pentalon guy who was so determined to get you only last week? How is it we can drive my abandoned car away without a care in the world—find it sitting by the curb like that, just waiting unwatched for us to come along and be on our way. It doesn't make sense with these stakes. Any of those guys who are seeking us could've traced my license plate."

"Maybe they just haven't found the car yet. You think we're being followed now?"

"I don't know. Possibly tracked somehow—the way Gretch must've followed your car back when all this started."

He leaned across her and flicked open the glove compartment. "Help me look in here for anything suspicious."

They found nothing but old maps and napkins and a few dusty ballpoint pens. Mickey pulled off at the nearest exit ramp and wove the side streets.

"Even if there isn't a tracking device, they know my car," he worried.

"So it's possible one of those cop sweeps would present a risk to us. What do they call them—an APB?"

"We gotta ditch these wheels before our next stop."

"Then how do we get around?"

"Well, I've been thinking. How do you feel about grand theft auto?"

"The video game?"

"The act."

"It's not on my list of things to do before I die."

"Maybe it's a thing to do so we *don't* die. I got a sneaking feeling anyone could've wired this car up the kazoo while it sat. Someone could be listening to us right now," he warned.

"Good. We could tell them to screw off."

"Screw off!"

"We could tell them we don't have the ape."

"We don't have the ape!"

"Did it help, Mick?"

"No. Are you with me, babe?"

"All right."

"Do as I do."

They cruised down a broad commercial avenue in Brooklyn, passing fast-food joints and gas stations and grimy strip malls. They pulled into a carwash line behind a maroon Jaguar SJR, from which a thin, middle-aged woman in high heels had emerged, a Louis Vuitton handbag looped over one arm and a Pomeranian clutched in the other. Mickey paid for a basic wash and they watched from inside as a belt pulled the woman's car through the tunnel.

Liane said: "You're not thinking what I think you're thinking."

"Our car reeks and I've always wanted an upgrade." Mickey beseeched the ceiling for forgiveness.

An attendant pulled the red car out of the tunnel and six workers fell on it with rags and spray bottles. As they neared completion Mickey took out a twenty-dollar bill and released it at the woman's heels.

"Ma'am," he said, "you dropped your money."

When she turned and chased the bill in the wind, Mickey and Liane took off toward her car, jumping in just as the attendants finished. Mickey floored the accelerator before they even had their doors closed and tore around the nearest corner.

"Radiance Metallic, I think they call this." He eased up on the throttle. "My brother has one. Love that new-car aroma."

"Beats baked chimp poop."

"You ain't kidding."

Forty minutes later the big Jag rumbled over Belgium blocks and pulled through Adnan Hammurabi's iron gates.

30

"*I'll drop you,*" Mickey said, "and hide the car around the corner that way." He pointed over the roof. "I'm in the neighborhood if you need me. Good luck in there."

Liane waited for him to roll away, then rang the bell.

Hammurabi answered, surprised. He wore an off-white Oxford button-down, open at the collar, brown slacks, stocking feet. It was the first time Liane had seen him without a tie.

"You alone?" she asked without preamble.

"My wife's out."

"Where's Pulsipher?"

Hammurabi guffawed. "He's not my best buddy. The house is empty. Just me."

Liane stepped over the threshold and into an ornate round foyer. There were a few suitcases at the foot of the stairs.

"My daughter's off with a friend's family," Hammurabi explained, "and we're packing for a trip—to get away for a while. They pulled my protection, thanks to you. Pulsipher was none too happy that I misidentified the bonobo. He thinks I tricked him. That was clever, Liane."

She followed him tentatively across the gleaming marble tile. "I can't take credit for the idea. Did it fool you?"

"Until I saw the outlines of the contact lenses."

He ushered her into a paneled library, where she sat on a leather couch.

"Can I get you anything to refresh?"

"It's not a social call, Adnan."

"I understand. Still, we can be civil. A drink?"

"Water, thanks."

He opened a cabinet to reveal a glass-and-granite wet bar and poured her an Evian. He mixed a scotch on the rocks for himself and settled into an armchair with a cigarette.

"So you figured out the ruse." Liane drank deeply.

"How does my wife like to say: I was born at night, but it wasn't last night."

"Yet you played dumb. For me?"

"For the bonobo. If you switched them, I figured you had a good reason. I know you have her interests at heart."

Liane looked up at the spines on the shelves, medical books mostly, many of them bound in tea-colored leather with Latin titles. There was also an entire section of poetry.

"Bea's carrying hemorrhagic fever," she said, seeking a big reaction but getting only a muted one.

Hammurabi shrugged. "It's tremendously deadly but hard to transmit. The mortality rate makes people a little hysterical."

"I guess they don't like the thought of dissolving into mush before their friends and family. You had to know, Adnan. How could you keep that from me?"

"What was I supposed to do, write you a memo? By the time I found out you were gone."

"But when we were all with Pulsipher, you might have let on."

"It's classified." He took a long pull from his cigarette and exhaled. "All this blasted secrecy! It's meant to protect us but it'll finish us one day."

"Maybe sooner than you think. I lost possession of Bea. She's out and about, but I don't know where."

"Escaped?"

Liane shook her head. "The FAULT organizers took her from me."

"You might have known you couldn't trust them. It's a far cry from animal welfare to animal liberation. They're fanatics."

"Now you tell me. At least FAULT won't cut Bea into pieces, as the supposedly mainstream scientists seem inclined to do. If I can get a hold of her again, I want to set her free in her natural habitat."

"Their range is limited to the Congo. It's a big country, almost the size of Western Europe. It's far off and largely impenetrable."

"I figure if she came out of there she can get back in there—somehow. I'll reunite her with her original troop if I can."

He shook his head.

Liane uncrossed her legs and pressed her palms together. "The reason I came is to find out what you know about the origins of those twins."

"I'll disappoint you. There's not much I do know."

"Were they bred in the States or captured in the wild?"

"They came from a dealer in Kinshasa. I've visited the city several times. It's crowded and chaotic, neither well managed nor well policed. The dealers fade in and out, all of them known to someone, but few known to everyone. The bonobo's transmission papers would show the chain of ownership going all the way back, but that file's locked up at Pentalon. Axel won't share it voluntarily, you can bet. I suppose the federal authorities could lay hands on it with a subpoena."

"The feds? What do you think they'd do if they captured Bea?"

"My guess, sadly, if they confirm she's a carrier of the fever they'll destroy her."

"In spite of everything?"

"Safety before science—it's a cover-your-ass kind of thing. Even if they do let her live, she'll be permanently quarantined in a hot zone and never see the light of day."

He sipped his scotch, the ice clicking against his teeth. "You're right, in a sense, that her best hope for self-fulfillment is a return to the jungle. She may spread the virus to some humans eventually, but it likely would burn out quickly, as the Ebola types always do. And one might view it as a comeuppance of sorts to whomever captured her in the first place. If no one goes near the wild bonobos then no one gets hurt, right?"

"So imagine a different kind of publicity than FAULT has in mind,"

Liane mused. "Imagine the world knowing she's out there in the wild—and people afraid to go near her."

"A warning of sorts. God's will, perhaps." Hammurabi took a final sip from his glass and became reflective. "I'm sorry to hear about your mother. It surprises me that she couldn't get a kidney in time."

"She was old and a difficult match, they said."

"She must have been if Axel couldn't help."

Liane's eyes widened. "What are you talking about? I never asked for his assistance."

"That kidney she almost got… Axel used his influence to push your mother's case near the head of the line."

Liane gasped. "I had no clue."

"Don't let it change your opinion. He didn't do it out of altruism. He was manipulating your stepfather to keep you in a box."

Narrow straits, Liane recalled.

Hammurabi extinguished his cigarette and thrust out his lower lip as a sound emerged from the kitchen.

"Ah, that must be my wife," he whispered. "Let me go for a moment. She's the jealous sort and on edge these days. I don't want her walking in on us without explanation."

"May I use the bathroom?"

"It's just through there." He pointed and disappeared through a paneled door.

Liane went to the powder room and washed up at the pedestal sink with a bar of soap shaped like a scallop shell. She sat on the toilet cover, fully dressed, with her face in her hands.

The news about Frank came as a hard blow. It meant she'd been right, in a way, not to trust him fully, but that he'd done what he did for purer motives than she might have expected. Perhaps she could forgive him. Another of Axel's pawns, struggling to make something right in his own world, he couldn't possibly have known how crooked Liane's straight and narrow would become.

She opened the door and looked into the library, but Hammurabi hadn't returned. She walked back to the foyer, through that to the living room. It had an alabaster fireplace with an ornately carved surround. The furniture, Louis-Something style, appeared little used. Oil paintings of country landscapes hung on the walls in gilt rococo frames.

The murmur of a man's voice reached her from far away. She folded a shutter aside and peeked out the window, seeing no sign of anyone— only green lawn and the wilting blossoms of red azaleas.

The sound came again, fainter but more compelling. Liane stepped back out into the foyer. She looked at the front door, still and solid. Colored glass panels hid her view of the entry steps. She turned and headed deeper into the house, tiptoeing, calling softly for Adnan.

From the edge of the butler's pantry she sensed his presence in the spacious kitchen. She heard something that resembles a wet slap then a deep moan. Her breath caught. She reached into her tote for the pearl-handled switchblade and closed her fingers. Clutching it unopened, she peered around the corner.

Hammurabi lay strapped atop the glass kitchen table, the chairs pushed aside as if a dinner party had just broken up. His shirt was torn open, and his mountainous abdomen, cleaved in two, showed a glistening valley of yellow fat and pink viscera. Blood ran along the table edge and dripped to the floor.

His head thrown back in agony and his eyes pinched, he spoke in a tight groan. "It's the girl you want. She's here."

Every instinct told her to run. Instead, she stepped around the corner, deeper into the kitchen, the switchblade raised in her clenched fist, its blade still sheathed, her arm trembling. She didn't feel the dark presence until it fell upon her, one giant vise of a hand encasing her fist, muscular arms and legs imprisoning the rest of her in a rigid hold. From behind, a chin dug into her shoulder. His wheezing tickled the down of her ear.

"In order to use this one," Gretch said, "you have to extend the blade."

He squeezed her hand so the blade shot out with a *swick*, pointing, to Liane's surprise, not upward but past the heel of her hand.

"Careful. You might cut yourself." An inch from her cheek, she could feel his grin.

She exhaled, and when she tried to draw restorative breath her diaphragm couldn't overcome the constriction of his hold. She struggled for air as he moved her hand down with overwhelming force and rested the flat of the blade between her legs, the coolness of it, felt through the chinos, stiffening the flesh of her pudenda.

"Get your panties back?"

She couldn't answer, couldn't breathe. She felt the subtle shift of his engulfing weight and knew he was poised to do a terrible thing.

Then came a crash from behind—shards sailing through the margins of her vision. Gretch's body relaxed. She shirked him off and he fell with a thud to the floor, landing among the remains of a broken planter.

Mickey looked nonplussed by his accomplishment.

Liane paused for her own confusion to dissipate. "I thought you were waiting in the car."

"It took too long. I worried."

"Mickey on the spot."

They stared at Gretch's hulk on the floor, then Liane looked at Hammurabi, who had slipped into unconsciousness. She ran to him and lifted his heavy, limp hand, averting her eyes from the mess of his torso. His face was still but not peaceful, his eyelids closed and gruesomely inanimate. She felt for a pulse and found none.

Mickey stood over Gretch. Though facedown, the rise and fall of his ribs suggested reserves of significant strength.

"This guy's gonna come to any minute," Mickey guessed. "We gotta get out of here before that happens."

"But what about Adnan?"

Mickey lifted the phone from the wall, dialed 911 and set it down on the counter. "They'll trace it back here. All we can do."

Just then Gretch stirred.

31

"Ahrw!" Liane groaned, leaning out the car window. It was the third time she'd had to puke in ten minutes, and there was nothing left inside her.

"You all right?" The big Jag had a canister of wet wipes in the storage compartment between the front seats. Mickey handed a couple to Liane.

She cleaned the edges of her mouth and ran a fresh one across her forehead. "To think of that man with his hands on me. And the sight of poor Adnan."

"Poor Adnan? He was out for himself. I heard him through the door. He betrayed you."

"He suffered from divided loyalties."

"You mean between you and Pentalon?"

"Between humans and primates."

"Sounds familiar. Well, that guy Gretch won't have such qualms. He's gonna wake up eventually and it seems like he's got a mean streak."

They looked out at the supermarket lot where they'd parked. It was half empty, people pushing grocery carts, pulling in and out of spots.

"We should get moving," Liane said. "I feel like a sitting duck here."

"All due respect, I need food, and so do you. Let's get some sandwiches."

"I can't think of eating right now."

"You'll need your strength, though, for whatever they throw at us."

"Gretch might find us here."

"He doesn't know the car."

"He might've woken up, looked out the window as we pulled away. He's everywhere, like a wraith. I'm scared."

"Far as I can tell, you do some of your best work in that condition. Let's just grab a few ready-made sandwiches. Then we'll hit the road again."

They climbed out and skittered across the parking lot, casting their eyes about. The interior of the Super Fresh—its wide aisles, crowded shelves, misted greens—conveyed a sense of satisfying normalcy to Liane. She wanted to buy everything, toss it all into a cart, go home, and fill the pantry. But a few minutes later, they emerged with only a soggy tuna on rye, a turkey club, chips and sodas.

"What about the car?" Liane persisted. "Even if Gretch doesn't know it, the local cops have to be looking."

"The car wash was just into Queens from Brooklyn. If anything, the *city* cops are the ones on high alert. We'll head away from there."

Mickey glanced over his shoulder, backed out and drove to the exit.

"Take the Whitestone Bridge and let's get off of Long Island," Liane said.

"We'll have to pass through two of the five boroughs."

"But if we go east, we'll run out of real estate."

Remembering Bea's RFID, Liane pried the E-Z Pass transponder from the windshield and threw it out the window as they drove. She checked her cell phone, for a fourth time making sure the battery was disconnected.

"This is no way to live." She massaged the leather seats, touched the smoothly polished burled wood of the dashboard. "Thanks for the rescue back there. I couldn't have done half of this without you."

"We're a team, right?" He shook his head. "Though it seems incomplete without the kid around."

Liane turned to him. "They can't win, Mick. Pulsipher with government secrets still safe...Flickinger and Gretch raking in the bucks with blood on their hands. And Corey and Sarita in possession of Bea, the catalyst for their long-planned revolution? They can't all win and we lose."

"So what are little old us gonna do about it? Bea could be anywhere in the universe at this point."

Liane wondered what she must be thinking right now, passed from hand to hand like so much chattel. Did she question, did she fear? Did she have an inkling of what was in store for her?

"Did you ever look at a horse at the racetrack, Mick, and wonder what it might be thinking? Did you ever wish it could just come out and describe to you how it felt?"

"Sure. All the time."

"I can't tell you," she said, "how many times I've wondered even what the rats were thinking, let alone the bonobos in my care at Pentalon. And there was Bea yesterday, just on the verge of being able to tell us. I would've liked to have a few moments of real communication with her."

"Yeah. 'One, two, three,' she said. The synapses starting to fire off more complexly, the way a growing child's mind gels. Wow."

"She was trying to communicate, even from early on, like she had this gift and knew it shouldn't be squandered. And there at the end it seemed like she tried to pass information along, didn't it? Thessaly, she said." She knitted her brow and sat forward, the insight dawning. "That's where they are, Mick! Can you remember what else she told us?"

Mickey scratched his chin. "It didn't seem meaningful at the time. It came so quick. Something about shaking, was it?"

"No. She said Thessaly, then Shaker. As in, Shaker Moyo, Corey's old accomplice."

"Shaking out. That's what it was."

"Or Shaker out." She stared at traffic for a bit then turned to face him. "They're going to break Shaker out of jail. That's how it begins. And Bea said 'belkin' and I thought it was a Lingala word of some sort, but it must be a street name. One-two-three Belkin. It's an address on Belkin Road or Lane or something. Why are you pulling over?"

"The lady who donated her car to us, she was nice enough to include a navigation system. But you can't look up an address while moving. Here."

He punched in the town of Thessaly, then 123 Belkin. No match. He tried it without the house number. No match. Tried neighboring towns, yet still couldn't find a match.

"We need to head up there anyway," Liane said, not allowing herself to feel discouraged. "But the Taconic's swarming with cops. Can we use this system to find our way to Thessaly without hitting the parkway?"

"Sure. I can confine conditions to avoid fast roads. But what'll we do once we get there?"

Liane took out the pieces of her phone.

Mickey reached over to stop her. "Wait a second."

He pressed the telephone icon on the steering wheel and a keypad illuminated on the dashboard touch screen. "Just as I figured. This chick sprung for all the bells and whistles."

"But can't someone trace the car phone as easily as my cell?"

"I suppose so, if they're looking for it specifically. But for my money they're not likely to engage the national security apparatus for a lifted car, whereas we already know they're after you personally—at least so long as they think you have the missing link. Plus, Pulsipher knows your cell phone number."

Liane was already hitting the buttons on the touch pad.

"So who're we calling?" Mickey asked.

"A guy I know in Thessaly."

32

First thing Saturday morning the visiting room was crowded. To pass through security, Liane used a false I.D. that she'd found in the cave. She bought fistfuls of Kit-Kat bars from the prison vending machine and gained an advantageous spot three-quarters down the screen, as far from any guard's earshot as one could get.

When he came to the Plexiglas, Shaker Moyo looked happy to see her. They exchanged smiles as she pushed the candy through the slide drawer.

"Thanks!" He tore a package open, broke off a piece and bit it daintily. "I eat well when you're around. How were the rest of those pistachios?"

"Divine. They almost got me killed."

"You didn't say anything about wanting to avoid trouble." He smirked. "If you sought peace then you should've taken my earlier advice."

"Was that *advice* or was it misdirection?"

"Ah." He clapped his hands. "Very good."

"You don't look so surprised to see me this time."

"The world's all abubble. You never know what's going to surface."

"Like old friends, maybe?"

"You could say."

She sat forward. "It's a mistake, Shaker. I did some research. You're eligible for parole in another two years with good behavior."

"And into what kind of world would I walk?"

"One you can countenance, where killing hasn't led to more killing. Where your conscience is clear."

"Hmm. Only the animals still suffering. Is that what you're saying?"

"You know I don't advocate that. You can do a lot of good if you leave here on the right terms. There's a two-million-dollar reward on Corey's head, for example."

"Blood money. Posted by the companies."

"You could make a second career with half of it."

"Are you asking me to betray my friend for cash?"

"I'm asking you to be true to your own principles." She bit the inside of her lip. "I haven't proved myself to be the greatest judge of character, but somehow I sense that revolution isn't your thing, Shaker. You know in your heart that revenge, if it means killing, won't bring back a single life. It won't bring back that policeman's dog."

"You remembered that story."

"Who're you protecting? Corey left you outside the burning lab to take the fall for him."

"Not of his own accord. I told him to go on without me. The cause is bigger than any individual. We always knew that."

"If I had a dollar for everything I thought I *knew* for sure, then I could post my own reward. All this certainty, it comes on like a steamroller, Shaker. Get in its way and be crushed. Where's the justice in that?"

"So stay out of the steamroller's way."

"But what if you don't have a choice? Did your uncle have a choice when he faced the certainty of the cop who shot him? Did the family of the security guard who burned in the lab have a choice? Aren't individual people and animals more valuable than the ideals that lead us to ruin their lives?"

He sat back with his arms folded, fixed his gaze on her. "You're pressing, Liane. You've dragged up everything you know about me to try to win my confidence. Why? Is it your own principles that brought you here or some other motive? Does it have to do with that bonobo I'm hearing about?"

"Of course it does."

"You want her to be happy, is that it? What of the others left behind?"

"You've tried this conflict on a grand scale, Shaker. Maybe, instead of making it bigger, you need to drill down to one entity at a time."

He rested an elbow on the table, wiped the corners of his mouth with two fingers, and frowned. "Tell me about this bonobo. Tell me everything—how you met her, the development of your relationship, what makes her special."

The request took Liane aback. She exhaled, puffing her cheeks, read the faux grain of the chipped Formica table, and raised her eyes to Moyo.

"Bea and her brother came in with a large troop. I don't know about the others, but the twins were lifted from somewhere in the Congo, presumably from the jungle there. They were all weaned prematurely. Although there's little biological effect from that, the psychological damage is hard to determine—maybe in this instance it made her needy. At Pentalon she lived in a cage with few comforts and nothing natural. It wouldn't take a primatologist to see how depressed she was, more so even than the other bonobos. Her only companion was her brother in a neighboring cage, too far apart to touch."

"But you were also her companion."

"It was my job to acclimate them to handling. It makes it easier to do procedures if they're used to human contact. In many labs, you probably know, they don't bother much with this—they just over-whelm the animals with brute force. Approaching more gently, in a more deliberate fashion, with more patience, so as not to stress them out and get the adrenaline flowing—that was one of Hammurabi's innovations."

"You sound like an admirer of his."

"We had a complicated relationship and now he's dead."

"Is that so?"

"It'll be a long time before I can fully evaluate what he meant to me. It was sort of like having an uncle with bipolar disorder. Just when you're sure you have him figured out, someone else shows up who looks exactly like him but acts completely different." She paused. "At bottom, I think he was conflicted. Like many of us."

"And Flickinger?"

"He cares for the animals like a strip miner cares for the mountain-top—something to scrape aside while digging for what he truly values."

"And you chose to defy him, but it didn't occur to you to do so when the subjects were mere rodents. Why at this moment with this bonobo? Was her talking the only reason?"

"Yes." She closed her eyes. "No." She opened them. "I don't know."

"You saw something else in her, didn't you?"

"I must have."

"Tell me."

"From the beginning, Bea was complacent. When I reached out to touch her she didn't recoil at first like the other bonobos. She always complied. I never had to call an attendant to pin her down when I drew blood. She held her arm out through the cage bars. She watched me do it, looked me in the eye."

"Liane, she trusted you."

She gaped down at her hands, which lay flat against the table. Her cuticles needed washing. "More than trust. Bea put her faith in me." Liane hesitated, corrected herself. "She put her faith in all of us."

"I see." Moyo's face grew serious, reflective. "You're saying she expected bigger things from mankind."

"Yes. Do you remember the jungle of your homeland, Shaker?"

"In Zimbabwe there's not so much jungle. There's a rain forest by Victoria Falls. Where I grew up, the bush, as we call it, was more a savannah. It's beautiful. Spiritual."

"They treat the animals better there?"

"Mostly no. It's not Eden, you know, the black man roaming around in naked innocence. There, too, animals for most people are a means to an end. But there are more wild areas. Some people respect them, all things being equal."

"Are all things ever equal?"

"Rarely, in my experience."

"I know so little of Africa. If I can lay my hands on Bea again, though, I plan to return her to the place she came from."

Shaker stacked the candy bars she'd brought and pushed them forward like a tower of poker chips. He took the empty wrapper and aluminum foil from the one he'd eaten and folded them into neat squares. Liane wondered whether he was again planning some kind of secret communication, but he appeared more than anything to be lost in thought. Finally, he looked up at her.

"Nelson Mandela spent twenty-seven years in prison, more than twice what I'll have in two years. The cash, if it comes, I'll take back to my country and spend on good works with God's creatures. Here? Now?" He threw up his hands. "Let our cause be this ape. This *particular* bonobo."

Liane closed her eyes in relief.

"I'm unfamiliar with the Congo," Moyo added. "It's far from Zim, toward the equator—in some ways, at the edge of all civilization. How else can I help?"

"The Congo's not my concern as yet. It feels farther away than the moon. Right now I need to figure out where Corey is—and where Sarita's taken Bea."

"They're all together."

"No. They said they were splitting up, to make it harder to find them."

"Listen to me. They always claim that. It's a feint, internal misinformation. Find one of them and you find the other."

"Where?"

"I don't know. Tell me what pieces you have."

"One-two-three Belkin."

He pressed his knuckles against his lips. "Where'd you get that from?"

"Bea told us."

"No kidding, the bonobo? She's paying attention. Belkin's the name we call a safe house not five miles from town."

"This town?"

"Yes." He gave her the address from memory.

"And one-two-three?"

"Beats me." He shrugged. "Maybe the ape's learning to count. Wouldn't that beat the band?"

"For sure." She stood to go.

"Do me a favor, Liane. Don't be too hard on Corey."

"Nothing gratuitous, if that's what you mean. But one thing I've learned from all this: We make our choices. We can't just leave others to face the consequences."

33

In quick succession, Pulsipher received at his desk some photos and three phone calls. The first call was about a female with an unfamiliar name who had visited Shaker Moyo. It was a heads-up, a courtesy, but Pulsipher wondered. All of sudden Moyo seemed too popular.

The pictures were of Hammurabi's body laid out on the kitchen table like an assassin's feast, his tongue already swelling from his mouth like a plump apple. Ugly as he'd been alive, Pulsipher thought, he looked much worse dead.

Then the guy who'd beamed the photos called. He told Pulsipher that Hammurabi's wife preceded the EMS techs into the house by thirty seconds and collapsed on the floor in hysteria. Too little information all those years, followed by an excess. *What the hell would she know,* Pulsipher thought, *a failed model turned store clerk who probably had no clue what went on inside Pentalon. And seeing your husband split open like a watermelon makes for a harsh introduction to anatomy.*

No sooner had he hung up than the phone summoned his attention once more. He lifted it on the fourth ring.

One of his agents: "We lost the girl."

"You told me that yesterday. You tagged the vet's car, didn't you?"

"That's what I'm saying. After we lost the tail on the girl downtown, we followed the tracking device to the vet's Beemer. We found it at an impound lot. We're walking back the cat to figure out how it got there. May take awhile."

Unbelievable! As Pulsipher cradled the phone he wondered how these guys pass their civil service exams. He was no closer to the magical ape, and the Undersecretary had begun riding his ass hard, knowing a timebomb was still out there, bound to go off at the worst possible moment, just when a pet project came up for funding or some such thing.

But it was the virus that really worried Pulsipher, the virus that the Undersecretary didn't yet know about. Changing man's perception of animals and, therefore, what agribusiness could do to them—that was big. But a man-killing virus that the federal government had failed to contain? That was bigger. If people in America started bleeding out of their eyes, then Special Agent Pulsipher had a feeling both he and the Undersecretary could kiss their jobs goodbye. And what next? Go work some private security gig like all those former law enforcement types who placed money—or worse things—before country, before everything? Pulsipher didn't think so. He sat up and put his feet flat on the floor, where they belonged.

If he reached the Undersecretary and they shocked the bureaucracy into emergency mode, Pulsipher figured he could sweep up all the primates at Pentalon in thirty-six hours, Axel Flickinger and his high-level connections be damned. Even the most self-serving politician in Washington wasn't going to stand in the way of an effort to contain a viral outbreak with eighty percent mortality.

From his desk Pulsipher picked up the telephone receiver, dialed the Undersecretary, requested a face-to-face and hung up. They'd have to notify CDC immediately, he knew, which meant all those guys in funny suits would descend on Pentalon faster than United Nations peacekeepers attending their first gangbang. The upside meant Flickinger would have no choice but to cooperate from now on—and on Pulsipher's terms—probably turning in Gretch if the CSI guys found evidence he'd done that evil deed at Hammurabi's house. And it had to be Gretch—who else? Pulsipher had looked into Ferrone's and Vinson's eyes; they were romantics, not killers. Besides, they'd turn up on their own eventually. *In what condition?* That was anyone's guess.

34

Off a country road and past a trailer park, a cluster of modest pre-fabs clung to one another like politicians in caucus, square and well cared for. Ribbons of walkway cut through neat patches of lawn, and freshly planted impatiens suggested aspirations beyond mere survival. But someone's survival, Mickey reasoned, was the exact purpose of the house with BELKIN on the mailbox in off-kilter, reflective, stick-on letters.

"Nondescript," Mickey assessed, peering through the windshield, "and doing just enough to fit in. It's two miles from the train station. Two and a half from the parkway. Thick woods a block away. Roads in all directions, yet still off the beaten path. There are neighbors nearby, but none too nosy, I'd bet. The perfect safe house."

"What do you know about that?"

"Just what I read."

"And what do the books say about how we get inside?" Liane glanced at her watch. "It's near the appointed hour."

"The windows are closed and there's no chimney. I say we ring the doorbell."

"They'll see us and flee."

"I doubt that. They don't respect us that much."

Mickey pulled the car into the driveway, blocking a black Pontiac Grand Am with old Dole-for-President stickers blistering on the chrome bumper. They got out and walked to the small concrete stoop. Liane missed the switchblade she'd dropped at Hammurabi's house. It never sat right in her hand, but it was the only weapon she'd ever owned, and she now felt exposed without it.

"Would you care to do the honors?" Mickey extended his palm to the doorbell.

Liane pressed the button. She closed her other hand around Mickey's and tried to find her center.

They heard the floor settle behind the door. After a pause it swung open. Corey.

"You two? What the hell. Get in here!" He pulled Liane inside by the sleeve. Mickey followed close by.

The house was as one would have imagined from the outside. They stepped directly into a living room with a cloth couch, three chairs, a coffee table buried in magazines, and a Sony television. Carpeting covered the floor, but the walls were bare.

"Where's Bea?" Liane said.

"Having her diaper changed."

"She doesn't wear diapers."

"She does now. How'd you find us?"

"The ape ratted you out," Mickey said. "She has a mind of her own, just like you hoped. Ain't that something?"

"It makes things interesting. I'll give you that."

"Or is an independent mind a complication for you?" Liane jibed. "Not something you want in your cadres."

"She's a bridge to another world," Corey said. "We accept her for what she is."

"Then how about accepting what she wants."

"You don't know what she wants any more than you know what a one-year-old wants. It's not in anyone's interest for her to make her own decisions at this stage."

"Certainly not in *your* interest, Corey. But a one-year-old wants to be a one-year-old. Doesn't a bonobo want to be a bonobo, live among its own kind? She doesn't want to perform for the cameras because it suits a cause someone else considers great."

"There you go again, Liane." He shook his head. "You're like a terrier bitch with a bone."

"Never mind the insults," Mickey said. "The ape's a danger far beyond what she does or doesn't stand for. She's carrying hemorrhagic fever."

"Oh, brother." Corey furrowed his brow. "At long last, don't try to pull that shit on me."

"It's true," Liane said.

"Then why aren't you dead? Why isn't everyone who's touched her dead or dying?"

"When you think about it, only a few of us *have* touched her. The virus might have a long incubation period or it might just be hard to transmit."

"You have this on what authority?"

"Blood analysis," Mickey said. "Now we all got a responsibility to limit further exposure to humans. So give her over."

"I find your logic a little too convenient," Corey said. "But we can take precautions. If true, it's a footnote in history."

"What history would that be?" Mickey asked.

"The history we're making."

"Do it without her," said Liane. "Bea's coming with us. Tell me where she is."

She went down the small hallway, past an empty bathroom, and opened a closed door. Bea was on the queen bed there in a diaper. She cocked her head and cried, "Liane!" She bounded across the space between them and leaped into Liane's arms, driving them both against the hallway wall. She reached up and fiddled with Liane's earlobe.

"Friends," she said.

"We're gonna get you out of here, Bea," Liane said. "Right now."

"Not a chance," Corey said, as Mickey reached for the knob of the front door.

A metallic snap came from behind. Unmistakable.

"Put the ape down!" Sarita shouted from the bedroom doorway. She balanced a sawed-off shotgun in one freckled hand and had her index finger wrapped around the trigger.

35

Sarita used the gun barrel to herd them to the center of the living room, Bea still clutched in Liane's arms.

"Drop the ape and let's get on with it," she said. "There's a crawl space in the basement with your names scratched in the dirt."

"Nuh-uh," Mickey said. "We like a room with a window. We'll check elsewhere."

"You're both a liability now," Sarita said. "You've outlived your usefulness."

"Usefulness to what," Mickey asked, "the revolution?"

"You never should've come," said Corey gravely. "You weren't cut out for this, neither of you. This powder puff with the tattoos—"

"Who you calling a powder-puff?!" Mickey said, but he didn't move.

Liane, engulfed in Bea's hairy arms, twisted around to look at her watch. Sarita noticed and shoved her gun forward.

"What've you got—a train to catch? I have news: You're not leaving, with or without the bonobo."

Liane thought she perceived the tinkle of dog tags and the sound of an animal whimpering outside.

"First off," said Corey, "give the damn ape over."

He stepped forward and closed a hand over Bea's upper arm, but she turned in a flash and scratched him across the eyeball. As one hand rose to his face, she caught the other and bit two fingers down to the bone with a crunch.

Corey let out a roar just as the front door flew open.

The first thing they perceived was a black blur charging into the room. Sarita turned to train her gun on it, saw that it was a Doberman, and hesitated. But the dog, seeing her tense with the weapon in hand, responded instantaneously, launching itself across the cocktail table and snapping its tyrannosaurus jaws onto her arm. Her sawed-off fell to the carpet with a harmless dull thud. Mickey went to pick it up, but someone shoved him aside and got there first.

"Help!" Sarita screamed over the dog's growls. "Ow! Get him off me!"

"That'd be a she," Handy said, passing Sarita's shotgun to Jerry and leveling his own twelve-gauge at Corey.

Left hand covering his right eye, bleeding right hand squeezed between his thighs, Corey appeared to be in no position to threaten anyone. He blinked in confusion with his good eye.

"Get him off me!" Sarita shrieked again as the Doberman worked its head back and forth, tearing her flesh.

"I said she's a girl," Handy repeated. "She belongs to my daughter. Off, Sheila!"

The dog let go but remained standing over Sarita, vermillion glistening on its jowls.

Handy frown-smiled like a proud father. "She's mighty glad to be untied from that tree," he said. "No worse for wear, though, that's for sure." He nodded toward Mickey. "That your boyfriend?"

"Yep," Liane said, surprising herself.

"Looks like a keeper."

"Couldn't live without him," said Liane. "You know what to do about the cars?"

"Sure. We wipe down the Jag real good, throw a few of their possessions inside, then call the cops."

Sarita, on the floor, worked in agony to piece the freckled skin of her forearm together.

"They need medical attention," Liane said.

"They should last past an hour."

"You'll be a hero in Thessaly, Hands."

"Who'd a'knowed it."

"We should split. We'll take the Grand Am," Mickey said, looking around for the keys.

"They're in it," said Jerry. "We checked."

He had on the same sweater Liane first saw him in, with the fishing flies attached. Besides Sarita's sawed-off he also held a big revolver that resembled a museum piece but, if it functioned, looked like it could drop a rhino.

Jerry handed the revolver to Mickey, who hated guns. He held it like a dead scorpion, with minimal skin contact. Handy reached into a coat pocket and passed Jerry two rolls of duct tape. Jerry dragged two metal chairs from the kitchen, and Corey and Sarita soon passed without resistance into sticky confinement. It didn't hurt that Handy had the shotgun pointed at them. And Sheila, eyes perched above jaws of death, followed their every move with profound concentration.

36

Liane stopped in Thessaly to use a pay phone.

When she was done, they drove south for an hour, pulling into a spot at a Park and Ride. She took out her prepaid cell phone and called Frank, but reached only his voicemail.

"Hi. Frank," she said, tears welling, the sound of his voice opening an emotional gate that she'd sealed shut until now. "Listen. I'm indisposed for another few days but I'm okay. I'll reach out again soon. My cell phone is lost. Don't trust anyone from Pentalon. And—Mom—if you can hold off on the funeral, I— Shit, Frank, it'd really do both of us a lot of good."

When she hung up she descended into sobs, and Mickey took a few minutes to massage her neck. She left the battery in the cell phone and tossed it onto the grassy median as darkness fell. Three hours later they found another Park and Ride, reclined the bucket seats of the Grand Am, and closed their eyes while Bea munched potato chips in back.

"The diaper's a good idea," Mickey said, as they fell asleep. "Let's keep it on."

37

It felt strange to be standing on the road to the Pentalon gate. Everything looked the same to Liane but somehow different, like the feeling you have when you dream about being in your bedroom and then sit up awake to see the place you always knew, but as if for the first time. Familiar, yet eerily unfamiliar.

They waited inside the Grand Am, which Mickey had pulled off to the shoulder. The sun scaled the wall of pines, knitting shafts of yellow light through twiggy branches. A buck with a small rack stepped on a dried stick in the woods and shied from the snapping sound it produced, showing his white tail to them as he bounded for the interior.

"You sure he's coming?" Mickey asked.

"Yes," said Liane. "I could hear it in his voice."

A few minutes later, the car pulled behind them, an unadorned silver Mercury Sable. Liane walked over to the driver's-side window and greeted Ronald Berg, still in his white smock. Hands trembling, he passed her a manila interoffice envelope closed with a red string-tie. She unspooled it rapidly, removed the few sheets of paper, and scanned their contents. *Pierre Sanza. Dikembe Kasa. Kinshasa.* It was all there, everything known about the twins' provenance.

"Thank you," she said, tucking the papers into her tote. She went around to the passenger door of the Sable and got in.

"What do you think you're doing?"

"It's not enough for me to have this information, Ronald. I need to be seen taking it."

He scrutinized the road. "Why can't you get your message across some other way, from outside somewhere?"

"It has to be credible and immediate. I can't leave anything open to interpretation. I need a camera in the core, where they constantly surveil. And I need you to put me there. There's no one else."

"That's not possible. I'd lose my job letting you in."

Liane pulled down the car visor and fluffed her hair in the mirror. It was limp, needed a washing.

"I know who you are," she said. She turned and fixed her gaze on him. "Is anything you told me true? Do you really have a significant other named Keith?"

"I never lied to you. Not a word."

"That's a relief. You didn't call me at my mother's house on behalf of Pentalon, did you?"

"No." He shook his head slowly.

"You provided me with a crucial bit of information then. In what capacity are you here now?"

"As a special friend. Truthfully, I sent up a flag after you called. No response came. I'm going on the presumption that you're working the right side of the equation."

Liane studied his face. He looked as lost as she'd felt for a long time, but she was beyond fretting now—not for herself, not for anybody. Only action would save Bea.

"Someone turned in Corey and Sarita yesterday," she said. "They'll be out of commission for a long time. That's probably why no one responded to your inquiry. One has to believe that a big law enforcement sweep will follow. We can imagine how that unfolds—cascades of information that won't be concealed from Flickinger and Gretch for long."

"All good things come to an end."

"Corey said he has moles in the strangest places. I thought of the way you stirred up the pot, sending Adnan those photos, calling me and steering me to Shaker. All very calculated. So I don't think you're the cynic about animal experiments that you claim to be. If I'm misjudging you…"

"My retirement account vests fully in three years. I guess it was wishful thinking to hope I'd make it that long on this precarious perch."

"You can hide me in your trunk. You don't need to be seen with me. But I have to get into that lab, and I have to do it now."

Ronald closed his eyes, took a deep breath and exhaled as if he were blowing up a balloon in one sustained effort.

"Okay," he said, "but please don't make me stick my neck out any farther than necessary."

She opened the glove compartment and pressed the trunk release button. When she got out of the Mercury she gave Mickey a thumbs-up. Bea, she saw, was sitting atop the dashboard, facing backward while eating grapes. She didn't notice Liane, who turned away and climbed into Ronald's trunk, pulling it closed.

Inside smelled like carpet shampoo and axle grease. Liane felt around in the dark for a tire iron, in case she had to fight her way out. The car swayed as Ronald pulled from the curb. He accelerated, turned, and stopped at the gate. They were a few minutes inching forward there, and she pictured Ronald exchanging conspiratorial hand gestures with the guard, but just as quickly banished that image from her mind. The car moved along, paused, swung around. She heard the crunch of gravel and it jostled to a stop. A moment later, the trunk popped open.

"There's the door." Ronald indicated the emergency exit where she'd first escaped with Bea.

The sight of it churned Liane's stomach.

"Give me five minutes," he said.

He got back into the car and peeled out toward the parking lot. Liane went to the steel door and crouched behind the bags of traction sand. The wait felt like an eternity, but at least she knew that Bea was safe this time. She slipped the papers from the envelope in her tote and clutched them against her chest.

The door clapped open, hitting the outside wall, but there was no sign of anyone. She caught it with her foot just before it swung closed, her pulse beating so loudly in her head that it took her a minute to perceive the horn of the alarm. She ran down the hall and, after two turns, flung open the door to the primate lab. A pair of technicians looked up, startled, as she burst in. They had a baboon laid out on an examination table, struggling against hands and arms gloved in leather to the shoulders, and one tech held a large syringe. Time slowed down. Liane saw with clarity the animals in their cages, begging for mercy with their eyes, smelled the stench of body fluids mingled with antiseptic, the essence of life leaching away. *What did I do?* she thought. *What was I part of?*

She ignored the dumbfounded technicians and stepped toward the tinted bubble that concealed a camera and microphone. She held up the papers one at a time, her hand now steady with rage. Lowering the last page, she stared straight into the circle of the lens, barely visible through the protective shell, and channeled her anger the way she'd seen Sarita do: "Axel, you bastard! If you want your bonobo, I'll see you in Kinshasa! Yes?"

In the hall, a cage full of white rats sat atop a utility cart. Liane grabbed the cage and stormed from the place, racing for the push bar to freedom without further hesitation. She burst forth and sprinted up the grass to the woods as a single security guard, emerging from a golf cart, gave chase.

Mickey, she knew, awaited her in the car on the other side of the woods, not far from the abandoned FAULT camp. He should have the engine running, ready to take off the moment she hit the seat. But the cage weighed her down and the guard was gaining. He lunged and missed her by inches, her knees burning, her momentum fading.

Just then, from behind, came the sound of more footsteps and something that resembled a rebel yell. Ronald Berg caught the security guard from behind and they tumbled to the ground, rolling backward on the grass in a tangle of limbs.

Liane didn't look again. She pressed forward, gasping for breath, and plunged into the woods.

FOUR

O, my offence is rank, it smells to heaven;
It hath the primal eldest curse upon't,
A brother's murder.

— WILLIAM SHAKESPEARE

1

—

Through a chain-link fence, Liane and Mickey stared at the Pentalon jet, a Boeing 747 sheathed in silver, the only plane of its size at Republic Executive Airport. It was three a.m. and the plane was dark.

"You really think—" Mickey began.

"It's Axel Flickinger," Liane interrupted. "He isn't flying commercial."

They went to the corner of the squat terminal and peered through its glass doors. A skeleton crew manned the facility at this hour: a receptionist in a red blazer and two uniformed TSA guards.

"There must be more somewhere," Mickey said.

"We just need to get to the other side before they notice we're here."

"Any metal on your person?"

"I tossed the phones."

"Straight through the portal, then. Ready?"

Liane had Bea on her back. Mickey wielded the rat cage.

The TSA workers were occupied with their own boredom over by the equipment, flicking spitballs through finger goalposts. When the receptionist turned away to fiddle with some brochures, Liane eased one door forward and Mickey snapped the cage open. In an instant, a dozen white rats scrambled into the terminal.

"*Dzikinuka,*" Liane whispered.

"What's that mean?"

"Be free. Shaker taught it to me."

The rats seemed to be everywhere at once, and the TSA workers came running. Heading in the opposite direction, Liane and Mickey used a door by a side wall. As the three employees scrambled, they hugged the wall with Bea and sprinted for the door to the tarmac.

No one saw them.

2
—

"Axel, you bastard! If you want your bonobo, I'll see you in Kinshasa! Yes?"

"Axel, you bastard! If you want your bonobo, I'll..."

The image mesmerized Flickinger. He aimed the remote control at the big digital screen on the bulkhead. Rewound. Played it again: Liane Vinson waving the bonobo papers, mugging for the security camera.

"Axel, you bastard! If you want your..."

Gretch had an awful headache. He let his attention drift from the screen and focused on the sharp lines of Axel's face, drawn into an isosceles triangle, eyes burning with icy fury.

"She is mocking me, yes?" Flickinger said. "Why?"

"Because she hates your guts? Because you mutilated one of her apes? Because she finally can?"

"But she went out of her way. What does she have to gain?"

"She's a live wire. I wouldn't read too much into it."

Flickinger unlocked his captain's chair with the press of a lever and spun around to face his security director across the broad aisle. "Have you so lost your edge, Mr. Gretch, that you cannot see she is up to something? She wants us in Kinshasa. Perhaps she *needs* us in Kinshasa. This is more than a snit fit. The question is: why?"

"I had a bad feeling from the start about her," Gretch said.

"One would prefer not to have made a mistake of this nature. But with living organisms and their occasional independence of mind, some misjudgments are inevitable. The important thing is to recognize the error and clean it up as soon as possible, yes?"

"With animals it's easier."

"Sure. It is what attracts me to them. All the same, we need to reassert control over this enterprise."

A stewardess came up and asked the men if they needed anything. She was all legs and blonde, just as Gretch liked them. He wished he had the energy to take her back to one of the two bedrooms on board and bend her over the dresser. But his strength level was so low he only wanted to sleep. The lingering effects of his fight with the bonobo and the blow to his head in Hammurabi's kitchen were things he could handle under normal circumstances, but he hadn't been able to refuel for forty-eight hours. Since his visit to the zoo, he couldn't keep food down. And his whole body ached, besides. He ordered three aspirins and a glass of mineral water.

"For you, Dr. Flickinger?"

Flickinger, distracted by the video, didn't acknowledge the stewardess. He pressed the power button on the remote control, blacking out the screen, but continued staring at the bulkhead. He fiddled one shirt button between thumb and middle finger and turned to study the floor of cottony clouds out the plane window.

"He'll have what I'm having, beautiful," Gretch said, winking. He loosened his collar and shivered as he watched her walk away.

Flickinger faced him again. "What do you know about the arrest of Corey Harrow and that accomplice of his?"

"Only that a couple of local cretins turned them in, possibly for the reward money."

"And the bonobo?"

"Evidence she was there at some point, but no confirmation of her whereabouts. The retards say she headed for the woods, but they don't sound too reliable. The feds'll be checking anyway, I'd imagine. It'll be hard to do any kind of real canvas, though, without getting the whole community roused up. More likely they'll scramble a few copters and send some snipers out there on a search-and-destroy mission."

"The government knows she's ours?"

"Of course."

"They're wasting their time, yes?"

Gretch reached into his pocket and placed the RFID on the leather armrest of Flickinger's chair. The boss dropped his hand to it and turned it over absently, mulling. "It might have been removed some time ago."

"Yeah," said Gretch, "and the Seven Dwarfs might've been living in that Central Park cave. But they weren't. The little beast is on the move somehow, somewhere, and that girl's providing the transportation. That's my analysis."

"I am inclined to agree. I did not ask you to join me on this flight in order to chase some wayward paperwork."

Gretch reflected. "Why come yourself?"

"The bonobo requires handling by someone she knows. Losing that animal has led us to this crisis. Regaining it will perhaps begin to make us whole again. The girl is another matter."

"Vinson will find that in the Congo I don't have many constraints. There are only the rules of the jungle. By luring us there on purpose, she's miscalculating real bad."

The stewardess returned with the aspirins on a silver tray. Gretch swallowed all six and took a few gulps of water. He thought he must have hit the floor hard when they beaned him from behind at the monkey man's house. He ached to the bone.

"If you'll excuse me," he said, wobbling to his feet, "I gotta go lie down."

"Alone?" Flickinger eyed the stewardess in the galley.

"Most definitely. I had a snack at the zoo that didn't agree with me. I'm still feeling the effects."

Gretch rose and walked back toward the bathroom. He pushed open the door and caught sight of his pale face in the vanity mirror. The bathroom, decorated with tumbled marble and chrome fixtures, stood in sleek contrast to the ratty image Gretch saw before him: uneven hair, bandaged ear, and three long scabs from temple to cheek, struggling to heal. He opened the cabinet and located a bottle of antiemetic pills, swallowing several of them dry. It had been a hell of a week, he thought, but as soon as he could hold down some food he'd be all right. Kinshasa was a web of fear. It should do him a world of good.

3

In the morning Dikembe felt achy and listless. He sat on the edge of the cot for a long time, Daniel looking on with concern. When he attempted to stand, a charley horse seized one of his legs. He fell back and sucked a deep breath. His ribs hurt.

"Hand me my shoes." He gestured to Daniel.

Dikembe ran his fingers through the lining of his work boots and found his remaining treasure intact.

They left the hotel in the afternoon, Dikembe limping along, feeling worse than miserable. The heat and pollution didn't help, car and truck fumes choking them for long stretches. They walked down Boulevard du 30 Juin, a broad modern thoroughfare, into the district known as La Gombe, past heavily guarded government buildings, large red-roofed residences half-hidden behind fences and hedges, shining office towers reflecting the glaring sun. Somewhere inside those towers, Dikembe knew, men traded fortunes of diamonds. He and Daniel paused by a revolving door.

The guard on the sidewalk waved a billy club to move them along. "Hey, no loitering here."

Dikembe looked down at his scuffed boots, the legs of his soiled pants, the sweat-stained shirt clinging to his chest. In the villages, his appearance would have gone without notice. Here in the commercial precinct of the big city it marked him as an outsider. As men passed in flowing suits and shiny shoes, his original thought—to attain a visit to one of those offices and sell his diamonds—now revealed itself as preposterous. He tugged Daniel along and they turned the corner.

"But why didn't we go in?" Daniel asked.

"We don't have an appointment."

They went on, Dikembe pondering the task before them. He needed a berth on a boat to get up to Mbandaka, from where he would follow the Ruki River into the area of Salonga. They would require food—or currency with which to buy food from others aboard—and maybe a *bambula* and charcoal for cooking. They would need some form of protection from the sun. They also could use something soft on which to rest their heads for the long journey against the current. And something with which to defend themselves, perhaps a machete.

Back in the neighborhood of the hotel, they found a variety shop, where Dikembe selected a tarp and some rope with which to make their shelter, as well as a fishing pole, which might also come in handy on the boat. He chose a canvas bag in which to carry the other small possessions they'd need for their journey. He placed his items on the counter and bent over to fiddle with his shoe.

The clerk, a Middle Eastern man with skin the color of road dust, calculated the bill on a scratch pad and gave Dikembe the total.

Dikembe rose with three small diamonds in his hand, uncut, brownish, cloudy as pond water. He held them out and the man forced a smile. "What am I supposed to do with those?"

4

___

The Pentalon plane had a two-story hold encompassing what would serve as the main passenger cabin and baggage stowage area of a commercial airliner. The size of the space surprised Mickey and Liane, even divided into cages and closets and cubicles. It looked like a narrow warehouse, the tops of curved exterior walls—eighteen feet tall—nearly disappearing into empty darkness. Extinguished halogen fixtures hung inert, shadowy disks in the gloom. The only light came from the faint orange glow of LED tubes, laid into the floor and woven through the beams of the windowless lower fuselage. The camera system appeared to be off. They found their way to a bank of seats that were bolted to the floor in one corner, and Bea ate a banana while the roaring whine of the engines echoed fiercely through the empty hold, causing her to grimace and cover her ears with her hands.

"Look at that," Mickey said. "Hear no evil."

Liane gulped. Being successfully airborne represented a step closer to danger, she feared, not away from it.

They struggled to make themselves comfortable, exploring their options, observing in dim light the massive aluminum hooks and steel cables intended for the management of animal transport crates and cages. Finally, they collapsed to the floor alongside a row of empty foot-lockers.

Mickey shivered. "Not for nothing, but it's probably like twenty degrees below zero at cruising altitude. It's gonna get awful cold in here over the next twelve hours."

Liane began opening cabinets, looking through closets. "They must store all the supplies off the plane," she said. "There's hardly anything here." She found a single thin blanket and held it up. "The exception that proves the rule. Where do we hide for the duration?"

"The footlocker," Mickey concluded. "We can't stay exposed. The one by the bulkhead's against an interior wall. It may not get as chilly."

Liane pulled off her sweater. "Layers," she said. "We'll squeeze into both of ours with Bea between us."

"It's for your own good," Mickey told Bea. "Cooperate."

They spooned with the bonobo between them, then managed to stretch Liane's sweater over their torsos, followed by Mickey's shirt and the blanket. They climbed with great effort into the footlocker, lying on their sides, all facing the same direction.

"*Butu*," Bea whimpered. "*Pio*."

"She's back to Lingala. Do you think she understands where we're going?"

"I don't know. Let's get some sleep."

Sandwiched so awkwardly, Mickey took forever to work down the locker lid with a heel. It clunked them into complete darkness.

5
—

"No kidding," Pulsipher said. "First name's Handel, like the composer?"

"I don't know anything about that," the FBI agent shrugged. "Handel Amadeus Wagner. That's what's on his driver's license. We ran a check. No priors. Owns his own home, inherited from his parents."

The agent's rolling eyes had a twinkle in them. *Not characteristic of the species,* Pulsipher thought.

"I got a guy going over there now," the agent continued, "probably find a meth lab in the garage or bodies in the root cellar, by the looks of him. But so far he seems to be just your average Joe Citizen with a shotgun and a taste for local adventure. Makes a living shuttling folks around without a hack's license. His father was a prison guard, I'm told. The friend's got a similar story, but he's just a follower."

"Couple a melon heads, then."

"You been looking for this guy Harrow, what? Ten years?"

"Nine, but who's counting?"

"And these two characters haul him in?"

"The Lord works in mysterious ways. Send Mr. Wagner around, will you?"

"Kid gloves, awright? He's no suspect, probably get a nice write-up in the regional papers. He's officially in *our* custody."

The agent disappeared around the front of the house while Pulsipher looked about the yard, amazed as usual by the quotidian nature of it all, murderers and terrorists living among us, happy as you please, watching ESPN and scratching their nuts while they plotted the end of civilization. He hadn't looked, but he'd have bet good money there was a fresh container of milk in the fridge and a couple sticks of butter. Always was. *Fry an egg, hide from the feds. Edit radical manifestos, drink your coffee. Oil your weapon, spread some jam on your toast. Then type your plans for total mayhem into the laptop so you can keep it all straight. Just another day at the safe house!*

There was a swing set in the yard, its frame and slide recently painted. Pulsipher pictured the ape atop it, Corey and Sarita standing nearby grilling veggie burgers in their own twisted version of domestic bliss. He'd get to Harrow soon enough, he thought—maybe tonight, when they finished setting up the quarantine room at the hospital. Meanwhile, there were other sources of information to cull from.

Two agents in surgical masks brought Handel Wagner around. He was short and square with a globular face. The agents retreated.

"You can remove your mask, if you want," Pulsipher said.

"Damn happy to."

The man pulled it free and balled it in his fist. His smile revealed a set of teeth that Pulsipher thought would revolt the English.

"I'd shake your hand," Pulsipher said, introducing himself, "but there's a fear of disease."

The man nodded. "The monkey."

"Right. We don't want to violate too many procedures at once, Mr. Wagner."

"You can call me Handy. Everyone does."

Pulsipher led Handy to a redwood picnic table in the corner of the rear lawn. They sat diagonally across from one another, the agent wishing suddenly that he was with his kids in his own yard in Arlington. *All work and no play makes Henley a bad father,* he thought. He had Harrow now, which was a major coup. Soon as he swept up the whole bonobo mess, he figured, it'd be time for a long-overdue vacation. He pondered the picture of Rome that Jimmy took, squinted at Handy to refocus.

"An unusual set of names you have there, friend. Who was the classical music fan?"

"My mother listened to opera all day."

"Then she should have named you after Rossini or Verdi or like that."

"That was my brother's name, actually. Ross. He passed away. I ain't under arrest, am I?"

"No. We just need to make sure you're on the up and up, if you get my meaning. The guy you turned in is very bad news."

"They took my daughter's dog, Sheila. Are they gonna give her back?"

"Honestly, I'm not sure," Pulsipher admitted. "She had blood on her jowls and there's this deal with the ape. Anyone in the vicinity—any *thing* in the vicinity of the ape—needs to be thoroughly checked out. That's why the house is sealed up."

"More than we bargained for, I guess."

"It's the theme of the month. Who's your friend, the guy who helped you?"

"Jerry? Baba au rhum."

"Baba what?"

"You know. Those Italian desserts, like a sponge cake soaked in alcohol? Sell 'em down at the deli in town. That's Jerry. Generally he goes where I point him."

"And you pointed him to this house, to apprehend a criminal on the FBI short list? Mind if I ask why you'd do a thing like that?"

"Personal reasons. It involves a woman."

"Not the redhead, Sarita?"

"Nope."

"You hoping for the reward money?"

"I don't care much, but what's mine is mine. I'll take my half, maybe buy a new car, some other things. Help out my daughter and her mom. Get Jerry a new sweater."

"And the other half?"

"I'm told it belongs to a guy in the prison over there."

"Who told you?"

"The girl. Says the guy in prison was an accomplice of Harrow's. I took her to see him once or twice."

"You're talking about Shaker Moyo."

"She never told me his name. I guess he gave up his friend."

Pulsipher thought of Moyo's recent new visitor and drummed his fingers on the redwood table. It was a nice stain job, he noticed, should last awhile, even in the sun.

"So Liane Vinson sent you to get Corey, is that it?"

"Yeah," Handy admitted.

"And the chimp didn't run into the woods like you told the FBI agents, did she?"

Handy furrowed his brow. "Do I need a lawyer?"

"Nah. Listen, just tell me flat out. Liane's got the chimp, hasn't she?"

"I suppose. She left with it in her arms."

"I'll be damned."

"She gave me a note for you. You're Pulsipher, you said, right?"

Pulsipher stared at Handy, whose cheeks had drooped into a fleshy frown. He thought of the federal employees he had scrambling all over the woods, the CDC guys about to descend on Pentalon, the vise closing on Flickinger, but neither tightly nor quickly enough. Gretch was still out there, too.

"The girl gave you a note and you're just getting around to telling me now?"

Handy reached into his pocket and Pulsipher flinched for his weapon. Handy raised a palm. "They patted me down already."

"You always wanna move deliberately in the presence of an officer." Pulsipher let his gun settle back into the shoulder holster. Handy already had the envelope in front of him, folded and wrinkled.

Pulsipher hesitated. "They didn't take that from you?"

"They gave me back everything that was mine, except the dog and the shotgun."

"I see." He thought of the virus, that great unknown. "They decontaminated it?"

"They put everything of mine through a big machine of some kind, bright lights inside and whatnot. Even my clothes. I never touched the monkey, though. Never got near her."

Pulsipher pulled on a pair of rubber gloves. "Those aren't your clothes?"

"Sure. They gave 'em back. You gonna take the note?"

Pulsipher tore it open and read it quickly. Written by hand on a plain sheet of paper, it wasn't long.

"Sweet Jesus." He adjusted his glasses. "You done good, Mr. Wagner."

He slipped the note into his jacket pocket as he stood to go.

By the time he reached the swing set, Special Agent Pulsipher found himself running at a dead sprint.

6

The thump of the plane hitting the ground jolted them awake. Liane's arm was asleep. It tingled as she wiggled her fingers. Bea pressed a knee into the small of her back as Mickey shifted his shoulders.

"Not yet," he said. "We have to wait. What the hell's that smell?"

"*Bosoto*," Bea said. "Dirty."

"It's her diaper."

"Oh, for cryin' out loud!"

"You couldn't expect her to hold it in. I have to pee, myself."

They squirmed for an hour, Bea squeezed between them, the stench nearly overwhelming, until Liane couldn't handle the pressure anymore.

"I'm gonna burst, Mickey. If they murder me, so be it."

She lifted a leg and kicked open the cover of the footlocker, which made an echoing crash against the bulkhead. They worked themselves up, wriggling out of the tight space and the shared clothes. No human sound emanated from within the plane, but the equipment ticked, expanding in the warming air.

Mickey was peeking up the stairs when Liane and Bea emerged from the lavatory. He waved her to a far corner. "Voices up there," he whispered, "inside the plane."

"We have to get out."

They decided to use an emergency exit that was situated up a ladder along the inside of the fuselage. Mickey went first with Bea hanging onto his back, Liane so close she bumped into his ankles several times. He pushed open the door and pursed his lips. "Nighttime."

Liane followed him through the door and onto the wing. The air outside felt thicker than porridge and there was no breeze.

"I'll lower myself down," Mickey said. "Toss Bea to me first, then I'll catch you."

He pushed Bea into Liane's arms and disappeared over the edge, his fingers clinging to the back of the wing for a moment, dark against the silver skin. Liane realized that the only illumination came from the moon and from a lone floodlight at the corner of the terminal building. Mickey's fingers disappeared and she heard a thud.

"Landed on my feet," he called. "Bea's turn. C'mon, Bea!"

Liane peered over the edge of the wing. Mickey was just a shadow there in the darkness, his features unreadable. She crouched on one knee, trying to guide Bea into his vicinity.

"No!" Bea said. "No no!"

Liane shoved her in Mickey's direction, but Bea grabbed at her sweater and Liane had to push a second time even as she lost her own balance. The effort spun her around on the lip of the wing. In her peripheral vision she saw Bea recede into the darkness.

"Got her!" Mickey called.

"Ahh!" Liane cried. Her hips passed the point of no return as she twirled. Her arms smacked against the top of the wing. She gripped the polished aluminum with her fingers but couldn't get traction. Her fingertips dragged across the rivets, slowly giving up their grip. Then she was off the wing, falling through the air, leaving her breath behind.

Oof! Mickey's arms engulfed her. He must have seen the terror on her face, even in the dark. "I gotcha, I gotcha."

They oriented themselves on the tarmac. There were several planes in this area, Pentalon's being the biggest, landing gear held in place by bright orange blocks. The terminal building, a low-lying yellow structure with a glass tower in the center, was a way off. They were near a chain-link fence, behind which lay scattered brush. Black mountains loomed beyond.

Out of the darkness, a figure emerged, wearing camouflaged military fatigues, a rifle strapped over his shoulder.

"*Mbote,*" he nodded, shuffling his feet.

Liane and Mickey froze in their tracks.

"Sir. Madam," the soldier added in French. "Follow me please. You are under arrest."

7

The soldier strode behind them, deliberate, as if it required great concentration to lift his heavy boots off the ground in the dark.

"*Kotala,*" Bea said. "*Sanza.*"

"*Parlez-vous* Lingala?" the soldier said to the side of Liane's head.

Mickey saw at once that the soldier presumed Bea's words came from Liane. "*Quelques mots seulement,*" he said. "Do you speak English, by any chance?"

"*Oui.* Where you from?"

"New York. We didn't have money for the plane tickets and we forgot our passports. Plus," Mickey shrugged, "the ape was a problem."

"Right. And my mother's a warthog. How do you come to have this little beast?" He reached out to touch Bea, who clung tight to Liane's shirt.

"She got misdirected in America," Liane said, "and ended up in a bad neighborhood."

"Ah." The soldier paused, turned to Mickey. "I know something about New York. I have a cousin who lives in Fort Greene, Brooklyn."

"Fort Green! No kidding? I got a cousin there, too. What's his name?"

"Cyril."

"Nah, mine's named Johnnie. Owns a restaurant."

"You didn't think we'd have the same cousin!"

"It seemed unlikely. Is yours happy in the States?"

"Very much."

"I could set him up with a good table."

"A table?"

"At my cousin's restaurant."

"That would be fantastic." The soldier stopped. "Hey, my feet are tired. Maybe you'd like to buy me a beer."

"Sure. Where's that happen?"

"No no no. You buy me the beer. I get it later."

"Corruption," Liane grumbled.

"I call it thirst," the soldier said. "You can buy me a beer now or buy one for the jailer. It's your choice—but the jailer drinks more, *vous comprenez?*"

Mickey pulled a wad of cash from his pocket and leafed through the bills in the darkness. The whites of the soldier's eyes glowed.

"I don't have any Congolese francs," Mickey said.

"American dollars are better."

"Not forever. You just wait."

"'In the long run,' said Keynes, 'we're all dead.'"

Mickey laughed. "That's right. How'd you know that?"

"I'm educated. But soldiering is the only job I can get. Forty American sets you free."

"Forty'll do ya," Mickey agreed, "if you'll guide us to a taxi."

He crossed the soldier's palm with the bills and they shook on it.

"You tourists have to watch out for taxis in this town," the soldier warned. "Don't flash your money. They'll drive you to the bush and leave you to die."

"But you'll take us to a friend, right?"

"Of course. In honor of Johnnie!"

"And Cyril!"

"Don't say a word," the soldier said.

"*Maloba*," said Bea.

The soldier turned to Liane. "That's *liloba*. *Maloba* is the plural."

"*Liloba*," Liane repeated, clearing her throat. "Thank you. *Liloba*. Word. I'll remember it."

"Now follow me on through," said the soldier. "Don't let anyone stop you. You're with *me*, understand?"

The airport was deserted. They crossed several checkpoints unmolested, the soldier escorting them past his colleagues. There were four scuffed and dented vans by the curb, their drivers asleep. The soldier used the tip of his rifle to rap on the side window of the second one.

"*Mbote*. Wake up!"

The driver stirred.

8

Liane let the hotel shower run and run, pouring down over her. She was halfway around the world, but she felt closer to returning home than she had in a long time—the closest since she'd set eyes on the bonobos and left that mythical path: *the straight and narrow*. Maybe forever.

She thought of her mother and sat on the edge of the tub with the shower running, crying into the hard water that stung her eyes. She regretted the way she'd spoken to her mother sometimes, and it was all now lost forever. She cried until the water ran cold. Then she turned off the shower and dried herself and dabbed her eyes with the towel.

She had to finish what she'd started, finish it and get home to Frank, as she'd promised. She had to say a proper goodbye at her mother's final place of rest, too. And both could only be done, she knew, when she was free of her obligation to Bea, free both from the light and the shadow that the mutated bonobo had cast over her.

When she was dressed Liane passed Bea, asleep on the couch, and joined Mickey on the small terra cotta terrace. The sky on the horizon, moments before sunrise, was vivid as the flesh of a blood orange, with layers of dark clouds building in the foreground. It seemed like a primal display—dawn as it once had been. Then the red rooftops and the deep green treetops of the city clarified below.

"The key to Bea's survival," said Liane, "is out there somewhere. If only we could reach down and grab it."

"We will, in our way. She's almost home."

Liane shook her head. "If we don't get her to the right spot—to the bonobos she was born among, her real family—she's good as dead. On the map Congo looked manageable. Now, from this vantage point, I sense its vastness. Hammurabi said it would be impossible."

"He told you that? Screw him. There's fate carrying us forward, Liane. Consider the odds we beat just to get here."

She took his hand in hers, thinking of Frank's gambling sheets. "What if we've used up all our luck just getting here, Mick?"

"Nah. Branch Rickey—guy who brought Jackie Robinson to the Dodgers?—said luck is the residue of design. We fell into this whole thing, both of us, but now we're turning for the home stretch under our own steam. The finish line? We'll find it."

"Or it'll find us." Liane looked through the door at Bea. "What so scares humans about the prospect of a talking animal, anyway?"

"You mean besides the plain freakiness of it? I've always thought it's because we don't really want to know what's going on inside their heads. We're a conservative race. We don't like to have our illusions shattered."

"There's something to that. But I think, more than knowing who *they* really are inside, we fear that they'll tell us the truth about *our-selves*—about who *we* really are."

"About who Axel and Hammurabi and their ilk are, I give you that. That's what *they* fear, maybe."

Liane blanched. "Me, too, then. I was one of them."

"I like to think that was under duress, just like me putting down horses."

"But I enjoyed it. I felt fulfilled for a while."

"Yeah, until the cutting started. You came to your senses quick enough after that. Should we finish what we began?"

"We're out of diapers."

"No more bonobo domesticity."

They rode the elevator down with Bea in Mickey's arms. Cracks showed in the walls of the modern lobby, and layers of ground-in dirt accumulated in corners where the floor-polishing machine wouldn't reach.

The concierge was a white man with a South African accent and a pinched face. He eyed Bea. "What can I do for you today?"

"We're wondering," Liane said, "where one would go to buy an animal like this one."

"That's a bonobo you have there, correct? It's illegal to traffic in them."

"We understand," said Mickey, slipping a bill into the concierge's hand. "We're looking for a particular dealer. Would you recognize if we mentioned who?"

"I'm afraid not. Do you have an address?"

Liane shook her head. "Just a man's name."

The concierge unfolded a photocopied city map and used a red marker to draw a circle in the midst of it. "You can try here. They congregate near the animal market, by the train station. It's crowded with locals. Tourists stand out as easy marks."

"Is it more dangerous than most neighborhoods?"

"It's a shakedown on every corner in Kinshasa. Seven million people live in this city, and most are desperately poor. The majority are God-fearing, but plenty others would kill you for your broken wristwatch. It makes life cheap." He frowned. "I can hire you an armed guard, but I need a day's notice. No amount of baksheesh will change that."

"We don't have a day to waste."

"I can call you a car and that's the best I can do. At least you won't have to walk."

"He'll put us in the animal market?"

"Yes. Door to door." He picked up the phone. "I warn you, though, getting two bonobos out of the country won't be easy. It requires entering another realm entirely, and not one where the faint of heart rule—or the indigent. You'll pay twenty thousand U.S. in bribes, I'd imagine."

"What if we're not planning to take a bonobo out? Rather, to put one back."

"I don't understand. It's a return?"

"You might say."

"Don't count on getting your money back."

9

Gretch sat on the mattress as the ceiling fan rasped through malodorous air, its spinning blades doing nothing to loosen the grip of heat or humidity. He pulled a beetle off his cheek, thinking the room felt like a sauna where someone had pissed on the glowing coals. He didn't comprehend how Flickinger could stand there looking cucumber-cool in his blue blazer, no inkling of sweat, playing with his coat button. *The man isn't human,* Gretch thought. *The atmosphere itself doesn't touch him.*

They stared together at a web in one corner with a large black-and-yellow spider guarding the center. Flickinger poked his fingernail into a sticky strand and they watched the spider flinch, assess the intruder, then freeze.

"It is not enough to wait," Flickinger observed. "One must be *prepared* for that which one awaits."

Gretch stood and walked to the window, using the barrel of his Kimber to move the battered shutter. He looked out on the street, still and gray under gathering clouds. In addition to a foul smell wafting from the river, the air now held the odor of ionization. Thunderstorms. They rumbled not far away.

"This is where they'll come," Gretch said. "Dikembe Kasa's the primary source, the name on the manifest papers."

"But this room appears to be unoccupied."

"Like anyone from the bush, Kasa probably carries all his possessions with him. You see these people around here lugging their stuff in baskets on their heads?"

"It is not what is on the man's head that worries me. It is what is inside it. From the account we heard, he means to make trouble. When we are done with him, it would be better—"

"No doubt."

"In fact, anyone who knows that the bonobo can talk must fall into permanent silence," Flickinger said.

"I'm on it."

"I am feeling impatient. I wonder whether they beat us to him."

"Impossible." Gretch looked out the window again. If anything it was darker, and gusts had begun to shove the dust around. "Even if they left ahead of us, the commercial flights all lay over in Paris. And we came direct."

"That sounds like conjecture. Your intelligence indicates no flight number?"

"They weren't on any lists—not under their real names. But if they had help from FAULT then they might have forged identities. Anyway, the nexus is here now. We'll wait right in this room. They'll come."

Flickinger slid his hands into his coat pockets and frowned. "I had a call while you slept on the plane from a source in the Department of Agriculture. It seems federal policy toward Pentalon is changing, and not in our favor."

"Don't tell me it's all going to hell," Gretch said, suppressing a cramp below his navel. It surprised him; he'd never had a nervous stomach.

"As for the girl," Flickinger said, "she is looking for the perfect solution for the bonobo, which is what brings her to Kinshasa, in my estimation. If we are to salvage this situation, our response must be equally perfect. We have allowed too much to slip."

Fear, Gretch thought. There seemed to be an epidemic of it. A contraction seized his lower bowel again, forcing him to pause his breathing. It took great effort not to grab for his abdomen.

Gretch holstered his pistol. "I gotta run to the john."

He walked down the hall and into a filthy bathroom with a cracked mirror and a sink hanging from rusty pipes. The toilet had no seat. A clammy sweat engulfed him as he squatted. He'd seen cleaner latrines among GIs in the desert, but it wasn't the state of the privy that grossed him out—it was the bloody stools he shat. Something was real wrong with his intestines. He yanked his pants up and buckled his belt hastily.

"No sign of them yet," Flickinger said when Gretch returned.

Gretch contemplated the person they were up against. *The girl,* he thought, *fears greatly what might happen to the bonobo—has always feared it—like a mother for her child.* This fear activated instincts that could overcome the most daunting obstacles. But it was a primate, not a human child, that she had in her possession, and a stolen one at that. The correct order of the universe was overdue for restoration, and the task fell to Gretch.

He sat once more on the cot, flipped open his knife, and tested the edge with a thumb. He liked that it was clean again, shiny and sterile and sharp as a motherfucker. He weighed it in his hand as they waited.

10

The streets in the animal market carried the reek of a dirty barnyard on a wet day, ripe with the perfume of damp fur and manure. Rickety pickup trucks rolled by, goats crammed in back standing on quivering bandy legs. Live chickens clucked in tight crates and schools of fish roiled tanks of cloudy water. Smoked monkeys hung from wooden poles.

In this environment, a bonobo on a man's shoulders didn't draw a second look. They trundled along the crowded sidewalks, inquiring after the dealer Pierre Sanza. A shriveled woman selling lizards and frogs knew him. She directed them to the other side of the street, a block away. In the crowds, Bea wouldn't settle down. She left Mickey's shoulders and walked along the ground holding Liane's hand and blurting out Lingala: *kotala* and *wapi* and *moto* and *bosoto* and dozens of other words beyond their understanding.

The skinny girl in front of Sanza's shop gaped at their approach. She had a fly swatter in hand made of meshed grass, which she waved lazily over the cuts of raw meat, never taking her eyes from the visitors.

Bea stared at the small crocodile thrashing on a chain. "*Mabe,*" she said. "*Bomo.*"

The bonobo's words, no longer lost among crowds or darkness, riveted the girl.

"*Mbote.* Do you speak English?" Liane asked.

"A little."

"Can you tell me what this ape is saying?"

"*Mabe*, bad. *Bomo*, fear."

"She doesn't like the croc. What does *bowling-go* mean?"

"*Bolingo* is love."

"*En-decko*?"

"*Ndeko* mean brother."

"I hate to interrupt the language lesson," Mickey said, "but is this the shop of Pierre Sanza?"

The girl stared at the tattoos around his arms, as if trying to parse their meaning. She turned to the butchered meat and waved the fly swatter about.

"We're looking for Pierre Sanza, the animal dealer," Mickey persisted, bending into her face. "It's extremely important."

"Always these days," the girl looked up, "for Pierre it is important. You want buy apes?"

"Tell us where he is."

Mickey dangled a five-dollar bill, but the girl only fluttered her eyes.

Just then a large man with a round face, dark-skinned, parted the beaded curtain in rear.

"I am Pierre." He smiled.

When they turned to him, the girl snatched the bill from Mickey's fingers. He let it go.

"We need a word," Mickey said.

"Who sent you?"

"Pentalon. Axel Flickinger. Sound familiar?"

"Again?" His smile became forced. "Okay. Please step into my office."

They ignored the feel of the girl's eyes on their backs as they passed a riot of animal-part curios, piled on shelves in the anteroom. Sanza wore a pinstripe suit with the collar open and polished black shoes with square toes. Thick gold chains hung from his neck, and he had a diamond-encrusted gold watch strapped to his wrist. He sat behind the big desk and waved a hand toward the guest chairs.

As they sat, Bea looked at the baby gorilla resting listlessly in its cage. She wrapped her arms around Mickey's neck. "Sad," she said. "Sad."

"Ah, the talking bonobo," exclaimed Sanza. "So they've found her."

"Not exactly," said Liane.

Sanza looked to Mickey, who spread his hands in the air, palms up. "We're here on a freelance assignment of sorts. You know how it is. Did you sell this bonobo to Pentalon?"

"Possibly. Who could say for sure?"

"Don't they get tagged with RFIDs?"

"Not by me. Somewhere in Europe or the States, they may. I don't ask too many questions about that."

"But you do sell animals to Pentalon," Liane said.

"I sell to anyone with the ability to pay in hard currency. Can I interest you in a young gorilla?" He gestured. "Unfortunately, it has become separated from its mother."

"The mother was killed, I bet," Liane said. "By poachers."

"You don't know that. Accidents happen in nature. A lion might've eaten the mother, a tree might've fallen on her. It's not my place to ask."

Liane bit her lip.

Bea took a lollipop from the elephant-foot bowl. "Okay?"

"Fascinating." Sanza nodded.

Mickey pulled the wrapper off the lollipop and handed it back to Bea.

"Thank you," Liane said. "Say thank you."

"Good," Bea said.

"If I did sell somebody this ape," said Sanza, reaching to slide open a desk drawer, "I undoubtedly charged not enough for her."

Mickey stretched across the desk and forced the drawer closed. "A little late for that, Mr. Sanza. We're interested in where she came from."

"And I," said Sanza, leaning back, "am interested in where she's going."

"Do you even know where she originated?" asked Liane.

"If this is the bonobo I think it is, then much time has passed. Months. I'm only a middleman. Sometimes the sources do tell me. Occasionally, what they tell me is actually true."

"Maybe we can ring a bell," Mickey said, reaching into his pocket. "The provider was named Dikembe Kasa. She's one of twins."

"So I now figure. You're not with Pentalon at all, are you? You're the people who stole this animal."

"No. Kasa's the one who stole her," Liane corrected. "And Pentalon exploited her. The term for what we did is *liberate*."

Mickey rested his fist on the edge of the desk, showing off a wad of bills. "I'm interested in confirming a saying I once heard." He began leafing through them. "The expression is that money makes the world go round. I wonder if you agree."

He held out a hundred-dollar bill.

"These people are dangerous," Sanza said through clenched teeth.

"We only need an address," Mickey said. "Soon as we hit the door, we forget where we got it."

"What are you looking to do with this bonobo?"

"That's our business, kinda like what you said. Let's just say there's no place like home."

"And you're asking me to jeopardize my livelihood for that?"

He reached for the drawer again. Mickey jumped around the desk and forced it closed with a knee.

"Your livelihood's already in jeopardy from where we stand," he said. "If you go after that drawer one more time you'll have the United States government on your ass. There's a special agent friend of mine not far behind us and he has an interest in seeing us leave your shop unscathed, with the chimp in tow. If that doesn't happen . . . well, his expertise is gumming up the wheels of commerce. No tickee, no monkey. Get my meaning?"

Sanza folded his hands across his belly. He looked to the gorilla in the cage then at Mickey. "Five hundred."

"Two."

"Two-fifty."

"The current address of Dikembe Kasa."

"Last known." Sanza frowned. "He was in a hotel as of two days ago. I can't promise you'll still find him there."

"He lives in a hotel?" Liane asked.

"Just visiting," said Sanza, licking his lips and taking the cash from

Mickey, "with his young son. I no longer do business with him. Both could be gone any minute."

He wrote the address on a piece of newspaper, slowly, in a fine hand.

"Also," he added, "you may find that Dikembe has company."

11

They met their driver where they'd left him and climbed into the van. Beads of sweat stippled the back of his neck. He wiped it with a rag and twisted the ignition key.

"You know it?" Mickey pushed the paper into his hand.

"Looks like it's by the water near the industrial part of town."

The van crept along at first, bodies pressing around them. Then they pulled onto a main avenue and watched from the rear window as the throngs receded. In front of them, newer buildings reared up, encased in glass, then the van plunged into side streets again, less crowded than the market streets, potholed and garbage-strewn, lined with open sewers and dust-stained colonial-era buildings.

Clouds thickened overhead. Mickey lowered the window halfway and they sniffed the metallic air. Miniature vortexes spun by carrying sand and stray plastic bags. Pedestrians picked up their pace, jogging down sidewalks, ducking into doorways.

The van turned a corner and drove past the boatyards along the river. The driver stopped by an old four-story building, weathered and neglected.

"You're sure this is it?" Liane asked.

"It could be," the driver said unhelpfully. "I think."

He went around the side and opened their doors.

"Wait here for us," Mickey said, slipping him ten dollars.

They paused by the front door. Shutters flapped on the facade. As a gust of wind arose, they turned away to see a man and boy approaching. The man was tall and lanky. He loped and the boy struggled to keep up.

"*Mbote*," Liane said. "English?"

"Yes, I do speak," said the man, taking the boy's hand.

"By any chance, do you know whether a person named Dikembe Kasa lives here?"

The boy chuckled.

"Not *lives*, no," said the man. "And soon leaving, we hope."

12

The closer they got, the more Pulsipher quickened his steps. Too many times recently, he thought, he'd come up a day late and a clue short. Not again. He didn't possess all the information he needed, but he had most of it, and he felt his power ascendant. Harrow was behind bars and the balance had tipped against Pentalon's excesses. Meanwhile, Vinson had reached out—sincerely, he hoped. Yet, when things shift like this, he knew, danger and opportunity wear similar masks. With their empire collapsing around them, Flickinger and Gretch would be more volatile than ever, something Vinson and Ferrone may not be counting on. And Pulsipher now found himself in Kinshasa practically alone.

"Around the corner here," the man next to him said.

Pulsipher kept his eyes on the street. On the military flight over he'd worked the phone, looking desperately for someone who could guide him around. The best he could do was the spy next to him, a Belgian whose guts Pulsipher had to admire for just being here, of all places, after the way his ancestors had raped this country. You'd think the Congolese would be lining up to rip his flesh off and eat it, as they were said to do upriver. But the man looked like he could take care of himself, broad-shouldered with a serious face and hair all over his neck. *A Cro-Magnon in a finely tailored blue suit,* Pulsipher thought. He'd rather have landed a black guy in a dashiki, a legitimate native who could blend in. Instead, the two of them must look like they just climbed out of a wormhole, he thought. But at least the guy had the city map in his head.

"Just another block."

Pulsipher grunted his approval and lengthened his stride, wondering about Vinson and what the endgame might look like. The note, he realized, could have been a feint to send him in the wrong direction. But he didn't think so. She used her phone, knowing he could trace it, and even though she'd thrown it away, he suspected that was only to buy a little extra time. She'd wanted to remind him she was out there. And if she and the boyfriend had planned to remain hiding in the States, Pulsipher reasoned, it would've made no sense for them to use their ATM cards, as they had yesterday. They learned quickly, and they'd only show themselves on the grid once they knew they were about to make a negating leap. Vinson, in her note, also said she was taking the bonobo "home." Pulsipher had an agent sitting in front of her apartment on Long Island just in case she meant something else, but he didn't see the woman turning herself into a sitting duck that way. Besides, Flickinger damn well thought they were in Congo, and that counted for a lot. He'd filed a flight plan at the last possible minute—direct, not stopping in London or Paris as he usually did, just pausing to refuel on Ascension Island.

"*Deluge,*" the Belgian said as they walked. "It's gonna rain like hell any minute."

Lost in his brooding, Pulsipher had failed to see the obvious. Beyond the river, clouds met the horizon in a gray curtain.

"Just up here now, on the left." The Belgian reached for the weapon under his jacket, ready for action.

Half a block away, four people stood in front of the fleabag hotel. One of the group had an ape on his shoulders.

"That's them!" Pulsipher shouted, unholstering his Sig Sauer and breaking into a run.

Even from a distance he recognized Liane Vinson, cleaned up and more beautiful than ever with the wind blowing her hair. Unexpectedly, he found himself rooting for her.

13

Gretch's head throbbed. He felt nauseated and his muscles were knots. His stomach, he suspected, was dissolving inside him, further transforming to pulp with each passing minute. And there stood Flickinger, spit and polish like he'd just left the barbershop, phone to his ear, chattering away.

"No, miss, I must speak with the Secretary immediately. It most certainly cannot wait, yes?"

Every syllable felt like a pile driven into Gretch's skull.

"Blast it," Flickinger muttered. "I am out of the country. Have him call me on my cell, please." He dialed another number. "This is Dr. Axel Flickinger of the Pentalon Corporation. Is the senator available? No, I will hold."

The micro cell phone looked smaller than a quail egg in Flickinger's fingers. Gretch watched the boss's steel-gray eyes casting absently around the room, frustrated, searching for invisible cracks. He looked like the monkeys did when they first arrived at the primate lab, probing silently for a way out of their confinement. And Gretch could relate. The waiting and the pain were making him crazy. He'd pick up his own phone, check in with his security team in the States for news, but the thought of an amplified voice in his ear brought him close to a freakout. He wanted to escape like he had from those Chicano kids in his old Dallas neighborhood, disappear like straw in the wind. Instead, he began pacing into the hall and back. It hurt to move, but no more so than to stand still. When he next looked into the room, Flickinger was holding the phone out and staring at it in disgust.

"Nobody is available for me suddenly. A million dollars a year in contributions and I cannot get a person of consequence to come to the phone. This is very bad. What do you hear?"

"Just a ringing in my ears."

"You do not appear well. I have seen people with malaria who look better, in fact. When was the last time you ate?"

"That fucking hot dog."

"No hot dog can do that, Mr. Gretch." He lifted an eyebrow. "What is under those bandages?"

Gretch felt for the spot and gritted his teeth. "Less ear than I had a few days ago, thanks to that damn creature of yours."

"An exchange of body fluids?"

"You didn't see the security tape?"

"Why watch it? He bit you?"

"That—and worse." Gretch looked at Flickinger, as if for the first time. The room went wavy. "I bit the fucking ape!" He sank onto the stained cot. "I swallowed its blood."

"Idiot!" Flickinger exploded. "It is hemorrhagic fever. The CDC is on its way to the lab complex. I thought it was a power play, but it is real. Nobody informed me." He scratched at the blazer button. "Of course! Only Hammurabi knew, that bastard."

His rising voice beat on Gretch's skull like a club on a kettledrum.

"Just shut up, Axel. I can't hear myself think."

"Oh, you want to think, you moron! It is a bit late for that. The girl—"

"Shut up!"

"How dare you!"

Gretch stood abruptly, vectoring through the dizziness. He snatched the phone from Flickinger and crushed it in one hand, dropping the shattered pieces to the floor—the sound hitting his ears like a thundering herd.

Flickinger, beyond intimidation, grinned as if he were in on a joke.

Just then they heard voices through the window. Gretch ran to it, drew his gun, and peered down as two men closed in on a group below.

One of the running men looked up, square to Gretch, and his face seemed familiar.

"Shit," Gretch said, dropping back. "I've been made."

14

The sky turned black. The clouds crouched low, rumbling.

Gretch bolted down the stairs and out the back door. By the time he hit the alley, the world was a washed-out blur, which he moved through like an insect caught in grease. Drops of rain big as malt balls teemed through the heavy air, thrumming on his head and shoulders, bouncing hysterically off the dirt.

Without breaking stride he glanced over his shoulder, seeing Pulsipher, a vague and ominous shadow moving toward him through the gray sheets. The fence between them, he guessed, would not be an obstacle for the agent. And by the time he'd turn to aim, Pulsipher might be upon him, a dangerous and preponderant force versus Gretch's depleted condition. Even sprinting down the alley as fast as his legs would carry him, Gretch felt the virus turning inside him. He needed to shit and puke at the same time, but the act of letting go would only slow him down. His lungs burned and with each heartbeat a twinge pierced his skull. His muscles had the responsiveness of split rubber tires, yet his limbs still pumped. He was running on pure instinct, fueled by pure fear.

This time it would not be sufficient. Pulsipher was closing. The street had become a river, churning wildly with its pillage: leafy branches, tufts of muddy grass, plastic fragments, sandals. The rain dripped into his eyes, half blinding him. And what was this? From a side street, a white man in a soaking wet business suit emerged, gun drawn, closer to Gretch.

"*Arretez-vous!*" he shouted through the din of the rain. "*Arretez-vous!*" As if Gretch would ever be that stupid. Bullets pinged around him, hissing through gunky air. A pang blossomed in his hamstring, hobbling him, but also delivering a jolt of adrenaline that propelled him around the corner.

The cars here, in tight formation, bumpers almost touching, created a narrow gauntlet that gave Gretch sudden appreciation of the plight of a rat in a maze. And he knew in that instant that his life was more endangered than it ever had been, more so than when the Iraqis had surrounded him in the Gulf War, more than when he'd taken a bullet to his shoulder in the Secret Service. Fear rose in the back of his throat. It had a delicious quality, lent him power. He ran down a narrower street, ignoring all pain now, concentrating only on the thrill that nourished him. It so sharpened his senses that he could perceive the footsteps of his pursuer through the rainy din, and he sensed the bullets that sought him before they glanced off the pavement. Gretch half turned and threw up his hand and opened his shoulder and pulled off three quick shots with the Kimber. The sound, even muffled by the teeming rain, pierced his inflamed eardrums. But his unknown pursuer went down.

Then Pulsipher appeared again through the grayness. Gretch pivoted and fired wildly in the agent's direction, noting suddenly how leaden the pistol felt. He was near the end of the block, on the edge of a vast shantytown built of corrugated tin sheets and piles of straw. If he could make it that far, he'd disappear into its warrens, but he sensed Pulsipher gaining, heard the hiss of bullets, then felt the sharpness of a new pain in his buttocks. Two yards away lay an open manhole. If he sprawled forward, he would touch it. If he could reach it, he might yet escape to wherever it led.

His soaked clothes weighed heavily on his weary limbs. The fear was now more than a taste in the back of his throat; it was something palpable, an entity. He took it wholly into his bubbling viscera as he strained toward the manhole.

A sharp sting exploded the back of Gretch's ribs, lifting him into the air. But he was at the lip of the manhole. With one step the void below him rose up, gurgling, along with a tremendous stench. He felt himself hanging in the air only for a second, then he hit a viscous wetness, the sewer water receiving him. In seconds he was gasping and choking and drowning as the current carried him off, and all he could think was how delectable the fear, how alive in him, how complete.

Ecstasy overtook him as the world went dark.

15

When he saw the men with the guns coming, Dikembe shifted his feet and spun his shoulders and reached out his hands—and Daniel materialized in his arms. Then he was running, aware of the puddle splashes soaking his pants at the shins, of the facades of buildings sailing by, of the people with the bonobo right beside him as he crossed the traffic-jammed boulevard by the river then turned down a side street heading away from the shipyards. And he continued fleeing—beyond all reason, with Daniel wrapped in his arms—in a straight line, leaving the Americans behind. When he finally stopped, gulping for breath, and set Daniel down, he was far from the waterfront. He stood with his hands on his hips.

"You—oh—kay, boy?"

"Yes, Papa." But dread still animated him.

Dikembe scanned the street. They could begin walking, he supposed, in the direction of the bush. It would take much time and success would depend entirely on his ability to trade the diamonds or find work in exchange for food. He rested a hand on Daniel's shoulder and for a moment saw Odette's countenance in the boy's, reproaching him, condemning the choices he'd made. Yet, when he refocused he saw that his son's faith in him still burned strong. It resembled, somehow, the trust he'd seen in the bonobo twins that he'd spirited out of the jungle.

They were special, those bonobos, children of God in their way, which was why he'd held onto them for weeks before selling them—why he'd spoken to them incessantly. And they'd answered back with their eyes, with a faith like that he still witnessed in Daniel's face, despite the very betrayal that had put them in his possession. He could still see it, too, in the eyes of the bonobo the Americans brought with them. Bea, the woman called her. He didn't understand traveling halfway around the world for an ape, but then again, it was quite close to the very goal that also had brought him so foolishly to Kinshasa.

"That bonobo," he said to Daniel, "was one of the twins I was hoping we could get back from Pierre." It couldn't be a coincidence, he thought. They had to have come looking for him, specifically.

Dikembe looked around. The rain had stopped, and the puddles began to recede. He and Daniel crouched by the curb, wringing the water from their shirts as the sun poked out. Steam rose from the pavement.

"Did you hear the pops as we ran?" Daniel asked. "The men with the guns killed someone. I hope it wasn't the woman. Are they like regular people, the Americans?"

"They are richer than regular people."

"Those two we met, they love the bonobo as much as you do, Papa."

"We don't know that."

"*I* do. I saw what passed between them. And—look! Here they come!"

Dikembe gathered Daniel to him again, ready to flee.

"Don't!" the tattooed man shouted, gasping for breath. "Please!"

He set the ape down and held up his hands in peace. While Dikembe assessed him the woman jogged up.

"We're glad—we—found you again," she gasped, smiling.

"You are still chased?" Dikembe asked.

"I don't think so."

"You heard the shots?"

"Yes. It was hard in the rain. Is there someplace we can go, dry off, talk?"

"The sun," Dikembe pointed, averting his eyes from Liane's clinging sweater. "The sun dries. Doesn't it work that way in your country?"

"That depends," Liane laughed, "on where you are, how cold it is, how much time you have."

"Here the rainy season is beginning and the sun can hide for hours. But when the sun is out, it dries. It doesn't take long."

Dikembe looked around for signs of trouble. It was hard to see past the people who had begun to clog the streets again. "Let's walk down this way," he said warily. "We ran mostly straight. If they continue to seek you, we are too easy to find here."

"Okay, champ," Mickey said. "It's your town. Where to?"

"This way, if you don't mind. We'll talk as we walk. You haven't told me your names, only the bonobo's."

They apologized and introduced themselves.

"I'm sorry about the shooting," Liane said, conscious of how lame that sounded. "I realize it's a heck of a way to start a relationship."

"What kind of relationship would that be?" Dikembe said.

"They want to kill you?" Daniel asked.

"Well," Liane said. "It's complicated. What they want most is Bea here. If they have to kill us to get her, then so be it. That's pretty much how they look at the situation."

"So why not give her up and get yourselves an animal with less risk?" Daniel asked.

"This kid's sharp," Mickey said. "What is he, about eight?"

"Yes," Dikembe said. "Exactly so. How'd you know?"

"It's a gift he has," Liane said. "We're a gifted lot. Mickey can guess anyone's age. I have a knack for getting out of tight spaces. Bea here, she talks."

Dikembe nodded. "They're a vocal species, the bonobos."

"No," Liane said, "I mean really talks. Like the dickens when she chooses to—English, Lingala. Human words."

Dikembe pulled at his shirt to speed its drying. "You've quite an imagination."

"We wish."

"Why haven't I heard her?"

"She tends to clam up around strangers," Mickey said. "And she's pretty quiet, too, when we're running for our lives—which happens more often than you'd think. But wait a while. You'll see what we mean."

"I thought she was different." Dikembe paused to study Bea. She reached out a hand, and they pressed their palms together.

"*Mbote*," he said. Bea didn't answer.

"If you thought she was different," Liane said, "why'd you sell her?"

"For the money. We had little. I was trying to better our situation. Only later did I begin to regret my decision." He cast his eyes down.

Mickey looked at him sympathetically. "Don't be too hard on yourself." He bounced a glance off Liane. "We've all made mistakes."

"What of the brother?" asked Dikembe. "Do you think he talks, too?"

"Listen," Liane said, "it's not a question of what we think. It's what we know. And, yes, the brother also speaks. He once did, anyway. Unfortunately, he's out of commission now, which is why it's doubly important to save this one."

Daniel's eyes widened. "Someone ate him?"

"No. In a laboratory." Liane bent down. "He was experimented upon by scientists. They claim that it helps people, but the evidence is thin. We don't want them to get Bea. We want to return her to the jungle, which we hoped your father could help us do."

"So she wasn't a pet."

"Not even close."

Dikembe said, "*Moduki ezangi masasi elelaka te, nzoka motema ezangi bolingo elelaka bilelalela.*"

"What does that mean?" Liane asked.

"An adage we have: A gun without bullets doesn't cry—that is, fire—but a heart without love cries like hell." He sighed. "We, too, are trying to get to the jungle, but we have no resources."

"If you'll guide us we'll pay you," Mickey said.

"It's quite distant, and dangerous for foreigners."

"We've come this far," Liane said. "Can you bring us to the very spot? We need to reunite her with her troop."

"That would be the only way. We'd have to take a boat upriver."

"Let's get going then," Mickey said.

"You have no luggage?"

"Just what's on our backs." He lifted Bea and adjusted her weight against his hip.

"We left in a hurry," Liane explained.

"Because of the men with the guns?"

"Yes."

Dikembe looked them over. It all sounded suspicious. But he thought of Odette and the neighbors who'd driven him from his village. He considered Pierre Sanza and the lonely baby gorilla in its cage. If there was any hope for starting a new life, he thought, he must get to the Englishman.

"We'll go straight to the port," he said, "stopping only for provisions."

"*Oui. Oui.*" Mickey said. "Lead on."

16

Sometime later, laden with armfuls of supplies, they came to a run-down cabin on a pier that served as the dock master's office. Dikembe went inside and waited for an hour until his turn arrived, then stepped forward.

The dock master stood behind a high counter. He wore a blue guayabera, half unbuttoned, stained with sweat at the armpits, and had a well-trimmed thin mustache that began at his lip and ended half an inch below his nose.

"Where are the other passengers?"

"Outside," said Dikembe, the American dollars trembling in his hand. "Watching their possessions."

"Tourists?"

"Yes?"

"You are their guide?"

"Yes."

"Let me see your papers from the Ministry of Tourism."

"I haven't any. It's an informal arrangement."

"How informal?"

"They are old friends. From when I was in the army."

The dock master stared at Dikembe, suspecting that wasn't the truth.

"Please," Dikembe said, pressing his money into the man's palm. "They are good people, come to see the wildlife. There's four hundred U.S. there to get us on the next barge. You can keep it all."

"You must have done something very wrong if you're in such a hurry," the dock master snarled. A thought crossed his face. "For another thousand I can put you on a speedy boat."

"No, thank you. We are prepared for the barge."

When Dikembe left, he found the Americans, the ape and Daniel huddled under the eave of a tin shack, sheltering from the high sun.

"You bring back any change?" Mickey asked.

Dikembe shook his head.

"Jeez."

"We must proceed now. It leaves shortly. There." He pointed.

"That heap of floating rust?" Liane said.

"Yes, it's our barge."

"I hope it'll stay afloat."

Dikembe frowned. "You have no passport, no documents at all. People chase you with guns, disturbing the peace. If you don't mind my saying, that barge may be the least of your worries."

17

The wiry girl sensed danger, yet stepped bravely into the intruder's path. Making no attempt to convince her to move, he grabbed her by the throat with one bony hand and flung her atop a table of antelope meat. She landed in a heap, toppling it. He pushed aside the beaded curtain and walked through the cluttered anteroom to the office.

"Dr. Flickinger," Sanza stuttered, "wh-what a surprise."

With his supply replenished since he'd seen the Americans and their bonobo, the tanks and cages in Sanza's office were nearly full: monkeys and snakes and exotic rodents, grey parrots and young red forest pigs and the lone baby gorilla, its lower eyelids beginning to swell, a symptom of malnutrition. There was a small crocodile, three feet long, tied in a corner, dozing.

"Tell me where they are headed," Flickinger spit.

"Who are you talking about?"

"You know very well who."

Flickinger opened a nearby cage and snatched a gray parrot by its throat, feathers flying as it attempted to beat its wings. Its large black claws scratched futilely at the sleeve of his blazer. He ran the knuckle of his free index finger across the top of the creature's immobile head, as if to comfort it. Then in one motion he tightened his grip and twisted, breaking the bird's neck. He dropped the carcass in the middle of the desk, its muscular dark tongue protruding. Sanza flinched, and the other birds screeched their alarm. Flickinger extracted a second parrot.

"I don't even know those people," Sanza protested over the din. "They were on their way to a hotel by the docks."

"They are gone from there."

"That's all I know. They could be anywhere."

Flickinger broke the neck of the second parrot and flung the dead bird across the room. It crashed into a line of cages, and the monkeys began screaming.

"That was uncalled for," Sanza whined, rising.

"Sit back down." Flickinger produced a 9 mm Walther PPS from his coat pocket and pointed it at Sanza's head. "I was at the end of my patience when I came in here, and you are trying me further. Bad enough I had to lay low for two days, hiding from a misguided federal agent while those thieves got away. I will not be lied to by scum like you, yes?"

He turned and fired into the side of a pig, causing it to cry out but producing little blood. The men watched while it suffered, its cloven hoofs sprawled out, scratching uselessly at the metal pan. A minute passed before the squeals died into silence.

"I was going to get fifty euros for that pig from a Frenchman," Sanza observed finally. "Now you pay me double or I'll call the police."

"The police?!" Flickinger barked. "You will be stiffer than that pig by the time they get here—if they bother at all to come. Tell me where Dikembe Kasa got the bonobo twins. That is where they are returning to, is it not?"

"Perhaps. They did ask about it. But they didn't tell me."

"You want money, is that it?"

"It may help my memory." Sanza smiled.

"After all the business I have given you."

"One can't eat the same meal twice."

Pocketing his Walther, Flickinger strode rapidly across the room and closed his hand over the small crocodile's long snout. He unclipped the chain and seized the animal by its front legs and swung the tail into the side of Sanza's head, cutting his ear and knocking him from his chair. He lifted the crocodile over his shoulders and brought it down on Sanza like a thick whip as the man raised his arms, struggling to protect his face and head, crying out, "Stop! Stop!"

By the time Flickinger had finished, the crocodile lay inert and Sanza's head and face were pulp. He sat on the floor, back against the gorilla cage, his forehead glistening with blood, looking up in wide-eyed disbelief.

Flickinger surveyed the room. "Such a collection. What have we in this case?" He slid the lid off a large fish tank on a shelf. He reached in with a flick of his wrist and his hand emerged with a tan snake, its two-foot body braiding itself around one arm. Flickinger squeezed the back of the neck between thumb and forefinger and the mouth opened, powder black inside.

"Oho! A visitor from a different part of the continent!"

He stepped toward Sanza and crouched beside him on the floor, waving the mouth in the dealer's face, fangs showing.

"*Dendroaspis polylepis.* The black mamba, yes? This will indeed make a nice gift under a Christmas tree in the industrialized world. What a surprise when he grows to eight feet, largest venomous snake in Africa! Did you know, Mr. Sanza, that the black mamba likes to strike multiple times about the head and neck? Not that it needs to. It carries enough venom in one bite to kill two or three dozen men."

Flickinger held the head a foot from Sanza's battered face, let the deep brown eyes of the African meet the beady slits of the reptile.

"There's a p-place," Sanza stuttered, "th-that Dikembe did mention."

"You have a map?"

"Somewhere."

He waved a cautious hand and pulled himself up along the cages and turned to his desk, opening one drawer after another, riffling through stray papers, dripping blood on them.

Finally Sanza found the map. Printed by the Interior Bureau, it showed small streams in detail, other topography and notable land-marks. He spread it open on the desk and peered into it. He located a place with his finger, moved to another spot, then another.

"I can't tell you exactly," he said, "but there is a rill coming into the river here, and Dikembe said something about a giant bombax tree by the fork, standing almost alone, clinging to the bank." He looked up to Flickinger. "That's all I know."

"You are sure? That is all?"

Sanza nodded solemnly as Flickinger took a step back.

"Your face." He shook his head. "It looks terrible, yes? You should put something on it."

When Sanza forced a bloody smile, Flickinger tossed him the black mamba. It sank its fangs into the dealer's neck and writhed across his chest.

A minute passed while it played out—first the panicked windmill of the man crashing about the room and last the look of shocked resignation. Before Sanza crumpled fully to the floor, his eyes bulging, Flickinger had seized the map and left.

18

From under their makeshift tent, Mickey looked out on the rabble strung across the barge deck: women clutching babies to their breasts, shirtless boys blacker than the dark of the jungle, traders with stuffed suitcases, and fishermen whose poles rested on the iron-pipe side railing, their lines disappearing into the river.

The Congolese called the tugboat a *pousseur*—a pusher—because it impelled from behind. Though old and dented, it had a fresh coat of white paint that made the rusty barge seem, to Mickey, unworthy of its efforts. A week earlier, he might have said the same for the ape, he had to admit. It hadn't been any particular argument that changed his mind, just a sense of how everyone responded to the *idea* of Bea and, what was more, the way Liane had committed herself to the high calling of the animal's defense. She hadn't acted as she did for what Bea *represented*, Mickey thought, but rather for who the ape *was*.

They'd been on the water for five days, floating in the oppressive heat past small shoreline villages and bosky uninhabited islands, colonial ruins and miles of dense jungle. Occasionally, squalls erupted from nowhere, forcing the *pousseur* to cast the barge adrift in the churning water and sending people scrambling to secure their possessions. On sunny afternoons, the deck got so hot that you couldn't touch it with bare skin. They lolled under the protection of the tarp, sprawled on thin foam mats that they'd bought at the variety store.

Bea had begun talking again on the second day, quietly, intimidated by the unfamiliar sights and smells of the barge, perhaps also disconcerted by its faint, constant vibration. Daniel worked to expand her vocabulary, but the Americans prevented ape and boy from touching, going so far as to tie Bea to an eyebolt with a canvas rope. Every time she saw Bea tug in frustration at that knotted rope, Liane winced.

"Look, Mr. Mickey," Dikembe whispered conspiratorially. In the shadow of the tent, he held out a handful of translucent granules.

Mickey squinted as Dikembe moved them around his palm with a fingertip.

"Pebbles?" They were unimpressive; they didn't even look clean.

"The hardest known to man," Dikembe hinted.

"Diamonds," Mickey whispered. "Never seen 'em in their natural condition."

"You like to buy?"

"What would I do with them?"

"You could trade them for big money back home. I can make you a good deal. Look, this one here—" He pushed it around in his pale palm, showing all the rough angles. "This one you could have someone cut. It's three carats, I estimate. You can give it to your girl. A souvenir of the trip—or something more!"

"You're a good salesman." Mickey laughed. "Lemme think it over."

He pictured coming home after this life-changing journey, drinking wine across the table from Liane, maybe showing off his sage-butter recipe with pumpkin ravioli. He thought perhaps he'd open his own veterinary practice, convince Liane to work as his tech—or stake her to vet school and then be full partners.

He watched Dikembe stash the diamonds in his shoe. Together they chased away a group of green bottle flies, waving their arms around, killing two with an empty charcoal bag that they'd rolled into a make-shift swatter. Dikembe used a towel to cover the smoked fish he'd purchased on board, protecting it from further pests.

"I can see life's hard here," Mickey said.

"You didn't know?"

"To be honest, we don't spend much time thinking about Africa in the States. It takes a major natural disaster to get our attention—or a genocide. And a week later we're back to forgetting."

"Here, some people think about the U.S. all the time. If you visit a bar in one of the bigger towns, you can watch American TV sometimes. CSI. Oprah."

"No kidding? When this is over, maybe we can arrange for you to come back with us."

Dikembe shook his head. "For me, even Kinshasa is too much. I am—how would you say?—a country boy. There's an Englishman studying wildlife in the jungle. I hope to work for him—and that he will teach my son all he knows. Maybe one day Daniel can go to America, if he chooses."

"He's a good boy."

"He's been through a lot."

"You should know something. We think the ape carries hemorrhagic fever. It's why we don't let them too close to one another."

"Liane told me." He nodded. "My wife died from it, probably from eating monkey meat that was not so well cooked. Every day I feel her absence afresh. Some of us seem to be immune. I wished at first that the virus would take me instead, but there's no accounting for the ways of the world, no point in wishing for what is not. That's what the witch doctor told me, and he's wise. The mystery of nature is that nature remains mysterious. I think it will always be so."

Mickey stared out at the glassy river. "Yet we have learned so much over the centuries."

"The witch doctor says man never steps in the same river twice. But what he forgot to mention, I've been thinking, is that the man doing the stepping doesn't change much."

"I know that quote. The same philosopher also said that a man's character is his fate."

"He makes a point." Dikembe laughed. He stood and ducked from the tent out into the broiling sun. He sniffed the air and looked around. Mickey crawled out and took a place alongside him. The tranquil river, at this wide point, was the color of strong tea.

"By tomorrow morning we will be at the drop-off," Dikembe said. "We have a little charcoal left. Tonight I will cook some fresh fish and rice on the *bambula*, but we cannot take it with us. Too much to portage. Shall I sell the items we can't carry?"

Mickey studied their fellow travelers. Some had been riding unprotected from the sun for nearly a week. Even those with tents lay listless on the deck. "Give it to those you think are the neediest on board."

"They'll be grateful."

"It's the least we can do. Don't make a big deal of it."

Mickey felt hopeful. He ducked back under the tarp and kissed Liane awake.

She sat up as Daniel and Bea looked on.

"*Bolingo*," Daniel said.

"Love," echoed Bea.

19

The next morning, Liane awakened to a foul smell. She stepped out from the tent to see that a heavy fog had engulfed them, so thick that the bow of the barge disappeared into it.

"What's that odor?" she asked Dikembe.

"The mangrove is near."

"It smells of sulfur."

"Like the devil. From the rot. It's a good thing because it means we are very close to a dugout I have hidden there. I've just come from talking with the first mate. They'll drop us a little farther up this way, where there's a pier by a small village."

Half an hour later the barge sighed into the end of the pier. It paused, but no one made an effort to tie it down. By the time they scrambled off, the *pousseur* and barge had disappeared almost completely into the mist, like ghost ships.

There were figures on the shore in the fog.

"*Mbote,*" Dikembe said. He spoke with them in Lingala.

When he returned, Liane asked, "Is this your village?"

"No, we are well past there. But these people are of my tribe. We are safe."

He purchased fufu cakes. They ate them on the pier while the river and the rising sun collaborated to chase off the fog.

"This bonobo," Dikembe said, "in the jungle she'll follow the instincts of her kind and head for the trees beyond our reach. If you want to save her, you'll have to tie her up."

When they finished breakfast they fastened Bea by the neck to Mickey's waist with the canvas rope, and he carried her in his arms, following closely behind Dikembe, who led with the machete they'd bought in Kinshasa. Supplies weighed all of them down—as much as each could manage without collapsing. Liane trailed in the rear, often glancing over her shoulder into the green monotony. Within ten or twenty feet the meandering path became a vague cleft, and shortly after that the mahogany trees and underbrush engulfed it completely, so that Liane thought it would be nearly impossible, if anything happened to Dikembe, for them to find their way out. She had the macabre vision of them dropping one by one to the jungle floor, their bodies feasted upon by wild animals and beetles and worms and fungus, turned to humus in the blink of a geological eye. And that made her think of her mother's ashes, by now sitting in an urn somewhere, and of the fact that she'd missed the funeral and Frank must think her to be a bad daughter, or worse. It was an odd feeling to worry about what he thought of her. She did wonder about him, though, as she watched the boots she'd bought in Kinshasa sink into the mud of the trail, listened to the animals calling ahead to announce a disruptive presence, felt the living spirit of the jungle creeping behind her like a stalker.

After more than an hour, they came to a clearing and Dikembe instructed them to wait while he scampered across the knobby roots that had become increasingly evident as they neared the mangrove. As they dropped their loads he disappeared so quickly that it seemed like an illusionist's trick, and the three of them stood silently with Bea, peering into the soughing walls of trees.

For a while Liane's skin crawled with dampness and insects and nervousness. Then Dikembe emerged as magically as he'd gone. He had a fresh welt on his cheek and several on his arm, thick as knots.

"Are you okay?" Liane asked.

"Some wasps made a home in my dugout. But they're gone."

"You shoulda screamed for help," Mickey said.

"And what would you have done for me?"

"I dunno. I've been known to exceed expectations now and then."

"The important thing is we have the canoe. Please follow me closely. Step only where the person in front of you steps. And watch out for critters, especially snakes."

"Spare us the specifics, Dikembe," Mickey begged.

"What was that you said back at the hotel—about making your own luck?" Liane jibed.

"From a thousand feet up this looked like a chessboard. But from down here, I've noticed a lot of stuff that's bigger and quicker and stronger than us."

They picked their way along, balancing above the water on arched roots resembling viaducts, vivid fish darting among the pillars. A startled white heron cried out and took sudden flight, causing Liane almost to lose her footing and her cargo. Neon dragonflies hovered in the air, investigating. Turtles dropped from logs and slid into still water.

"All the animals run away," Liane observed, when they came to a patch of sand by a clump of tall reeds. "Everything fears us."

"Not everything," Dikembe said. "Not everything."

He slapped the water noisily with his machete, then found a big stick and threw it halfway to the canoe, making a giant splash. He paused, holding up a hand, peering forth. Then they waded to the dugout and climbed in, stowing their gear. The dugout was large—ten feet long at least, hollowed from a giant tree—but it was a tight squeeze and they weighed it down, obliging Dikembe to pull them by foot into a greater depth. When he finally climbed aboard, the river nearly crested the gunwales.

From his place in the rear Dikembe used a long branch to pole them through the mangrove, then switched to a paddle when they neared the main river. He knocked the paddle against the side of the boat and looked attentively ahead, assimilating everything down to the smallest detail. When hippos rose to investigate, Dikembe cut a wide berth around them.

"Why are we going downstream?" Liane asked, after watching one of the beasts give a giant yawn. "That's where we came from."

"They dropped us past the point we need for the bonobo. There was no closer place to disembark."

"So the village is in the wildlife preserve?"

"We're on the edge of the bonobo range. The preserve is at least a hundred kilometers inland from here. But wildlife knows no borders. Neither do many people."

He paddled them across part of the river to an island with an inviting patch of sand and a small clearing where men had beaten back the undergrowth. Their arrival spooked several birds and a crocodile sunning nearby. The birds squawked and flew off while the crocodile plunged away. They dragged the canoe ashore and piled their provisions in the grass. Daniel began gathering wood for a fire.

"It looks like there's a spot around there," Dikembe said, pointing. "I can watch the bonobo if you'd like to bathe."

"Ain't there dangerous animals around?" asked Mickey.

"There are no hippos right here," said Dikembe. "And the crocodile has gone for now. Just keep an eye out. Remember, when it comes to hippos and crocs on land, not to get between them and the water. They don't like that."

"Which they'll express how?" Liane asked.

"They will kill you." Dikembe smiled. "Or try to."

"He's not kidding," Mickey said.

"That settles it. I need to get the grunge off, but I'm not going alone." Liane dug for the soap in a box of supplies. She stood with it in her hand—Ivory. "Let's go, Mickey."

"Me?"

"Who else?"

"Don't wade too far out and don't drink the river water," Dikembe warned as they disappeared around the corner.

Mickey took Liane's hand. They helped one another maintain balance as they climbed over branches and rocks. They soon came to a place where flat, round river stones covered the shore like tiles.

"I guess this is it," Liane said.

They looked out on the placid river, which mirrored sky and trees. Off the point of the island, hippopotamus nostrils and eyes monitored the fork in the river. A fish eagle swooped low, yellow talons extended, seeming to chase its own reflection. Closer to where they stood, a water bug danced along the surface, hesitated, and continued on. Liane stared across to the opposite bank, where a bushbuck emerged from the undergrowth and drank cautiously.

"It's like Eden," she said.

The eagle struck. He looked so majestic with his white head and dark wings, gliding far off, disappearing into the trees, that it was easy to ignore the plight of the fish he had wriggling in his grasp.

Mickey took both of Liane's hands and they kissed.

"Wouldn't it be nice," he said, "to make love right here?"

"For someone, not us. There's an eight-year-old just around the bend."

"Can I help you undress, at least?"

"You're incorrigible. Turn around."

Liane removed her clothes. She'd never felt so exposed, and despite the hot air her skin tingled with goose pimples. The river mud, however, soothed her blistered feet. She squatted in three feet of lukewarm water, lathered her body and hair, then passed the soap bar to Mickey, who'd snuck in when her eyes were closed. When he turned toward the far shore and lathered his own hair, she gave her head a final dunk and waded out, pulling on her clothes while still wet. A few minutes later she watched Mickey as he climbed ashore, hands covering his privates. She observed that his stomach was flatter than it had been when she first saw it. *Inadvertent starvation and long marches,* she theorized. She forced herself to look away.

When they'd fully dressed, they sat on the warm river stones for a bit, trading kisses. Though late afternoon had come upon them, the sun floated halfway up in the sky.

"It gets dark fast here," Mickey noted. "We should go back."

"They have no word in Lingala for evening. Just day and night, Dikembe told me. The sun drops as quickly as the ball in Times Square."

"Yeah, but much prettier. It's a natural. Like you."

"Oh, shut up."

"Nice. You're blushing."

20

When they returned they found that Dikembe had strung the tarp among trees to make a spacious tent and had caught two medium-size fish and impaled them on sticks. They roasted them over a blazing fire and ate them with cans of beans. As night fell the mosquitoes descended in clouds. They put wet wood and reeds in the fire and sat close together in the smoke it cast off, getting little sleep.

In the morning, Mickey and Liane had a contest counting mosquito bites as Daniel officiated. Mickey won with twenty-eight to Liane's twenty-three, but Liane argued that she had more bites per pound. She had to explain until Daniel grasped the logic. He giggled and declared Liane the winner. Mickey pretended to pout and marched off to Bea for sympathy.

"Poor Mickey!" she cried as he approached. Her squeaky laughs ceased when Mickey untied her from the trunk of a nearby tree and fastened her to Liane with the rope.

"Notice that she's stopped fighting having the rope around her neck." Liane frowned. "In the animal testing trade they call that 'learned helplessness.'"

"She'll be free soon," Mickey assured her.

Dikembe finished packing the dugout and Mickey clasped a weathered board he'd found among the trees, intending to help paddle.

It was still early when they cast off. The eastern sky—gradations of orange like a slice of ripe pumpkin—sprawled behind them as they eased into the current.

"I don't like this weather," Dikembe said.

"But it's beautiful," Mickey said.

"It will likely rain before the day's out. We don't want to be caught on the river then."

They paddled deeply to cross back to the main shore, then they allowed the gentle current to carry them, Dikembe steering only occasionally with his paddle. Within an hour they came to a narrow promontory formed by the convergence of the river and a rushing stream. They stroked hard to fight across the current that poured in, and they grabbed onto overhanging branches to fix their position.

Dikembe stepped out and dragged the canoe into a riot of vines and thorny bushes and thick muck, hacking out a space with his machete. On the tip of the promontory a fourteen-foot-long crocodile awaited the full sun. Dikembe pointed it out to warn them.

"Make noise," he said as they waded along the shore. "At the base of the stream, predators come down to feed. We don't wish to surprise anything."

A few yards farther along, the underbrush yielded to rocks and red sand. Standing nearly alone, the trunk and roots of a giant bombax held the shore like the talons of a gargantuan webbed claw. Beside it Liane saw the opening of a game path. Bea, clinging to Liane's back, adjusted her weight to peer over her shoulder. Together they followed the path with their eyes as it ascended into the jungle and disappeared in deep green darkness.

21

"Let's wait here awhile," Dikembe said, inviting everyone to pause by the shore.

As they sat with their legs crossed, Bea sniffed the air. She seemed restless and Mickey held the leash tight as she climbed into Liane's lap. Liane handed her a stick and she worried it between her teeth.

Dikembe rose and walked to the edge of the clearing then back to the river. He crouched, pinched the soil of the shore. "A leopard came through here," he said, "not an hour ago. Everything would have fled, but the leopard has moved on and life returns. Can you hear them growing closer again—the birds, the monkeys, the small game? They are like musicians reclaiming their chairs in the orchestra."

"That's a beautiful image," Liane said.

"I've thought about it for a long time. I find the sounds comforting. They communicate a kind of balance."

"And, in that view, what side of the scale are we on," Mickey asked, "— mankind, I mean."

Dikembe reflected. "Hmm. Percussion—more disruptive than we appear to be at first. When we aren't careful, we overwhelm the balance."

A rustle came to the bushes nearby.

"See here," Dikembe said. "A herd of duiker is there."

Liane peered through a thicket of tall grass and brush and saw the antelopes, tawny and leggy and skittish.

"As Liane suggested yesterday, these do fear us," Dikembe said. "But at this moment they are trapped between us and the river and the place where the leopard walks, somewhere over that natural hedge there. It makes them uncertain, but—because they can see us and only smell the leopard—their fear of us will win eventually. Their instinct won't allow them to stand there much longer. And a female will lead them first over the hedge."

"A female? How do you know?"

"It's always this way. I don't understand why." He chortled. "Like so many of us men, maybe the bucks won't stick their necks out."

Soon after he said this it happened: a doe first leaping over the hedge, rapidly followed by the rest of her herd, floating in arcs as if borne by springs.

"You called it!" Mickey said. "Impressive."

"*Moto*," said Bea.

"*Moto?*"

"Afraid of humans," Daniel interpreted.

"*Moto* means afraid?" Mickey asked.

Dikembe shook his head. "Humans. The rest—how you say—she implied."

Liane turned to him. "You're sure this is the place?"

Dikembe nodded and let out a cry, so unexpected that it startled them all. "*Hoo-hooo!*" It sounded like the intonation of a living French horn, if such an instrument could be made animate.

Bea sat up, alert, peering into the jungle with wide hazel eyes.

"It's how I lure them," Dikembe said sadly, watching a termite struggle through some weeds. "Did Bea's brother suffer much?"

Liane hesitated, meeting Mickey's eye. It seemed pointless to tell the truth to a contrite man.

"I don't know," she said. "I wasn't present when the worst happened."

Dikembe called out again. "*Hoo-hooo!*"

If his emanations resembled the bonobo's, it was a vocalization that Liane hadn't heard before, like the glissando of a tenor, echoing through the jungle. For all its beauty, no reply came.

"How did you catch them?" Liane asked.

"It was wetter during the dry season than it should have been. The tamarind in this part of the jungle was sparse and didn't produce much fruit. Finding any would be a real treat for the bonobos. I camouflaged some traps and put tamarind pods inside—one of their favorite foods. I expected to get an adult and would have been lucky to capture any at all. I sat in the jungle near here for days, calling from afar during the day and coming closer to check the trap at night. I was very surprised to find two—and so young—and twins, very unusual."

He twisted the tip of his machete into the ground as he spoke, digging a small hole in the red dirt, but avoiding the crawling termites.

"There is so much death here along the Congo for everyone and everything. People eat the monkey, but the monkey, sometimes, will eat its own kind from another troop. Very few things simply lay down and die. The strong pick off the weak—that is nature."

"We know that," Mickey said. "We know about the natural cycle of life, the harshness of it. Don't we, Liane? But so often it seems like a far-off theory. Here you feel it everywhere, even in the city."

"When I sold the bonobos," Dikembe said, "I knew that they were likely to end up in a wealthy country. I presumed in a zoo, maybe, or as pets or for a circus show. I never imagined that I was sending them to a secret life where they would come to harm for little purpose."

"I understand," Liane said.

"The Englishman would be very cross if he knew."

"Don't tell him."

"I had the bonobos in a single cage. I sat with them first for days, getting them to acclimate, to start eating again. They looked at each other a lot—and at me. I don't know why I spoke with them, perhaps because they seemed to have an understanding in their faces that I had never seen before in their species. Not that I could have imagined…"

He reached out and touched Bea's chest. She nodded her head.

"Home," she said, looking from Dikembe to Liane to Mickey and back to Liane. "Bonobo."

"We're trying, kid," Mickey said.

"I took my time bringing them to Kinshasa," Dikembe concluded. "Like a tourist out for a float. And I spoke to them quite a lot, all the way down river."

He stood and let out another call. "*Hoo-hooo!*" He leaned toward the densest part of the jungle and cupped an ear.

A faint call wafted back.

"You hear it?" The words caught in his throat.

"The bonobo," Daniel whispered.

"*Bolingo,*" Bea said, scrambling atop Liane's shoulders. "*Wapi mama. Miliki.*"

"What's she saying?" Liane asked.

"She seeks her mother's milk," Daniel said. "And her mother's love."

Dikembe bracketed his mouth with his hands and issued another call. The response came right away, louder, closer. Bea jumped from Liane to Mickey and back, embracing Liane in her long arms, rubbing her genitals against her side.

"Not that again," Liane said, embarrassed. "It's been a while."

"I'll say," Mickey deadpanned.

"She's very happy," Daniel said.

"*Bolingo*," Bea exclaimed. "Love. Love."

Dikembe extended his arms to the group.

"Come." He stood and brushed himself off. "They won't draw much closer. We must go to them and make sure they find her and accept her."

The game path narrowed as they walked, necessitating heavy use of Dikembe's machete. Mickey and Dikembe took turns swinging the big blade from side to side in the humid air, now grown oppressive. The exertion had them all breathing heavily, and by the time they came to a clearing, they ran with sweat.

Dikembe settled himself and issued another tenor call.

Having come to expect an answer, they were surprised to be met by silence.

22

A gust passed through them—warm and damp as the exhalation of a giant—ruffling their hair. Clouds scuttered across the sky, flat on one end and puffy on the other, like silent waves. Behind them, the sun was an angry white molten ball. Dikembe called again like a human French horn, and again he received no answer from the bonobos in the jungle.

"It could be the wind shift," he speculated, resting the flat of the machete on his shoulder and staring up into the trees across the clearing. "They may have picked up our scent. My cry is as much the poacher's call these days as it is theirs. It makes them wary."

"Maybe we should free Bea now," Mickey said. "See if they'll come to her."

"But we have to make sure it's the right troop," Liane warned.

"If I saw her again, I would know the mother," said Dikembe. "She has a scar across her shoulder, a long pink stripe. And her eyes have a shine to them. Last time I saw them, they were flashing anger and she—she was crying. She ran at me but I got to the water in time. They won't swim."

He called out again.

Bea responded as she had before, elevating her alertness, clambering as high as she could up Liane's back and shoulders, seeking movement in the high branches.

Dikembe approached her closely. "Let's take the collar off but hold onto her tight."

Mickey stepped forward and obliged while Daniel continued peering across the clearing, a hundred yards wide. From across the expanse of grass, the thickest part of the jungle appeared as a dark green wall, impenetrable. A few birds flitted in and out of the treetops.

When the collar came off, Liane felt a shift in Bea, an increase of relaxation and intensity at the same time. She bade her come around. Bea hugged her but continued looking about the jungle.

"*Hoo-hooo,*" Dikembe called out. He looked directly at Bea. "*You do it.*"

"Yeah, that's right." Mickey nodded. "C'mon, kid. Call mama."

"*Hoo-hooo,*" Dikembe said. "*Kobenga.* Call her. *Hoo-hooo.*"

"*Hoo,*" Bea said tentatively.

"It's like she needs to learn to be herself again." Liane fought the tug at her heart. "Do it, Bea. Let go."

"*Kobenga. Hoo-hooo!*" Dikembe cried louder, still looking at Bea.

"*Hoo-hooo!*" Bea finally let loose. "*Hoo-hooo! Hoo-hooo!*"

"Right on!" Mickey whispered. "You did it, kiddo."

They waited, hearing a rustling in the bushes behind them. Then, from the thick of the jungle in front of them, a response arrived.

"*Hoo-hooo!*"

"It's nearby!" Dikembe exulted.

"Just in time, then, yes?"

Liane snapped her head around. She'd have known that voice any-where.

Axel Flickinger trained a pistol on Liane and Bea.

23

In a blousy khaki safari shirt, perfectly creased, and flowing matching slacks, Flickinger looked thinner than Liane remembered him: a twist of sinew with the head of a steel screw. The eyes were the same, however: lasers of light that seemed to violate the jungle with a single glance. They were reductive, she thought, in the sense that a potent laser reduces matter to ash. And in this way Flickinger transformed every-thing before him into his subject. His presence made Liane feel like a caged animal, helpless as Bea had been when she clutched her Curious George toy for false comfort. It came to mind in a split second. Then her attention returned to the gun, held steady in Flickinger's hand, the muzzle as fathomless as a mineshaft.

At first the silence lay over them like a suffocating cloak. Flickinger tore it open.

"Some news," he said, tapping his canvas boot on the ground. "Mr. Gretch is dead. Killed by his own government, yes? The animal dealer Pierre Sanza, too, has passed away, bitten by a deadly snake. Thus, Ms. Vinson, you leave quite a trail of destruction behind you. Your father, when he finds out, will no doubt be deeply disappointed."

"He's not my father."

"Is he not?" Flickinger took a step closer. "He vouched for you as a father would."

"He always liked a long shot. He gambled on you, too."

"Too bad about your mother, then, yes? She came up on the losing end of both bets. There was a kidney as recently as last week that would have made a perfect match. Alas, at the last moment it was not to be."

"I won't believe that. You don't have that power."

"No? Remember that the croupier at the roulette wheel may not have the power to choose the number, but all he needs is a nudge of the table to keep the ball away from *your* cup. The issue of control is an uncertain thing, yes?"

"I won't accept that anyone like you can control everything."

"Certainly not everything, or we would not find ourselves here now. But, on the other hand, nature is a mess. That which we do not control can easily overwhelm us. It is the history of the world."

"Of the human world," Mickey corrected.

"Ah. The helpful veterinarian now heard from. I was told that you are smarter than you look. Finally meeting you, I see that this is a low bar to clear."

"Yeah? Well, I heard you ain't as smart as you think you are, so maybe we're even."

Flickinger waved his free hand in an arc. "But by any objective measure, Dr. Ferrone, we are far from even. And there is the additional factor that I hold the gun and you do not. It has eight rounds in the clip, in case you are wondering. More than enough."

"It depends how good your aim is."

"When you are done tying up that bonobo, you can be the first to find out."

"The ape's not going back. If that's what you're asking for, you *will* have to shoot me."

"It is not about what I *have* to do. It is a matter of what I choose."

"Is that why you cut out Isaac's larynx?" Liane said.

"No no no, foolish girl. I was curious to see what was in that most unusual Adam's apple. He certainly did not need it for anything of use to us. And he might have lived without it for a good long while but for his mean streak. He was never the same after you stole his sister, Ms.

Vinson. The will to live left him. Another victim along the road of your good intentions."

"I don't understand," Dikembe said. "So you killed the brother twin?"

"Killed? What is death, Mr. Kasa? Merely the absence of life. By that measure, knowing your sentiments, the brother was dead the moment you captured him, yes? Just as this one, 673B, is already the walking dead because of your actions. That is how Liane looks at it, too, is it not, Ms. Vinson?"

"I was dead. Now I'm risen."

"Ho! How scriptural-sounding of you. So you are saying the straight and narrow is no longer for Liane Vinson? She has left the straight and narrow forever? We must insert that observation into your file. It can be the very last entry."

"How do you know about that?" She paused, hugging Bea tightly.

A great blue turaco glided in and alit on a branch, not far from Liane. It had aquamarine feathers and a handsome black crest. Its eyes were large and its yellow beak was tipped with red, as if someone had messily painted lipstick upon it. She ignored the bird's *cawr cawr*.

"Oh, sure, now I see. You spied on my psychological records. Why wouldn't you? When would a small thing like doctor-patient confidentiality stand in the great Flickinger's way?"

"If only I had thought to look sooner. A criminal record, Ms. Vinson. Tsk-tsk. By the way, she was not even a doctor, your psychologist. She held only a masters."

"You've studied her too? There isn't an item in the world that's off-limits for your kind, is there? Everything on earth invites your violation by its very existence."

"Do not be so dramatic. We are an exploitative species. Some of us just acknowledge it more honestly. There is an order to the world, yes? In our society it places some people above others. In nature, if you will, it puts the majority of humans ahead of all other species. Thus!"

He swung the Walther around and fired. They watched the great blue turaco fall from its perch and sputter through the tree, crashing against leafy branches until it hit the ground like a brick.

Flickinger smirked. "You see? We call that an exercise of authority. Now what brings us all together for this discussion is a piece of property that belongs to the shareholders of Pentalon. When that is settled, a bit of revenge may be in order, as I have by now seen enough of my plans disrupted by you and your crew. Your termination will assure me that this does not happen in the future, yes?"

"Maybe you can do us as easily as you just offed that bird," Mickey said. "I sure wouldn't put it past ya. But the ape carries hemorrhagic fever. You take her back to Pentalon and she could infect the rest of the troop."

"What makes you think they do not all have it already?" Flickinger sneered. "Clearly it is asymptomatic in these animals or they would be dead down to the last organism. And transmission to humans is difficult or you would also be in the grave. Besides, I do not intend to return to Pentalon, which the government has undoubtedly made a hash of by now. I will use this animal to begin a new company, a new lab, conceived in the long boat ride to our rendezvous. Imagine a creature that can be trained to report to its handlers the more subjective symptoms, such as pain and suffering. How very useful and valuable indeed."

"You won't hurt that ape!" Daniel shrieked, speaking for the first time in Flickinger's presence. "Never again! Let her go, Liane." He spun around, extending his arms to the jungle. "*Hoo-hooo!*" he screamed. "*Hoo-hooo!*"

"And a child shall lead them," Flickinger mocked. "Oh, what nonsense!"

"*Hoo-hooo!*" Dikembe called into the jungle.

"*Hoo-hooo!*" Bea imitated.

"Enough!" Flickinger shouted, waving the gun around. "Tie the bonobo up! Tie her!"

"*Hoo-hooo!*" It came not from the clearing but from the jungle. And not far off. "*Hoo-hooo!*"

Bea, hearing it, jumped from Liane to Dikembe, rubbing her genitals on him. She bounded back to Liane, nearly knocking her over.

"Hoo-hooo!"

"Shut up! Tie her!"

A sign of movement came high in a tree. *"Hoo-hooo!"*

Two bonobos appeared, settled on their haunches and looked down on the clearing. Then a third joined them nearby. This one had a thin pink scar on its shoulder, barely perceptible at a distance.

Bea stiffened. She jumped to the ground, using Liane for a springboard, and began running through the grass in the direction of her mother. Liane watched in relief as one stride followed another, then another, quickening.

She turned to monitor Flickinger and saw the ice of his eyes clarify. He raised the pistol toward Bea.

Not pausing for thought, Liane lunged for him.

In midair she barely perceived three sharp pops and felt the spray of hot powder, burning pinpricks on the skin of her arms.

24

The white-clad captain leaned in to say something, but Pulsipher waved him back, indicating the noise. The captain smiled and nodded his head, pointed to a triangle on the GPS monitor and gave a thumbs-up. The engine of the small navy cruiser was so loud that the roar made talking, even from a foot away, nearly impossible; you had to get right up to someone's ear and shout. Pulsipher had had enough trouble with the captain's accent yesterday, back at the port, where the only aural distractions were an occasional thunderclap and the distant shouts of stevedores. Here, on the water, hand signals and facial expressions worked better. Pulsipher chopped the air with two fingers to request that they press on, then left the wheelhouse to sit in the stern.

It's a ball-buster, he thought, *to tail someone in a boat on a river.* Engines made noise and hulls threw wakes and cabins were visible from a long way off. You needed to hang back, making it easy for the target to duck among dense reeds or the deep recesses of mangroves. If the image on the monitor were reliable, however, the boat Pulsipher followed had taken the straightest possible path.

The agent looked out at the curtain of endless green on either side and thought that a person could easily lose a bonobo in there—and maybe that wouldn't be so bad for the American people. Let a few generations pass and—if her descendants survived—maybe the world would be ready. But the Undersecretary still wanted the ape, virus and all, so Pulsipher had a job to do. The Undersecretary had stopped palling around with the Pentalon CEO, and done so fast enough to prove that friendships in the District had the half-life of francium-233. Blood now stained Flickinger's hands, human blood. The Undersecretary requested that the CEO be brought to heel before Pentalon's recklessness set the animal-testing infrastructure back any further. Pulsipher, despite the vast jungle, thought he could oblige.

He looked to the gathering clouds and wondered whether they were in for another soaker. Capturing the attention of one of the two soldiers who accompanied them, he pointed to the sky and spread his hands for a question. The plump soldier shrugged and shook his wide grin noncommittally—not willing to venture a guess about the rain. *That soldier's not still alive,* Pulsipher thought, *without having learned to keep his head down.*

The second soldier ducked into the wheelhouse and popped right back out. He was thin with blue-black skin and looked sharp in starched camouflage with a kelly-green beret. He held up a finger and Pulsipher read his lips—*un kilomètre.*

The special agent decided that he was fortunate to have thought both to bug Sanza's office and to tag the right boat in Kinshasa harbor with a tracking device. Sanza, already known as the bonobo's dealer, was a no-brainer. But tracking the boat required the instincts of a high-caliber investigator, one who knew, after some reflection, that there was only one boat in Kinshasa Harbor that would meet both Axel Flickinger's needs and his standards. Having conceded a three-day head start to the ape's protectors, that boat now represented Flickinger's sole hope. It stood out amid a flotilla of rotting heaps: a new twin-cabin Glastron GS 269 Sport Cruiser. The sleek red-and-white cruiser, twenty-seven feet long with 315 horsepower and a maximum speed of 58 mph, wasn't the fastest boat on the planet, but it was the fastest nonmilitary boat in the harbor—and by far the most pristine. It was available for hourly charter, but Flickinger had bought it on the spot for a fistful of diamonds and a leather pouch stuffed with American cash. He'd overpaid by thirty thousand bucks, according to a Congolese source, and he immediately hired the seller as skipper. *Well,* Pulsipher mulled, *we'll soon see who got the better of that bargain.*

An arm extended from the wheelhouse window, the captain's large hand flapping from the wrist. Pulsipher accepted this as his final signal. He lifted the Mini Uzi off the bench next to him and checked that the clip of thirty-two 9 mm Parabellum cartridges nested properly. He set the gun for semiautomatic, leaving the safety engaged, and leaned a shoulder on the corner of the wheelhouse as they came beside the anchored Glastron. The soldiers jumped off with remarkable alacrity and pointed their rifles in the surprised skipper's face. They tied him up without a fight and the captain of the military boat cut his engine. In the sudden quiet, the slapping of water against their hull sounded infernal.

A lingering cloud of burnt diesel choked Pulsipher as he climbed into the rubber dinghy they'd thrown into the river amidships for him. He waved for the soldiers to join him and they shook their heads in unison. He called for the captain, who said something Pulsipher couldn't exactly understand, but the tone of voice was enough. These guys didn't do land. Not here.

Alone in the dinghy, Pulsipher turned the key and yanked the starter rope, engaging the two-stroke engine. He pointed the craft straight for a giant bombax tree fifty yards away.

Except for an overturned dugout, driven repetitively up against the shore by the current of the merging rill, the scene looked pristine at first glance. Herons waded in the shallows. A colossal crocodile dozed on the tip of the promontory, perfectly still, as if it had petrified. In the diffuse light of cloudy skies, the jungle offered a thousand shades of brown and green, leaves trembling in the faint breeze.

Pulsipher ran the dinghy aground and pocketed the key. He saw footprints leading to the game path—then, as he entered it, came upon freshly hacked vines and limbs that bracketed the narrow trail. It was uphill and tough going. Cursing and crashing along, he became aware that he couldn't sneak up on a deaf man at a rock concert for all the noise he was making. Then he heard something different.

"*Hoo-hooo!*"

It sounded otherworldly, like a heavenly instrument whose tone wasn't meant to tickle human ears.

"*Hoo-hooo!*"

Next he heard human voices, he was sure. He accelerated into a jog, then a run as he broke through the shoulders of the jungle path and burst into a clearing. He saw Flickinger with his arm extended and a pistol aimed at the cantering bonobo, trigger finger flinching, Liane taking a remarkably athletic step, then throwing herself, arms outstretched, into Flickinger's line of fire.

In a single motion Pulsipher flicked off the safety and leveled the barrel of the Uzi from his hip. Some time had passed since he'd last fired one of these little death dispensers, so he was amazed anew by the subtlety of its report, the tightness of its recoil. *More than the sum of its parts,* he thought. Like the poetry rendered by a Leica camera. And that was the last thing to cross his mind before Liane and Flickinger went down in a clatter of flying bullets.

25

Flickinger's weight on Liane's back felt more solid than she would have imagined, narrow and skeletal but possessing the density of a steel beam. It pressed her into the ground, where the grit of damp grass and ferrous dirt invaded her mouth. She lifted her eyes and through sparse vegetation saw Bea propelling herself on hands and feet, closing in on the place where they'd seen the other bonobos, which were no longer visible from the clearing, having ducked into the leaves upon the sound of gunfire. Bea arrived at the base of a low-limbed tree, looked up with one hand resting on the bark of the trunk, glanced back toward Liane, then climbed out of sight.

It should be a moment of triumph, Liane thought.

Instead, pulse racing, flush from the surge of adrenaline, she had to fight the crushing weight before it suffocated her. She felt Flickinger's torso shift and noticed blood on her arm as she twisted around. Not her blood—Flickinger's. Through a jagged tear in his khaki shirt she saw the lurid exit wound, high on his chest, like a surprised red iris. Their faces were inches away, and he was smiling down at her. He shifted his weight again and grabbed for her left wrist, which was trapped behind her back and between them. He wrenched her arm to the limit of her shoulder joint and quickly enveloped her in his limbs. Then in a flash of elegant motion they rose together and she succumbed to his overwhelming force. He was behind her, his left arm wrapped across her upper chest, his cheek flat against hers, the hot tip of the pistol searing into her right temple, steady as a drill press. His fingernails, seen out the corner of her eye, appeared perfectly manicured, glistening improbably. He exhaled and the smell of fresh mint fought the sour odor of cordite.

His embrace had her elevated, toes brushing the ground. Her legs flopped like a rag doll's as he skittered over to a large mahogany tree, alone in the clearing, and flattened his back against its scaly trunk. Now she knew how the primate felt when it sensed the cage's impenetrability—paralysis induced by deep despair. Yet she'd done the good thing, the right thing, she thought. She'd left the well-trod path and freed Bea. Even if Flickinger pulled the trigger right now, no one could run back the reel on the actions Liane had taken.

In unison she and Flickinger surveyed the clearing: Mickey on his knees twenty feet away with his hands out, as if in supplication; Daniel fallen to his side on the ground, staring up in panic with wide young eyes; Dikembe out of the picture, perhaps having fled into the jungle at the moment of chaos; Pulsipher inching forward, his compact black machine gun raised to shoulder level, peering at Flickinger and Liane over the short barrel.

He held out a photo I.D. with his free hand, an almost comical gesture, given the circumstances.

"Special Agent Henley Pulsipher, United States Department of Agriculture." He returned the I.D. to a back pocket without removing his eyes from them.

"I know who you are," Flickinger snarled across Liane's ear.

"Drop the gun, Dr. Flickinger." Pulsipher worked the barrel around, seeking a clear line of fire, but Flickinger adjusted with him, shifting Liane's face, cheek-to-cheek, like a depraved parody of dancing lovers.

"Drop the damn gun," Pulsipher repeated. "It's over. The chimp's gone. There's nothing to gain by more killing."

"Speak for yourself," Flickinger snapped. "Even that which is seemingly gone can be recaptured. In the lab we have induced cardiac arrest and brought primates back to life a hundred times. The bonobo was captured once and can be captured again."

"Pentalon is finished. You've nowhere to bring the ape back to—even if you had her."

"The power to regulate is the power to destroy, I grant you." Flickinger tightened his grip on Liane. "But here is something you will never understand: Pentalon is not a building or an institution. I carry my laboratory with me. It is a state of mind."

"You can carry it with you to prison, then, or to a shallow grave in the jungle, for all I care. But you're not leaving here alive except in my custody. Start by letting the woman go."

Pulsipher walked around in an arc, maintaining his distance from Flickinger, who rotated in response, bringing Mickey better into Liane's line of sight. He was struggling up from his knees, and a trickle of blood ran from his forehead and down a sideburn to his chin. It dribbled into the grass. But when Liane met his eyes she saw euphoria there.

"Did you see her, babe?" Mickey said. "Did you see Bea going for the prize? She looked back at you. She knew you did it and that you were right and that it's good. All of it, babe. She's free and this automaton ain't gonna get his hands on her again." He teetered on his heels and stumbled toward her.

"Stay back!" Pulsipher shouted, but Mickey took another tentative step, wiping the blood from his face and onto his jeans without removing his eyes from Liane.

"Please, Mickey, don't," she pleaded, but he stumbled forward again, stiff-legged, like a man raised from a coma who was just learning to walk again.

"Now I'm gonna take you outta here the way you freed Bea," Mickey said, "the way you freed me."

He began to run at them, stumbling stupidly through the grass, taking an oblique angle, and Flickinger swung his arm around, pointing the pistol at Mickey's chest while Liane squirmed and Flickinger tightened his grip.

Pulsipher twitched at the unfolding action, shouting instinctively, "Freeze! Stop! Everybody freeze, goddamn it!"

With a direct view down Flickinger's arm, as if it were her own, Liane saw Mickey's stumbling tattooed form rising past the lip of the muzzle, his bleeding head cresting the gunsight. When Mickey filled the whole background, Liane cried, "NO!" then watched in deep terror as Flickinger's bony index finger tensed on the trigger.

26

In the prolonged moment, everything happened at once and Liane perceived with all her senses. First, a surge of undiluted rage vesting in the body that engulfed her. Along with that, in the space between her and Mickey, a palpable surge of pure love. Then the fire erupting from the pistol muzzle. Mickey falling. The deafening percussion in her ears.

But there was something else, barely perceived. There was a flash of shiny metal to her right, a fleeting glimmer in her peripheral vision, followed in almost the same instant by a blur of every color in the universe. And also a wet thwack of the kind she'd heard when they cleared the vines away, hard and soft at the same time.

Then came a cry of pain in her ringing ears and a violent push from behind that sent her sprawling onto her face on the ground again. Mickey popped back up just as she fell. He ran over and cradled her in his arms, but she was so numb she could barely feel him. Her ears jangling, she could hardly hear him. But she managed to read his lips, and he was saying, "Liane! You all right? I love you, Liane. *Bolingo. Bolingo!*"

At the same time a flash of khaki blurred past them into the crease of the game path, yelling like a snared dog.

Pulsipher looked at the two of them, then took off in fast pursuit.

Mickey and Liane rose together, trembling from the shock of it all, unsure where next to direct their focus. They looked from the head of the game path to the other side of the clearing, where Liane would swear she'd seen one last movement in the trees and a bonobo hand reaching out in a gesture of farewell. But it was the unmoving thing on the ground that soon seized their attention. It was a forearm—Flickinger's arm—the fist still clenched around the pistol butt, the bony index finger threaded through the trigger guard, the starched khaki cuff encircling the wrist, a fancy single gold button holding that cuff together, and the gash at the elbow dripping blood and marrow.

Beyond it, still half-hidden by the tree trunk, stood Dikembe, waving his machete in midair as if to apologize.

27

He ran. He ran. The motherfucker ran. Pulsipher couldn't believe it. He'd seen the African behind the tree—saw him consciously the whole time, careful not to tip off Flickinger with any change of expression, not even the lifting of an eyebrow, hoping the African might come in useful, if only as a timely distraction. But not this—not stepping out like the king's executioner with a sweep of the big blade. There'd been something primitive in it, Pulsipher thought, like a reptilian explosion of movement that kills as much by surprise as by pure violence.

But in that moment of stunned immobility, while every human present struggled to make sense of it, Flickinger clutched for his severed arm, let out a visceral yell and ran—glided across the clearing so sharply and swiftly that it struck fear into Pulsipher's heart. He didn't like the feeling. He suppressed it and pursued, the cut ends of vines whipping his shins, his ankles turning on the uneven path.

Occasionally he perceived a flash of khaki and thought that he was gaining on Flickinger. Then the sight disappeared again, swallowed by the dark jungle.

Pulsipher couldn't imagine anyone ducking into the trees here, where the jungle was thick as callaloo soup. But, then again, until moments ago he couldn't have imagined a man taking off the way Flickinger had without his newly severed arm. So he worked to keep his peripheral vision attuned, lest the psychopathic scientist jump out at him. And this was why, before he felt anything happening, he saw the trees dancing, whipped to action by a relentless whirling wind. All at once, the jungle was nearly dark as night. Pulsipher heard the rain before he saw it, clattering on the limbs and giant leaves above like a thousand gossiping birds. Then the drops began to pelt his head and shoulders. They were exploding bomblets of water that obliterated vision even to the middle space. But Pulsipher pressed forward down the path, splattering through ankle-deep mud, holding the Uzi as steady as he could before him—ready, he hoped, for any and all surprises.

He hadn't the luxury of cursing the rain. He viewed it as interference, like snow on a television monitor or static on a phone line. But that was the foreground. In the background, somewhere, information persisted, and it was the investigator's role to find, to reveal, to amplify until it could be heard, ignoring the noise. And he thought of what he knew about Flickinger, searched the mental file thoroughly as he ran.

Relentless, ruthless, brilliant—these were the adjectives that came to mind. Adaptive, focused. The man should know he can't survive long without a tourniquet and might stop to apply one, perhaps using a pliant twig or young vine or long, wide blade of grass. Yet he also knew he was pursued and that the wild animals of the jungle would smell fresh blood and come for him. At least, that was what Pulsipher presumed—his specialty was the human jungle and what the hell did he know about tropical trees and animals with their own varied intentions? Still, he ran all out, as if no questions harried him. He sensed there was only one means of escape for Flickinger, the boat that the scientist believed waited with its skipper at the shore. The game path was the most direct line to that boat, and Flickinger would stick to it so long as he had the strength to move forward. So Pulsipher pressed on, half blind in the rain, slipping and sliding and stumbling until he arrived, almost unknowingly, at the shoreline of the Congo River.

Flickinger was there with his back to the trail, his rent sleeve bright red with blood, the boiling river lapping at his feet. The downpour, as Pulsipher emerged from the trees, retreated abruptly to a smattering of large drops, and a ray of sunshine brimmed the darkest cloud, illuminating Flickinger's clinging soaked shirt. His pale flesh glowed from beneath, stark and rigid.

The soldiers in the navy cruiser stepped out of the wheelhouse just as Pulsipher emerged with his gun raised to Flickinger's back. Pulsipher shouted, "Hold it, Dr. Flickinger!" The soldiers, raising their Kalishnikovs and taking positions on bow and stern, barked out, *"Arretez-vous! Arretez-vous!"*

Flickinger ignored them. His attention shifted from the skipperless Glastron to the river, assessing the possibilities. Pulsipher narrowed the gap between them to six feet, his Uzi aimed squarely at the scientist's spine. Flickinger's left hand was closed around the stump of his right arm like a vise, but his skin had gone ashen and his knees wobbled. Taking nothing for granted, Pulsipher checked his safety. Flickinger peered over his shoulder, emitting cold hatred from steely eyes.

"You didn't have to do it," Pulsipher said.

"Do what?"

"Any of it. You didn't have to go as far as you did. Why would you?"

Flickinger sneered.

Pulsipher raised the Uzi barrel to target Flickinger's forehead. The soldiers, too, shifted their aim at the pale and bloody apparition.

Flickinger turned abruptly back to the water, let go of his arm stump and sprang across the rushing merging stream in the direction of the Glastron, anchored beyond the narrow promontory. One, two, three enormous strides across the water toward that spit of land, with Pulsipher unable to pull the trigger and shoot a man in the back; the soldiers, not personally threatened, waiting for the agent's lead. By the fourth stride Flickinger had splashed his way to the promontory, flying water dousing a log that he was aiming for, a last solid footing from which possibly to launch himself across and into the main river water, where the empty boat drifted at anchor.

The log moved. The jaws of the giant crocodile levered open and snapped closed across Flickinger's thighs and he brayed an inhuman yowl as the crocodile rolled and dragged him into the depths of the river.

Pulsipher watched the great beast thrash in foaming water with Flickinger's lone arm beating at the dragon head until he was drowned, torn to pieces and consumed. It lasted several agonizing minutes, the agent all the while wondering whether to try a shot at the crocodile with his Uzi but continually thinking better of it. A school of fish quickly gathered round and pecked up the scraps. Nothing wasted in the jungle.

When it was over the crocodile pivoted and glided to shore, dragging its long body into the shallows, where it lurked half underwater.

Pulsipher turned back toward land, where four survivors stood at the head of the game path in wonder.

28

They huddled on the shore near the rubber dinghy and the dugout canoe. Daniel began weeping first, followed by Dikembe and then Liane and then Mickey. The convulsions spread over them like a contagion, every cell in their exhausted bodies releasing its pent-up tension.

"You didn't see that," Liane said, poking Daniel. She turned to Dikembe. "Please tell me he didn't see what just happened with that crocodile."

"He has seen worse than that in his young life," Dikembe said. "Today, though—all at once—what horrors!"

"You saved my life," Mickey said, extending a hand to Dikembe, who shrugged as he accepted it.

"What could I do? The man was about to shoot."

"It was the worst and the best—all wrapped together in a single instant," Liane reflected, tears streaming down her cheeks.

Pulsipher shook his head and examined his Uzi, unwilling to take any credit on himself. "What a rat fuck," he said stoically.

"A rat fuck?" asked Daniel.

Liane was the first to laugh through her tears. She found a rag washed up from the dugout and wiped the blood from Mickey's forehead.

"Looks like a flesh wound," Pulsipher observed. "You got grazed is all. Might've made you a little silly for a while there, Dr. Ferrone. Nobody'll hold that against you."

"He might have a scar to complement the other one," Liane said, still dabbing.

"A real rat fuck," Pulsipher repeated.

Liane thought he didn't look happy.

"I still don't understand," said Daniel. "What did rats have to do with it?"

"More than anyone would've imagined just a few weeks ago," Liane said.

"You two have made yourselves into serious pains in my ass," Pulsipher grumbled, using a shirttail to wipe his glasses clean. "Going forward, I wouldn't mind if you'd both stay away from any enterprise that's regulated by the Department of Agriculture. It's no fun killing American citizens, even maniacs like Gretch and Flickinger. Next time it occurs to you to save a chimp, think twice. There was a better way."

"Would it have freed Bea?" Liane asked.

"Doubtful." With the toe of his shoe Pulsipher pried up a river stone. Water seeped into the depression it left behind. "Hell. Another part of me—maybe this was all inevitable in some way. Maybe people who play with scalpels deserve to get cut themselves now and then."

"So are we square?" Mickey asked. "Or is this only the beginning of our troubles?"

"This?" Pulsipher said, returning his glasses to the bridge of his nose and casting his gaze off into the jungle. "In two weeks the vegetation will have filled in and memories will fade."

"Whose memory?" Mickey said.

"Listen," Pulsipher softened his tone. "The guy should've known better but it happens all the time, right? A man goes for a walk in the jungle unprepared and gets in over his head. Dude looked like Dr. Livingston without the safari hat, for fuck's sake. Did you see that? Some genius."

"He was a perfect specimen until an hour ago," Liane said.

"No, he wasn't. He didn't even have a canteen with him, see what I'm saying? And the croc ate his passport, I'll bet. It's an unforgiving world. Things don't always work out on these spur-of-the-moment expeditions."

"I get your drift now."

"Speaking of which, we gotta send the Pentalon plane back. Repatriation and all...court order. You two need a lift?"

"Depends," Mickey said. "Do we have to ride in the animal hold again?"

"So that's how you got here? Nah. But you'll have to spend a couple nights in Kinshasa, courtesy of Uncle Sam, while I have a doctor check you out and we wait for the results. Separate rooms, by the way. No funny business until you're both deemed virus-free."

"Jesus, I can't catch a break," Mickey sighed.

The captain on the naval vessel waved frantically at them.

Pulsipher threw up his hands. "Haven't been able to understand a word this guy's said since we set out."

"He's talking about the crocodile," Dikembe said. "He says someone has to kill it before it swims off. It has the taste of human flesh. It must be avenged."

"The final insult," Liane moaned. "How old must that creature be?"

"That fellow?" Dikembe said. "Sixty years at least. He was in this river before man walked on the moon."

"Damned shame," Mickey said. "Flickinger's final victim."

Pulsipher waved to the captain and gave a thumbs up, but the captain called back.

"They see it as your responsibility," Dikembe said. "They don't wish to waste ammunition."

"Terrific," said Pulsipher, walking over to the rubber dinghy and inserting the key into the engine. "How much more of this guy's shit am I gonna have to clean up?"

"Approach from the front," Dikembe instructed. "Circle around, then cut the engine and let it drift. At thirty feet, hit him between the eyes. Try not to miss."

"Get the kid out of here. He shouldn't have to see this."

"Let's take a walk," Liane said.

They wandered behind some bushes as Pulsipher yanked the engine to life. While it purred in the background they exchanged goodbyes.

"We must be going," Dikembe said. "It's a hard paddle upstream to the place we can next make camp."

"I'm sorry we involved you in this," Liane said.

"I was always involved," said Dikembe. "All of us down to the last man: We are all involved. It's a cycle from which too many benefit. Maybe we've broken a part of it now."

"Don't count on that," said Mickey. "But we did save one animal, and a very special one."

"Very special indeed." Dikembe sighed. It may be true that the cycle could not be so easily broken, but at least, he thought, he'd paid his own debt.

The sound of the engine cut off and the silence grew oppressive. Even knowing what would come, they flinched when the report of a single gunshot cracked across the water.

29

With his guests gone, the large dugout felt empty to Dikembe, and Daniel too light in the bow. He would swap it, he decided, for a smaller one that he and his son could portage past shallows and rapids where necessary, when they left the main river to get to the place where the Englishman maintained his permanent camp. Perhaps in the trade he would gain a few more provisions, as well, though he also had some money that Mickey had given him and the fancy button from the bad man's arm, which looked like solid gold.

The incident echoed like the memory of a dream where there is no normal, only surprises that turn reality upside down all around you, where events only make sense if you consider what lies below the surface.

He thought of this as he tapped the gunwales, watching for rising hippos—squinting into the glare of a falling sun—and pulled the dugout through the water with long strokes.

Back in his rebel days, when fighting for one's life sometimes required ending another's, he could kill only when the dreamlike state overtook him. The gunshots in the clearing, hours ago, had brought him back to it. From behind the tree he'd had a perfect view of the bonobo as she cantered across the grassland, and he believed that when he had the luxury to close his eyes again—when he could let go his river vigilance—he would be able to conjure that vision of her on command, the way a snake charmer always gets the snake to leave the basket. She was a miracle, that bonobo, a miracle that he almost smothered with his selfishness. She waved from the tree—at him, at Liane, at a spirit among them—who would ever know which. But that simple gesture affirmed his power to do what he'd done with the machete, because in that wave from the tree he'd recognized how close they'd all come to making the wrong irreversible. And, as he thought of it now, maybe it had not been a human being but the spirit of her brother to whom the bonobo had waved, her brother the sacrifice that had set her free.

Dikembe knew how to be quiet as a cat. He'd stood in wait behind that tree, not crouched like a lion but as ready to spring when the moment called him. He was so close that he might have reached out and pulled the bad man's hair or tugged on his ear. He'd moved when they moved, staying exactly behind them, seeing the margins of what they saw, with the tree trunk blocking a direct view. One wrong step, if perceived from behind, would probably have led to Liane's death—maybe to all of theirs. It had crossed his mind for a moment that they deserved to die—all but Daniel—in a kind of retribution, to fall into silence the way the last trill of an orchestra fades away. But he knew also that it wasn't for him to decide, but for the conductor who at that moment seemed greatly distant—farther even than America looked from the bush. When Mickey went into motion and the bad man extended his arm, Dikembe knew he was the only one with the power to make the pistol drop. He let the dream force overtake him then, so much so that he'd barely sensed his muscles moving, only saw the whoosh of the sharp blade slicing the air. And he felt no resistance in the handle until the tip of the machete had sunk well into the red earth.

When the navy boat pulled away, the cruiser in its wake, Dikembe went back and buried the arm, pronouncing the Lord's Prayer over it while Daniel looked on, putting special emphasis on the words *forgive us our trespasses*. It had been easy to cut off the gold button, but getting the pistol had been another matter, quite a job to pry away the stiff fingers. When he'd finally accomplished this, he laid the arm in the hole he'd dug, placing it palm up, and though a different color, it reminded him of the severed gorilla hands that trade in the animal market. Some buzzards were circling and the flies had already found the dead flesh, landing relentlessly, each determined to have their taste. The dirt, as he'd covered the waxen skin, gradually frustrated them, until the futility chased them away entirely.

The captain of the navy cruiser had had a spare paddle, which Mickey insisted on buying for Daniel as a parting gift. Meant for the dinghy, it was well proportioned to Daniel's body size, and it made Dikembe proud to see his son pulling his own weight, especially in the face of so strong a current. It would have made Odette proud, too. But it also meant that they would require more food to replace the expended energy. In this way, it seemed to Dikembe, nature reminds us that we are not so different from the crocodile and the turaco and the fish and the duiker. Everything has its consequences. You tear the fabric and you mend it—or nature will, and with her own prejudices.

"My arms are getting tired," Daniel whined.

"Rest them. I will paddle myself."

"Are the Americans home yet, do you think, Papa?"

"No."

"But they have motors where we have only our arms. And they also have the current with them."

"Even when the current is behind you," Dikembe said, "it can be a long way home."

Water dribbled from Daniel's resting paddle, tracing an aqueous line as they moved.

"Papa?"

"Shhh. Do you hear it?"

"What?"

"The chorus of the bonobos."

"I do hear them. What are they saying?"

"I don't know."

"Could it be thank you? Bea's out there somewhere."

"Yes, she is."

"So one day we may know what they're saying."

"One day, perhaps." Dikembe lost himself in the curtain of trees. "Or maybe we already know."

EPILOGUE

I believe that man will not merely endure: he will prevail. He is immortal, not because he alone among creatures has an inexhaustible voice, but because he has a soul, a spirit capable of compassion and sacrifice and endurance.

— WILLIAM FAULKNER

1
––

Pulsipher put them into a Lincoln Town Car at JFK before catching his own flight back to Washington.

"If you should happen to pass me on the street one day," he said, "don't be offended when I act like I never saw you before. Just part of the job."

"Better that way," Mickey said.

Liane smoothed the fabric of her dress. In Kinshasa they'd tossed away their old clothes—funky from the jungle and deemed a total loss. Liane wore home an African-print shift, while Mickey sported a colorful dashiki and ivory cotton pants.

Pulsipher held the door as they climbed into the back seat. He leaned in. "You look like a couple of Congolese who got dunked in bleach."

"I'm sorry . . . do I know you?" Liane said.

They rode home in anxious silence, Liane tracing doodles with an unpainted fingernail on the back of Mickey's hand.

When the Town Car dropped them, they ignored the mailboxes. Holding hands, they took the elevator straight up without a word. They had an awkward parting in the hall. Liane walked into a mess and sat on the edge of her overturned couch, wondering where Nicholas could be. She heard Mickey outside, bellowing from the window for Einstein.

When he knocked on her door five minutes later he looked pale and sweat glazed his forehead. "I feared this would happen. Any sign of yours?"

Liane shook her head as Mickey gazed around for the first time.

Pieces of furniture lay on their sides, and someone had put a chair leg through the screen of the television. Utensils and pots were scattered over the kitchen floor, drawers thrown atop the heap. Framed posters with broken glass hung askew or rested against the walls where they'd fallen.

"I guess they were trying to send a message," Mickey said.

"Too bad I never received it." Liane shrugged. After all they'd experienced, some broken furniture seemed trivial.

"We'll have it straightened up in no time."

Mickey had changed into jeans and a light flannel shirt with the sleeves rolled up. He went to work righting chairs and putting pots away, not waiting for Liane, who stood watching him in a near trance. When he said he couldn't get the couch onto its feet by himself, she snapped out of it and they cooperated. Then she found a box of trash bags among the piles in the kitchen and began to put the shards of broken plates into one of them. She worked slowly, distracted with watching him. The tattooed muscles she'd once thought coarse she now found cute. The scar on his cheek made her think of the thread of idealism that all his worldly toughness couldn't hide. She caught herself hoping that the forehead wound, now a dark scab, would develop into another permanent scar, a memento of their shared experience.

When she came over and tried to relieve him from the effort of putting away the silverware, he waved her away. *He wants to help,* she thought. *Let him help.*

2

The next day, at the big pet store around the corner, the Humane Society had organized cat adoption day. There were four lines of cages, stacked three high, each with a litter box and a bowl of water and something soft inside. A gray-haired volunteer hoisted herself from a folding chair and offered assistance.

"Thanks, but we're just looking," Liane said.

Mickey stuck an index finger through the bars of one cage, and a fluffy Persian named Pearl drew herself up on her hind legs and batted at him playfully.

"Please don't touch," the volunteer warned. "Most of them have claws. And they all have sharp teeth."

"My bad. You're right." Mickey turned to Liane. "This is depressing."

"It is, isn't it?"

"I just want my Einstein back."

"I know how you feel."

They returned home in a bubble of aimlessness, pausing at the entrance to the apartment building as an airplane roared overhead. When it was gone they smiled at one another like conspirators. The Pentalon plane had barely reached cruising altitude when Liane had decided she had to have Mickey inside her, right there, right then. She'd grabbed for his waistband and they fell into the bedroom that Pulsipher had left vacant for them. Mickey stopped everything to dramatically check the spot on her breast where Bea had bitten her. Not finding even a lingering mark, he determined to kiss it and make it better anyway, and he did so until she couldn't stand it anymore. They made love for six hours, using their tongues and their hands and even their feet when the other equipment needed a rest.

When they finally collapsed in exhaustion, Mickey said, "Now that I see what a guy's gotta do to get your attention, I think I'm in over my head. The heart is willing, but the body, my Lord . . ."

"Oh, shut up," Liane said. "Now that you do have my attention, you won't soon lose it. Loyalty's one of my strong suits, remember?"

"Bea certainly remembers."

"You think?"

"I imagine her up in the trees, telling the whole sordid tale to a rapt audience of bonobos."

"Stop!"

"Too bad, at the very end, she wasn't there to see Flickinger get his."

Now Liane watched the contrails overhead and thought she'd never think of a plane the same way again. She knew the world more thoroughly than she ever would have dreamed. When the plane passed into the clouds they turned to go inside, but a rustle in the bushes caused them to stop again, and a pair of cats dashed to them from a nearby hedge.

Nicholas and Einstein.

Liane and Mickey crouched to receive them, but the cats were stand-offish. They rubbed their cheeks against human shins but refused open palms.

3

A week later Mickey found his BMW keys hanging from the door-knob of his apartment with a note:

Dr. F., Cool it on the car washes. —P.

The car was spotless. Mickey checked the VIN number against the registration to make sure it was his.

"They even got rid of that monkey shit smell," he marveled on the way to the cemetery.

"As Pulsipher never tired of pointing out, these people are professionals."

Mickey took Liane's hand. "You okay?"

"Why wouldn't I be?"

"You nervous?"

"Yup. It was hard enough on the phone—twice this week. I don't know if I can look him in the eye."

"He ain't gonna take your head off, Liane."

"Maybe he should."

"You risked your life and your freedom to get back to her at the end."

"If I'd just shut up and done my job, she might be alive now, with a new kidney."

"You don't know that. You can't rely on the bona fides of a sociopath."

At the cemetery gate they got directions to the mausoleum. The day was clear and comfortable, the warming sun illuminating headstones and flat green lawns and setting the breeze in motion through the flowering crabapple trees.

A priest awaited them, wearing a navy blue suit with white clerical collar. He was young and handsome and slightly effeminate. Liane didn't catch his name.

"Do you have the ashes?" she asked.

"No. The husband's bringing them."

"You know which vault?"

"It should be marked inside with a Post-It. Engraving comes later."

She walked in ahead of them. The wall of vaults was faced with marble and had an unnatural sheen. Liane admired the random veins of the stone, a full complement of color brought out by fine polishing. There were three yellow stickies. One of them, at shoulder height on the south wall, had her mother's name written on it. *You'd think they could do this with a bit more dignity,* Liane thought. But she decided there was nothing dignified about death.

She heard a rumble outside and stepped out again through the glass door as the sound grew louder. It was Frank, pulling up on the old Harley. He had a cardboard box strapped to the back with bungee cords. He took off his helmet, and his hair was mussed. When he saw Liane he broke into a smile.

"You got the bike back," Mickey observed.

"They called me earlier this week. I brought it in for a tune-up the other day and it's riding good as new. Helen always loved this motorcycle." He patted the cardboard box. "Her last ride."

It should be funny, Liane thought, but no one laughed. She formally introduced Mickey to Frank. They carried the box inside and the priest unpacked it. Liane expected an urn, but her mother's ashes rested in a silver cube. She touched the top before they placed it in the vault. It felt cold.

When the priest intoned a few prayers Frank looked shaky. Mickey, still holding Liane, sidled up and braced Frank with his other arm. They stared at their shoes until the priest finished.

"I have a one o'clock," he apologized, and left.

"We never had a family cleric," Liane said. "Who was that guy?"

"He comes with the cemetery," Frank said. "Would you two like to sit down somewheres?"

"We could grab some lunch," Mickey volunteered.

They followed the Harley in their car.

"You had to tell him that," Liane said.

"What?"

"Suggest lunch."

"He's lonely, babe. Can't you see it in his eyes? Have a heart."

"You don't understand, Mick."

"The man's trying."

They ended up at a diner, wrestling with giant menus. The food was vapid and lukewarm, like the conversation, Liane thought. Frank rambled on about nothing in particular.

Liane interrupted. "The thing I don't understand, Frank—why didn't you just tell me we needed Flickinger's help to get Mom the kidney?"

"Because I didn't want to put any more pressure on you."

"You were afraid I would crack, is that it? Leave the straight and narrow?"

"No. I was afraid you'd blab to your mother. I didn't want you lying to her, but I didn't want you telling her the truth, either. The idea that she might jump the line—I don't think she would've accepted the unfairness of that."

"And she'd be right. Why should she?"

"Only to live."

"So you lied to her."

"She didn't need to know that jerk was helping her."

"The jerk that you encouraged me to work for?"

"Yeah, that one. We didn't have a lot of good options. And who would've anticipated all this craziness with the bonobo and all? In the long run, when she was better, I figured I'd back off helping you with further career advice and everything would settle down straight away."

Liane caught herself. "I promised Mom," she said, "that I'd stop resenting you after all these years."

"They say resentment's like drinking poison and waiting for the other guy to suffer."

She chewed the inside of her lip. "Tell me it isn't too late."

"Of course not."

She grasped his hands across the table, appreciated their warmth. Mickey had his face buried in his empty plate, as if he were trying to read the scratches. She tugged his sleeve and he looked up.

"Maybe you two would like to be alone for a spell," Mickey said.

"No," Liane said, "you're part of this now."

They sat quietly together a while longer.

"I was wondering," Mickey said finally. "Maybe we all take a road trip to Atlantic City, have some fun, get to know each other a little better."

"No, thanks. I'm done gambling," Frank said.

"Yeah. All right." Mickey gazed into his plate again, leaned back in his chair, sunk a hand into his pocket.

Liane sensed that he was up to something. "Any more ideas?"

"Just one. I was gonna ask you something."

He held out a small box with velvet skin. "If you don't mind, Frank—and if she'll have me—well, you know." He popped open the lid. The gold ring had a rock in the center, plenty large but cloudy.

Frank looked as confused as Liane felt.

"Back on the barge," Mickey explained, "me and Dikembe conducted a small man-to-man transaction. He needed the dough and I needed something for my girl. It's three carats but it's got occlusions up the wazoo and stuff, so it ain't worth much, technically speaking. The jeweler practically laughed me outta the store when I asked him to set it. He wouldn't cut it either, not into less than a million pieces. Still and all…"

"I love it."

"I wanted you to have it."

"I love it and I love you."

"You do?"

"I do."

"So you will?"

"I will."

"And you, Frank, you'll be the best man, I hope?"

Frank grinned at Liane. "I said I wasn't taking any more chances, but I have a good feeling about this guy."

"*Bolingo,*" Mickey said.

Liane slipped the ring on and peered into the diamond. It was lumpy and uneven and there were specks of black inside, but it had an aura. She felt as if she could lose herself for hours inside the gem, and she knew in an instant that she would cherish it forever. It was perfectly imperfect, like immutable love. Like grace. Like a primate gene gone awry.

To any expert, she thought, the rock now on her finger may be something to discard or to grind into dust. But Liane knew better. She peered into its jungle of occlusions and inclusions and flaws and saw a beam of light, the path straight through.

It had been so well hidden that she'd almost missed it.

AUTHOR'S NOTE

The author is neither a scientist nor an animal rights activist. Those who wish to explore the merits of animal research might begin with The National Anti-Vivisection Society (www.navs.org) or People for the Ethical Treatment of Animals (www.peta.org). The NAVS website, in particular, offers a great deal of information about animal testing and experimentation, including links to government agencies and players in the industry. The Institutional Animal Care and Use Committee (www.iacuc.org) is the self-regulating entity that the federal government has established to oversee the care of animals in laboratories. The American Association for Laboratory Animal Science (www.aalas.org) represents the experimenters in this country. The United States Department of Agriculture maintains a web page (www.aphis.usda.gov) providing information with regard to federal regulation of the treatment of animals.

The above list is by no means definitive or complete.

People in the animal research field often distinguish between experiments performed in the interest of "pure" scientific research and the testing of animals for explicitly commercial purposes. Often these activities happen in different facilities. This book, however, makes no such distinctions.

The animal research landscape has changed and certainly will continue to change over time, in response to evolving human ethics and other considerations. In any case, experiments on living creatures go on as you read this and will continue to occur until society as a whole decides that they must stop.

One other point: So far as the author knows, primates can't speak as humans do. There is a bonobo in Georgia named Panbanisha who purportedly "knows" thousands of words, though these words do not emanate from her mouth.

Still, as Mickey might say, that ain't nothing.

ACKNOWLEDGMENTS

For teaching me how to listen when animals talk: my wife, Pamela Biddle.

For rooting for me every step of the way: my daughter, Macklin, whose world is always "tinkling with magic that made us."

For believing in me without pause: my parents, Sandra and Arthur Fishman.

For his early encouragement: Brian DeFiore of DeFiore and Company.

For reading imperfect drafts and providing suggestions: Cynthia Bell, Jamie Biddle, Patricia Connelly, Marla Grosswald, Ralph Grosswald, Mitch Higgins, John Hubner, Ken Jones, Josh Leicht, Cindy McKean, Beth Moore, Kimmell Proctor, Scott Proctor, and Courtenay Valenti.

For expert weapons advice: Robin McKelvey.

For peer-to-peer feedback: James Rahn and members of the Rittenhouse Writers Group.

For friendship and professional counsel: Jane Dystel and Miriam Goderich of Dystel & Goderich Literary Management; Raphael Sagalyn of Sagalyn Literary Agency; and Heide Lange of Sanford J. Greenburger Associates.

For going to bat for me: my agent, Paul Bresnick of Paul Bresnick Literary Agency.

For bringing me up to speed: Mary Ann Naples of OpenSky; Richard Nash of Cursor; Marysarah Quinn of Random House; Robert Riger of Simon & Schuster; Marly Rusoff of Marly Rusoff Literary Agency; Bruce Tracy of Workman Publishing.

For crackerjack editing delivered with unbridled enthusiasm: Patrick LoBrutto.

For the best jacket and interior design ever: Whitney Cookman and Jennifer Daddio, respectively.

For putting this book into your hands: Clint Greenleaf and the rest of the Greenleaf Book Group.

For invaluable business advice, freely and generously shared: John Moore, Jeff Morris and Chris Saridakis.

Bolingo, my friends.